James Brown

Life of William B. Robertson, D.D., Irvine

James Brown

Life of William B. Robertson, D.D., Irvine

ISBN/EAN: 9783337054663

Printed in Europe, USA, Canada, Australia, Japan

Cover: Foto ©Raphael Reischuk / pixelio.de

More available books at **www.hansebooks.com**

Yours most truly
W B Robertson

LIFE

OF

WILLIAM B. ROBERTSON, D.D.

IRVINE

WITH EXTRACTS FROM HIS LETTERS AND POEMS

BY

JAMES BROWN, D.D.

AUTHOR OF "THE LIFE OF A SCOTTISH PROBATIONER"

WITH TWO PORTRAITS

𝔉ourth 𝔈dition

GLASGOW

JAMES MACLEHOSE & SONS

𝔓ublishers to the 𝔘niversity

1889

PUBLISHED BY

JAMES MACLEHOSE AND SONS, GLASGOW.

———

MACMILLAN AND CO., LONDON AND NEW YORK.

London,	*Hamilton, Adams and Co.*
Cambridge,	*Macmillan and Bowes.*
Edinburgh,	*Douglas and Fouiis.*

———

MDCCCLXXXIX.

PREFACE TO THE FIRST EDITION.

WHEN I undertook to prepare this Memoir, I was aware that it would be difficult to make those who did not know Dr. Robertson understand what manner of man he was. It seemed best that he should be made to reveal himself by the incidents of his life, by his letters, and by his poems. Those who had the privilege of listening to the brilliant preacher and yet more brilliant talker, are not likely to be fully satisfied with what is here presented. I shall be content if they think it in any measure worthy of the man they loved.

I am grateful to the many friends who have placed at my disposal more material than it was possible to use, and especially to those who entrusted me with letters which they received when they were in sorrow. The very tenderness of these letters made me shrink from publishing more than a few of them.

In addition to the friends whose services are ac-knowledged in the course of the narrative, I desire to express my gratitude to Dr. Walter C. Smith, and Mr. David M'Cowan for their efficient help.

The study of Dr. Robertson's head at the beginning of the volume is by the late Mr. Robert Herdman, R.S.A., who most generously offered it for the Memoir. The engraving, by Mr. James Faed—in the prepara-tion of which Mr. Herdman took a lively interest—now stands as a memorial of the distinguished painter, as well as of him whose features it so vividly portrays.

As the engraving represents Dr. Robertson in his later years, a likeness taken in 1870 is also given.

St. James' Manse,
Paisley, 1st November, 1888.

PREFACE TO THE SECOND EDITION.

I desire to express my gratitude to those whose generous appreciation of this book has made the publication of a second edition necessary. I have availed myself of this unexpectedly early opportunity of making some slight corrections.

24th November, 1888.

CONTENTS.

CHAP.   PAGE

I. Birth-place and Early Surroundings, . . 1

II. At College and Hall, ... 17

III. In Germany, ... 47

IV. In Germany, Italy, and Switzerland, . 63

V. The Beginning of His Ministry, . . . 78

VI. Pastoral Work, ... 99

VII. Growing Power, ... 117

VIII. Life in the Manse, ... 139

IX. Letters and Poems, ... 161

X. Revival and Church-Building, . . . 183

XI. The Closing Years of His Irvine Ministry, 208

XII. The Valley of the Shadow of Death, 242

XIII. Hope Deferred, ... 258

CONTENTS.

CHAP.		PAGE
XIV.	In and Around Florence, ...	288
XV.	In the Engadine, ...	318
XVI.	Again in Italy and at Home, . . .	334
XVII.	At Bridge of Allan, ...	362
XVIII.	At Westfield, ...	389
XIX.	The End, ...	442

LIFE OF WILLIAM ROBERTSON

OF IRVINE.

CHAPTER I.

Birth-place and Early Surroundings.

WILLIAM ROBERTSON was born at Greenhill, in
the parish of St. Ninians, on May 24th, 1820. His
birth-place stands on the high ground to the south
of the Carse of Stirling. The field of Bannockburn, with the Gillies Hill and the Bloody Ford, is
a little way to the north-west, and the Torwood
is as near on the south-east, while at greater distances in the same directions are Stirling Bridge on
the one hand and Falkirk on the other. The quiet
homestead is thus on the edge of the battlefield of
Scotland—the scene of all the most famous fights in
the War of Independence, and now distinguished
among Scottish landscapes for the abundance of its
peaceful harvests.

S   A

The house, shut in by garden trees and well-trimmed beech hedges, has not an extensive view ; but the prospect from the open ground near it, and especially from the road to Stirling as it descends on the village of St. Ninians, is peculiarly beautiful. North-eastward, across the many-coloured carse, lies the range of the Ochils, like a mountain wall shielding the plain from northern blasts. To the westward of the Ochils there are in the foreground Abbey Craig, the Braes of Airthrey, the heights of Keir, and the Castle-hill of Stirling, with the ancient town clambering up its sides, and rendered picturesque by the old tower of the Church of the Holy Rood. In the background there rise in impressive majesty the summits of Ben Vorlich and Stuch-a-Chroan, with the heights of Uamh' Var to the right, and occasional glimpses to the left of the Braes of Balquhidder, and the summit of Ben Ledi peering above the trees that crown the Gillies Hill.

William Robertson often told how he used to drink in the beauty of that landscape as it lay bathed in the light of Sabbath mornings, when the family were finding their way from Greenhill to the Back Row Church at Stirling. Near the end of his life, when his sister and he were returning from a visit to Auchenbowie, she said to him—"Surely we did not in the old days realize how beautiful this is?" He answered—"Did we not ?"

But he owed even more to the influences within the house than to its impressive surroundings. Pictures

of the quiet "interior," and sketches of John Robertson, the venerable head of the house, have been given
in another memoir,[1] and need not be repeated here.
He was factor on the two estates of Plean and
Auchenbowie, and manager of the joint coal mines
wrought by their proprietors. This position had long
been held by his father, Andrew Robertson, and when
he was installed as his father's assistant and successor
he was spoken of as "the young factor." By the time
I knew him he had become the old factor, and the
other title had been transferred to his eldest son,
Andrew, who was in turn associated with him in
office.

It is difficult to write of John Robertson's qualities
of head and heart without seeming to exaggerate. His
natural abilities were of a high order, and they had
been cultured by a liberal education. At college he
excelled in chemistry and mathematics. It was
intended that he should enter one of the professions ;
but though failure of health led him to return home
and follow his father's calling, he remained a student
to the end, keeping himself abreast of the best
thought and literature of the time. He early
devoted his chief attention to sacred themes. While
still a young man he made a profession of the
Christian faith, and from that hour his life was consecrated. Those who knew him felt that certain deep
words of St. Paul and St. John concerning the

[1] "James Robertson of Newington : a Memorial of his Life and
Work." (Edinburgh : Andrew Elliot.)

Christian life had become more intelligible to them. His unobtrusive piety gave him a commanding influence in the district. His employers implicitly trusted him, and counted him among their most honoured friends; while his men looked on him as a father and a counsellor to whom they could confidently go in every difficulty. The estimation in which he was held was quaintly expressed to me by his minister, the late Mr. Steedman, who, after speaking of Greenhill, where I had been visiting, looked at me with the peculiar expression which those who knew him will remember, and said, in the vernacular which he could use so effectively, " Do ye no' think, Mr. Brown, that John Robertson is just as guid a man as there's ony use for ? "

By birth connected with the Secession Church and with its mother congregation, to which Ebenezer Erskine had ministered, that church was his Jerusalem, rather than forget which he would have had his right hand forget its cunning. Its ministers were counted as his personal friends, and were always welcome at his fireside. But his outlook could not be limited by sectarian boundaries, and it grew wider as he advanced in life. One of the last books he read was the life of Frederick William Robertson of Brighton. When he laid down the second volume, those about him noticed that he sat for a time absorbed in thought. They had learned by experience that if they wished him to speak freely it was better not to question him. By and by he said,

"They say that man was not orthodox, but it seems to me that he occupied a platform intellectually and spiritually so much higher than common men that he cannot be judged by common standards."

Margaret Bruce Kirkwood, whom Mr. Robertson wedded in 1809, was in all respects an helpmeet for her husband. Sharing his earnest convictions and his spirit of self-consecration, she brought into the family characteristics the touch of genius and the play of humour. Belonging by descent to the straiter sect of the Secession, the Anti-burgher,[1] she yet inherited no narrowness of sympathy. William used to tell that the Burgher Kirk of Denny was founded by his maternal grandfather and grandmother, who, being threatened with rebuke by the Anti-burgher session of Dennyloanhead for some harmless violation of stern Puritanic custom, were driven to seek a larger room.

There is a pleasant glimpse of Mrs. Robertson, as well as of the distinctive characteristics of her two

---

[1] It may make this and some other paragraphs more intelligible to English readers if we note that the church of the Secession, founded by Ebenezer Erskine and his associates in 1732, was in 1747 rent in two by a dispute as to the lawfulness of an oath, required of burgesses in certain of the burghs, to maintain the Christian religion as established in Scotland. The sect, composed of those who held the oath to be lawful, was popularly known as the Burgher Church; while that composed of the opposing party was known as the Anti-burgher. The two sections were brought together in 1820, and formed the United Secession Church, in connection with which William Robertson was ordained. In 1847, three years and a half after his ordination, the United Secession joined the Relief Church, which had finally separated from the Established Church in 1761. The Church thus formed was named the United Presbyterian.

most noted sons, in the following story preserved in the family. When William was about eight, and just after James became tutor to his younger brother, a change of servants took place. This was an unwonted event at Greenhill, and there was great curiosity among the children to see a new and tall domestic—Nannie Brash, by name—who then came for the first time, but remained a friend of the family and frequent visitor at Greenhill to the end of her life. She had gone into the byre to look after the cows. William stole in to have a look at her; and was impressed with her great stature. He came running into the house and cried, " I have seen Nannie, and her head is up to the couples "—the joisting of the roof. James was shocked at the tendency to exaggeration thus revealed, and proceeded to deal with William for an offence against truthfulness, insisting that to say that Nannie's head was up to the couples was a lie. William stoutly defended his hyperbole, and refused to confess a fault. Ultimately it was agreed to refer the matter to the mother, James as prosecutor, stating the case against William, and asking that he should be punished, and William being heard in his own defence. The good mother gave verdict of acquittal on the ground that in Scripture there is warrant for such figurative speech, as it is there written that the cities of the Anakim were walled up to heaven.

When I first went to Greenhill, lines of pain were already deep on Mrs. Robertson's face, and ere I

returned again she had passed away. But her maiden
sister, Miss Kirkwood—without notice of whom no
picture of William's early home would be complete—
survived both her and Mr. Robertson. She was not,
till a comparatively recent period, an inmate of
Greenhill ; but the little ancestral cottage where she
lived was close at hand, and she was from first to last
a notable factor in the family life. With her erect
bearing, her keen eye, her shrewd insight, her ready
wit, and her unresting needles, she was a fine
specimen of the maiden lady of the old school. As
she clung to her ancestral cottage, so she adhered
to her ancestral church, going regularly, in fair
weather and in foul, to worship in Denny—and
stoutly maintaining the superiority of the minister of
Denny for the time being, over every other member
of the profession. It was not easy to get the better
of Miss Kirkwood at repartee. There was a tradition
in the house, that when a probationer of many years'
standing was visiting at Greenhill, he was on a wet
day pacing up and down the parlour floor, while Miss
Kirkwood sat erect and busy with her knitting
needles. He stopped in his walk and laying his hand
on her shoulder, said, "You and I are just alike,
Miss Kirkwood, you never got a husband, and I never
got a kirk." "How many calls had you, sir ? " she
quickly asked. "Oh," he said, "I never received a
call at all." "Then don't you be evenin' yourself to
me," was her reply.

Mr. and Mrs. Robertson had fourteen children,

but of these five died in infancy; and of the rest, two died before their mother, and four before their father. The eldest son, Andrew, after being educated at Mr. Browning's school at Tillicoultry, became, as I have said, his father's assistant. He was the only one of six surviving sons who did not go to college with the view of entering the Christian ministry; but few ministers have done more to advance the interests of true religion than Andrew Robertson did in the sphere in which his lot was cast. Diligent in business and faithful to the interests of his employers, he passed among his men like a sunbeam, brightening their countenances and lightening their burdens by a kindly word. He was never weary of laying plans for their improvement. The school-house in which their children were taught became a centre of well-directed effort. Lectures and weekly sermons were provided, temperance and other societies were formed, and a singularly effective Sunday school was conducted. In the neighbouring village of Bannockburn where forty or fifty years ago the means of grace were scanty, Andrew Robertson was mainly instrumental in organizing a new congregation. When all preliminary arrangements were completed, and the opening day had come, it was found that no money having been left to provide a beadle, that functionary was wanting in the little sanctuary. The question occurred as the hour of worship was at hand, who should, according to Scottish custom, carry up the Bible, and shut the minister into the pulpit. Andrew

Robertson at once volunteered to do the service. His whole life was an illustration of the words, " He that is greatest among you let him be as the younger, and he that is chief as he that doth serve."

When the long day's work was done, Andrew would retire into the cottage of Avenuehead, that had been tenanted by his grandfather whose name he bore, and where he had taken up his abode ; and there, behind the sheltering screen of flowering trees and shrubs which almost hid it from the highway, would carry far into the night the work of self-culture. His books were well chosen, and thoroughly mastered. The college-bred brothers were eager to testify that Andrew was to the full their equal. In his careful study for the work of his Sunday school, he had gained a knowledge of theology that would have put many a professional theologian to shame. His modesty gave his attainments a peculiar charm. In his unselfishness he would not even burden those he loved with the knowledge that he was a habitual sufferer. For years he had borne in silence and solitude severe heart spasms, till at last on a February evening a hurried message came to Greenhill that he was dying, and ere they could reach him he had passed away.

The second surviving son of the family, James Robertson of Newington, has had his portrait drawn so faithfully and so lovingly, in the memorial to which we have already referred, that it is unnecessary to say anything of him here. William was the third of the surviving brothers. George, his companion at college and hall, was the fourth.   The two younger brothers were Robert and Ninian.   Of three sisters, Sophia died when William was a lad of fifteen.   Isabella was his faithful housekeeper and accomplished companion through the greater part of his ministry; and the youngest was privileged to minister to him at the end, and survives to mourn him. No home could have been happier than that in which these sons and daughters grew up together, under the care of their father and mother, who so trained them by the influence of love that harsh or ungentle words were never heard. Clouds often rested on the dwelling, but they were such clouds as are tokens of the Divine presence. Alienation or bitterness never came to mar the family joy.

I am permitted to add the following: "If the children in the Greenhill family were guided not so much by command, as by strong persuasive influence, the same principle held in a degree over the domestics of the household and servants labouring outside on the farm. 'Orders,' in the common sense of the word, were seldom heard, and yet authority was always maintained and never disputed. The relation between master and servants was on a much higher level than that of mere 'work' and 'wages.' The 'place' was soon found to be a 'home,' where yearly or half-yearly engagements were never known; and in several instances the service was life-long, the servants in such cases usually developing into 'characters.' Prominent among these was 'Hugh,' who came a young lad from Fort-William, in tartan coat and hose, with nasal tone and Gaelic accent, and full of weird, romantic tales of his own Highland glens, to the constant delight of the children who listened with silent wonder to his stream of Celtic eloquence.

"There was an air of self-importance about the little man, with, occasionally in later years, an assumption of authority that was amusing rather than provoking, for his heart was ever loyal and true. Nothing surprised Hugh. 'I ettled[1] that, maister' was the unfailing explanation of the most atrocious blunder or the most unlooked-for accident. On one occasion when Hugh was employed in building a hay stack, Mr. Robertson was quietly looking on, and observing that it was growing alarmingly like the 'leaning tower,' he said, 'Hugh, that stack is considerably off the perpendicular.' 'I ettled that, maister,' was the quick reply. No more was said by the 'maister,' who calmly awaited the result. In a few minutes over went Hugh and stack into the yard. 'Did you ettle that too, Hugh?' said Mr. Robertson with quiet humour, as he turned round without another word of rebuke and walked into the house, leaving Hugh to rectify matters as he best could.

"At the 'catechising' on Sabbath evenings Hugh, on first coming to the house, took his place with the family in the usual round of the Shorter Catechism. 'What is man's chief end?' was asked. 'I dinna ken

---

[1] Meant or intended.

thae questions, maister,' was the reply. ' Probably not, Hugh, but you'll have some idea of your own on the matter. What do you think should be the chief end of man ? ' ' Weel, maister, I may be wrang, but I'm thinking it should be his heid.'

"To the young people growing up around him Hugh was simply devoted, and was wont to speak of them as his own personal property. 'Do ye ken *my* young men ? ' was a question frequently asked of the casual passer by. Indeed everything about the place belonged to Hugh after this fashion. It was 'my fields,' 'my crops,' ' my beash ' (beasts), and ' my young men.' Nor was his faithfulness unappreciated by the circle, old and young, among whom for nearly forty years his lot was cast. He lived to be esteemed by them as a friend, and when he died in a good old age he was mourned as one of the family."

Other and younger servants became characters all but as quaint as Hugh. One of them, Jamie by name, had unbounded faith in William's power to solve all intellectual and spiritual perplexities, and used to store up every difficulty that occurred to him in his sermon-hearing and Bible reading, against "Maister Weelam's" next visit. On one occasion his difficulty was in connection with the enumeration of David's mighty men, where it is recorded of Benaiah, the son of Jehoiada, "who slew two lion-like men of Moab," that "he went down also and slew a lion in the midst of a pit in time of snow." " I'm no clear about that story ava, Maister Weelam," said Jamie, as he was driving the young divine from Stirling. "It's ma opeenian that as the grun' was a' covered wi' snaw the puir brute wad be snook-snookin' about seekin' for a drink o' water, and wad gang doon into the pit thinkin' he wad maybe get some there, and the man wad just gang doon ahint him, ye see, when he wasna lookin' and get the better o' him. I wus' that beast had fair play, Maister Weelam!" William was accustomed to tell this as illustrative of the reverence for Scripture and the love of fair play, which are both characteristic of the Scottish peasant, and which, when, as in Jamie's case, they seem to come into collision, occasion serious perplexity.

It was in this genial atmosphere and amid those pleasant surroundings that William Robertson spent his boyhood. The only school he ever attended beyond his father's roof was at " The Camp," a row of colliers' cottages at the foot of the road leading up to Greenhill. It was there, with colliers' and farm labourers' sons as his companions, that he got between his sixth and seventh years the rudiments of educa-tion. He often said that he did not learn much within the school, but he learned a great deal outside from his elder schoolmates—Bob Davie, and Jamie Durham (pronounced Dürie)—with whom he went bird-nesting. Jamie had gathered somehow a collection of Norse legends, which he told to William as they rambled by the hedge-rows. These legends made a deep impres-sion on the boy, and he treasured them among his precious possessions. To the end of his life he was in the habit of repeating them, always maintaining that Jamie's versions were much finer than those he found in books. This Jamie had in the after days a son who won high distinction as a scholar both at school and college, but died early.

It was no slight advantage to the future minister that his education was thus begun at a common school and in the companionship of the children of the poor. Indeed it is one of the secrets of the power which the Scottish clergy exercise among their flocks that the great majority of them have enjoyed a like advantage. No subsequent part of their training, at grammar school, college or hall, is more valuable than that which makes them feel their oneness with the class that generally forms the major portion of Scottish con-gregations. They can preach the gospel to the poor all the better that they know them as only school-boys learn to know each other.

Even at this early period the delicacy of health, which, to the end, hampered William Robertson's power of work, had made its appearance. The gastralgia which was his enemy through life and the immediate cause of his death, afflicted him when he was a little boy. Often in later years when this or the other cure was spoken of, he would say, " You need not think of curing this, I have had it since I was a boy at the Camp School, playing with Bob Davie."

When he was about eight he was withdrawn from the school at the Camp, and placed with younger members of the family under his brother James, as tutor. James was only four years his senior, but, along with Andrew, he had gone to Tillicoultry, and had enjoyed the advantage of nearly two sessions in the school of the Rev. Archibald Browning, who was known in all that district and beyond it, as a teacher of rare intelligence and freshness, devoted to learning, and with a peculiar power of awakening enthusiasm. In the brief curriculum which his constitutional delicacy permitted, James had acquired sufficient knowledge to qualify him for the charge of pupils the eldest of whom was only eight ; and no one who knew James Robertson in later life can doubt that he would have, even at twelve, sufficient gravity to command respect, or, that whatever might be wanting in gravity, would be more than made up in winning gentleness.

William's education made progress on Sundays as well as on other days. Not only, as we have seen, did he begin, on the weekly journey to church at Stirling, to experience that keen delight with which natural beauty always inspired him ; but, when the ancient town was reached, and its castle-hill was ascended to the sanctuary founded by Ebenezer Erskine, the air was filled with influences powerful to mould the thought of the eager boy. The vast congregation, gathered from a wide stretch of country, and composed of men and women who were still in living sympathy with the contendings of their fathers for truth and liberty, was itself an inspiration ; and of the two ministers who then preached in this his-

toric church, one at least had power to stamp his
individuality on the minds of his hearers. Dr. Smart
of Stirling attained a reputation in his own district,
and throughout the whole Secession Church, which
is sufficient guarantee of his power. Only a volume
of posthumous sermons remains to attest that power ;
but with all the disadvantages under which such a
volume is produced, no reader of these sermons can
fail to recognize rare gifts of imagination and eloquence. Those who have heard William Robertson
at his best, would be interested in tracing on the
pages of the old minister, to whom he listened in his
boyhood, unmistakable marks of a parental likeness.

CHAPTER II.

At College and Hall.

THE education at Greenhill, under James Robertson's tutorship, made such progress that in the autumn of 1832 William and George were enrolled as students in the University of Glasgow. William was then only twelve years of age, and George was two years younger. As they were both below the average stature and of slender build, the appearance of the little fellows must have excited some interest as, clad in their red gowns, they took their places on the benches of the Latin and Greek class-rooms. We have no record of how William acquitted himself in Latin; but his fellow-student, Mr. Andrew Duncan, now the venerable minister of Mid-Calder, says, "William and his brother George were both distinguished in the Greek class by the excellence of their metrical translations which were sure to be read from the chair; and I remember how greatly delighted the professor, Sir Daniel Sandford, was with William's render-

B

ing of one line in Anacreon's song about
women :—

> ' To man she gave a thinking mind,
>   Wisdom and courage well combined.'

And I have an indistinct recollection of a very lively
poetical version of one of the Dialogues of the Dead.
He got the fourth of the prizes awarded by the
votes of the students. I voted for him each time till
he stood highest."

One of his class-fellows was William Barlas, well
known in after years throughout the Church as a
blind preacher, whose gentlemanly bearing and un-
feigned goodness made him welcome at the fireside
of every manse he visited, and whose ability and
earnestness, made him no less welcome in every
pulpit he occupied. William soon noticed the blind
boy seated on the bench of the class-room, and on
an early day in the session found him standing at
the door as the class was dismissing. He went
to him and asked if he was waiting for any one.
Mr. Barlas replied that he was waiting for his brother.
William put his arm through his, and saying " Come
along, I'll be your brother," led him homeward. This
was the beginning of a friendship which only ended
when Mr. Barlas died.

At the close of their first session William began a
correspondence with Mr. Andrew Duncan which was
continued for some years. Three of his letters
have been preserved. They are before me now, on

their faded paper. In the earliest of them, dated "Greenhill, Saturday, 17th August, 1833," he announces that it is not his intention to attend college during the approaching winter. "I had once thought," he says, "of taking the Logic; now, however, I think it more advisable to try what I can do at home for a season, as I shall have the assistance of my brother, who is at the Hall at present. . . . I think myself scarcely fit for such a course as the Logic; you know I have no inclination to study hard." He then gives his fellow-student a sketch of his recess studies, which seem to have been sufficiently varied, and, it is to be feared, somewhat desultory. Logic and Hebrew, with "a glance at the elements of Moral and Natural Philosophy," divided the attention of the boy of thirteen! "Of these," he says, "I think the study of Hebrew is the most pleasant and easy."

William and George Robertson returned to college for the session of 1834-5. Besides the Greek class they attended during that session the class of Logic and Rhetoric. Among William's papers there is a descriptive essay entitled "No Fiction," to which this note is appended in a handwriting familiar to all Glasgow students of Logic for nearly forty years. "Given in, April 1835—Rob. Buchanan." In his lecture on German Burschen Life, written during the earlier years of his ministry, he says: "I well remember studying Logic (or what I thought Logic) in the Glasgow College, and being cheered through weary hours of study in the mysteries of syllogism by the music of the *night waits*[1] underneath the window."

The brothers again intermitted a session, but returned to Glasgow for the session 1836-7, and enrolled as students in the class of Moral Philosophy. George writes to Mr. Duncan, who was spending that winter in Edinburgh, of date 16th January, 1837 : " For a considerable time we thought of attending Wilson and Forbes in Edinburgh. In that case I should have enjoyed your company during the session. But several weighty reasons determined our return to our old *Alma Mater*. We have, besides Moral, taken Natural Philosophy in the Andersonian University ; and thus this session completes our preparation for those more congenial and ennobling studies which are themselves only preparatory to something beyond them nobler still."

William Robertson's course in Arts was thus somewhat irregular. It consisted of three sessions, spread over five winters. Except in the Greek and Logic classes, he does not seem to have entered with any enthusiasm into his work. He was accustomed to speak in after years of the absurdity of a boy of twelve being sent to study at a university. There is evidence in letters written to him by fellow-students that even at that early time he had im-

---

[1] The night waits are a band of aged, and, I believe, blind musicians, who, under license of the Lord Provost and magistrates, play through the silent streets of Glasgow at midnight for some weeks before and after Christmas.

pressed them with a sense of his power; but his intellectual quickening did not come till a later date.

He and George had brought, from their father's catechizings and James's teaching at Greenhill, a deeply religious spirit which led them to seek fellowship with those like-minded. Mr. Duncan writes in reference to their second session: "They were both members of a students' prayer meeting which was held in the vestry of Duke Street Church. Among the other members of the society were Mr. James Fleming, now of Whithorn, Mr. William Barlas, and Mr. William Cuthill, a relative of mine, who gained the highest honours in the classes of Mathematics and Natural Philosophy, studied at our Hall, and had resolved to be a missionary, but died after his fourth session." Mr. Duncan adds that the records of the meetings of the society which he has preserved are meagre, but in them he finds that on one occasion "one of the members having wondered if Lazarus would die again, this gave rise to a long and keen disputation about Hades, a subject which William and George Robertson had been studying with the guidance of their brother James, and in which they evidently felt a very special interest."[1]

They worshipped in Greyfriars' Church, and were drawn, like so many of the worshippers there during

---

[1] About this time George Gilfillan published some now forgotten sermons, in one of which there was the suspicion of heresy about Hades. This may account for the peculiar subject on which James Robertson had been instructing his youthful pupils at Greenhill.

Dr. King's ministry, to take an active part in church work. In a letter to Mr. Duncan, accompanying the one from his brother already quoted, and dated 17th April, 1837, William speaks of an epidemic of influenza as " ravaging the city widely." He says : " The funerals are literally crowding our streets. The poor people say ' It is as bad as the cholera,' not so mortal perhaps, but more general certainly. Our agents of the Christian Instruction Society find in every house not ' one dead ' as in Egypt of old, but generally more than one sick." He adds : " I sometimes spend an hour in the business of this society, and such hours are, perhaps, the most interesting of my time. I can scarcely think of an employment better calculated for the stimulus of personal religion. When you turn to the abodes of wickedness you naturally connect sin with the wretchedness met in its company. When you meet a Christian character in a hovel you are as naturally led to admire the power of that religion that makes the heart, even under burdens of distress, to hope and rejoice. And then the thought so often recurs, what if this person or that should find, or should see ' afar off,' his counsellor on the left ' that day.' "

During the winter between their second and third sessions, when George was detained at Greenhill by illness, William entered on an engagement as tutor in the family of Captain Aytoun, of Glendevon, among the Ochil hills. There is no record of the precise date when he went, but we find him established there in May, 1836. An undated letter from his father bearing the post-mark "11th May, 1836," and addressed to him at Glendevon, has been preserved. It is written to announce the death of an intimate friend, James M'Laren, whom both George and James had been visiting on his deathbed. It suggests reflections on the solemn event, and very earnestly urges him "with all the affection, and even authority of a parent," to "attend rigidly to the use of means necessary for preserving health and strengthening the constitution." The letter goes on to say—"Your brother George is again almost quite well. He intends going this afternoon to converse with Mr. Stewart on the subject of the approaching communion at Stirling. I know your own thoughts have been turned to this important subject, and I should have been happy in seeing you go together. In your present circumstances, however, this cannot be. But although he should get the start of you in publicly obeying the dying command of the Saviour, this is no reason why you should be behind in being prepared for it; and if this is so, an opportunity may soon, in the course of Providence, be given you of observing it." In a later letter the same faithful correspondent says: "When you feel yourself surrounded with all the charms of fashionable life, I hope you will remember that 'one thing is needful,' and that 'the fashion of this world passeth away.'"

William retained his connection with Glendevon till near the close of 1840. His curriculum at the

Theological Hall of the Secession Church began in
1837 and ended in 1841, but the sessions of the Hall
were in the autumn, and only lasted for eight weeks,
so that it was easily arranged to make the holidays of
his pupils coincident with them.   Longer absences
were, however, rendered necessary by his attendance
at the university during the winter of 1836-7, and by
more than one serious illness.   But the remarkable
power he had of closely attaching to him all with
whom he had any relations had so charmed Captain
Aytoun and his family, that even lengthened inter-
ruptions to study were cheerfully borne rather than
part with one who had the happy art of making study
a delight to his scholars.

The following characteristic invitation to exercise his
gift in another direction will be read with interest :—

AVENUEHEAD, 15th December, 1837.

My Dear William,—You do not need to be told that I
never write either to friend or foe except on business, and
seldom even then, if I can help it.   My reason for addressing you at present is to call your attention to the following
bill of exchange which will be returned, I trust, duly
honoured :—

COLD WATER COMPANY'S WRITING CHAMBERS,
15th December, 1837.

On Monday, the 25th current, deliver to us or our order,
in Auchenbowie School, between the hours of 4 and 8 P.M.,
a speech 20 minutes long, " de omnibus rebus et quibusdam

aliis," for value to be then received in tea, sugar, oranges, etc.—DURHAM, MACKENZIE & CO.

To Mr. WILLIAM ROBERTSON,
    ABC Prof., Glendevon.

To be serious, I presume there is no doubt you will be here at Christmas, and there can be just as little doubt that you will, at the earnest desire of the committee hereby conveyed, give us a lift at our second temperance soiree, which is to come off on the evening of that holiday. As no refusal will be taken it will be needless to offer any. If it were not that your humility, such as it is, might suffer shipwreck in consequence, I would have told you a secret, which is that the time of the soiree was fixed mainly to suit you. . . . .

And now that I have finished my business what shall I say more, except that I am, my dear William, your ever affectionate brother, ANDREW.

I am keeping this unsealed till I go into Stirling in case George should have anything wherewithal to occupy the blank space underneath.

George, who had been William's companion in all his college classes, was then town missionary at Stirling. No student preparing for the ministry ever dreamed in those days of spending his recesses in idleness. Bursaries were not so common as they are now, and there are some who think that we have lost something in our ministry since the pressure of necessity, which forced students to labour for their own support, has been lightened. It was characteristic of the two brothers that while William chose a situation in which he had larger opportunity of study, George preferred to enter directly on the work to which he had devoted his life. This was not because he was insensible to the influences which were so powerful with William. It is remembered that when he was toiling hard among the poor of Stirling, his favourite retreat for quiet thought was underneath the bridge by which the Glasgow road crosses the little Bannock, just after it has passed the Bloody Ford, and before it skirts the holm on which stands the house where James III. was slain.

William's gifts as a public speaker were in request in the neighbourhood of Glendevon as well as at Auchenbowie. Mr. Harvey, the Secession minister at Muckart, writes to him on 12th March, 1838, saying: " You will be obliged to give us a speech on Thursday. It is expected, everybody wishes it, nobody will be pleased without it. If a petition were necessary to be made up to secure it, I would get as many names as we can command for those that are to take the road to London. But as it would be insulting your goodness of heart to suppose you needed to be petitioned to do a good and right thing, which only proud peers and perverse parliamenteers expect, I shall not hint one word more about petitioning you." We have a glimpse into the matters of public interest in those days, in the postscript: " Take any of the subjects you incline, the abuse of human beings in the colonies, or the [here follows the drawing of a mouth wide open] for endowments, or both."

The speeches delivered on such occasions were fully and carefully written out, and, as no aspirant to a Secession pulpit in those days ever dreamed of reading a discourse, they must have been committed to memory.

So early as the spring of 1836, William had suffered from weakness of chest, and in 1838 disquieting reports reached Greenhill as to the state of his health. His father visited him in May, and in June the family physician, Dr. Johnstone of Stirling, was sent to consult with the medical attendant at Glendevon. The report was so far favourable that it was not then deemed necessary that he should leave his situation. His father writes to him on 16th June, urging the greatest possible carefulness, and adds, " I hope our gracious God may see it meet soon to restore to ordinary health, and to make your present and late distress a blessing to you by training into subjection to His holy will, and leading you to take up your rest and refuge in the hope set before you in the gospel. If these be the happy results, the medicine of affliction that now tastes bitter, will in the end be sweet, and be the subject matter of thankfulness and praise to Him who sent it."

A return of the more distressing symptoms later in the same summer compelled him to resign his position for the time. The regret with which his kind friends, Captain and Mrs. Aytoun, parted with him found expression in several letters which he fondly preserved along with those of his father and brothers. But the separation seemed inevitable, another tutor was found for the boys, and William, after only a few days attendance during the autumn session of the Divinity Hall, settled down for a winter's rest at home.

It was some time before this that his enthusiasm for literature began. He owed his intellectual quickening not to any learned professor or other accredited agency, but to the accident of his lighting on one or two of the works of Dickens, then being issued as monthly serials. The reading of these was like the revelation of a new world. He found himself in a large room, and began to wander at will through the wide realm of our English classics. There are among his papers various copies of verses belonging to this period. One of these is a poem on " Imagination " in which we recognize the combined influence of the metaphysical lectures of the Logic professor at Glasgow, and of the melody of Shelley's poetry. Another is a "Lament on the death of a favourite dog," and an " Epitaph " for his grave in the garden. From a letter written to him by Mr. Steedman (afterwards of Stirling) on 28th November, 1838, we gather that they and others of their fellow-students had a literary project in hand—the publication of some miscellany of which William was to be editor, but which, of course, never saw the light. Mr. Steedman writes in true student style : " You are to be pilot. Mind you have the management of the vessel, and I warn you beforehand, you have engaged a most unruly crew, M'Kenzie, Wylie, and Steedman ! If you venture from shore with these you will have to throw them overboard, else the poor crazy wherry will suffer ship-wreck. Peace, Prudence! thour't all a liar and as false as—Norval. Will Robertson can guide the helm 'where whirlwinds madden and where tempests roar.' La, how poetical! la, how metaphorical! Send me a long letter soon and give me all the particulars."

The impression made by him on fellow-students was, as might have been expected from the intellectual progress we have noted, deeper at the Theological Hall than at the College. Dr. Ker thus refers to a sermon he prepared for Professor Mitchell on the text "This is that King Ahaz":—[1] "He drew the picture of a man moving in the dark along a burial path till a grave stops his footsteps. He stoops to examine it, and gropes out the epitaph. It is the tomb and character of the wicked King of Judah; and then he proceeded to sketch his deeds and his doom, till there crept over us a feeling of *eerie awesomeness.*" It must be to the impression received from reading the sermon that Dr. Ker refers, for it was never delivered in the class. The state of his health only permitted William Robertson to attend the Hall for a few days about the middle of the session, and Dr. Mitchell agreed to accept his discourse in writing. After William had gone home the sermon was handed to George, who kept it in his possession till the end of the session, and freely lent it to his fellow-students. I have found among his papers the faded MS., and can well under-

[1] "Scottish Nationality and Other Papers," p. 244.

stand the feeling that crept over the students when
they read it. The written criticism of the Professor
is characteristic of its author. It thus begins :—" This
is a beautiful discourse, full of tender feeling and
original thinking.   It is the product of genius and
sensibility.   Nor do I know that the author could
have chosen a better method of illustration than that
which he has, by causing the character, like tints from
different parts of the fair canvas, to start into life and
lineament from the different passages of his history.
Yet when I take the discourse in connection with the
end—the edification of a Christian audience, perhaps
an humble and illiterate congregation, where there are
many ignorant, and few persons of a refined taste, I
cannot but feel that the delineation is too fine and the
language too figurative to meet the case or be suitable
to their edification. I beseech my young friend to
rein his imagination and study more plainness of
speech."   He then proceeds to give examples both of
beauties and of excesses of figure and colouring.   He
characterizes the fine passages he commends as " pre-
eminently beautiful and altogether original."   Of the
last of the passages noted as " excesses," which are
only three in number, the criticism is specially
interesting.   After speaking of the burial of Ahaz
" not in the sepulchre of the kings," and glancing at
what comes after death, the young preacher said—
" Why should we limit the power of mercy ? We may
yet, when the visions of hope are realized—we may
see him arguing a higher right to gratitude with the

thief upon the Cross ; or he may stand by the Throne and receive his crown of glory while the tale is swelling to an anthem, and we hear in the music of Heaven, ' This is that King Ahaz.' " On this passage the Professor remarks—" I fear we may not venture to indulge such a supposition, beautiful and benevolent though it be ; " and then the criticism thus ends— " But I feel that I am intermeddling with a fine embroidered fabric."

The Rev. Henry Erskine Fraser writes :—" It was during those few days' attendance at that session of the Hall in Glasgow (1838), which was his second and my first, that I saw him for the first time. During the next two sessions in Edinburgh he and George and I lodged together, and it was then that I became so intimate with him. During his fourth session he delivered a lecture before Professor Duncan, which caused some sensation. It abounded in condensed poetical expressions and abrupt literary allusions, of great force and beauty when the meaning and reference were caught, but very difficult at times to follow. I can remember the puzzled look of the Professor as he listened, and his saying at the close—that he had sometimes been at a loss to catch the preacher's meaning, but what he understood he very much admired. The opinion expressed among the students was that he might attract and interest a cultured few, but would never be a popular preacher. But that opinion was greatly modified the following session, which was his last, and in which the high esteem he was held in by his fellow-students was shown by his unanimous election as censor. The discourse he preached before Dr. Balmer on 'Pray without ceasing' (to which I believe Dr. Cairns alludes in his funeral sermon) was the gem of the session. It was listened to with breathless attention, and in its combined simplicity, poetry, and unction stamped him as one who could touch the chords of all hearts. It gave me, besides, an insight into his own spiritual experience, such as from his natural reserve and playful humour I had not had before, but of which glimpses were often afterwards obtained. A peculiarity about him was that he scarcely ever seemed to study. His reading was mostly miscellaneous, and there was apparently not much time given to it. And yet on every topic he was well informed, and expert in all theological and philosophical questions, on which, when they were under discussion, he would throw out original and vivid gleams of light. It was difficult to observe when and how he prepared his Hall exercises, but he was always ready with them when they were wanted, and had them carefully and thoroughly thought out. He told me once, while he was still a student, of a discourse he had mentally composed, even to the minutest expression, and which he carried in his memory without putting pen to paper. He had the power apparently of carrying on trains of thought, while outwardly engaged about something else."

A friend who has been searching into the records of the Edinburgh University Library sends me lists of the books taken out by William Robertson from 1836 to 1839, as well as those taken out during the same period by his friends, Dr. Ker and Principal Cairns. Robertson's list is the most voluminous, and it is also the most miscellaneous. The only systematic reading which it reveals is in the department of Roman history. Hooke, Gibbon, and Goldsmith were all laid under contribution. They are intermixed with Molière, Byron, Shelley, Shakespeare, Scott, Moore, Hogg, Cervantes, and a History of Chivalry. There seems to have been an occasional diversion into science, as we find Joyce's Scientific Dialogues, Haller's Physiology, and a work on Botany; while some vague purpose, which never led to anything, is probably revealed by the fact that he took out Walton's "Complete Angler," and "The Fly-Fisher's Guide."

While studying in Edinburgh, Robertson formed a friendship more influential on his intellectual future than the books he was reading. The "English Opium Eater," Thomas De Quincey, was, in these years, when health and fortune had alike declined, living at 113 Princes Street, in the house of his lawyer, Mr. Thomas M'Indoe, S.S.C. He had been in lodgings within the precincts of Holyrood, but desiring to consult Mr. M'Indoe, he came one night to call at his house. Mrs. M'Indoe, finding that some essential part of the dreamer's outgoing raiment was wanting, had asked him to stay till next morning. He accepted the invitation, and remained her guest for three years!

William Robertson, being Mr. M'Indoe's second cousin, was an occasional visitor at the house, and discovering who was the mysterious inmate occupying the bed-room by the side of the dining-room, he persuaded the good hostess to give him an introduction. The inter-course to which he was thus admitted, he always reckoned one of the greatest privileges of his early life. It led him into a new world of thought and speculation. It quickened his imagination, and left its mark on his style of speech and writing. He often said that if he had any power of expressing himself in good English, he owed it to Thomas De Quincey.

The following fragment has been found among his papers :—

De Quincey, whose literary style is in the English language—more perhaps in his later than his earlier works —perfectly unrivalled. From him, through so early an acquaintance with the old man eloquent, I, still young, learnt far more than from all other earthly masters of mine. And as his writings and low-toned, weird, musical speech— to which I would, alone with him, night after night, listen for hours together—were all upon the side of Christianity (unlike the sceptical and godless *litterati* that babble around us now-a-days), this had for me an indescribable charm which, like the charm of a beautiful child of his (it is long ago, but "a thing of beauty is a joy for ever") has never passed away.

The young student sought to repay his debt

to the illustrious writer, by every ministry of kindness he had the opportunity of rendering. He gladly spent hours in his company, and lightened the gloom of his strange solitude ; so that the dreamer learned to look for his coming.

To few besides was the door of his chamber opened. Mr. Robertson's youngest sister dimly remembers the awe with which, when she was a very little child and on a visit to her kinsman, she regarded that door and the mysterious man behind it, who put forth his hand to receive his meals. The little girl asked the servant why she handed in the gentleman's meals and did not go into the room. The reply was, "The last body who went in there was put up the lum, and never came out." Once when she was playing in the lobby with his daughter Emily, the door of the dreaded room was opened softly, and the gentle voice was heard. Emily said, "It is you he wishes," whereupon she ran screaming into the kitchen, and hid behind the servant. But Emily followed, and dragging her from her hiding place to the door, pushed her in. She has in her mind a vivid picture of the aspect of the room, with its awful "lum," up which she expected to be thrust. There was not a spot which was not littered with papers. De Quincey spoke kindly, and said, "I do not wish to frighten you, my dear, but only to ask you whether your name is Robertson, Robison, or Robinson," putting the emphasis on the distinctive syllables.

In 1883, when a new club-house was about to be

built in Princes Street, and the house in which De Quincey had sojourned was doomed to be taken down, William telegraphed to his sister to tell him by return whether the number was 113 or 114, and he wrote a few days later, " I have had a sketch made of the wall of 113 Princes Street, including the ' lum ' up which you should have been put."

There was at that time no lack of intellectual stimulus among the students at the Secession Hall. In addition to those with whom Robertson had formed friendships at college, he was now admitted to a goodly fellowship of the sons of the prophets. He had among his chosen companions, in addition to the two already named, John Cairns and John Ker, such men as Alexander MacEwen, A. L. Simpson, William Graham, and Alexander Renton. The professors of 'the time were men of note in their denomination, and one of them, at least, Dr. John Brown, has left his mark on the theology of Scotland. But we can well believe that Robertson was even more indebted to the men with whom it was his lot to associate in that peculiarly delightful intercourse which only fellow-students know how to enjoy.

During his Hall session in 1839 a proposal reached him from Captain Aytoun that he should return to Glendevon, and, after consultation with his father and mother, he resolved to do so. Captain Aytoun wrote of date 9th October, 1839 :—

I hope you will come here as soon after you receive this

as may be quite convenient for you. It will really be delightful to have you once more amongst us; but you must submit, I tell you, to very strict military discipline. I shall have all the lights out, particularly yours, at half-past ten every night; and you must fall asleep precisely at eleven o'clock, and not presume to awake one minute before 6h. 15′, 3″·1298764328777777—one minute did I say? I meant not one of the last decimal of seconds which stands above, which, if you can turn into words, it is more than I can do. . . . I really think your ministers ought to interfere to prevent that self-murder amongst so many of your students by over-exertion. . . . How great a mistake to suppose that the mind can acquire much if the bodily health be neglected, or rather ruined, by want of sleep and neglect of exercise, not to speak of over-excitement of the nervous system at its centre—the brain. I do hope, my dear young friend, you will allow me to keep you a little in order. I shall have no dissipation, no going out in winter nights, no sitting up till daylight, etc. In short, I am afraid you will mutiny; but, if you will follow my advice, you will acquire more in half-an-hour with proper care of your health than in a week without care.—Ever affectionately yours, etc.

It would seem from the hour at which the following letters were written that even Captain Aytoun's "strict military discipline" failed to overcome Robertson's early acquired habit of sitting far into the night.

To Mr. Henry Erskine Fraser.

GLENDEVON, Midnight, Hallowe'en, 1839.

My Dear Erskine,— . . . . When one is going to write to a friend, he has to wait till the kitchen chimney go a-fire, or the next river go a-flood, or the mercury rise, or the rain fall, or something occur that may be worth the telling. Neither is he likely to wait long, I trow, since Nature, like the most of her sex, has so much of the " varium et muta-bile semper." Though, if he do, he is quite entitled then, to be sure, to make a letter out of his disappointment ; and in that case, too, it is recommended that the post be just a-going as he writes, this being always the best excuse for not writing more or having begun earlier. So while I had at first been meditating the latter expedient for you, since, indeed, nothing *would* happen at all . . . did the old earth stumble in the hurry and treated us to a ***. Now I had meant to shroud that word in all the mysteries of gram-matical astrology until I might have burst forth upon you from some corner (of a page) in the dignity of having felt an *earthquake !* But in the meanwhile I came to learn that your own citizens had felt the shock. Well, thought I, this is very provoking. . . .

Seriously, I had written fifty lines of blank verse on the subject, with " Dear Erskine " for the first three syllables and " Here's a go " for the next three. As I sacrifice them to the flames now—(Oh, dear ! but it's all out of spite, you see, for your having felt the earthquake too)—I mark such words as these very prominent—" Death ! ghosts ! church-yard ! knell!" (How very grand it must have been !)

Talking of " knells," you must know that we have strange music here by way of accompaniment to that grand opera of Nature—(the earthquake, not the poem). Tradition says it is the dead of former ages singing at times their own for-gotten dirges, and probably from this *wailing* sound the Ochils have taken their Gaelic names. It may result from the vapour heated in their bosoms, breathing sonorously through their porous rocky lips. Perhaps it is only the winds of heaven vibrating into music between these glens.

But, hark you ! there it is, booming away at this midnight hour. So I was just thinking, as I threw me back in my chair to listen, that *you* must have often looked towards these hills amid the sports of your childhood,[1] and in your early fancies, I suppose, they may have assumed many fantastic similitudes. But perhaps you never thought of them till now, as the chords of a magnificent Æolian lyre, framed by the hand of Nature, and tuned to her own ear and moved into music under her own breath, and played to her own wild dance of an earthquake !

" How do you like Glendevon now ? " You see, as to the geography of the matter, I may still like it very much, though it be at this season of the year, when (to be poetical once more), the country, with its sudden alternations of smiles and tears, its fitful breathing and ruddy flush over the face of all things (not to mention its well-stocked farm yards !), exhibits all the symptoms of consumption. But I have written a fearful word, and must go to bed, for the one candle is out and the vital spark of the other will be fled almost simultaneously as in the case of the Siamese twins, or Pyramus and Thisbe, or Romeo and Juliet. . . . . So then good night ; 'tis pleasant to utter it though you cannot hear. The thought of living friends, like the remembrance of the lost, comes upon one more sweet and soothing and sacred at the gentle fall of the hour of sleep. (To be continued.)

Saturday Night.

A letter from home has brought me the first notice I have had of the death of William Thomson, and you will not doubt that it has saddened me. It has indeed cast a gloom over mirth, defying one to laugh at it, and given melancholy

---

[1] Mr. Fraser was a son of the Rev. William Fraser, of Alloa, about three miles from the foot of the Ochils.

a deeper shade of sadness, and you may easily conceive how everything around seems to have caught up the strange sympathy. It is a foolish thought, I know, but I cannot help it,—the cold blast without appears to blow more wildly and fall more fiercely when I think how they have laid him in the cold ground. And then that wailing sound I told you of, it never seemed so mournful before. Oh, the grave ! the grave !

It is easy to say we had expected it all,—this will not satisfy the heart. I have known it, even when the dead was yet unburied, think itself less lonesome. Let that moment come as softly and long lingering as it may, it is still the passing of a spirit into the presence of its God ! away from all our fondness and sympathies and prayers. Then as we begin to think how our thoughts and feelings had mingled with his, and that *he* has gone to his account—if there is not a deeper seriousness settling down upon us, Erskine, we are mad.

To Mr. Thomas M'Indoe, S.S.C.

Glendevon, Midnight, Hallowe'en, 1839.

Writing to a friend to-night I have made an engagement which presupposes my being in town about Christmas (not sooner), being conscious of no inducement to this above that of spending an hour with you, and, by your permission, De Quincey (of course to write that name with a " Mr." would argue as much ignorance of literature as to write mine without it). By the way, if Mrs. M. will still insist that the opium eater possesses all the attraction that ever draws me to 113 Princes Street, I should like to be told how I first came to meet him there at all. She seems to suspect I look on her as something like that cipher in arithmetic which is 0 in itself, but acquires a value from the figure beside it.

Very well; but then, you know, it multiplies that other by ten again, and indeed so did she by the indulgence she gave me to see him so late and so often, and as you know every opportunity of this kind could only enhance his ——. But I am becoming mathematical when I should be sentimental, and should only say that I am very thankful to them both.

To Mr. Henry Erskine Fraser.

Glendevon, 23rd April, 1840.

My Dear Erskine,—— . . . . You brought me so far onward from Alloa as to have left little scope for dissertation on the sequel of the journey in the style of your first unanswered letter that lies before me. About half-way up the glen a sleepy herd boy started from the silent hillside, and sung out in hearty welcome a cock-i-lecrie-la! This salute I of course charitably construed as a compliment, and at once conceived myself to have been greeted as the morning sun returning from the east with a light and with a gladness to the natives of this benighted glen!

Nothing of more importance crossed my way, unless it were an old man fishing beneath the Black Linn Bridge. A real Isaac Walton he was, and altogether I should think rather a queer fish in the stream of time.

He complained that the day was so bright and the river not a-flood! What will somebody not be complaining of! I wondered that so very old a man should be trifling his days away with such amusements. He told me he was weary of the world altogether, and very glad of any recreation in which he might forget it. I asked him how he could be weary of a gently coming summer, bright streams and soft breezes, and the flowering earth and the beautiful sky; and when he took off his hat and looked up devoutly into heaven, I understood him to say that green fields and stream-

ing music and his friends and his hopes were all there.   I
loved the old man, and wished a blessing on his hoary head,
especially as he had given me a snuff.

But I won't lead you further into the glen as you have
been here already, and I daresay, whatever you may have
gained in reality, must have been all lost in romance.   Besides, I know you will have no patience just now with anything but revivals,[1] and I hope you will give me credit for
sympathizing with you.   To be sure I hate all sentimental-
ism in real life.   I admire the character that can even frown
on you while he is doing a hidden kindness.   And you do
not *talk* to a mourner about his grief just because it is so
very deep; but there is a restraint upon your actions, a better
tribute than words, and a whistle or a jest would be an insult
and a mockery.   I have always felt a great temptation to
carry the same principle into religion, but it will not altogether do,—when motives may be mistaken, they must be
stated,—where God is forgotten He must be acknowledged,
—where a Saviour is unknown He must be preached.   I
have seen nothing in the least extravagant to quarrel with.
There may be not so much artifice in a revival as is suspected by those who are unacquainted with the " demon-
stration of power," and if there were I do not know how
much it should be condemned.   Sighs and starts and tears
are certainly not conversion.   There is a great difference
between the features and expressions of a living countenance
and the hideous mimicry produced by galvanism on the
dead.   But the latter experiment may yet issue in resusci-
tation.

Soon after the date of this letter, he was compelled
again to leave Glendevon for a time.   He returned to
Greenhill suffering from an illness which developed

---

[1] Meetings in Alloa in which his brother James took part.

into small-pox, one of his brothers being also laid down with the same disease. The remarkable recuperative power, which, spite of the delicacy of his constitution, always distinguished him, enabled him to throw off the malady and return to duty in the month of June. But he finally resigned his situation at the close of that summer, his place being taken by his friend, Mr. Erskine Fraser. The winter of 1840-41 was spent in Edinburgh, where we find him busily engaged with a number of his fellow-students in the study of German, and, in supplement to the theological education provided by the Secession Church, attending the lectures of Dr. Chalmers in the University.

From valuable notes of his conversations, kindly furnished to me by his early friend, the Rev. John Haddin, I find that so late as 1882, William Robertson thus estimated, with perhaps the exaggeration of off-hand speech, the various influences that contributed to mould him at the period of which I am writing. "I have had two kinds of education, that derived from books and teaching, and that derived from play and the exercise of my own mind. The latter I can testify is that from which I have obtained the most profit. If I have developed into any power, it is by casting aside all to which I was trained, and cultivating every faculty that was repressed. I gained enthusiasm from Sir Daniel Sandford, but no Greek. I gained no theology from Dr. Chalmers, but I gained enthusiasm. I gained no theology from Dr. Brown but what I gained was encouragement. I gained more from De Quincey than all I obtained from all my teachers. Dr. Brown said after hearing my first discourse that it was such a discourse as De Quincey would have written had he been a student of divinity."

Pleasant traditions have been preserved of the thorough enjoyment with which he entered into the "play" of which he spoke to Mr. Haddin. We hear of him now in Alloa with Mr. Erskine Fraser or Mr. Ramsay, and now at Cairneyhill, where the Secession manse was brightened by the presence of young ladies sent from far and near to get good learning and motherly kindness combined, at the hands of Mrs. More, the minister's wife. But it was at Green-hill that he was at most pains to exercise the happy art of bringing brightness into the lives of those with whom he was associated. As we have seen, he first went to college when he was a boy of twelve, became a tutor when he was sixteen, and was never afterwards, except for one winter, a continuous resident under his father's roof. But Greenhill was still his home, and his visits, at Christmas and other holiday times, brought to himself and to all the household keen enjoyment. Sometimes he would make elaborate preparation, and select and arrange a classic play to be performed by himself and his brothers and sisters; or have readings from Shake-speare or Milton or Cowper. The manner in which he succeeded in putting on the family stage, and having acted to its close, the Mask of Comus, was a fond tradition in the house. And yet it is noteworthy that he never claimed the freedom, hardly denied even to students of theology, of occasional visits to the theatre. One of his friends remembers that late in life he told him this, and added the reason, "I somehow always felt that my mother would not like it."

During his winter in Edinburgh, 1840-41, he enjoyed frequent intercourse with De Quincey. He often met, and talked of the books they were reading with Mr. Halkett—afterwards of the Advocates' Library, and his partner, Mr., afterwards Sir George Harrison. Alexander Logan, a rising advocate, and then the acknowledged wit of the Scottish bar, was his frequent companion. He and his brother John, being sons of the Relief minister of St. Ninians, had been the friends of his boyhood. Samuel Brown, the chemist, of whose marvellous genius and early death he used to speak to the close of his own life, was then in Edinburgh following his speculations, and dreaming his dreams, and Robertson was much with him. Samuel Brown's kinsman, Dr. John Brown, the author of "Rab and his Friends," had not then risen into fame, but his genius and his tenderness had already drawn very close to him a circle of friends, among whom Robertson was one of the most appreciative. Robertson and his friend, Mr. Simpson, had begun to cultivate that love of art, which made both of them in after years so com-

petent guides in the study of the great masters. In
their early days, they enjoyed together the friendship
of David Scott, when he was laying the foundations
of the fame which even his early death did not render
evanescent. From shreds of correspondence which
have been preserved, we can gather that amid these
congenial surroundings he was not merely receptive
but was trying to give expression to his thought. Mr.
Simpson writes to him of date 17th November, 1840,
" How is your poem advancing ? Let me have a
stanza or two in your next, and let your next be
forthwith."

CHAPTER III.

In Germany.

WILLIAM ROBERTSON was now qualified, as far as the requisite attendance at classes in arts and theology, and ability to pass the requisite examinations were concerned, to offer himself for license as a preacher. But he was only twenty-one years of age; and there had come to him a great thirst for wider knowledge, and for deeper insight into the problems with which it was to be the work of his life to deal. On the advice of De Quincey he resolved to study for a year at one of the universities of Germany. It was an ancient habit of Scottish theologians to complete their studies at continental seats of learning. The habit had fallen into disuse for fully a century, and Scottish religious thought had in consequence tended to become to some extent insular. To William Robertson belongs the honour of reviving the ancient custom. He was followed to Germany by a long succession of students, headed by his own friends, John Cairns, John Ker, Alexander MacEwen, William Graham, and Erskine Fraser.

The difficulties he described in his lecture on
" Burschen Life " as thrown in the way of the young
student proposing to study in Germany were not
encountered by him. Mr. Robertson of Greenhill,
though deeply and intelligently attached to the doctrine of his church, was too wise to fear the effect on a
student of theology of contact with divergent or even
adverse forms of thought. From a paragraph in a letter
to William dated 17th September, 1839, we gather that
thus early he was looking forward, not disapprovingly,
to what took place two years later. He says: " If
yourself, or George either, is desirous of learning
German, let any necessary books be got for the purpose, and perhaps some general instructions from a
living teacher might be had before you leave Edinburgh. James has some money to give you when he
arrives, and if more is wanted let me hear and it will
be sent next week."

William Robertson was accompanied to Germany
by his friend, Alexander Renton, afterwards minister
at Hull, and subsequently theological tutor in connection with the Montego Bay Academy of the United
Presbyterian Mission in Jamaica. Like Robertson,
Mr. Renton was the son of remarkable parents, more
than one member of whose family have done distinguished work in the Church. His mother was widely
known in Edinburgh and far beyond it for her keen
insight and unwearied philanthropy ; and his brother,
the Rev. Henry Renton of Kelso, was an honoured
minister, and fearless champion of the cause of civil

and religious liberty, while other brothers and sisters
in less public spheres were no less faithful and
effective in service. Robertson had a peculiar affection for this companion of his youth. Addressing the
annual missionary meeting of the Synod in the Music
Hall of Edinburgh, in the year 1864, he spoke of him
as :—

A missionary of your own on whom the grave has
closed and heaven opened some six months ago. He was
my dearest friend and fellow-student twenty years ago in
Germany. A man of gentlest manners, princely bearing, rich
gifts, and rare accomplishments, he gave himself with all
his gifts and accomplishments to the comparatively humble
task of teaching your poor blacks over in Jamaica, and
literally worked himself to death at God's work there ; and
when he had come home in the green summer time to die,
and, as the winter darkened, to place an honoured
missionary's grave in the Grange Cemetery, "beside the
grave of Chalmers," I said to his venerable mother who still
survived at his return, "Your son is really a martyr to the
missionary cause." "Yes," she said, "and if I had a hundred
sons, I would be proud to see them all the same." The
noble spirit of the Spartan mother has not died out yet !
The spirit of the brave old Roman mother that could give
her sons to die in battle for the commonwealth and conquest
of the world—or rather, shall I say, the spirit of the
Abraham, who, "by faith offered up his son upon the altar,"
and of those holy women also, in the days of old, that "by
faith received their dead raised to life again," as this most
noble mother also did—following her martyr son in a short
time to glory.

William Robertson has left a record of his voyage

to Germany, of his arrival in Halle, and first experiences and impressions there.

THE STEAMBOAT.

I sailed from Hull by the "Tiger." It was in the dark of a November afternoon. The lamps were lighting up the quay and the neighbouring streets, and I was reminded that it made . no difference at all to Hull whether I stayed or went away. "But there are hearts," said I to myself, "that may have been touched with my farewell—one—beautiful —— " "Hold out of the way there," said a sailor roughly, who was slipping a rope along the quarterdeck. The roar of the engine was suddenly stifled into a hollow thunder. The boat moved off, and stopped again—splash, splash—and I took a farewell look of my native shore—that is to say, of a very dirty stone pier, including certain wooden posts, and chains, and cables, and a heap of coals, and an old woman selling gingerbread. Splash, splash, splash. . . . .

A few hours later and we were really at sea. I was sitting half asleep over a volume of the "Mysteries" (which, by the by, is the safest way of reading that book), and felt myself suddenly pitched right into the floor. I looked round and the cabin was now empty, save only a very fat Dutch captain "spinning a yarn" over a bottle of porter to a tall gentleman, who was growing pale in the face, and not paying the least attention to what the fat captain was saying. . . . .

I went on deck. A solitary passenger, muffled up closely in his topcoat, was attempting to walk up and down as swiftly and as straight as possible. Suddenly he retreated to the one side, and leant over. I heard a deep drawn breath, and recognized the voice. "Ha, ha, Renton," said I, "what are you doing there?" Of course he was only looking at the bright phosphoric stars that were dancing in the paddle foam.

I walked on deck till long past midnight. The wind filled the white sails, and tossed up the white waves also. I looked at the bright stars above, and then I turned to look at the last red light in the mouth of the Humber, which, like a faint star, was twinkling and disappearing, and then I went to look at the phosphoric stars in the paddle foam also. . . . .

Next morning all assembled at the breakfast table. We had entered the Elbe. The river is very shallow, and the navigation difficult. We took in a pilot at Cuxhaven. Presently he came on board, he threw off about half-a-dozen suits of clothes without seeming to come at all nearer to his skin, and then, taking his station upon the gangway, commenced a series of sundry motions and gestures with his legs and arms, which were faithfully copied off into the helm by the steersman abaft.

. . . . The wind, rain, and darkness had all passed off together. The sunshine glanced on the river and the fields, and made a hazy brightness in the air. The country on the Hanoverian side is flat, offering nothing of more interest to the view than a simple sloop of war, riding in a ditch hard by, from which several figures in red coats came out to challenge toll for his Majesty of Hanover. The Danish side is more picturesque, with here and there cottages among trees, or a painted wooden village with its church and spire. Under the clear cold light of a November morning, it lay like a quiet landscape in water colour. The scenery grew bold and even romantic. We had all got on deck to admire it, and a heavy dark cloud burst over us, which for a moment or two enhanced the effect, and then, in a shower of hail, we were swept into the port at Hamburg.

"And this is Germany," said I, as our droskey came to a sudden stop under one of the gates of Hamburg. "What is your name?" inquired a dirty-looking fellow, poking in his head at the coach window. The answer to this and other such queries being given and spelt over to his satisfaction, and recorded on the fragment of a slate which he rested on his coat sleeve, the coachman was roused up, and once more requested to get along. "Yes, to *Streits* on the *Jungfernstieg*," replied he, by way of showing that we were quite mistaken if we supposed he had been asleep, and then drove off quick enough, performing a series of loud ringing cracks with a heavy whip to the manifest discomfiture of his own horses and the dismay of all dogs, porters, and old ladies in the immediate vicinity. "It *is* Germany," I repeated, pulling up the window again.

The next day was the Sabbath, but to me it seemed more like a Saturday. There was the same clattering of carriages and cracking of whips, the same knocking with invisible hammers and sound of street music, and voices in conversation, with song and laughter, quite out of the grave and solemn Sabbath key. It was only by the ringing of bells you could know it to be Sabbath at all, and to me the sound of the deep-mouthed bells, quite jars on the hum of the city. In the quiet of a Scotch Sabbath they mingle with their own echoes. Here they seemed more like the growling of angry spirits from the vaults of the old cathedrals. . . . .

HALLE.

We had come by a very early morning train from Magdeburg, and to think of the place we had left was much like looking back through the deepening twilight of a tunnel, upon dimly lighted streets at the far end and the red glare of the engine and the flickering of the guard's lamps to and fro upon the *Eisenbahn.* We were glad enough at the Halle station to commit our bags to the railway porter, and feel ourselves once more in open daylight, as you may sometimes have seen a collier deposit his picks at the pit mouth, and extinguish the little black lamp on his forehead as he looks up and sees the white blazing lamp of the sun, hanging high on the forehead of Heaven.

It rained heavily, so that we saw Halle first in its glory. For you must know that Halle is celebrated over Germany for many things, chiefly for its dirty streets. Everybody talks of *schmutzige Halle.* "Schmutzige" is a Christian name indeed, as it has been baptized in rain a thousand times. . . . .

After two months here I can feel pretty much at home. Have taken lodgings in the *Kleiner Sandberg;* stuck up my card outside the door; carry the key in my P.-coat pocket. My landlady is a respectable old dame, who swears a good deal without thinking any harm of it; her husband is an officer retired on a pension. He has fought in the battle of Leipsic, was present at the field of Waterloo, and declares our Scottish Highlanders are the finest soldiers in the world. The old gentleman makes himself useful in the way of cleaning my boots, running out for cigars and the like; or when such duties fail, he sets a-scouring and polishing at the brass handle of my sitting-room door, till he can see himself laughing in miniature inside. I can now recognize the voices of the different church bells in the vicinity, have got quite reconciled to the invisible being who practises the piano in some adjoining room every night, have exchanged nods with the old gentleman in a window opposite, who lies the most of the day with his head and shoulders out into the street, smoking a meerschaum and smacking his lips like a rabbit eating clover. "How do you do, old boy?" This is what I call feeling at home.

Almost the first acquaintances I made in Halle was with
H————, a student and member of a *Burschenschaft* in '34.
At that time these societies fell under suspicion of the
Government. He was arrested, and along with seven others
condemned to death. Subsequently his sentence was com-
muted into imprisonment for life ; and on the death of the
old king, I know not how, he has regained his liberty. All
the while he had never seen his accuser, nor known what
his crime had been. I believe it consisted chiefly in singing a stupid song, with a chorus of Trara, Trara, or some
nonsense of that sort.

He is a good-looking young man of 28, speaks English
well, and is altogether very accomplished. He had just
about finished his studies in law, but, of course, can never
practise now in the Prussian court ; and from so long con-
finement in the darkness of a dungeon, has almost com
pletely lost his eye-sight.

How fond his mother is of her handsome son who was
confined so many years in that fortress on the Baltic, and
she had never seen him all the while ! Every other minute
she rests her knitting on the table, and looks at him so
fondly, for she is a widow and he is her only son. The
story has something romantic in it besides. A young lady
of Colberg, the castle in which he was immured, had by
some chance seen the handsome prisoner, and become
passionately attached to him. They are betrothed now, as
the custom is in Halle, and she is at present on a visit to his
mother's house. She sits on his knee sometimes, and
pushes back the black hair from his brow playfully. I even
think I saw him kiss her once or twice to-night, and
that I could excuse, for he is going to leave her for a long
while. He goes into Switzerland to-morrow. A thorough
romp in the eyes of everyone else, yet how tender and
gentle she is with him.　.　.　.　.

And he is not one of your peevish, sullen spirits that refuse to be amused. He talks, and sings, and laughs too, whenever they want him; but I have observed that he slides back as easily into melancholy again, as if it were the constant habit of his mind. I suspect his spirit is broken.

To-night I prevailed on him to play me that forbidden revolutionary air, and joined with all my heart in its stupid chorus of Trara, Trara. Still while I was laughing at it, his fingers had mechanically begun touching the soft notes of a *Sehnsucht* waltz of Beethoven's, and then passed into a wild and melancholy air which Oginsky, the Pole, wrote before committing suicide. In the silence that ensued I felt embarrassed and took my leave. "That is my favourite music now," he said to me, as we shook hands at the door.

Letters to his brothers Andrew and George, and to his friend, Mr. Erskine Fraser, supplement the record from which the foregoing extracts are taken, and give us yet more vividly his early impressions of Halle and its university.

To Mr. ANDREW ROBERTSON, Auchenbowie.

HALLE, 14th January, 1842.

Your digest of general information was just the very thing that was wanted for a couple of poor fellows that had been two months out of their own country, and had no certain means of knowing that it was not all swallowed up in the Atlantic! . . . .

Tholuck took me the other day into a reading room, and brought me some English periodicals. In a little he came and asked if I had got anything to amuse me. I showed him a passage in the *Mirror*, extracted from the *Stirling Advertiser*. " Ah," said Tholuck, "the *Stirling Advertiser!*

That must please you very much, although I suppose it is *no great shakes.*" How comically this sounded from Tholuck you cannot think. I have laughed at it ever since ! . . . .

You wish to hear of the university and its professors— orthodox and rationalistic, and the difference between them. There you have proposed to me a task. I have not yet been into one third of the lecture rooms, and I suppose scarcely any two professors here have the same opinions in philosophy and theology. This, which confuses one at first, turns out to be a great advantage. Here you can study the German mind in all its shades and distinctions. We have come to the right shop for that. "Halle is the Menagerie of German Philosophy," said Tholuck, the first time we saw him. Here you have .Rationalists and Supernaturalists, Pietists, Mystics, Fichteans, Schellingians, and Hegelians of all kinds. To explain these in the shortest manner possible, would require one to begin from Kant at least, and write a few volumes. This you must excuse me doing till I come home. . . . .

I have been sitting for half-an-hour translating my ideas into English, to see if I might not give you some account of this Hegelian system—but I understand it much too partially to give any comprehensive view, and as the remaining page cannot contain *all* I know about it, I shall defer the task.

Hegel has his best expounders in this University, Hein- richs and Erdmann. More than half of the students, and these the most gifted (Tholuck says), are his followers.

Gesenius belongs to the old school of Rationalists. He is driving away at Genesis just now, and is paying a great deal of attention to it for a man who does not believe the half of it to be true. It is pleasing to turn from these to Tholuck. He and Müller, professors of theology, and Leo, professor of history, all very talented men, are the defenders of Evangelical religion in Halle. Leo was formerly a Deist, and highly esteemed among his party. I have heard that he has been brought over by Tholuck's instrumentality. I should think the evil influence which may be derived from hearing the other professors may be much more than counterbalanced by mingling with these men. Tholuck has his answer ready for them all. He enters on every difficulty you propose to him with the fearlessness of a man who has studied the subject and quite made up his mind.

It is noble to hear him tell it in the face of a class, two thirds of which are opposed to him, that he knows they reject the Bible just because they have no heart to it. The warm glow of passion, that runs through all his discourses on Sabbath, and addresses to the students, is even more delightful than the cool clear light in which he places a subject of criticism or philosophy.

To Mr. George Robertson.

HALLE, PRUSSIAN SAXONY, 25th January, 1842.

I have found Germany very much what I expected. People with broad faces and very long pipes, waggons with four horses, a boor astride the hindmost and a peasant girl sitting on the top, bands of apprentices with knapsacks singing as they pass, linden trees and windmills. Halle is a good specimen of a university town—wooden houses with low flat windows, old ladies sitting inside knitting, or a lazy student smoking his meerschaum, with his head and shoulders thrust out into the street, reminding one of those beavers we used to read about in the Plean school collection. Halle contains some fragments of antiquity, besides such as are to be found in the heads of Gesenius and Tholuck. It has one old castle several old churches, and a great number of old women with their heads done up in towels.

As a modern town, Halle is not a very busy one. Excepting the salt works, perhaps, which are its chief support, the principal trade seems to be done in coffins! I have seen about a dozen shops with the doors and windows full of them. They are gay-looking articles, with nothing that is black or dismal about them. The Germans are very particular about that sort of thing. The churchyard is a favourite walking place in Halle—"God's Acre" they call it, but I hate that name. The ground is thickly planted with crosses over the common buried dead. The side ranges of family vaults are more interesting. You look in through the iron grating upon an ascending series of coffins in historical order—a gloomy calendar. The parents of some remote century side by side at the bottom, and their family in its successive generations piled one above another on their breast. Loose flowers are scattered on the topmost, or wreaths are hung round about on the walls, but as it is winter time, the flowers are withered, and nothing but snow wreaths are going just now.

. . . . Renton has just finished an appendix to his letter, and he urges that we send them immediately, or some of his remarks will be out of date—and we are going out just now to "Tholuck's Encyclopædia," which is a very interesting series of lectures and I could not pardon myself for missing one. Then we have yet to practise "God Save the Queen" for that dinner to-morrow which Renton has told you about. I cannot tell you how many songs I have had to sing in parties here—songs which I never dreamt of being able to sing at home. The Scotch ones are greatly in request. Of course I have the words to make for myself in many cases; and already I have written two songs to the music of the *Rowan Tree*, that favourite of yours, and of mine also I may tell you, and of several other people here besides, "though I say it that shouldna say it." . . . . Be sure to write if you want to hear from me again at full length. Meanwhile, I must refer you to Andrew for information on the civil and philosophical department, Erskine Fraser on the literary (I shall write to him immediately), James on the ecclesiastical, and I shall send a packet of the miscellaneous to the care of G. Mackenzie.

From this letter it would appear that the gift of writing verse, of which we have already found traces in earlier student days, was still cultivated. The following song, written to the music of an old Scotch ballad, probably belongs to this period. He was accustomed to sing it in later years. The tune to which it was sung gave a most ludicrous effect to the refrain of each verse.

The Guid Auld King.

The guid auld king went a May wooing,
And oh ! but the beggar lass was bonnie,
The auld king said—my very pretty maid,
I'll marry you rather than ony.
    Marry you, marry you, marry you, marry you,
I'll marry you rather than ony.

The bells did ring, and the choirs did sing,
And they rade to the kirk on the causeway,
And the guid auld king had a merry wedding,
When he married the bonnie beggar lassie.
    Married, married, married, married—
When he married the bonnie beggar lassie.

The guid auld king was a waefu' man,
And oh ! but he lo'ed her rarely ;
When aff she ran, with a gaberlunzie man,
And the auld king grat fu' sairly.
　　　Grat—grat—grat—grat—
And the auld king grat fu' sairly.

She hadna' been but a fortnicht queen,
When the bonnie beggar lassie grew weary,
She took aff her croon, and she laid it doon,
And she said, "Whaur's Jock, my dearie?"
　　　Jock—Jock—Jock—Jock—
And she said, "Whaur's Jock, my dearie?"

Oh ! there comes Jock, wi' his auld meal pock,
It was in the mornin' early ;
And afore the king rase, and had gotten on his claes,
She's up and she's aff wi' him fairly.
　　　Aff—aff—aff—aff—
She's up and she's aff wi' him fairly.

Oh ! whaur are ye gaen, my bonnie, bonnie wean,
But Jock said, " Never to mind him ; "
So aff they ran, the gaberlunzie man,
And his ain true luve behind him.
　　　Luve—luve—luve—luve—
And his ain true luve behind him.

To Mr. Henry Erskine Fraser.

Halle, 27th January, 1842.

I hope when I return to be able to give you some sort of
information also which may save you a good deal of trouble
and expense when you come to make this journey, for until
very lately we have been going on quite at random and in

the dark. To be sure I like that sort of thing very much, and if it had only been in a country where I could not understand one word of the language I might just have liked it all the better. " But the dollars," Erskine, " the dollars," as Renton says—aye, there's the rub, when you don't understand the language and have to change your coin every two or three days. A Jew on board the steamer to Hamburg asked me if I could speak German. " Very imperfectly," said I. " Sovereigns, my dear sir," said the Jew, " English sovereigns are the thing. They speak all languages on the Continent." " But they suffer very much in translation, I believe," said I. The Jew laughed immoderately—I daresay the rascal knew it very well. . . . .

You must come to Halle, of course, and take a session at Berlin also, if you can afford it. These are, out of question, the two best theological schools. Halle represents best the German mind in its present moods and variations. . . . Gesenius holds on by the old Rationalistic school. I hear him now and then. . . . . If you only saw the old fellow coming into his lecture room with a P.-coat fringed with fur, and boots and spurs, or cutting capers on horseback. The best Hebrew scholar of the age ! He is quite a man of the world is Gesenius, and they say a little avaricious withal. . . . Tholuck I like best of all yet. I know him almost better than any one in Halle. I had a request from him yesterday morning, as I have very often, to bring Renton that we might have a walk with him, in half an hour or so. I wrote in reply that we would certainly come, but as a heavy shower of sleet was falling at the time, hoped the weather would change within the half hour. Tholuck doesn't seem to understand these scruples about walking in wet weather. " To be sure," said he, after we did go, " I expect to catch cold in this walk, but I must walk for the benefit of my health ; so, if you please, come away." And we did walk, and the sleet did fall, and we kept ourselves as warm as possible talking about English fires and German stoves. . . . . But I must tell you what like he is. Tholuck is slightly made, and bears in his appearance the marks of ill-health and severe study. . . . He is very short-sighted, and in the class wears sometimes a pair of round-eyed spectacles with a black rim, which gives him a very odd appearance. When you bow to him in walking he takes off his hat in a great hurry, looking straight before him all the while, and without having the least idea who you are. He does not dress very elegantly, and throws a mackintosh over all when he goes out. He walks with a quick, irregular and springing motion, in which his hat seems to describe a succession of parabolic curves. But you cease to observe such oddities when he begins to address you, and by and by you forget them altogether. His conversation is exceedingly engaging. Altogether, his manner is rather earnest than great. A deep passion runs through his discourses. It breaks out sometimes in the midst of cool exegesis, when he comes upon a passage that has been desecrated by the opposite party. In his descant on the Psalms to his private meeting of students on Wednesday evening he is peculiarly impressive.

CHAPTER IV.

In Germany, Italy, and Switzerland.

IN the record of his German experiences, resumed three months after the date of the extracts already given, William Robertson gathers up some of the results of his observation and study.

HALLE, 9th April, 1842.

The everyday religion of Germany is a very ambiguous kind of thing. It seems to consist very much, for one thing, in swearing. I am quite serious in this remark. It is one of the first, indeed, that might occur to a stranger in this country. You can hardly talk a minute with any one of these Germans, without hearing him use such expressions as "God save us!" "Lord Jesus!" "Dear Heaven!" and so forth. Tholuck does not do so. He is almost the only exception I have met with. . . . In a former age, when a living piety had spread itself among social and family circles, they have been brought, perhaps, very imprudently into colloquial use, and now they remain as the dregs where the better spirit has been quite drained off.

After describing the Christmas trees with their lighted tapers, etc., he goes on to say :—

The idea of the symbol, as Tholuck explains it, is this :—
" As the evergreen in winter, as those lights burning in the
dark night, even so came Christ upon our desolate and
blighted world." I thought the whole affair looked very
childish, but I was told the beauty of it just lay in this—it
was a season for Christians to "humble themselves and become as little children."

The present festival of Easter, again, is celebrated chiefly
with magnificent music. I have already heard several
oratorios performed in public. A friend of mine, of whose
sincere piety I have no doubt, assures me that to him these
are always seasons of the deepest devotion. I cannot well
understand this, for although there were certainly passages
of overwhelming power such as I have never heard before,
yet in general the blowing of French horns and scratchings
of fiddle strings, seemed much too profane a mode of expression for subjects so sacred. . . . .

I wonder under what mutilated forms real Christianity
may appear. I wonder how much a man may disbelieve
without being an unbeliever, for there are yet many among
those I am describing whose real Christian character I should
not like to call in question, till I was a little more confident
about my own.

I find a very instructive chapter in the history of Rational-
ism. The longest and stoutest opposition to its outspread
seems to have been given by the practical clergy. Whatever
dreams might please the philosopher in his study, something
else was necessary for them. The truth of the Bible only
could avail, when they came to deal with the hearts and
consciences of living men.

At Easter he began to keep a journal. It would
seem from its earliest entry that in doing so he acted
upon the suggestion of one or both of the correspond-

ents—Wiliiam Barlas and George Gilfillan, from whom at that date he received letters. A note on the title page of the journal warns any stranger into whose hands the book may fall from peering into it. We shall so far respect the warning, as to give only a few extracts. These, with a letter to his brother Andrew, will complete our account of his student life in Germany.

HALLE, April 11, 1842.

Received a letter from W. B., with an appendix from G. G. Resolved therefrom to begin this journal. Tholuck sent for me to have a walk with him yesterday, and quarrelled with me very tenderly for my reserve. The *Frau* had remarked that there seemed no bridge between us. I promised to build one. Renton he would excuse, as he was *schweigsam* at anyrate. Once he thought I was coming out on Coleridge, but the moment he touched me I retreated like a snail, and had kept my shell ever since. (He had asked if I had had many struggles with infidelity.) I said snails only came out in wet weather. He supposed I had found *him* very dry, eh !

. . . .

13th.—Finished Schleiermacher. . . . . Sent a note to Ulrici, and followed it up by walking with him at 12. He likes Lanssing most, of their modern painters ; all that he does is *ausgeführt*. In Berlin I must visit Count Rancischky's Gallery, and see particularly the *Battle of the Huns*, by Kaulbach. The spirits of the slain armies rise at midnight and resume the battle. . . . . Saw Koch from six to eight, and read " Wilhelm Meister " till ten.

14th.—Dreamt a good deal last night and unpleasantly, though I have forgot what about. The thoughts of the

E

day are said to reproduce themselves in dreams. This seems to be a stating of the truth in one of its subordinate illustrations, in too limited a form to be quite exact. It is the disposition and character in general which works itself out thus unconsciously, creating and then realizing its own pleasures and punishments. The state of health, of course, being always taken into account, and the same conditions required as in judging of character in waking life, for it were too bad to refer a frightful dream to some dreadful sin or sins unknown, when the greatest sin in the case may have been eating toasted cheese to supper. . . . . Spent the evening with Treuherz. He tells me that when young he heard Schleiermacher preach. He was about four feet high, and had a large head and nobly chiselled countenance like a statue. He leant forward on the pulpit and spoke almost in a whisper. But he was distinctly heard, and seldom used a gesture. . . . .

17th:— . . . . Yes, I must confess I would be ashamed to tell all that I dream. I dreamt last night that I was a boy again. My younger brothers and sisters were eating something nice, and they were not very sure about the propriety of it, and I as greedy as any of them, though a little more reserved, as became my more advanced age, I suppose. Then hearing my mother's footsteps approaching I began walking very determinedly up and down the room to let her hear just as she was entering. "Now," says I, " you will see what mother will say to all this." "Oh, poor things," said she, when she saw what it was, "let them eat it ; it will do them no harm." This was dreaming my childhood back to the life. I can almost say it without shame, as Lamb has said, one can talk of what he was when a child without egotism. In future years will I be so much estranged as this, I wonder, from my present self. Thou, William Robertson of 18—, if perchance thou deignest to cast an eye upon these pages, say do I seem to thee as quite another being. Dost thou think of me as the German student whom thou mightst yet find in his *Wohnung* of the *Kleiner Sandberg* by the dim light of his oil lamp? Yet, believe me, my dear sir, the best wishes of my soul are quite concerned about thee! Aye, sir, and let me tell thee if thy faith and hope and love are not the same as mine, only greatly more sincere and true and ardent, thy past self of the K. S. Halle—this 17th day of April, 1842.—W. R., Esq., student, rises up, sir, as an accuser against thee. " I would wish my days to be, ' Bound each to each by natural piety.'" I do not know if I quite agree with Wordsworth in the word *natural,* but it would be unfair to mangle a quotation by leaving it out, and the whole passage, " My heart leaps up," etc., has to me a deep and sacred meaning, let Lord Jeffrey and all critics say what they can.

But eleven has struck, the watchman is blowing his whistle, and the remaining reflections of this night I shall shut up in the secret chambers of my soul, or tell to One alone.

21st.—" Fast," or rather I should say *Busstag,* in Halle and over all Prussia—the one annual fast. Walked with Ulrici at twelve. We met Tholuck. He asked me if I had *hingegeben* myself to the *Gefühl* which such a day as this *entspricht.* Now, the weather being exceedingly beautiful, and the question exceedingly long and intricate, and Ulrici laughing in the middle of it, I thought he must certainly mean if I was quite in the mood for walking. But I asked him what *Gefühl?* and he then asked me if I had been doing *Busse.* I said " No," or not very much. Ulrici said I did not acknowledge Prussian fast days. Tholuck then asked Ulrici " if he found anything so laughable in that." Ulrici lifted his hat and begged Tholuck's pardon, but argued his point very seriously nevertheless that

I was in the right. On parting, I thought Tholuck said to me, rather coldly, " Good morning, *Herr* Robertson." . . .

Tholuck was an intense student, and could not understand any one who did not work hard. He never, Mr. Erskine Fraser tells us, understood William Robertson. When his name was mentioned Tholuck would shake his head gravely and say, "Ah! he will never come to anything ; he is a great idler." Mr. Fraser was in Germany about a year before Tholuck died, and called to see him. His face was shrivelled up like a mummy's, but his intellect was clear. They talked of Robertson and of his brilliant career as a preacher ; but the old man shook his head as of old, and said, "Ah! but he never did any work. He was a great idler."

To MR. ANDREW ROBERTSON, Auchenbowie.

HALLE, 29th April, 1842.

I received your letter, as I was saying, on Sabbath at breakfast time, and as the morning looked very well, and as I myself looked nothing of the sort, but, on the contrary, rather pale, from having sat up too late the night before, I just, look you, took a walk out to the village of Giebichenstein, in the outskirts of which is a very neat and pretty cottage of the Roman Catholic priest, in which Renton has taken lodgings and is going to hang out for the summer. Now, if you could only think how precious we reckon a letter from home, you could easily divine the purpose of this morning's visit.

But Renton had just gone out at nine to morning service.

On a knoll at the distance of a few stone casts stood the church with its old steeple and churchyard, and already the deep breathing of the organ, with the accompaniment of many voices, might be heard, though somewhat faint and distant like. I cannot tell you how lovely it was—so much so as to make me sad and thoughtful. No other sound but that of the Psalm, now swelling, now fainting, the worshippers unseen. The morning was exceeding beautiful. I rested myself in an arbour in the garden which looks over to the church, and read the diary of an old Pietist while the service lasted. Did you ever linger in the neighbourhood of a church at the hour of prayer and feel how lonely it was? A little dog came snuffing about my feet, looked up in my face as if surprised, but without barking, and ran away as quick again.

By and by the congregation thronged across the churchyard and down the sunny slope, while the organ music swelled louder and faster and seemed to be rushing out at all the doors and windows.

Then the people disappeared in the dell, among the trees, and by the stream side. Here and there, after a little, appeared a straggling party on the neighbouring heights—only some children were left laughing and playing about the churchyard. Why I should be wasting a whole page describing all this to you I do not very well know; but I had your letter still in my hand all the while, and that its contents and associations mingled themselves up with the stillness and the scenery, is that which, most of all, I cannot help remembering.

Nothing of importance has occurred since I last wrote you, except the arrival of your letter. I have been, indeed, to Leipzig, and seen that great Easter fair. It has lasted for more than a month. As the Highlander could not manage to see London for houses, so one might find it difficult

to see the Leipzig fair for stalls and crowds of people. Indeed I could not feel like being in a fair at all, till I had got
into the confectionery division, or still more into the corner
where the man with the miniature organ and the three monkeys was exhibiting, and the half groschen peep show, and the
great show with the giant painted outside, and the circling
hobby horse ! Oh, ye joys and dreams of the young heart !
Ye remain the least unchanged by climate or country all the
world over. I have indeed been often struck by the simi-
larity of the rhymes they use here in play upon the streets
to our own at home, but you will say, " What has all that
got to do with the purpose of a Leipzig fair ? "

The common streets were almost superseded, each of
them comprising ranges of smaller ones—built up in one
place, of shoes, in another, of pots and pans, and so on
through all the branches of merchandise, towards the market
place as a centre, which comprised within itself a duodecimo
edition of a city with streets, the booths and stalls crowding
up through all the streets, clustering even outside the gates,
on the promenades, and under the linden trees. . . .

This is the only instance in which I have been beyond
the distance of a walk from my *Kleiner Sandberg.* In Halle
itself I have witnessed one of those things I have heard and
read about—a torch procession. On Monday evening one
was given in honour of one of the wealthiest and most
esteemed fellow-citizens, by the burghers of Halle. There
were not fewer than 1,000 torches in the procession, with
flags and bands of music, and gendarmes riding about in all
directions to clear a passage. From a point of view which
I occupied in the market place the effect was very striking.
The procession moved slowly. Its approach had for some
time been announced by a lurid glare covering the sides of
the houses. Every window and every sort of eminence and
crevice, when lighted up by the gleam, disclosed scores of

curious faces packed together like the angels' heads in a baby's picture, and presenting a most grotesque appearance. The procession stretched itself across the market place, and looked like a long stream of fire banked in by the black and pressing crowd on either side, above whose heads the torches were seen undulating like waves of flame and moving to the sound of music.   .   .   .

Returning by accident into the market place between ten and eleven I found the procession just filing back, from the other side.   Directly, the torches were formed into a large circle, the music playing in the centre, from which point also I could hear something like the sound of speech-making from some person or persons unknown.   Then the national air was sung, thousands of voices joining and the bands accompanying.

Finally, the torches were all thrown rather riotously towards the centre to be burned in a heap.   The horsemen riding about among the fire and smoke, attempting to keep some sort of order, were very picturesque ; and ere all was over, the pale moon, whose interference in the matter was very much dreaded all along, was already looking over the roofs of the houses.

Having completed his course at Halle about the middle of August, 1842, he planned a journey up the Rhine, thence through Switzerland and over the Alps into North Italy. A portion of the money he had got still remained, though not enough to enable him to carry out his project ; but a letter to Andrew brought such supplement as was necessary, and so he set forth with a glad heart to make the grand tour before returning to address himself to the work of his life.

TUESDAY, 16th August, 1842.

I paid no parting visits of form. If attachment may be measured by the unwillingness to part, I parted most unwillingly of all with Koch, Ulrici, and the Frau Räthin.[1] The "God bless you" of the last especially was uttered with such fervour, exquisite and touching, most like the blessing itself. I could not feel as if my wish were any equivalent in return—as if my prayers were half the value.

On the other hand, my *Wirthin* kissed me most passionately on the cheek at parting, wept, and called me her second son, and yet I could almost leave her without any regret at all. Is love such a selfish thing? Is mine?

His journal from this point becomes fragmentary, consisting of little more than jottings by the way, from which, however, we are able to trace his course, and to learn something of the impressions he gathered, and to obtain here and there vivid glimpses of what he saw. His travelling companions at the outset included a certain Herr Lechermann, of whom he says :—

Lechermann used to play with Prince Albert when a boy. A most lovely boy was the Prince, about twelve, had a little horse he rode on, the beautiful boy of Coburg. They used to joke him and say he should have the Queen of England for a wife.

From Halle they went by Leipsic, Naumburg, Jena, Gotha, Eisenach, and Frankfurt to Mayence. A great part of the journey was on foot.

19th August.—Walked to Kuhla and Rudolstadt.

[1] Tholuck's wife.

Thoroughly lame. I was so ashamed of it. When at school I used to practise standing on my head a little and walking on my hands, but, unfortunately, never got on so far with it as to be able to turn it to any practical advantage now.

At Mayence he was joined by two of his Scottish friends—Mr. John Ramsay, of Alloa, and Mr. Curle, of Melrose, who were his companions on the Rhine for about a week.

HEIDELBERG, 2nd September.—Ramsay and Curle went off to Mannheim. I was dull out of endurance, and unwell into the bargain. . . . 3rd September.—Ascended the valley of the Neckar, eating fruit all the way from the trees, and resting when weary. I was recovering from *parting* sickness. . . . 4th September.—Crossed the Danube.

At Munich he met by appointment his friend, Mr. Renton, with whom he spent some days in the picture galleries. Here, too, he had his first view of the distant Alps—

From September 13th to 20th.—Walked over one of the principal passes of the Alps with a guide.

It was on the last of these days that the incident so vividly described in his lecture on German Burschen Life took place—

We had crossed a mountain pass on the High Alps, with dazzling pinnacles of snow on either side, skirted by the dark pine woods, out of which ran the rivers of ice, the deep blue glaciers, down into the meadows with their sheep-folds, their cattle with the tinkling bells that lined on either side the mountain torrent, up whose steep course we were climbing : a scene that everywhere repeats itself in Switzerland, but all bathed, that morning, in the yellow mists of sunrise behind us, and the dark purple of a thunderstorm before. One gets to feel amid these Alpine solitudes and silences, broken only by the scream of the eagle, the shout of the chamois hunter, the ringing song of the herd-boy far down the vale, as Moses may have felt amid the solitudes of Midian, till every hill becomes a Horeb, every bush is burning with God's presence, and every spot is holy ground, where you must put your shoes from off your feet and commune with the living Presence and the living Voice that speaks to you out of the burning glory, saying, " I AM THAT I AM." In such a scene I was walking with this Pantheist, my fellow-tourist, the denier of the personality of God. And as we walked along I asked him—" Vanslow, did you ever pray ? " " Pray, pray ! " said he, " What's that ? " " Pray to God ! " " What's God ? That cloud is God, yon rising sun is God, that ground there (kicking it with his feet) is God, and I am made of that, and so I am God, and when I pray I summon up myself ! " The scorner laughed, I shuddered ! And the thunder pealed along the cliffs as if God called " I AM," and the reverberation of the distant mountains answered " Yea, Thou art ! " And after a little while we had a narrow escape from a considerable danger. An Alpine waggon, heavily laden with timber, and dragging up the steep incline of zigzag terraces before us, suddenly broke its traces, and down it came with a terrific crash not far from where we were. I said, " Vanslow, had you been killed just now where would your soul have gone ? " And he said, " My soul gone ? gone, gone to the Absolute, relapsed into the All, mingled with the elements, melted like a snowflake in the ocean, melted into wind and rain and sunshine, gone to feed the flowers, I suppose, the worms perhaps." He laughed and I shuddered ; and we two walked on. And again the thunder pealed along the cliffs, as if God called " I AM "; and the reverberation of the distant mountains to the Brenner and the Bernina answered " Yea, Thou art !" After a little it came on to rain heavily, and we had no shelter, and no view through the curtain of cloud and mist, and Vanslow was very angry, and lifting his dark face to heaven he spat into the cloud, and said, " If there be a God above us, it is thus that I would treat him," and he laughed wildly. I shuddered and shrank aside lest a thunderbolt should leap from the cloud and smite down the blasphemer; but the thundercloud passed and all was silent, and nothing was heard but the tinkling of the cattle bells and the rushing of the torrents and the deep music of the pine woods, "the silent magnanimity of nature and her God." I tell you that I turned back eagerly upon the Alpine waggoners, rude Roman Catholics although they were, I turned kindly to the hooded monks who had come down begging from the mountain hospice. I turned with unutterable relief to the Alpine woodman who greeted you as he passed with " Praised be the Lord Jesus Christ," expecting you to answer " For ever, Amen !" To these rude Roman Catholics I felt a thousand times nearer than to that dark-souled blasphemer.

Entering Italy by Trent, he passed along by Padua and Verona to Milan and Como—

21st September.—I leapt for joy when I saw the Adriatic, and ran for half a mile with my hat off.

Parted with Vanslow on Sunday the 2nd. He took me into the thicket that the soldiers standing near might not see our parting—kissed me, and asked me to forgive wherein he had been hasty—to think on him that morning four weeks. I said I should be in Scotland and going to prayer at that hour, and asked, "Shall I pray for you?" He smiled, thought a moment, and assented—bowing back to me till he disappeared.

Robertson crossed the St. Gothard into Switzerland, reaching home on 20th October by way of Lucerne, Basle, and Paris.

To the REV. ADAM L. SIMPSON, Forres.

BERNE, 14th October, 1842.

The occasion of my writing you from Milan was this—I had just been taking a walk on the roof of the Cathedral, and been calling to mind some of your architectural criticism written me from some preaching excursion in the north of England; for ever since that time your image has haunted me in every cathedral I have visited. Your face has grinned down from all the groined arches, though not the face of a saint or angel by any means, nor even of a sinner doing everlasting penance on a pillar. No, no. . .

And home I am coming, and no mistake. The whistling wind which to-day is bitter cold, the yellow leaves showered into the running streams, put me in mind more than anything else, that I am just a year from home. For in that year I have lived many. Even the seasons have been multiplied. I have found a summer in Italy after the German one was over, and twice I have crossed winter slumbering on the summits of the Alps.

Three days ago I was on the top of the St. Gothard, and have scarce got warm again since. I can scarce think that it is more than a week since I was wandering among vineyards and orange groves, under the deep azure of an Italian sky. Waggons laden with black grapes were standing in the lanes, or drawn slowly by white oxen, their flanks stained with the juice. Children were singing in the vineyards, young men were treading the wine-presses, and the girls smiled archly from beneath their broad straw bonnets, and handed grapes to the passing traveller. The slanting rays of the sun fell through the arch of the neighbouring church tower and reddened over the deep green of the citron and acacia leaves—a scene of loveliness sweet as a dream—a dream not to be forgotten. . . . .

GREENHILL, by STIRLING, Wednesday Morning, 5th Dec., 1842.

What interrupted me at this point I remember was that having succeeded in getting an excellent fowl served up for supper, the delightful odour steaming up into my brain rendered me all at once quite oblivious of dreams and citron groves, and Adam Simpson. Having hunted it out now— I don't mean the fowl—I wish it were !—but the letter, I make no scruple of sending it off without apology.

I did come home almost directly, only spending a few days in Paris by the way, and have been here already a week or two.

To find you a minister in a manse with a Mrs. Simpson, and I a poor vagabond of a student still, floundering on among trials for license—I don't know what to think of it. I wonder what you will, and am anxious to know if you may still acknowledge me. . . . .

When I publish my "Wanderin' Willie," in three volumes post octavo, I shall be able to repay you in some sort for your portfolio of sketches which still continue to illustrate our best parlour table.

CHAPTER V.

The Beginning of his Ministry.

IN the spring of 1843 William Robertson was licensed
to preach the gospel by the Secession Presbytery of
Stirling and Falkirk. To distinguish him from another
William Robertson then on the list of probationers, he
adopted the maternal family name of " Bruce," and from
his entrance on public life was known as William Bruce
Robertson. His first appointments to vacant churches
led him into Ayrshire. He was sent to the county
town, and to Irvine. When he appeared as a candidate in the pulpit which he was destined to occupy
so long, his stock of sermons was confessedly slender.
Even if he had not returned so recently from his
studies in Germany, and his long excursion among
the Alps and into north Italy, it is questionable
whether it would have been larger; for he never could
bring himself to prepare any kind of discourse till the
time for delivering it was close at hand. Be this as
it may, he said to Mr. Haddin in 1884, "When I
went to preach as a candidate in Irvine, I had only

four discourses. My appointment was for two Sabbaths, and three sermons each day. I had a prayer
meeting address. This I turned into a sermon, and
made one new sermon, and so got through. At the
prayer meeting I gave an account of some religious
meetings I had been attending. They asked me to
preach on the Fast-day following, but from this I
excused myself."

When he was fulfilling a preaching engagement in
Shrewsbury, a call to become the Secession minister
of Irvine reached him and, after due consideration,
was accepted.

In those days the Church of the Secession, on the
ministry of which William Robertson was about to
enter, was agitated by a doctrinal controversy, which
at one time threatened to rend it asunder. Mr. James
Morison, whom all the Churches now honour for his
personal worth, and for his contributions to the exposition of the New Testament, was then a youthful
preacher noted for his zeal in evangelistic labour. In
connection with that department of work, he had
preached and published certain statements with
regard to the extent of the Atonement, which were
reckoned at variance with the Calvinistic doctrine of
" particular redemption," as set forth in the Confession
of Faith. This led to some hesitation on the part of
the Presbytery of Kilmarnock when they were about
to ordain him. Explanations were given which
removed the difficulty for the time, and the ordination
was proceeded with. But in a few months the

charges against Mr. Morison were revived, with the result that in May, 1841, he was suspended from his ministry. This did not prove a settlement of the question. Three ministers avowed their adherence to Mr. Morison's views, and were also excluded from the Church. But still the spirit that had been awakened was not laid. Two of the professors of theology, Dr. John Brown of Edinburgh, and Dr. Balmer of Berwick, while consenting to Mr. Morison's exclusion, gave expression to views on the question at issue which greatly alarmed some of their brethren, and stirred bitter controversy. But threatened division was happily averted, and the Church emerged from the controversy with a recognized liberty of opinion as to certain aspects of Calvinism which, more than thirty years later, was regularly formulated in a Declaratory Act anent the Subordinate Standards.

When William Robertson appeared on October 31st before the Presbytery of Kilmarnock to undergo trials for ordination, he found as might have been expected that the trials were not to be in his case, as they so often are, a mere form. His reverend judges were abnormally vigilant. It was they who had first ordained and then deposed Mr. Morison, and they were resolved thenceforth to proceed more warily. There were, besides, certain circumstances which seemed to justify special caution in dealing with the minister-elect of Irvine. It was known that his elder brother, Mr. James Robertson, had been associated with Mr. Morison in evangelistic labour, before the latter came into collision with the courts of his Church; and though the orthodoxy of James, who had by this time been for three years minister at Musselburgh, was established beyond suspicion, who could tell how far the evil communications of his earlier years might have corrupted the theology of his younger brother? And, moreover, that brother had just returned from a German university, and there was no saying what strange doctrines he might have brought from the land of Hegel and of Strauss. The members of presbytery were therefore on the alert when he rose to deliver his first sermon; but he had not gone far when he was relieved by hearing one of them, of whose zeal for the form of sound words he had been specially warned, whisper to his neighbour, "That young man is perfectly orthodox." From that point he felt himself safe. The discourses, five in number, were accepted without cavil. In the examination which followed, one of the fathers of the court, examining in church history, bethought him that this opportunity should be employed for obtaining a distinct disavowal of sympathy with Mr. Morison's peculiar "heresy." He asked the candidate to state the five Arminian points condemned at the Synod of Dort. Having got the required statement, he then asked, "Was the Synod of Dort right or wrong in condemning these doctrines?" Robertson emboldened by the reception his sermons had met with, and feeling that the time had come to claim some measure of freedom, replied that he did not think

F

that was a fair question in an examination on church history. So entirely had his discourses disarmed suspicion, that his objection was sustained, and his examinations, as well as his sermons, pronounced satisfactory. His ordination was fixed for the 26th of December, 1843.

All his friends will recognize it as characteristic, that in setting out for his ordination, he was late for the train. Hugh had gone on before with his luggage in a cart, and being always punctual, had arrived at Castlecary station a good while before the hour. The faithful servant was in great anxiety as the time drew near and there was no sign of the young master, whom he had left to follow with one of his brothers in the gig. The train, the last by which he could be conveyed in time for the ordination, was standing at the platform when the gig appeared. The starting whistle had sounded, and the gates were locked. Hugh shouted, "Jump that yett," but before the command could be obeyed, the train was off. What was to be done? It was discovered that a train of cattle trucks was presently to pass, and in the urgent circumstances leave was obtained to travel by it. The last his brother and Hugh saw of him when he started from home to begin the work of his life, showed him standing in the last truck of the train, with his hand at his mouth, uttering " Bey," in imitation of the cry of his fellow-travellers.

Irvine, the name of which was thenceforward to be linked with his, proved a congenial residence. Lying

along the level, and on the old shore line of the
Ayrshire coast, overlooking the sandy dunes through
which the Irvine and the Garnock find their way to
the sea, it is very different, in its air and in its outlook, from the heights on which stands the home of
his boyhood. Yet it is not wanting in a sense of
breadth, or in grandeur of view. Across the sand-
hills and the belt of blue water, there rise the peaks
of Arran, which, evening by evening, are bathed in
splendour as the sun dips behind them. Up the
Garnock, and across the breezy moor, the level is
bounded by the Eglinton woods—to the glades of
which, all comers were in these old days welcome ;
while, on the other side, the fields through which the
Irvine flows, lead upward to the heights of Dun-
donald. The outlook was not marred, but rather
made more picturesque, when in the course of years
ironworks were founded at the safe distances of
Kilwinning and Ardeer, and furnace fires gleamed
out on the western horizon, blending not inharmoni-
ously with the colours of the sky at sundown.

The ancient burgh itself is by no means unsightly
in the Dutch quaintness of its principal street, that,
widening out at either end and narrowing at the
centre where once its continuity was broken by the
old Tolbooth which has in recent years been swept
away, presents a strange medley of crow-stepped
gable ends, thatched cottages, last century mansions
with outside stairs, and new buildings for banks and
shops and residences of well-to-do burghers. When

Robertson went to Irvine, and during the greater part of his ministry, its chief industries were seafaring and weaving; and so it wore for the most part the aspect of a sleepy hollow. Even down at the harbour, there was little bustle, and at most hours of the day, a cannon ball might have been fired along the High Street without peril to life or limb.

The place, quiet as it was, had a measure of intellectual activity. An academy, founded by King James out of the revenues of the White Friars, whose memory lingers in the "Friars' Croft," has sent a succession of scholars to the universities, and kept up the standard of education in the burgh. Irvine claims with the county town, and with Kilmarnock and Mauchline, a share of the lustre which the genius of Burns has shed on Ayrshire—though in truth she has little reason to be proud of the part she took in his upbringing. John Galt, whose "Ayrshire Legatees" and "Annals of the Parish" are themselves sufficient to disprove the charge that Scotchmen are devoid of humour, was a native of Irvine. But she has traditions yet more congenial. The memories of the saints Winning and Inan are associated with her twin streams; and not the least saintly of the apostolic men who, in the heroic days of the Scottish Church, had their centres of influence in Ayrshire towns, was minister of the parish. John Welsh of Ayr, William Guthrie of Fenwick, Robert Baillie of Kilwinning, and David Dickson of Irvine, together sowed the good seed which flowered the Ayrshire

moors with martyrs. Robertson was wont playfully
to speak of Baillie riding through Irvine as he set out
to attend the Westminster Assembly, and to speculate
what the effect on the future creed of Presbyterianism
might have been had the delegate's horse stumbled
and fallen. But his enthusiasm was more stirred by
the memory of David Dickson, who laboured two
hundred years before him in his own favourite field,
bringing from the ancient and the mediæval Church,
material to enrich our treasury of sacred song. It is
remarkable that the quiet burgh should have had no
fewer than four sacred singers so noteworthy as
David Dickson, the author of "O Mother, dear Jerusalem," James Montgomery, the author of "Hail to
the Lord's Anointed," Mrs. Cousin, the author of
"The sands of time are sinking," and William
Robertson.

Though he was to wear David Dickson's mantle,
Robertson was not called to be his successor in the
church that crowns the one rising ground in the burgh.
His light was to shine from a lowlier and less visible
candlestick. The Secession Kirk stood out of sight in
a back lane named Cotton Row. It was utterly free
from architectural pretensions, though not altogether
ungainly in its square simplicity, with its two arched
windows facing the narrow street. Between these was
a wooden box, where sat the imprisoned elders who
watched the collection plate into which the congregation put their offerings when they had entered by the
gate, and before they parted right and left to go into

the church by the doors on either hand, or by that at
the back of the building facing the pulpit, or by either
of the outside stairs leading to the gallery. In the
right hand corner of the pleasant enclosure in which
the church stood were the session-house and vestry,
built soon after Robertson's ordination, and near them
a pump well, from which the worshippers refreshed
themselves before and after sermon. This well was
the subject of many a characteristic reference ; it was,
of course, a fountain " fast by the oracle of God," and
especially at the time when the old church was left for
the new, it was likened to Beersheba—the well of the
oath.

The congregation worshipping in this humble
sanctuary, which had the wit to discern the gift of
the boy-like probationer, had an honourable history.
It was founded by men who cherished the memory
of David Dickson's evangelical fervour, when that
memory had for the time died out of the sanctuary in
which he ministered. In the 18th century there was
no church of the Secession nearer Irvine than Kilmaurs, a distance of eight miles, but thither the Irvine
Seceders had cheerfully gone. In 1802 six of them
began a movement for a congregation in the burgh,
and by 1807 the congregation had been formed. Its
early meeting place was a malt barn, or rather kiln,
in which grain was made into malt for the innkeepers
and beer sellers of the burgh, and for the use of which
the congregation paid a weekly rent of two shillings.
In his speech at laying the foundation stone of Trinity

Church in 1862, Robertson referred to this primitive
sanctuary " that had no windows, and the door must
be left open to admit the light, when some worthy old
minister—young man then, dead now—Ellis of Saltcoats, Schaw of Ayr, or Blackwood of Galston—rode
over on his pony to Irvine on Sabbath, and preached
to the little handful of burghers clustering for worship
in the dusk and chiaroscuro of such manger cradle—
such outhouse of an inn."

On the same occasion he thus referred to his pre-
decessor, the first minister of the congregation :—

Under the ministry of Mr. Campbell, a homely, hearty,
hale, and, I believe, a heavenly-minded man, whose portly
person I have never seen, but yet with whose portrait I am
familiar as pictured and preserved in gown and bands, with
his bluff face and silvered head, in several houses, and as
pictured and preserved in fond remembrances in many
hearts, though these too now are dying away ; under his
ministry the congregation grew, first outwardly, then
upwardly, for thirty years and more.

When the young minister occupied the pulpit on
the Sunday following his ordination, it was felt by all
his hearers that a new era in the history of the congregation had indeed begun. The Scripture reading was
the first eight verses of the sixth chapter of Isaiah—a
passage which was chosen by him many a time for
reading and preliminary exposition to crowded congregations in the after years. His text was from Luke
x. 42—" One thing is needful "—a word, it may be
remembered, sent to him by his father in kindly coun-

sel when he was a student.   A lady, then a girl in her
teens, thus writes of the sermon :—" I do not remember a single sentence of it, but it touched the key-note
of all his after ministry.   It was like a new atmosphere
come into the old church at Irvine.   Instead of the
dry doctrines that we young people had found it so
hard to follow, we got the figure of the living, loving
Saviour constantly set before us."

The following letters, written to Mr. Erskine Fraser,
who had just returned from Germany, illustrate well
the period of transition through which the light-
hearted, merry student passed into the hard-working,
devoted minister.   It will be seen that he carried the
brightness of his student days into his ministry, and it
was one of the peculiar charms of that ministry that
this brightness never died out of it.   His latest holidays were enjoyed with as much zest as was the first,
of which we have a glimpse in one of these letters.

To the Rev. Henry Erskine Fraser, M.A.

IRVINE, 18th April, 1844.

.   .   .   .   By this time, if I am not mistaken, you are a
licentiate of " the Church of the Erskines," and sickening in
the agonies of your first discourse !   By a letter from Greenhill I learn that you are to be licensed on Tuesday—the
first notice I have had of your being in the country again.
How glad I am to hear it !

Do you remember what you said to me at parting ?
" When I come back " (so you said) " I will visit you at
Irvine."   The words were prophetic.   Often have I remem-

bered them since, often have I repeated them here, and
many people are quite impatient to see this marvellous
prophet, so soon as he shall come from the land of prophecy
and mist. *Es ist ja wahr !* I *am* the minister at Irvine.
Since I saw you the *Aufgabe* of my life has wholly changed.
It is not yet a year since we parted, if you calculate time by
the Belfast almanacs ; but if you calculate it, as Locke says,
by the succession of one's thoughts, it is a great deal more
than that. In the last few months I have lived through
many years of changes—years of thought and experiences,
sick headaches, and sleepless nights, lone Saturdays, and
bustling Sabbath days, strange new anxieties, and newer and
stranger joys. Since I saw you I have become, by many
years of thought, older, and wiser too I trust, and better.
The idle, reckless "wandering Willie" has become the
sober, staid minister—drinking tea with old maids, baptizing
and marrying and funeralizing, preaching to the sinner and
visiting the sick, comforting the dying and the mourners for
the dead—into all this I have grown since I saw you last.
But let me tell you the *so-genannte* minister at Irvine *ist dir
eben so gut* as when of old we roamed hand in hand by the
banks of Devon, or slept together in the garret of 21
Broughton Place. Heigh-ho ! these were delightful days in
their own way, and I look back on them as into a former
world. Now look you, *mein Theurer*, I suppose your first
day is engaged for Alloa, and that's right ; but if you don't
come to Irvine for your second I declare I shall never speak
to you again in the flesh ! *Die Sonne des Lebens werde ich
auf meinen Zorn untergehen lassen.* It is not so much to have
your sermons as it is to have yourself; it is not so much to
have that highest of preacher's favours, commonly called a
" day," as it is to have the "week" of the context—days
and nights of glorious *Zweigespräch* of Halle, and Tholuck
and his Tholuckism, and *Frauen*, and *Mädchen*, and

Studenten, and *Heften*, and *Vorlesungen*, and *Seyn* and *Nicht
Seyn*, and dear old *Deutschland*.

And withal this is just the place you would like—a quiet
town and a loud sounding bay—some of the streets not
unlike Halle ! and warm firesides and warmer hearts.   Do
come.   .   .   .   .

I would gladly write on.   I have 1000 things to say, 999
of which I must leave till I see you.   I go to Dundee on
Sabbath eight days.   Logan is to be with me in the beginning of the week after next.   He is coming through to the
Ayr Circuit.   This might help to tempt you to come. . . . .

And now I sincerely hope you will be strengthened and
sustained through the trying duties of your first day.   *Gott
segne dich ! und hüte dich, mein lieber* Erskine !   It is a
solemn work.   May God acknowledge and assist you in it.
I can sympathize with you.   *Ich werde deinetwegen nicht
entlassen viel zu beten.   Es hilf dir Gott !* .   .   .   .

IRVINE, 4th July, 1844.

Dr. Balmer dead !   I had the note of it on Tuesday
evening when going in to my meeting.   It gave the tone to
the meeting.   The services were all in a doleful minor key.
I felt it keenly and so I feel it yet ; and so I am sure you
do.

August, 1844.

I have come home to-day from the Western Highlands
—parted from my fellow-tourists yesterday at the head of
Loch Long.   We were a party of five.   Messrs. Ramsay and
Curle with a sister each ; a happy party you may guess.
The anniversary of our meeting on the Rhine on the
27th August, two years ago, was celebrated with a dinner
at Inveraray on Tuesday last.

The details I shall give you when you come.   Some of

them will be interesting to you as they have been most intensely so to me. The scenery romantic—the colouring of the season most beautiful—the lights and shades of the weather just the thing—clear moonlight at nights, and blue shining Highland lochs; all in a little boat passing in and out from the shadow of the black rocks, with the light dash of oars; and voices in song. . . . I am just awaking as from a dream.

But I cannot afford to be sentimental for want of time, and as it is getting on the road to Sabbath I cannot dream any longer. I shall expect you here as soon as you can possibly come. I'll be at home till George's ordination—12th September.

The ordination, to which he refers, of his brother George as minister at Busby, took place on the expected day. It is memorable as the beginning of a ministry, which, lasting only six and a half months, was yet so earnest and so spiritual, that it left a fragrance which still lingers in the hearts and homes of the people of the village. William had of course a very special joy in the settlement, so near him in the West, of his brother who had been his fellow-student and companion at college and hall. He had the pleasure of his presence, as well as that of his elder brother James, at the first anniversary of his own ordination. But his joy was soon clouded. George died suddenly at Greenhill on 1st May, 1845. On that night Mr. Ronald of Saltcoats was addressing the prayer meeting at Irvine. William, ill at ease on account of a thoughtless remark he had made on the way to church, was haunted, as he listened to Mr.

Ronald's discourse, with a distressing fear that, if occasion called, he could not bow in submission to the divine will. Next day brought the heavy tidings from Greenhill. This was the first of ·a succession of family trials and bereavements, which, without taking any of the brightness out of his ministry, gave that ministry deeper consecration.

The exhilarating effect of "the new atmosphere come into the old church at Irvine" soon became manifest. The members of the congregation began to bethink themselves that the Christian Church exists for other ends than self-improvement. Their old building, with only the accommodation necessary for the Sabbath assembly, was fairly symbolic of the conception of a church which had till then prevailed among them ; and the first sign that they were attaining a worthier conception, was that before the end of the first year of Mr. Robertson's ministry a movement was set on foot to build a hall and vestry. This was immediately followed by a successful effort to liquidate a debt which had from the first burdened the church property.

When the necessary accommodation had been thus provided and when the restraining incubus had been removed, a Sabbath evening school was organized in August, 1845. Soon after this a morning school was opened in the same premises ; and ere long other premises were secured, and teaching was begun, in one of the narrow vennels that open on the High Street.

The new hall and vestry were also utilized for

meetings in connection with enterprises of yet further-reaching beneficence, in which the interest of the congregation was enlisted. It was in these opening years of Mr. Robertson's ministry that Foreign Missions began to engage the earnest attention of the Scottish Church. Early in the century good men in all the branches of that Church recognized their duty to the heathen; but they had hitherto chiefly wrought through societies with no direct ecclesiastical connection. At the time of which we write the churches as churches had awakened to a sense of their responsibility. The missions, begun by the outside societies, had passed, or were passing, into their hands, and, with new missions then instituted, were being conducted under the supervision of their supreme courts. The cause of missions lay near the heart of the young minister of Irvine. In writing with regard to the arrangements for the social meeting which followed his ordination, he had said that "the subject of missions must not be omitted," and at his first anniversary soiree the same subject had a prominent place. In response to his call, and stimulated by his example, the congregation began to subscribe liberally.

These and other signs of quickened life appeared as the fruit of the new minister's work, even before he had acquired that peculiar power by which he was distinguished in later years. He was accustomed to tell that, not long after his ordination, he was led to change his style of preaching. We are indebted to the Rev. John Haddin for the following memorandum made immediately after Dr. Robertson gave him the information it contains :—

Mr. Robert Bartholomew, an extensive millowner in Glasgow, during the early years of Dr. Robertson's ministry, occupied, as his summer residence, Montgreenan House, near Kilwinning.   Mrs. Bartholomew was a Miss Graham, of the family of the Grahams of Lancefield, Glasgow.   From the first they placed themselves under the ministry of Dr. Robertson, with whom they soon became very intimate. Mrs. Bartholomew was a lady of great ability, and distinguished for cordiality of spirit and frankness of speech. After she had heard him for some time, she called on him one day, and said, "Mr. Robertson, in your preaching you fail to do yourself justice.   Your manner of speaking in the pulpit is not in harmony with the structure of your mind and your peculiar talents.   It must be altered.   In conversation you are most natural and powerful.   Bring your conversational manner of thinking and speaking into the pulpit.   Adopt it there and your discourses will be much more effective.   The result will surprise both yourself and your people."   Mrs. Bartholomew talked on in this strain, and made such an impression on his mind, that he determined to follow her counsel—he would make the attempt.   Next Sabbath accordingly, taking as his subject of discourse, the appearance of Christ to Mary at the sepulchre, he spoke in a way which riveted attention, and satisfied him that he had found wherein his strength lay.   The improvement was unmistakable, and from that day his former mode of preaching was laid aside.

The change of style involved a change in his manner of writing his sermons. His earlier sermons are written out fully and continuously in long hand, just as his college essays and hall discourses had been. But at the period when the change we have noted took place, he began to write in broken fragmentary paragraphs, with an admixture of shorthand, and on only one side of loose sheets, which he pinned on to successive leaves of the pulpit Bible, and turned over as the discourse proceeded, though he hardly ever even glanced at the notes thus kept before him.

His preparation was made at high pressure. He seldom began till the afternoon of Friday, and he was accustomed to say that he considered that he had made satisfactory progress, if, by the time he went to bed—which he never did till well on in Saturday morning—he had reached the point of thinking that his text would not do at all, and that he would need to look for another. On Saturday he appeared at meals, but hardly ever spoke, and only made a pretence of eating. The whole day—which, however, in his case, did not begin till near noon—was spent in his study, and he seldom retired to rest till four or five o'clock on Sabbath morning. He wrote at a small bedroom table on which a portable writing desk lay open. Somewhat late in his ministry he bought a study table—saying to a friend whom he met in Glasgow, when he was on the way to make the purchase, that as he had been more than twenty years a minister he thought it was time to begin to study! But the study table was never used except as a repository for books and papers. He wrote to the last at the portable desk on the small table, which he could easily shift about from the window, beside which he sat during the day, to the neighbourhood of the fire and the gaslight at night. A Bagster's pocket Bible, so well thumbed through the long years that some of its pages were hardly legible, invariably lay open to the left of his manuscript, his arm resting on it as he wrote. So long had it undergone that pressure that the binding had acquired a set, and the Bible would not remain closed.

On the Sabbath morning he seldom rose till the hour of service was perilously near. He hardly left himself time to dress, and often did not even attempt to breakfast ; but had to hurry away as soon as he came down stairs, followed on the road by the straggling members of his household, who had all been occupied to the last in the effort to get him ready in time. On one occasion when he was assisted at a Communion by Dr. Johnstone of Limekilns, one of the calmest and most methodical of the elderly ministers of the Church, that divine, who had withal a gift of kindly humour, said with a smile that the manner in which the household found their way to church reminded him of the close of the record of St. Paul's shipwreck : "And the rest, some on boards, and some on broken pieces of the ship. And so it came to pass that they escaped all safe to land."

When Robertson reached the pulpit, generally, it must be admitted, a few minutes late, there was no sign of haste or flurry, but the most becoming reverence, as with deep sonorous voice he, after the good old Scottish manner, announced and read the opening psalm. Sometimes, if a thought struck him as he read it, he would throw in a word of exposition to make the service of song more intelligent and hearty. This was a survival of another Scottish custom, now obsolete, but in which some of the old ministers greatly excelled, of "prefacing" the morning psalm. When the psalm had been sung he rose—the congregation in those early days rising with him—and with clasped hands began the morning prayer. No liturgy ever excelled the stately march of his well-ordered sentences, or the deep spirit of devotion which they breathed, as with perfect freedom in the words and arrangement, he yet embraced all that should be remembered in common prayer. Then followed the reading of the Scriptures, which he generally accompanied with some comment or· exposition—often the most impressive and instructive part of the service. After another psalm or hymn, came the sermon. He did not read it, neither did he deliver it *memoriter;* but, though every sentence was prepared, and every thought represented by some marking more or less legible on the manuscript before him, he spoke as one who was at the moment in communion with the truth, and setting it forth as it revealed itself to him. I once asked him with reference to a powerful description I had heard him give of the passage of the Israelites through the Red Sea, how he had given it. He said that he had called up the scene before him. The church, the listening congregation,—everything was for the time

G

out of sight, and he was looking on at the procession
of the tribes through the depths, simply telling what
he saw.

The effect which his preaching produced may be
judged of by the testimony of two men of widely
different temperament, when they had heard him for
the first time. One of these was Dr. Andrew Sommer-
ville, the foreign mission secretary of the United
Presbyterian Church, a man of great shrewdness and
intelligence, but entirely unimaginative. He had
been assisting at the communion services at Irvine,
and on his return to Edinburgh met Mr. James
Robertson, who asked him what kind of sermon
William had preached. " Sermon ! " was the reply,
" it was not a sermon at all ; it was an epic poem."
The other was Dr. John Service, himself a preacher
of no mean distinction in after years, but then a
student of theology. He wrote to the friend on whose
recommendation he had gone to hear Robertson, that
the sermon sent him away in the same mood as the
Campsie fiddler who having heard Paganini, hastened
home and thrust his own fiddle into the fire.

CHAPTER VI.

Pastoral Work.

THE power which Mr. Robertson acquired in Irvine was not won by his preaching alone. He had peculiar aptitude for the other departments of pastoral work. The Sunday schools which, as we have seen, were the first-fruits of his ministry, were fostered by him with loving care. It was his delight to be among children, and he had, in a rare degree, the gift of winning their affection. On one occasion when he was leaving Johnstone, where he had been visiting the Rev. James Inglis, Mr. Inglis opened for him the door of a railway carriage, and he was about to enter, when, seeing two or three children, he drew back and went into another compartment. Mr. Inglis said in astonishment, " I thought you were very fond of children ? " " So much so," he replied, " that I don't want to know these children, it will be such a pain to part from them." But that was when he was older, and had experience above most of the pain of parting. In earlier days he sought the company of children. It was a refresh-

ment to him, even after two long services, to visit their
schools and address them; and at their annual excursion into the country he was as happy as the youngest
scholar.

He had special joy in hearing the children sing, and
was in the habit of writing little carols specially
adapted for their young voices. Some of these were
the germs out of which grew later poems that will be
given in their order. On the death of one of the
female teachers, whose work in the school he greatly
valued, he prepared a little dirge and set it to music—
teaching the children to sing it. It contained at least
one verse which lingered in their memories through
the after years:—

> Children's little hands will dress
>   All the sod with lilies round,
> Children's little feet will press
>   Softly on the holy ground.

It was one of Mr. Robertson's earliest efforts to in-
spire his congregation with his own love of sacred
song, and gradually to make the service of public
praise more worthy. When he entered on his pastorate,
the singing was led by a precentor of the old school,
and till he could see his way to introduce a really
effective reform, the young minister was in no hurry
to disturb the time-honoured arrangement. But he
early addressed himself to the task of preparing a
choir which should in due time take its place in the
church. He had a high ideal of a church choir, both

as to Christian character and as to musical attainment. To realize as far as possible his ideal in the
first particular, he had it laid down as a fundamental
rule that no one should be admitted to the choir
who was not a member of the church : and to realize
it in the second particular he spared neither time nor
pains in the work of instruction. The young people,
whom he carefully selected, met for weekly practice
in his lodgings. It was three whole years before he
pronounced them qualified to sing in church ; and he
would sometimes insist on their practising a tune for
six months before he would permit them to introduce
it in public worship. The fruit of his labour was
reaped not only in the excellence of the first choir,
which thus enjoyed the advantage of training at his
own hand, but in the establishment of a high standard
which has ever since been maintained. He found it
impossible, as his labours multiplied, to continue the
work of training ; but he was at pains to secure the
appointment of conductors who could sympathize
with his aspirations and understand his methods.

The following has been furnished with regard to
the Irvine singing and the principles upon which it
was guided :—

In the matter of choosing a precentor he used often to say
that congregations almost invariably looked out for a man
with a *voice*, instead of a man who could train other people's
voices, and select and arrange them so as to blend harmoni-
ously in a choir, instead of letting them go off like a volley
of fireworks, or the general cracking of fiddle strings. He

would often tell that one of the best precentors they ever had in Irvine was a man who could not sing at all. Then, with regard to chanting, he maintained that it was not only the most scriptural, but the most natural and intelligent mode of praise. "Get a man," he would say, "to feel what he is singing, and he is sure to chant well, although he has no education whatever." Perhaps the most impressive part of the Trinity Church praise in later days was, when at the communion table, the congregation, without help of choir, chanted in unison, to some old Peregrine or Gregorian, the 53rd chapter of Isaiah. He was peculiarly sensitive to the intelligent rendering of the words; and after one of these occasions, on going into the vestry, he said to the precentor, "James, I didn't know you had given up the doctrine of substitution." The man asked what he meant. "Because," he said, "you did not emphasize the proper word. You should have led it so: ' He was wounded for *our* transgressions ; He was bruised for *our* iniquities.'" The hint was taken, and the emphasized word was remembered ever after.

The rule which made church membership a condition of admission to the choir was held binding; but when younger voices were wanted they were accepted, on the principle explained by him in the following note to the secretary, written in answer to a question as to whether two candidates who had been nominated were eligible :—

Your rule is that none but church members are admissible to the choir. Both of those you name are church members by baptism, though not in full communion ; and, belonging as they do to my class, are on their way to that too it may be presumed. If, then, the choir really wants them, they may, I think, be chosen, since in one sense they are both members of the church. It would be better, however, if such cases were exceptional, and if the entrance to the choir and the Lord's Supper took place as nearly as possible to each other. . . . The persons not to admit are those who are expressly not church members. If others who are partly so, and who are on their way to be so fully, ask admission, they may be accepted, just as students who are on their way to the pulpit are sometimes admitted to preach, and the nearer to the end of their course, the more so.

Most of Mr. Robertson's early hymns were written to be sung by the choir. Of these the earliest we have found is the following, which was sung, according to his own arrangement, to the grand old German chorale, *Straf mich nicht in deinem Zorn* :—

Evening Intercessions.

God's bright temple in the skies,
  Night is opening slowly,
Let our song like incense rise
  From a priesthood holy.
    Sacred flame, in Christ's name,
  In our censers laying,
  We come humbly praying.

For our loved ones all we pray ;
  Thou God looking hither
Dost see the near and far away
  In one glance together ;
    Seen by Thee,—they and we,
  Both that one eye under,
  Are not far asunder.

When the sailor on the deep
  Rests on his rude pillow,
Rocked a little hour to sleep
  On the heaving billow ;
    Save, Lord, save from storm wave,
  Guide with gentle motion
  Through the pathless ocean.

Where the sick lie wearily
  Tossing in their sorrow,
Murm'ring oft the plaintive cry,
  " Would that it were morrow !"
    Oh ! repress sore distress,
  Give them calm, sweet sleeping
  In their night of weeping.

Where the tempted may have strayed
  Into scenes of danger,
Let not virtue be betrayed,
  Rise, Lord, to avenge her !
    With strong arm, shield from harm,
  Or from the trial rather
  Keep them, Holy Father !

Where the penitent has gone
  To his chamber weeping,
Leave, ah ! leave him not alone,
  Bitter vigil keeping ;
    Breathe, oh Lord ! some soft word,
  All that true peace speaking,
  His vexed heart is seeking.

Star lamps now are filled with fire,
  Heaven's broad dome revealing,
Lord, we are a lowly choir !
  At Thy threshold kneeling,

> Yet our song, even among
> Angels' songs ascending,
> Holds Thine ear attending.

Another department of pastoral work in which he laboured most faithfully was the teaching of his Bible class. It met on Sunday evenings in the little hall, built in the corner of the church grounds, and was attended chiefly by the young people who had left the Sunday school, and had not yet entered into the full communion of the church ; but there were not a few who valued the instruction so much that they clung to it after they had passed the usual age. It was conducted as a real class, and not, like many advanced classes, a mere lecture or third service of preaching. The members had lessons prescribed to them and were expected to prepare them carefully.

One of his favourite exercises was to go through a book of the Bible, taking a chapter, or prescribed portion of a chapter, each evening. The pupils were required to tell him the doctrines or duties taught in the lesson, indicating in what particular verse the doctrine or duty was set forth, and answering any questions he might put to them as to the deductions they had drawn.

He was accustomed to defend his method as in all respects preferable to the common one of asking pupils to bring texts in support of certain doctrines or duties formulated for them. That method he condemned as tending to foster the habit of looking

at Scripture texts in isolation from their context, and
without reference to the person by whom, or the time
and circumstances in which, the words were uttered.
The method he adopted, fostered, on the other hand,
the habit of reading the Scriptures with attention, and
with intelligent desire to ascertain what they really
teach. He found the exercise profitable to himself, as
it enabled him to see how the Word, which it was his
calling to expound, presented itself to the unaided
minds of the young people under his charge. There
are traditions that there was sometimes an attempt to
make practical application of something in the lesson
for the admonition of the teacher. On one occasion
when he had been absent from his pulpit with more
than usual frequency, the subject of lesson was the
12th chapter of the Acts of the Apostles. A young
woman, being called in turn, said—"We learn from
verse 25th that when ministers require to go to other
places on the business of the Church, they ought to
return to their own congregations as quickly as possible : 'And Barnabas and Paul returned from
Jerusalem when they had fulfilled their ministry.' "

Another exercise given to the class was to prescribe
passages of Scripture apparently divergent, or contra-
dictory, and to ask the pupils to exercise their judgment or their ingenuity in suggesting a possible recon-
ciliation. He was much interested in noticing how
native shrewdness was often sufficient to get over
difficulties that had perplexed the learned. And he
was sometimes amused by the use of the forcible ver-

nacular, as when he asked them how to reconcile St. Matthew's version of our Lord's words, " Are not two sparrows sold for a farthing ? " with the version given by St. Luke, " Are not five sparrows sold for two farthings ? " and received in reply, " Becus' ye get them cheap if ye tak' a wheen."

His relation to the Sunday schools and Bible class endeared him to the younger members of his flock. As he passed along the street, they would stop at their play and smile to him, taking pains to attract his attention if by chance he failed to notice them. Once when he was hurrying to the train with a literary friend who had been visiting him, a little child ran up and touched the skirt of his coat, and was sent away happy with a kindly word. His friend quoted Goldsmith's lines :—

> " Even children followed, with endearing wile,
>   And pluck'd his gown, to share the good man's smile."

On another occasion when a distinguished preacher was his guest, a young woman, running across the street carrying a pat of butter, gave him kindly recognition. His friend said, " One of the pillars of your church, I suppose ? " " No," said he, " she is a flying butt'ress."

The custom of " pastoral visitation " is one of the secrets of the strong hold which the Scottish Church has on the affection of its people. That Church which makes light of any artificial " Apostolic succession," has always been careful to follow apostolic precedent, and therefore deems it incumbent on her ministers to teach not only publicly, but from house to house. Mr. Robertson's kindliness of disposition and his conversational gifts specially qualified him for this part of his duty. It was no weariness to him to go among his people and speak with them at their own firesides; and as he went, not in professional routine, but in friendliest, most brotherly spirit, he never failed to receive a cordial welcome. His annual visit was eagerly looked forward to; and when it was over, his sayings were fondly remembered and repeated, till the time of his next visit came round. Though his talk was altogether informal, yet he never lost sight of the object of the visitation. It was a veritable "teaching from house to house." He would refer to some Scripture scene or incident, bringing out its lessons in their bearing on family duties, or as giving warning or comfort in relation to some peculiar family circumstances. We have a little glimpse into the manner of his visitations, in the report of one of them by a good woman known to be somewhat of a "character." After Mr. Robertson had left her house, one of her neighbours said to her, "Ye had your minister the day, what was he saying to you, na?" "O'd woman," was the reply, "he had an unco wark wi' that family at Bethany the day."

His visits were peculiarly welcome where there was sickness or sorrow in the house. The depths of tenderness which were in his heart welled out in sympathy with the suffering. He never reckoned up the number of his visits to the dying, or counted them matter of "duty" at all, but would go daily, and often several times in a day. To see him, as he went out and in, burdened in spirit, where there was special suffering in any of the homes of his people, helped one to understand the Scripture which St. Matthew tells us was fulfilled in Christ, " Himself took our infirmities and bare our sicknesses."

When I was a student of theology, I enjoyed the great advantage, on more than one occasion, of accompanying Mr. Robertson on his rounds among the sick, and I can never forget the light that came into wan and weary faces as the minister appeared at the door of the room. His entrance was like a beam of sunlight—a light shining in a dark place. His manner was perfectly natural. He did not school his features or his voice into the expression or tone deemed appropriate in a sick room, neither did he put on that affected cheerfulness, which some visitors of the sick think it the right thing to assume. There was nothing of the patronizing air, which strength sometimes wears toward weakness. He would inquire with an interest which was manifestly real into the case of each, and would somehow, by a few well-chosen words, succeed in lifting part at least of the burden from the sufferer's shoulders. One case dwells in the memory: A poor woman, with some sad internal malady, had been sent to Glasgow in the hope that an operation might save her; but "the professor" had pronounced the operation impossible, and she had come home to die. He let her tell him her story, and made her feel that he thoroughly understood how hard it is to say, "Thy will be done"; but he managed so to lead her out of herself, and away from the sense of disappointment, that when his prayer was over, and we rose to go, the look of hopelessness had gone from her face, and the light of a better hope had taken its place.

Some interesting reminiscences of his conversation have been furnished by Mrs. M'Cunn of Liverpool, whose friendship, when she was Miss Florence De Quincey Sellar, he valued not only for her own sake, but because she was a friend of Dr. John Brown, and moreover bore the name of her godmother, one of the daughters of De Quincey. With reference to the time, and to the department of his work, which are now in hand, she writes :—

I remember two beautiful anecdotes he told of his early ministry, one of which shows his unrivalled power of bringing the Scriptures into close relation with daily life. I am sure you know it, but I can't deny myself the pleasure of telling it over again. During his ministry at Irvine, among the pupils of the "minister's class" was a girl whose special glory was her long beautiful hair. She fell ill of some fever—brain possibly, but I don't remember; and the doctor and her friends thought it necessary to cut off her hair. But she, girl-like, would not part with her glory, and they did not like to press the point for fear of exciting her. Such was the state of affairs when Mr. Robertson came to see her. "I'll soon put that right," and in he went, and said nothing, but sat down beside her, and read her the story of Mary Magdalene washing the Lord's feet, and wiping them with her hair. When he had done, he saw by the girl's face that she was considering, and said, "How long and beautiful your hair is. If Christ were here, and asked for *your* hair, wouldn't you be glad to lay it at His feet." "Send in the barber," said the girl, and the victory was won.

The other has a delightful element of humour in it. A few young students in his company fresh from church history were talking of the quaint old scholastic question, How many angels are supported on the point of a needle? "Five," said Dr. Robertson, with decision, and justified his answer with the following story. One wild stormy night he was coming home late through some side street at Irvine, and saw a light burning in the window of a low room where he knew a poor woman lived whose husband was at sea. He wondered what kept her up so late, and looking in, he saw her busily sewing by her dim lamp— while the five fair rosy children were sound asleep round her. "And there was a needle supporting five angels!"

Irvine being a seaport town, he had a large number of sailors among the members of his flock. A good old lady, a sailor's widow, remembers when he, "very boyish looking in a long coat," paid his first visit to the Friar's Croft, which was the sailors' district. He said when he came into her house that "he didn't know that his congregation was so much afloat." He used to boast playfully that it "was like the British empire—the sun never set on it." The good old lady just referred to remembers being at " a skippers' tea" at the manse, when Mr. Robertson entertained all the sea captains and their wives belonging to the congregation, who were then on shore. There were thirteen of them, including the harbour master.

This peculiarity of his congregation involved a painful duty. He had often to go to mothers and wives, and break to them the tidings of the loss at sea of sons and husbands. To one poor mother he went on this sad errand three several times. He used to speak with admiration of her calmness. She always received the intelligence with a silent tear.

Early in his ministry he wrote the following verses, which he described as "a story from real life in the Irvine churchyard." The parish church and churchyard are on a height from which the harbour bar can be seen.

"Tall and Alone.'

Tall and alone, on the flat headstone
 Where her sailor husband lay,
She stood looking down o'er the sloping town
 To the harbour and the bay,
With face set fast 'gainst the biting blast,
 And the freezing sleet and spray.

The only son of this widowed one
 Was toiling to cross the bar,
And she saw his boat to the leeward float,
 With the breakers stretching far ;
And she held her breath, for she knew that death
 Must be where the breakers are.

Still slowly he rowed ; oh ! pitiful God !
   The widow and orphan's stay !
A strange hour passed, and the bitter blast
   Still drove the boat away
To the leeward far of the harbour bar,
   And the entrance to the bay.

And there she stands, with her praying hands,
   Like sculptured marble form,
Statuesque on the tomb of the husband, whom
   They had laid in the earth, one morn ;
While her boy to save, from a watery grave,
   She prays, and he fights the storm.

Darkness came down over bay and town,
   As the steeple clock struck three,
A heavy rain squall so blackened all,
   That nothing could she see ;
And a hollow roar went down the shore,
   Where the hollow breakers be.

But still she stands, with her praying hands
   That succour from heaven sought,
Till after the rain, when it cleared again,
   Oh, God ! where is the boat ?
Gone down a wreck—and only a speck
   Is seen on the waters afloat !

She did not shrink, she could not think,
   She stood, like marble, dumb ;
Only tears to her eyes in silence rise,
   Not floods of tears—but some,
While the spirit moans with the speechless groans,
   That with deepest anguish come.

H

They brought her down to her house in town
    And laid her on a bed :
She never spoke—for her heart it broke,
    And no more tears were shed ;
But, like marble still, as pale and chill,
    Next morning she lay dead.

On the brown seaside, at the ebb of tide,
    A breathless form was found.
When the hollow roar went down the shore,
    Had the noble boy been drowned !
So not alone, by the flat headstone,
    They rest in holy ground.

I hope all three, where there's no more sea,
    Have met before the throne,
And that the twain, now living again,
    Shall hear Christ say, to the one,
Behold thy mother, and to the other,
    Woman, behold thy son !

He had above most the gift of consolation. He used to say that the secret of power in that direction is silence. To sit and be an interested and sympathetic listener while mourners tell the story of their grief, is much better comfort to them than any words. When he did speak he had the rare art of so speaking as to reach the heart. Once he was asked to see a young widow, not of his own congregation, who had only enjoyed a few months of wedded happiness when her husband was taken from her. She was sitting in a stony, tearless grief, and her friends had failed to rouse her. Mr. Robertson went and sat down by her side. When at last he spoke he said to her, "I am sure you must be most thankful that you were married to him and had these months of happiness." She said at once, "O, why has no one ever said that to me before," and then the fountain of her tears was opened.

As he went about among his people he came across many an incident which appealed to his keen sense of humour. On his first visitation among the farmers and farm-servants in the country, the young scholar, fresh from Germany and full of literary enthusiasm, was towards afternoon beginning to find the talk about the crops and the cattle a little monotonous. Entering a farm parlour before the master of the house came to him, he was delighted to find a copy of "Paradise Lost" lying on the table. He said to himself, we shall get something else to talk of now; and, taking an early opportunity of turning the conversation, he said, "I see you have Milton here. Are you a great admirer of his poetry?" "Ou, aye," was the reply, "but there's ane John Thamson o' Kilmarnock that has written some rale fine things tae." He let the talk return into its wonted grooves.

On another occasion, he went on a Sunday evening to see a newly-made widow, who was not specially noted for regularity in her church attendance. He found her brother seated with her when he entered. This brother was a zealous elder of the Relief Church, who was earnest that his sister's bereavement should be improved to her, and especially in the matter of "observing ordinances." The sister on her part was as resolute that the conversation should not be allowed to take an inconveniently practical turn. And so, as Mr. Robertson, following his usual course, was willing to be a listener, she started certain difficulties of a philosophical kind, which she said had been perplexing her very much of late. One of these was this—"What for had God nae beginnin'?" "What would ye bother the minister wi' sic a question as that for?" said the brother; "it wad be mair like ye if ye wad gang reglar to the kirk than tak up yer mind wi' nonsense like that." "It's nae nonsense," said the widow, "it's a question I'm sair troubled wi'. What for had God nae beginnin'? I can understand his havin' nae end, for I can think on and on and on, and no stop. But that He had nae beginnin'—I canna get at it ava." "An awfu' like question that!" exclaimed the brother at last, losing all patience, "What for had God nae beginnin'? For a very good reason. He had no need o' ane; He was there already."

One other feature of Mr. Robertson's pastoral work falls to be noted—his faithfulness in the exercise of church discipline. He inherited from his father a high ideal of the Christian Church, and of the conse-cration involved in church membership; and, even when he was a young minister, he was never tempted by the desire for an increasing communion roll to lower his ideal, or to permit open inconsistency to remain unvisited by censure.

CHAPTER VII.

Growing Power.

DURING the first decade of his ministry Mr. Robertson
lived in lodgings. His three landladies, the Misses
Cochrane, were enthusiastic in his service, and made
his rooms a real home to which his friends were always
welcome. It was then that he began to dispense the
unstinted hospitality for which he was distinguished
to the end. His early companions had standing
invitations to visit him, of which they did not fail to
avail themselves. Even De Quincey plucked up
courage to face the journey to the west, that he might
renew his fellowship with the youth whose presence
had lightened the gloom of his solitary chamber in
Princes Street. It was a grievous disappointment
to Mr. Robertson that he missed him. De Quincey
came unannounced. The youngest Miss Cochrane
opened the door to the stranger. His appearance did not prepossess her in his favour, and she
told him curtly that the minister was not at home.
He offered to await his return, but was told that he

would not be back that night. He then proposed to
leave a note, but the landlady dreading that the
stranger might have felonious intentions with regard
to the minister's books, showed him into a little side
apartment with only a table and a chair, and fetched
him writing material—standing guard over him while
he wrote. Whether this annoyed him or not, he tore
up what he had written and went away somewhat
abruptly, leaving his name, the foreign sound of which
confirmed her suspicions. She went into the room of
her eldest sister who then lay dying, and told with no
little satisfaction how she had disposed of the suspicious looking visitor with the strange name. Her sister,
whose literary tastes had led her to take an occasional peep into the minister's books, recognized the
name as known to fame. At her request Gilfillan's
"Gallery of Literary Portraits" was brought, and on
the likeness being turned up, the self-complacency gave
way to self-reproach; but the distinguished man,
"whose picture was in a book," had gone beyond
recall, and there was nothing for it but to await with
trembling the minister's return. The minister had too
much imagination not to fully appreciate the situation,
and pardon the well-meant caution; and an early post
brought a charming letter from De Quincey, in which
he took upon himself the whole blame of the *contre-
temps*, and said it would not now be so difficult for
him to bestir himself to visit his friend, since he had
seen the "quaint, clean, quiet old town." But he never
came.

A friend who had written to him in these days to consult him as to the furnishing of his library received a reply from which we make this extract :—

To Mr. John Ramsay.

IRVINE, 1847.

Sterne is a blackguard, morally speaking; a pleasant enough sort of person in other respects. His "Sentimental Journey" must, with all its wickedness, have impressed me much, for although I have not read it I am sure for a good many years, its successive stages and incidents are about as familiar as those of our own tour along the Rhine. That monk, that imaginary prisoner, that dead ass, that melancholy girl, Marie, I think, that grace before meat, I am sure I shall never forget them in this world. I wish I may be able to forget them in the next, for there's a dash of the "earthly, sensual and devilish" in them, that makes them unsuitable companions for a better world. It strikes me that Sterne *is* sentimental at times—at least I liked him extravagantly at that age when *I* was—when to me Beauty was a pale form, walking in evening twilight, crying into a white pocket handkerchief, and dying of consumption. My ideal has died of its consumption and been buried now some years, and instead of it, a healthy laughing girl, rather inclined to be fat than otherwise, with more of common sense than genius, and equally ready to give you a kiss or a box on the ear as you deserve. . . . . I should like to read Sterne again. I doubt if I should like him so well now. If I remember he has much of that inimitable pathos that is closely allied and "next-door neighbour" to great humour, which are indeed but opposite poles, positive and negative, of the same thing; and the power of his scenes lies in the mixture of the two, something as in "Hyperion," who however is much inferior to Sterne in that; very much as in Paul Richter, who is far superior to both of them; very much as in real life which is immensely superior to the whole of them. But the truth is as you will see very well—as I might just have said at once —I am not prepared to give any definite opinion of Master Sterne.

To another friend who had written to tell him of the death of an infant daughter, he sent an answer, which is interesting, not only in itself, but as the first specimen we have of a kind of a letter which he wrote more frequently and more carefully than any other. The sorrows of his friends drew forth his tenderest sympathy. If he could not go to them in their grief, he never failed to write. The variety which we find in his letters of consolation is marvellous. He entered into all the circumstances and surroundings of each individual case, and thus sent letters which were as cold water to souls thirsting in the wilderness of grief. The recipient of one such letter said to me, " She would be a rebellious mother indeed who would not be made submissive by such a letter as that."

To the Rev. Alex. MacEwen.

IRVINE, 13th March, 1848.

Your " little daughter dead," you say. Not dead, but sleeping. What a brief waking for her, and a long sleep ! A sleep on the cold bosom of earth, that shall yet unveil her bosom and give her forth again in a second birth, most beautiful, to die no more. So you must have thought when you put her into that black cradle for her first and final sleep.

Such an event as that in the mystery of human life is surely quite inexplicable, except under the light of the gospel. One may wonder why God does not make an angel at once, rather than a mortal to be changed forthwith, by death, into one. It must surely be to honour the Lord His Son, by adding to the number of His redeemed, by swelling the retinue of palm branch bearers, the band of chorus singers in the temple. For children's voices, with their clear, sweet trebles, seem to be wanted in that choir! God plants lilies in earth's gardens that His "beloved" may go down and gather them, and wreathe them in His chaplet. God hides precious pearls in earth's dark chambers, that the Saviour of the lost may seek them and find them, and set them to shine, star-like, in His crown. For their own sakes, too, for there are joys never to be known but by those that have tasted first the bitterness of sorrow. The gate to the very summit and to the very heart of heaven's joy is *Death*, and your infant child has been sent round to come in by that gate—has stooped a moment into the sphere of sorrow that she might rise by the reaction into higher joy—has been plunged a little moment into grief that she might come out of tribulation and have a place "before the throne." Mysterious little stranger! She has risen very quickly out of her baptism of sorrow, and put on her white robes!

For your own sake, too. If you cannot have a daughter living it is much better to have a daughter dead than none! Let there be no truth in the fancy that departed babes become guardian angels, no objective truth, but there is a great deal of subjective truth and meaning in it. Having laid up treasure in heaven, your first and your only pearl, where the treasure is there will the heart be also. . . .

Mr. Robertson not only kept up his intercourse with old friends, but was soon on terms of brotherly kindness with his new neighbours. The ministers of the Presbytery, having once had their suspicions of heresy set at rest, began to discover that the minister of Irvine, at whom they had been disposed to look askance, was fast taking possession of their hearts. They carried home from Presbytery dinners reports of his geniality and humour, till his promised visits to their manses were looked forward to with eagerness ; and when at last he arrived, it seemed to many of the young folks of these manses as if there had come into their little worlds a sunlight and a music of which they had not dreamed before. When he went to assist his neighbours at communions, the " new atmosphere " that had come into the old church at Irvine spread itself abroad over the Ayrshire towns and villages. Just then a new atmosphere was needed ; for the air was heavy with the smoke of the Morisonian controversy. That local incident in the controversy of ages had greatly exercised the minds and hearts of the good people in the Secession Presbytery of Kilmarnock. Those who remained within the Church of their fathers had ranged themselves on two sides as supporters of the " old " and the " new views " respectively; while in almost every district some had withdrawn and formed little communities adhering to Mr. Morison. To those who heard Mr. Robertson the all-engrossing controversy seemed to fall out of sight. Here was a man whom neither side could claim. He led into regions of thought in which distinctions between old and new views somehow disappeared ; and it began to reveal itself that in Christ Jesus neither old views nor new views availed anything. It was noticed that of all considerable towns in the district, Irvine was the only one in which there was no attempt to plant the new sect. Mr. Robertson was asked at a Presbytery dinner if he could explain this. He replied that the explanation was easy enough—the people got all they wanted in their own church, without going to seek it elsewhere.

And yet, withal, the highest Calvinists in the Presbytery were his warm friends. There was never any disposition to recall the early verdict, " That young man is perfectly orthodox." Rugged old men like Mr. Elles of Saltcoats, and Mr. Cairns of Stewarton, keen-scented theologians like Mr. Robertson of Kilmaurs, and gentle-hearted dreamers like Dr. Bruce of Newmilns, were at one in their affection for this new presbyter who had come among them. He, in turn, found delight in their marked individuality, and there was no one who more sincerely mourned their loss, as one after another of them was gathered to his fathers.

In the year 1849 his work was interrupted by an attack of scarlet fever. The first of the following letters was written when he was under the fever. He had no recollection afterwards that he had written it.

MY DEAR FATHER,—As they wrote you yesterday by the doctor's order, so I write you to-day by my own hand, to assure you of my being better, almost quite. It was a smart attack, but brief. If none of you have set out for this, I think it would not be right for you to do so at this time of the year. May God preserve all *your* healths to you, as He is restoring mine to me, and we shall both thank Him together.

To the REV. ALEXANDER MacEWEN.

IRVINE, 18th January, 1850.

For more than three weeks I have been ill of scarlet fever—a sharp and somewhat dangerous attack. For a few days I was not quite myself. How terrible are the wanderings of fever! What an Apocalypse of horror its burning hand throws open! The soul, like the "spirit" in the parable, wanders through dry places seeking rest and finding none. Once or twice I lost the consciousness of identity, and mingled and melted away into the universal spirit. I seemed to become the god of Hegelians, pervading all things, yet evermore having a keen sense of grief unutterable. After a few days, sleep came—gentle sleep, it was like music from the lyre of David, disenchanting the evil spirit—and I awoke refreshed.

I am now recovering slowly, but steadily. Yesterday I crossed the threshold of my prison for a minute and breathed the free air, and though I' did not just feel like the convalescent, of whom it is said :—

> "The common air, the sun, the skies
> To him are opening Paradise,"

yet I feel greatly pleased with myself and with my exploit. . . .

My poor landlady, Miss Cochrane, who had been very ill for some time, got much worse, they say, with anxiety about me. Perhaps this snapped the thread which was already worn and wasted. She died on Tuesday morning peacefully. The funeral has just gone from the door. It snows heavily; the black coffin and the white snow remind one of the contrast between death and glory. She was a good woman, and the sky has resolved to clothe her mourners in white.

To the spring-time of one of these years belongs a carol which, thirty years later, he expanded and printed as a triptych, which may be given as illustrating his Herbert-like love of conceits, revealed also in his correspondence, as for example at the close of the letter just quoted. In sending a copy of the carol to a friend, he speaks of it, and of some other verses he had previously sent, as "the leaves that have dropped in great numbers, in the shaded woods of the past—my Ayrshire Vallombrosa," and thus continues :—

The triptych (three leaved) written thirty years ago, was made to show how easily the divinest sacred history could be rendered into natural myth, which blockheads of the Strauss school might regard as all the root or germ from which the history had grown, and which other blockheads of the orthodox school might regard as an irreverent parody with a decided ritualistic meaning and broad school significance, neither of them having an ear to discern the hidden harmonies that underlie all " nature and grace " in creation and redemption, and give a beauty (as of subtle echoes) to the most remote and delicate, and even fanciful resemblances betwixt them.

Innocent children that belong to neither party sing it to the pretty carol it is set to, and for the rest it was thrown aside out of sight of any Unintelligent People, *i.e.* not, of course, U.P.

Easter Echoes.

I have seen the buried corn,
Under ground in Spring-time borne,
Rise with Christ on Easter morn.

When the sunlights and the rain,
To the tomb where it has lain,
Coming, find it risen again.

Angels in those sunlights seen ;
While each weeping shower between
Is a weeping Magdalene.

She sweet spices brings with her,
For the corn in sepulchre,
But the stone she cannot stir.

Frozen ground is hard as stone,
Under which the seed lies sown,
With the seal of frost thereon.

Ne'er can rain pass with her spices,
Valued at most costly prices,
Through the glittering guard of ices—

Guard, with glittering shield and spear,
Keeping watch around the bier,
In the moonlight cold and clear ;

Keeping watch till break of day :
And the sobbing sisters say,
Who shall roll the stone away ?

Lo ! at dawn from Eastern skies,
God's strong Angel, Morning, flies,
With his flashing, flaming eyes,

When the keepers fall as slain,
Seal and stone are all in vain ;
The dead corn is up again.

From its husk and winding sheet,
Where, behold at head and feet,
Sunlights twain have ta'en their seat.

And those shining sunlights twain
Tell the weeping, sobbing rain,
The dead corn is risen again.

So the Christ, and so the corn,
Under ground in Spring-time borne,
Rise again on Easter morn !

As he cultivated the art of writing verses, the habit
so grew upon him, that in the preparation of his sermons his thoughts often took rhythmic form. This
was the origin of the lines he entitled, "Able to Save."
They are really part of a sermon on Hebrews vii. 25,
which was preached in the winter of 1850. The
second last couplet was added in 1858, in which year
Donati's comet was visible on many successive nights.
With reference to these early verses, he thus wrote in
1884 to a friend—the same to whom he had sent the
carol—who had asked leave to print them :—

They were broken off from a sermon on "Christ able to save," out of which they had flowed in the preaching, as not seldom with me in old Irvine a song did flow out of a sermon, when at a certain heat the speech would boil up, or rather the glacier, descending, melt down when crossing the snow line, into a stream of rhyme; which stream most commonly (like that which issues from the mountain ice) flowed brown and turbid, and filled with rolling stones from the debris and the moraine above, so that it could seldom afford to be severed (as those lines can) from the sermon it belonged to.   For which reason few of these things have gone out into the world by permission, nor have they been collected and sent out.   How little that is spoken is worth the printing—how much less that is printed is worth the speaking?   Amid the more than tropical luxuriance—of weeds mostly in these days—I really am not ambitious of adding to the wilderness and undergrowth of hymns and other such herbs. I subscribe to the horticultural, but never exhibit except in my own garden.   .   .   .   .

Able to Save.

A lowly Man,—He takes my sins, and bears the heavy load ;
A lowly Man,—He takes my hand, and leads me up the road ;
And when I know the lowly Man is my Creator, God !
Oh ! this has solved much darksome speech, and loosed
    tongues that were dumb ;
For all creation round me now a gospel has become,
And what had seemed to me, before, mere wild confused Babel
Is now a fire-tongued Pentecost, proclaiming "Christ is able."

The thunders in the crashing skies announce it as they roll,
The lightnings on the black storm wall write it in lurid scroll,
And stars repeat it down the dark, in mystic gleaming light,
The Urim and the Thummim on the breastplate of the night.

And strong Orion shouts to me, what slumbered in old fable,
And echoes from eternal night-vaults answer "Christ is able!"
And comet, cresting bended heavens, wafts echo to the word,
Like waving white plumes in the star-mailed helmet of the
    Lord ;
For all creation its evangels utters forth abroad
In man's ear, when I know in truth my Saviour Christ is
    God.

To the same period (1850) belong the following verses, which had evidently a similar origin. In sending them to a friend in Mentone, when he was residing there in 1872, he prefixed this note :—

In the fourth century Ephraim the Syrian used to preach in metre. So did mediæval preachers frequently. Dean Ramsay (in his "Pulpit Text Book") asks why clergymen may not do so still? Why not? asks the pew opener. She will try it herself. She has a habit of dissolving the sermon in part, after hearing it, into rhyme. She did so last Sunday. Take the text 1 Cor. vii. 29-31 and try. "The time is short." Literally, compressed—shut in—by the expected second coming. "It remaineth therefore," etc., "for the *fashion*," *i.e.*, *stage scenery*, "of this world passeth away."

Stage Scenery.

Scenery, nothing more I ween,
Painted on a shifting screen,
Painted river, wood and hill,
Painted city, sun and star,
Things that rather seem than are—
Nothing real—hearts to fill,
Mere illusion for the eye,
Stage play and stage scenery !

I

Stage griefs are not really sad,
Stage joys are not really glad,
Real bargains are not made
On the streets of masquerade.
Crown'd kings, when the play is ended,
Lay aside their robes of pride,
Sceptred, throned, and slave-attended,
Yet poor men enough outside.

Weddings on the stage !   No !   Both
Bride and bridegroom plight their troth,
Endless as the ring between :
Yet full soon the marriage oath
Comes dissolved behind the screen ;
For these stage brides are not wed,
And their dead, too, are not dead,
Though across the stage with pall
Sadly borne by mourners all
In a doleful funeral !

Then—" the time is short "—the time
Shut in by a second coming,
Deeds of long years, deeds sublime
In a little night play summing,
And droll little Pantomime
Playful plucks, in passing by,
Thy black robe ! grim Tragedy !

On—the mystic drama moving—
Hoping, fearing, hating, loving,
And the angel over all,
With the trump of God down-bending,
At whose blast the screen shall fall,
And another curtain rending,

'Twixt the seeming and the true,
Brings the Eternal Real to view !

How, then, does the lesson run ?
" Having wives as having none,
Weeping as not weeping be,
And rejoice not merrily.

" Buy—thy grasp on bought things loosing,
Use this world as not abusing ; "
For, as actors well should know,
It is all mere passing show—
Passing show, and seeming all,
And the curtain soon to fall
On things seen and temporal !

Weep ! weep truly, for dead souls,
Lest when bell of judgment tolls,
Darkness, with her hearse and pall,
Gives them dismal funeral ;
For the rest refrain from weeping,
For they are not dead but sleeping.

Rachel weeps no more at Rama
In the last act of the drama,
For her children's shroud and clay
Are the things that pass away.

He sent to the same friend, at the same time, another copy of verses of early and probably similar origin, prefixing the words :—

With such plain chant the Ritualist pew opener ventures to go on, in measure without measure.

" Et Came to Pass."

Passing ! all things come to pass,
As we often thoughtless say—
Generations are like grass,
And our fathers ! where are they ?
Cross'd the stage, and passed away.
Marriages have come to pass,
Funerals have not come to stay,
Nothing ever comes to stay,
All things only " come to pass."

On—flows the phantasmal river,
Passing always—pausing never,
Joys and sorrows, mingled ever.
Bridal dresses glancing white,
And black hearses plumed in night ;
Now red lips and laughing eyes,
Now clasped hands and bitter cries,
Now the ringing of sweet bells,
Now the tolling of deep knells
With most sorrowful farewells.
On—flows the phantasmal river,
Passing always—pausing never !

Pausing never !—like the stream,
And yet pausing—like the beam
Shining with a steady gleam,
Shining in that running stream.

For amidst this whirl and flow,
In which all things come and go,
What remaineth ? Lord, 'tis Thou !
In Thine Everlasting Now !

Though the days are passing ever,
Yet " to-day " departeth never ;
And though withereth the grass,
Grass anew the fields are giving ;
And though men—*men* come to pass,
Yet "*the man*" is always living.
Liveth the Divine Ideal,
And the ideal shapes the real ;
And the rest is shadow, all
Passing and phantasamal.
Liveth the creating Word
Of the I AM,—of the Lord,—
Who amidst all change is true,
Evermore makes all things new !

It was about the same date that Mr. Robertson
delivered his first public lecture, and thus entered on
a department of service in which he peculiarly excelled. His power as a lecturer was not attained
without great labour. He was at pains to make himself thoroughly master of his subject, and in the con-
struction of his lectures he gave full play to that
dramatic power which, as those who knew his preaching are aware, he did not restrain even in his sermons.
He was not content with one writing, but re-cast and
re-wrote from time to time, so that there are extant,
fragments of many versions. As in the descriptive
passages of his sermons, he seemed to be telling what
he was vividly seeing—nay, he often seemed to be
himself the actor in the events he was picturing.

The subject of his earliest lecture was " German
Student Life," for which, as we have seen, he had

ample material in his note-books. The lecture
opened with a life-like picture of the Rev. Mr.
Burgher's manse, at the tea-table of which the
good minister, with the aid of Mrs. Burgher, and
Uncle Antiburgher, the elder, discusses with his son
John, a student of theology, a project which has
come into the head of the said John, to complete his
studies at a German university. Then came a description of "how things have gone in Lutherland
since the Reformation era," illustrated by a conversation between the lecturer and a German student—a
disciple of the Hegelianism of the left—with a most
vivid description of the mountain pass in the High
Alps where the conversation took place, and of the
incidents that befell as it proceeded. This was followed by a picture of the *Bursch*, leaving the *Pfarr-
haus*, the German manse—which a few touches
brought before the audience—and approaching Halle
by the Leipsic road. Then his characteristics were set
forth, and he was shown at work as "he stands
at his writing desk enwrapped in his long *Schlaf-
rock*, and the long pipe depending from his lips."
The audience were invited to follow the *Bursch* as,
"exchanging his pipe for a cigar, his dressing gown
for his velveteen, he sallies forth to hear the lectures."
They were led to the university, and in succession
into the class rooms of Gesenius, Wegscheider, Erdmann, Heinrich, Müller, and Tholuck. Then back
with the *Bursch* to dinner, and out with him again
to church on Sunday, where the Lutheran service

proceeds and Tholuck preaches. They had even a glimpse into the Sunday evening theatre to which he goes, and into the concert room, and the oratorios at St. Ulrich's, where he finds better influences to guide him. They were introduced to Louisa, the *Bursch's* betrothed, and overheard a conversation between the lovers as to the mysteries of the Hegelian philosophy, which closed with a song by Louisa, and answering verse of Schiller by the *Bursch*. Then followed a most marvellous description of the *Bursch's* funeral (for "there are two doors to go out by from the University—the door of doctorship and the door of death"), attended by a torch procession ; and the lecture closed with a hopeful outlook on the future of the religious life of Germany.

Another lecture, prepared somewhat later, was on "Poetry." Taking the well-known line from Collins' Passion Ode,

"Pale melancholy sat retired,"

he showed how that could be expressed equally well by Canova in sculpture, by Coreggio in painting, by Beethoven in music, and by William of Wykeham in architecture, there being the three fixed and the two flowing arts that are in essence the same. He then discussed the question, What is poetry ? He showed that it is not mere rhyme or rhythm; neither is it mere imitation, or copying after nature ; it is creation —fictitious creation, which has the power of giving life to its creations, and the exercise of which is lawful, but limited by reality, reason, and revelation. Prepared originally for an Ayrshire audience, some of the most striking illustrations of the successive points of the lecture are taken from Burns and " that fearful rider Tam," who, though " Burns is dead and buried in Dumfries kirkyard, still lives, and must hold on to ride so long as this strange life of ours can sport with its own misery, and blaze out rockets of wild, drunken laughter upon the very night of its terrible despair."

In a lighter department of service, Mr. Robertson early acquired a great reputation among the Ayrshire churches, and latterly, alas! for his health and peace of mind, in more distant places. As a speaker at church soirees, he had a unique power of combining serious instruction and stimulating address, with the sparkling fun that never failed to set the tables in a roar. As the fun generally came first, and was, moreover, the part of his speeches most interesting to the gentlemen of the press, it happened that often in the reports of such gatherings, the minister of Irvine was represented only by a succession of jokes or mirth-moving anecdotes ; but in reality he never did speak on such occasions without leaving a deep and profitable impression. A favourite theme was the seven departments of Christian service, set forth in Romans xii. 6-8, which he likened to the seven branches of the golden candlestick in the temple— the prophets or singers, the ministers or managers the teachers, the exhorters or preachers, the givers, the rulers or elders, and the mercy showers, or deacons, Dorcas visitors, and the like. Often he never got beyond the "prophets," for he deemed it one of his special callings in the church to seek to improve the service of worship. At other times he would give peculiar prominence to the givers, and to the apostolic exhortation addressed to them, that they should give " with simplicity," on which he based a condemnation of bazaars and such like devices for raising money.

Gradually his fame spread beyond his own neighbourhood, to the great cities, and wherever he went to preach, crowds gathered to hear him. In Glasgow, especially, where there is a close connection with Ayrshire, he early attained popularity, and in 1851 a strenuous effort was made to get him to accept a city charge. The congregation of Shamrock Street which called him was an extension charge, founded to meet the wants of a growing population in the north-west of Glasgow, and offered as eligible a sphere of labour as any hard working minister could desire. The church was so situated that it had rich and poor within easy reach on either hand. Among its prominent office-bearers were some of Mr. Robertson's earliest friends. Great, therefore, was the anxiety among the people in Irvine lest they should be deprived of the minister who had taken such hold of their hearts. The comings and goings of Glasgow deputations were eagerly watched, and the face of the minister was scanned for any indication of

what his decision was likely to be. But he showed
no sign to relieve the anxiety of his flock, nor were
the Glasgow deputations more successful. It is told
that one of the members of Glasgow Presbytery, Dr.
James Taylor, having gone to Irvine and spent hours
in a vain endeavour to get from Robertson some indication of his mind with regard to the call, was at last
leaving by the train, and Mr. Robertson was seeing
him off, when Dr. Taylor put his head out of the
carriage window, and said, "Good-bye you're a queer
fish, Willie"; to which he replied, "And you're a
queerer fisher, Taylor."

On the day of the decision—which, according to
Presbyterian order, had to be given at a meeting of
Presbytery at Kilmarnock—omnibuses were hired,
and all the members of the Irvine congregation who
could leave their employments attended the meeting.
When his resolution to remain with them was de-
clared, and the call which had disturbed their peace
was set aside, their joy knew no bounds. Meetings
were held for thanksgiving—in which it is remembered that an old elder prayed that the Glasgow congregation might be forgiven for their covetousness ;
poems were written and printed, and resolutions
were adopted to give substantial evidence of the
gratitude which filled the good people's hearts.
Among other additions to his comfort, it was determined to build a manse, that he might be no longer
a mere lodger, but an accredited householder among
them.

CHAPTER VIII.

Life in the Manse.

IN the early summer of 1852, the year following his refusal of the call to Glasgow, Mr. Robertson was sent to preach in London. This was his first professional visit to the metropolis, where, as in other districts of England, he was ultimately recognized as one of the most powerful of Presbyterian preachers. On this occasion his appointment was to Albion Chapel, London Wall, an old centre of Presbyterianism now swept away.

His autumn holiday that year was spent in Switzerland, his travelling companions being his old friends John Logan and Alexander Anderson, who were both office-bearers of the congregation whose call he had declined, and Mr. Smith of Hamilfield, a prominent member of the Irvine church.

On his return he set himself to a kind of work which he could seldom be induced to undertake. The Synod of the United Presbyterian Church had, in the May of that year, sanctioned a collection of hymns for use in public worship, and Mr. Robertson consented to review the book in a series of articles in the denominational Magazine. The first of the series appeared in November, 1852. Its most memorable passage is a footnote in which he expresses strong doubts as to the propriety of versifying the Psalter. He asks, " How could Rouse, Sternhold, Tate, or any man however gifted, succeed in discoursing the varied and ever-changing music of the many-stringed lyre of inspiration on the solitary string of a quatrain stanza ?"

Of the further articles projected only one appeared. It was published in April, 1853, under the title, " On Praising God in Hymns," and contains the germs of many lectures and addresses afterwards delivered on his favourite theme of church music.

Meanwhile the manse, which his congregation had resolved to build in token of their gratitude that he had not left them, was approaching completion ; and he was busy making the necessary preparations for entering it.

He had such horror of the initial letters " U.P.," to which common usage had reduced the somewhat unmeaning name of the Church of his fathers, that to avoid the otherwise inevitable designation " U.P. Manse," he resolved to give the house a name, and so he called it " Ravensbrook." There was a Ravens-croft not far away, and the rookeries in Eglinton woods sent enough of crows across the plain to justify the former part of the name ; but his friends were puzzled to know where he found the "brook." He was quick to defend himself by pointing to a slow runnel, which crosses the road at a little distance from the manse gate, and which a tradition, preserved in the name "The Minister's Cast," says was cut by good David Dickson, for the drainage of the waste land on Irvine moor.

To His Younger Sister.

IRVINE, 17th January, 1853.

Miss ——— has a laburnum in her garden called Mary ——— destined to be transplanted into the manse garden— and she is now ready for transplanting. The spring is almost in sight, and I can scarcely tell you how busy I am with planning and counterplanning shrubbery, gravel and grass walks, belts of limes and poplars, ivy screens for Major Todd's old wall, climbing rose and clematis rails, etc. I wish I had Andrew's ingenuity or the loan of it for six weeks. The manse is nearly ready for habitation . . .

You mind old Jean in the back court—the "old witch?" She died yesterday—strange old creature! She was afraid she would die of want, and to save a little money half starved herself and brought on illness. Palsy with its hammer struck her—felled her like an ox, and they found her the other morning, lying half dead on her cold hearth-stone. Great quantities of unused clothing were found in her house and between one and two hundred pounds! The neighbours agreed to use the money in getting for her soups and wines, and all such things as the doctor ordered, and old Jean partook of them very heartily, under the idea that her neighbours had provided them, and seemed recovering fast till, wakening up her attendant two mornings since at 2 A.M. to ask after her money, she was stunned to hear

that she had been eating and drinking her "ain siller"—
and so shocked was she that she swooned away and died
soon after.   What a mystery is human life and character !
Queer specimen of it this ! I tried again and again to speak
to her of the most solemn things, but her heart was sheathed
in gold and silver ; and let no one defer these matters till the
last !

At the beginning of summer he took possession of his
new home, and Isabella, the elder of his two surviving
sisters, came to live with him. Her coming brought an
element of peculiar grace and tenderness into his life.
She was his equal in grasp of mind, and in that love
of the beautiful in poetry and music for which he was
distinguished ; yet she was so shrinkingly modest that
the casual visitor would never discover that she had any
other qualities than those which were revealed in the
quietness and dignity and refinement with which she
ordered the house. The relation between the brother
and sister was very beautiful ; and as the years passed
with their joy and sorrow their lives were linked
together by sacred bonds.

He had the delight of receiving his mother—whose
health had been causing him anxiety in the earlier
months of the year—as one of his first visitors in the
manse.   Her presence gave him the deeper sympathy
with his fellow-student, William Barlas, and his brothers
and sisters, in the sudden death of their mother, of
which intimation had reached him when he was on
a preaching tour in Ireland

To Mr. James Barlas.

Irvine, 10th September, 1853.

Accept, dear friends, my sympathy, which though belated in the expression of it, is not assuredly the less sincere. Though I do not know what it is to lose a mother (God grant that sorrow may be long postponed), I look up to her across the table where she is sitting now quietly knitting, and try to fancy for a moment how awfully distressing it would be, to see that calm face which for more than thirty years, since first it hung radiant with maternal love over my cradle, has always seemed to me the sweetest and most expressive in the world—to see it muffled up in the white veil! No I cannot think of it, and if the very thought be so repulsive, what must it have been to you to have it realized. . . . .

His first year in the manse was like all the years that followed it in one particular. He was never without visitors. Thomas Aird, the author of "The Devil's Dream," and of the charming idyllic sketches collected under the title, "An Old Bachelor in a Scottish Village," came to join George Gilfillan of Dundee, and John Cairns, then of Berwick, round his table. In some interesting reminiscences of these years the Rev. John Kirkwood of Troon, says :—

Dr. Robertson was specially kind to the younger brethren ordained in his neighbourhood, and friendships were formed with some of us which lasted through life. Soon after our settlement we were asked to take part in some service that we might become mutually acquainted. My first opportunity was, I think, the evening of a Fast-day, when I preached for him ; for that ordinance which has now ceased

altogether amongst us was then consecrated by three diets
of worship.   That was to me the beginning of nights.   I
learned then that an " evening " with Robertson embraced
nearly all the hours of darkness, and yet always seemed too
short.   His flashes of genius and humour were a new revelation to me ; and yet he was perfectly brotherly, putting me
at once on a footing of equality.

To the Rev. John Kirkwood.

Irvine, 26th September, 1853.

Thursday evening first, at six o'clock, we have a conver-
sazione of Sabbath school teachers at my house.   If you
are not better occupied I shall be glad to introduce them to
you, and to get better acquainted with you myself.   The
form of the meeting is quite extemporaneous.   The chief
elements are tea, music, and palaver—the latter conversational only, not oratorical.   You might enjoy yourself, and
would certainly help to increase our joy.

Mr. Kirkwood remembers that "several had prepared speeches for the occasion, but whether from the
novelty of the circumstances or from inexperience
there were a few breaks down.   The genial way in
which Robertson helped them through, removing all restraint, and making every one feel at home, was a study
and a model.   When the company departed the richest
treat remained in the private chat till morning."
In the year 1854 he published specially for the use
of his own Sunday schools a collection of hymns for
children and teachers under the title " Hosanna."   In
the preface he says :—

It may be thought that a somewhat severe taste has governed the selection, to the exclusion of some well-known children's melodies; but it is to be remembered that good hymns for children are something else than hymns for adults written after a childish manner.

He was much exercised by the writing of this preface. Then, and to the close of his life, it was only by a great effort that he could bring himself to prepare anything for publication. For about six months before the hymn book appeared, he constantly pleaded the writing of the preface as an excuse for not visiting his friends. Great was their amusement to find, when at last the book appeared, that the preface extended to some thirty-two lines!

The collection has long been out of print, but it will bear favourable comparison with any that has since appeared. It is manifest that the compiler had a high ideal, and that he was seeking gradually to educate the Church in Scotland to a worthier service of praise. It was in this little volume that he gave his earliest translation of the "Dies Iræ," a fuller version of which was included in the Presbyterian Hymnal of 1876.

At the close of 1855 he was called to bear the great loss, the very thought of which had so distressed him two years before. His mother died on 7th December, aged 68 years. The trial was the greater that he was suffering from an attack of gastric fever, and could not see her during the closing weeks of her life, or be present at her funeral. I remember being with him about

K

three years later when he was recovering from an illness. The first evening he was to come down stairs I had prepared the little back drawing-room for his comfort, bringing the sofa near the fire, and putting up a screen to shelter it. When he came down he asked me, abruptly as I thought at the time, to alter the arrangement of the room. He explained afterwards that I had put it exactly as it was when his mother was dying and he lay there in sorrow, unable to go to her. On the day before the funeral he wrote :—

To the REV. JAMES ROBERTSON.

IRVINE, 12th December, 1855.

MY DEAR JAMES,—" Peace !" You read this in a solemn place and at a solemn hour. " How dreadful !" but is it not the " gate of heaven" ? Alas ! that I cannot be with you—not to give comfort, but to get it. I almost feel as if I could—in spite of all the doctor says—but all is well, and I submit.

There is deep snow on the ground here—reminding me (how forcibly) of the white vestures of those who have " washed their robes," and are therefore " before the throne ;" for when I was recovering from scarlet fever my mother was here, and Miss Cochrane was lying in her shroud, and there was then deep snow on the ground, of which we could not choose but talk in that way. May the hand of Love gather up all these sweet, though sad, remembrances, and knit them together for the times of restitution and re-union in the blessed future !

I will be with you to-morrow all day—in spirit. May the Lord, the Comforter, be with you in deep, deep reality, and the " peace of God that passeth understanding."

Thanks for your train-written letter and all the beautiful and consoling things it says. I should say something in reply, but cannot elevate my mind to the power of thinking anything whatever, and therefore your letter is the more acceptable. I can only lie in my weakness and see a funeral moving, and faces—dear faces—bitterly weeping, but with glimpses of contrasted glory overhead, when our wailing in the valleys is answered by shouting on the mountains, and One in the midst saying, " Fear not, I am He that liveth and was dead." Give them all my sorrowful love at this sad time. " We sorrow not," *certainly* not, " as those who have no hope." Thanks over again for your kind visit.

In one of his conversations with the Rev. John Haddin at Westfield House in February, 1882, Dr. Robertson said, " The best sermon I ever preached was that which I preached last at Irvine from 2 Timothy i. 10, ' Our Saviour, Jesus Christ, who hath abolished death and hath brought life and immortality to light through the gospel.' It was first delivered twenty-six years ago, after the death of my mother. It is substantially the same, and had not to be altered in any way in regard to matter and spirit. It is striking how free it is from specialities of doctrine, and how completely it accords with my preaching at the present time."

His time of mourning for his mother had its outcome not only in powerful preaching, but in verses which often in the after years he sent to friends in sorrow, whom thus he sought to comfort with the comfort wherewith he himself had been comforted :—

Departed.

Departed, say we? is it
    Departed or come nigh?
Dear friends in Christ more visit
    Than leave us, when they die.
What thin veil still may hide them
    Some little sickness rends,
And lo! we stand beside them—
    Are they departed friends?

Their dews on Zion mountain
    Our Hermon hills bedew,
Their river from the fountain
    Flows down to meet us too,
The oil on the head and under,
    Down to the skirts hath run,
And though we seem asunder,
    We still in Christ are one.

The many tides of ocean
    Are one vast tidal wave,
That sweeps in landward motion
    Alike to coast and cave;
And life from Christ o'erflowing
    Is one wave evermore,
To earth's dark borders going,
    Or heaven's bright pearly shore.

Hail! perfected immortals!
    Even now we bid you hail—
We, at the blood-stained portals,
    And ye, within the veil.
The thin cloud veil between us
    Is mere dissolving breath,

One heaven surrounds and screens us,
And where art thou? O Death!

About the same time, and probably in connection with some ministry of consolation to which he was called, he wrote the following for the comfort of stricken parents :—

The Child's Angel.

"In heaven their angels do always behold the face of my Father which is in heaven."

Elder sister, elder brother,
Come and go around the mother,
  As she bids them come and go:
But the babe in her embrace
Rests and gazes on her face,
  And is most happy so.

Christ, our Lord, in his evangel,
Tells us how the young child's angel,
  In the world of heavenly rest,
Gazes in enraptured trance
On his Father's countenance,
  And is supremely blest.

Other angels come and go
As the Lord will, to and fro,
  Some to earth on missions fleet,
Some stand singing, some are winging
Their swift flight, and homeward bringing
  The saved to Jesus' feet.

Angel hosts, all mingling, changing,
Circle above circle ranging,
  Marshalling, throng God's holy place;

But the children's angels, dearest
To the Father's heart, come nearest,
　　They always see His face.

And oh ! if every beauty beaming
From frail mother's face, rush streaming
　　Deep into her infant's heart,
What rare beauty theirs must be,
　Heavenly God, who gaze on Thee !
　　Who see Thee as Thou art !

It was probably in the days when, under the shadow
of his mother's death, he was recovering from the
fever, that he wrote the following powerful verses ; or,
they may have been struck off in the heat of preparing a sermon, after his return to duty. In any
case they belong to the period of which we are now
writing.　　They are included in the notes of a sermon
of later date on " the Desire of all nations " ; but there
they are manifestly introduced as a quotation and are
not an outgrowth of the thought.

" Skin for Skin."

Well said the devil in days of old
" Skin for skin," and gold for gold !
" All that a man hath will he give,"
Only to live ! to live ! to live !

Who would leave life's bright warm halls
For death's dank, dripping, mouldy walls ?
Who would exchange life's laurel wreath
For cypress black as thine ? O death !

Go to the slaughter the silly flocks,
Goes to the slaughter the stupid ox,
But shall *man* quietly yield and go?
Never—oh never, never, no!

Loth were I to lie as a clod,
Trodden, and rotten, and—Oh! good God!
Give me breath, and tears, and strife,
But only give me life! life! life!

To the same period when the shadow was over him
belong the following :—

Beneath o'erhanging mountains
   The stars are hid from view,
Those light besprinkling fountains
   That fret the vaulted blue ;
But as the pilgrim passes on,
   The mountains fade from light,
The starry hosts return anon
   And march with him all night.

And stars are lofty centres,
   That spread their golden rays,
Where nothing earthly enters,
   To break or mar their blaze;
So griefs are passing showers and storms
   That haunt our earthly road,
But joys are ever-during forms
   That dwell in heaven with God !

The friend to whom the following letter is addressed
was one of his fellow-students to whom he was drawn
by kindred sympathies.   The fact that Mr. Graham,

probably induced by his example, went to Germany
to complete his course of theological study, was
another link between them.   After they became
ministers, the one in Irvine, the other in Liverpool,
distance did not hinder frequent intercourse and exchange of service.   They had much in common.
They both brought great freshness and originality to
bear on the theology which it was their calling to
study and expound ; they both recognized its place
in the circle of the sciences, and enriched their
private conversation and public teaching with the
results of a wide and varied culture ; they both over-
flowed with genial kindliness and ready wit, and both
of them were distinguished for their readiness to
sympathize with and be helpful to any brother in
sorrow or in need.   Their friendship deepened as the
years went on. Graham, who had by that time become
Professor Graham, of the Presbyterian College in
London, was one of the last who visited Dr. Robertson when he was dying, and in little more than a
year he followed him to the grave. It was then
revealed that there was yet another point of resem-
blance between the friends.   Both of them had long
hidden, beneath a veil of sunny mirthfulness, sore
internal pain.

To Rev. William Graham, Liverpool.

Irvine, 2nd October, 1856.

My Dear Graham,—If you were ashamed at not writing
me sooner, to have replied immediately would have made

you more so, and that, of course (out of tender consideration for your feelings) is the reason of this belated reply to your last.

I was glad to find that you were not implacably angry with me for making you preach twice—no other body was—and hundreds would have been disappointed sorely if you had not mounted the second time. Your sermons, I think, have done real and much good, and so I am happy to learn that you are not totally *vollendet*, but still able, after your extra exertions here, to do a little at home.

Thanks for the journal of your tour among the ruins of a world that was. I found it very interesting, both for their sake and yours, and it strengthened in me the desire to have a ramble among ruins with you somewhen and somewhere. Let us keep that in view, pray, unless, to be sure, we get numbered among ruins ourselves.

Ruins ! Will any antiquary, I wonder, ever think it worth his while to renew the letters on our headstones? It doesn't matter. Let there be as much life and laughter in the world as ever ! Let us do our work and consent to be forgotten. *One* is not unrighteous to forget. The Lord will remember us (I hope) when He comes into His kingdom. To that extent I confess to a desire for immortality !

For the last week there has been a shadow over me. Dr. Samuel Brown is dead. Eight days before, I went into Edinburgh to see him, but failed, as he was having something done to him, and was very ill at the time I went—so that I had to slip away in spite of his wish that I should stay till he could speak again. It was Friday, and I was hastening home to preach. Some memorials that he has left for me have come to hand this morning. They recall some of at once the wisest and the wildest hours of my life, spent in his company.

What a brilliant life has been quenched ! and that, too,

when it had been purified by sore affliction into "a burning
and a shining light," in which we had been willing to
rejoice; not quenched indeed, but risen as a star upon
some higher firmament, yet set too early upon *our*
horizon. I suppose God can do his work well enough
without any of us, however gifted. Mind *you* that. There
are others on whom the rock at Arthur's Seat may be in
much less danger of falling.

You should read Dr. Samuel's "Itinerating Libraries and
their Founder," not scared by the unpromising title. He
has revised it on his deathbed, and it has come to me with
the dead man's blessing! I believe he has been "chosen
in the furnace," and, after long wrestling with the angel in
the "night of weeping," has vanquished, and won the blessing. The image of the "fairest of men" has been deeply
graven on his spirit by the encaustic of grief; or rather,
being there latent and invisible, though real, it has been
brought out in its beauty and fulness by the fire. May we
meet him in the Hesperides of the future!

You have now set to work, I suppose, in earnest for the
winter, and are reckoning it winter. It is not that here.
The finest season perhaps in the circle of the year still lies
before us. To be sure, the morning service of the singing
birds is over, and the first course of the feast—green peas,
vegetables and the like; but the golden tables of Autumn
are now drawn out, a finer tapestry is hung upon the
woods, purer lights are in the sky, the dessert of fruits in
leafy baskets is serving up (not to speak of vintage and
October ale), while the evening service of the black friars
and the crows, and the occasional solo of the red-caped
cantor, the robin, are very much to my taste. Were you
only with me to hear and see!

The week before last I spent not far from you at the
lakes, but had to return and preach twice on Sabbath. We

were a six-fold party, two thirds of it belonging to the
fair sex, and we were very merry.   Isabella would have liked
vastly to go on to Liverpool and you, but that I hope lies
in the *Zukunft.* . . . .

In these years he was engaged with a course of
Sabbath morning lectures on the Epistle to the
Romans. He had already by his vivid picturings
won the younger members of his flock; and their
elders were not only well pleased to see the juniors
so deeply interested in the sermons, they were themselves charmed by the beauty of the preacher's
thought and the earnestness of his spirit. But when
he successfully grappled with the theological problems of St. Paul's great epistle, their admiration
grew. Old men, who found their hearing not so
sharp as once it had been, would change their seats
and draw nearer to the pulpit that they might not
miss a word of his argument, as he led them to the
standpoint from which to see the harmony between
the apparent contradictions that had perplexed them
so long. The great truth by which he solved the
difficulties that beset the doctrine of predestination
was the eternity of God. He was wont to insist that
it is only because of the poverty of our language that
we speak of past or future in relation to the Eternal.
He is not only the same yesterday and to-day and
for ever, but yesterday and to-day and for ever, which
are distinguished to our finite minds, are with Him
one eternal now. He set the thought to music :—

Hymn to the Eternal.

The dead still live to Thee, O God !
   The unborn are living now,
O'er past and future, spread abroad
   Eternal wings dost Thou !

To Thee, old priest, by altar fires,
   His sacrifice still brings ;
And still to Thee the prophets' choir
   God's holy anthem sings.

Our fathers' morning song gone by,
   Thou still, O God, dost hear ;
And still the crucifixion cry
   Is sounding in Thine ear.

And so Thou seest us in our shrouds,
   And standing at Thy bar ;
Already with Thee all the crowds
   Of unfleshed spirits are.

The risen dead in white array
   Are singing round Thy throne,
As if already judgment day
   A thousand years were gone.

With Thee, who driest the mourner's tears,
   Great God to whom we pray !
One day is as a thousand years,
   A thousand years one day.

He had at this time a special stimulus to the writing of hymns. The introduction by Mr. Curwen of the tonic sol-fa notation had led to a revived interest in church music. William Robertson welcomed

the new system because it made it much easier to
teach the art of singing. He used to say that
students of the art had long been discouraged by
finding across their path a five-barred gate, with
curious looking creatures called minims, crotchets,
and quavers, grinning at them through the bars ; and
that it had cost himself thrice as many years to learn
music as to learn any of the languages he had acquired. He believed that it was only through the
sol-fa notation that there was any hope of teaching
congregations to sing correctly. He accordingly did
everything he could to encourage the use of it in his
own congregation, and had at this time classes for
teaching it. It was for these classes that he wrote
and set to music several of his hymns. In addition
to the one we have just given, he wrote at this time a
baptismal hymn, which was ultimately sung in part,
at the public dispensation of the ordinance. It followed the rhythm of the German *Seelenbräutigam.*
Its first and last verses were :—

> Sprinkle, sprinkle, now,
> Blessed Saviour, Thou !
> Thou baptize this young immortal,
> Ent'ring through the church's portal ;
> Hands, and feet, and brow,
> Sprinkle, sprinkle, Thou !

> .   .   .   .   .   .

> Come then, blessed Dove !
> Through cleft heavens above.

> Crown this babe, white-robed, ascending,
> While we on this shore, down-bending
>   O'er the depths of love,
>   Cry, Come, blessed Dove !

For the same classes he also wrote :—

The Smoking Flax and Bruised Reed.

When evening choirs the praises hymned
    In Zion's courts of old,
The high priest walked his rounds, and trimmed
    The shining lamps of gold ;
And if, perchance, some flame burned low,
    With fresh oil vainly drenched,
He cleansed it from its socket, so
    The smoking flax was quenched.

But Thou who walkest, Priest Most High,
    Thy golden lamps among,
What things are weak, and near to die,
    Thou makest fresh and strong ;—
Thou breathest on the trembling spark,
    That else must soon expire,
And swift it shoots up through the dark,
    A brilliant spear of fire !

The shepherd that to stream and shade
    Withdrew his flock at noon,
On reedy stop soft music made,
    In many a pastoral tune ;
And if, perchance, the reed were crushed,
    It could no more be used,
Its mellow music marred and hushed ;
    He brake it, when so bruised.

But Thou, Good Shepherd, who dost feed
  Thy flock in pastures green,
Thou dost not break the bruised reed,
  That sorely crushed hath been ;
The heart that dumb in anguish lies,
  Or yields but notes of woe,
Thou dost re-tune to harmonies
  More rich than angels know !

Lord, once my love was all ablaze,
  But now it burns so dim !
My life was praise, but now my days
  Make a poor broken hymn ;
Yet ne'er by Thee am I forgot,
  But helped in deepest need,
The smoking flax Thou quenchest not,
  Nor break'st the bruised reed.

I am indebted to Principal Cairns for an account of
a meeting of the Evangelical Alliance at Berlin which
Mr. Robertson attended :—

The meeting of the Evangelical Alliance, held in Berlin
from 9th to 17th September, 1857, is one of the most
picturesque of all the meetings of that great confedera-
tion. It succeeded the first ecumenical meeting held in
London in 1851, the year of the first Exhibition, and the
second held in Paris in the agony of the Crimean War in
1855. A violent effort was made to stop it by the High
Lutheran party; but King Frederick William IV. stood
fast to it, assisted by Baron Bunsen, his friend, and Dr.
Krummacher, his chaplain, and it proved a great success,
dealing a final blow to that fraction as a Church party.
The *Garnison Kirche*, holding nearly 3,000 hearers, was filled

with a most various audience, addressed by many of the
most able men from all parts of the Protestant world, the
great majority of whom were Germans, though about 100
were from other parts of the Continent, 20 or 30 from
America and about 170 from the United Kingdom, the
whole enrolled members being nearly 1,500.   John Henderson and David King, the founders of the Alliance, were
present.   Many remarkable papers were read and discus-
sions held on the state of theology and the Christian statistics
of the world ; and one unusual feature was a greeting,
extending over a whole meeting, from different missionary
societies.   But the most singular incident was the reception
of about a thousand guests by the King in the new Palace
at Potsdam, followed by an address to them on the green
sward, amidst associations connected with Voltaire and
Frederick the Great.   The closing meeting was attended,
as several others, by the King and other members of the
Royal Family.   The late Emperor William—then Crown
Prince—was present at an earlier meeting.   Dr. Robertson,
whose name stands in the list of delegates (Robertson,
W. B., Prediger, Irvine), contributed a striking account,
especially of this last meeting, to *Evangelical Christendom*,
and speaks of the royal party rising up to sing " *Nun
danket alle Gott* " as a homage of the world to Christianity.

CHAPTER IX.

Letters and Poems.

THE year 1858 was one of great mental activity to
Mr. Robertson. He was much interested in the
phenomena of the summer,—in the excessive heat, in
the thunderstorms of peculiar splendour by which it
was followed, in the richness of the foliage, and, last of
all, in the comet which blazed in the heavens for so
many weeks. He often spoke to his friends of his
growing delight in nature, and of how it is not true
that our joy in "the green-leaved earth" is greater in
childhood than in later life. It was in that year that
I first heard him read his "Dream of the Foolish
Virgin," and I have the impression that it had just
been written.

Dream of the Foolish Virgin.

Hair with lilies braiden,
  All for marriage drest,
Bridegroom-waiting maiden
  Laid her down to rest;

L

Why tarries he so weary long?
   A little slumber sweet,
To bridge the night, until the throng
    Comes sweeping through the street !
     Slumb'ring all the number,
      Wise and foolish both,
     Sin may come with slumber,
      Sisters sin and sloth.

White enclasping fingers
   Round her lamp are clenched,
Leaping light that lingers,
   Ah ! how quickly quenched !
And not by blasts nor dropping rains,
   Nor thick besmothering damp,
But all because no oil remains
   To feed the dying lamp.
     Oil the lamp is needing,
      Oil for wasting fires,
     Grace the heart's flame feeding,
      Grace the heart requires.

Through sleep's ebon portals
   The maiden walks in dreams,
Life to dream-eyed mortals
   Is not what it seems ;
Through flower'd arcade in citron grove,
   To the hidden sound of flutes,
A fair youth leads her, talking love,
   Under the golden fruits.
     Flick'ring lamp is burning
      Dimly and more dim,
     Faithless heart is turning
      More and more from Him.

Rosen wreath he chooses
   For her braiden hair,
Laughing then he looses
   Lilies wreathen there ;
" Hold back ! rash youth, this lily knot
   The Bridegroom's friend gave me,
And it were ill exchanged, I wot,
   Fair tho' the roses be."
     Flick'ring lamp that burneth
       Mingled bright and dim,
     Heart's temptation spurneth,
       And yet not true to Him.

More to tempt the maiden,
   Softer sound the flutes,
Arching branches laden
   With the golden fruits
Lead to cushioned banquet hall,
   Blazoned with pearls and wines,
Ah ! maiden wake—if wake at all !
   How dim the watch-lamp shines !
     Flick'ring lamp is burning
       Dimly and more dim,
     Faithless heart is turning
       All away from Him.

Tinted lights are glancing
   Over floor and wall,
Shapes of beauty dancing
   Round and round the hall ;
And music runs in thrilling showers,
   Dissolving heart and brain,
Till she has lost all will and power
   To drive him back again.

Flick'ring lamp is burning
  Ne'er till now so dim,
Faithless heart is turning
  More and more from Him.

Strokes the tressed maiden,
  Strokes her arched brow,
" Give me, queenly maiden !
  Give the lilies now."
Languid denial murmur'd half,
  His honied words have drown'd,
He plucks the lilies with a laugh,
  And strews them on the ground.
    Out ! the lamp it burneth
      Never as before,
    Grace abused returneth
      Never, never more.

Lightning !   Cracking thunder !
  Lights out !   Black as death !
Flooring split asunder,
  Red hell glares beneath.
Spectres' arms her waist enclasp,
  In snakes her tresses stream,
And downward drawn in lightning's grasp
  She shrieks, and breaks the dream !
    Oh, the doleful waking !
      Now the lamp is quenched,
    Heart with anguish breaking,
      Face with weeping drenched.

Dream ! still rolls the thunder,
  Bridegroom in the street,
Dream ! 'twas that shout stunned her,
  Shouting Him to meet.

His train—a shining river flows
  Between black shades of night,
And in the midst the Bridegroom goes
  Attired in blaze of white.
    Midnight cry that summeth
      Every joy and woe,
    Lo ! the Bridegroom cometh !
    Out to meet Him go !

Torches brighter blazing,
  Louder sound the hymns,
Now her dead lamp raising
  All in vain she trims ;
The vessel's oil is spent, and none
  Has any oil to spare ;
She runs—for they have bid her run
  To buy—in wild despair.
    Tresses all dishevelled,
      Bridal dress all torn,
    The laughter of the street is levelled
    All at her in scorn.

Knocking stands she, knocking,
  Knocking at the gate,
Echo answers mocking,
  " Maiden comes too late."
" Too late," words from within declare,
  " Too late," " I know thee not ;"
No wedding guest can enter there,
  When once the door is shut.
    Saints in glory singing,
      " Blest are they who wait ;"
    Hands with anguish wringing,
      Sorrow cries, " Too late !"

Mr. Smith of Hamilfield, who, since Mr. Robertson s removal into the manse, had been his nearest neighbour, spent the summer of 1858 in America, leaving his daughters, who were at school in England, under the minister's special care. Mr. Robertson wrote to them regularly, and arranged for their enjoyment when they were at home on holiday.

To Miss Agnes Smith.

Irvine, Friday (early in 1858).

Your little letter was a very welcome one. It met me at the " landing stage of Monday morning," and was the first to salute me on coming ashore from the Arabia (the happy) of my bed. I understand your hints on " early rising," and hope I may profit by them and by your example. In fact I have improved already, and though you may not know it, I owe it all to you, and to that present you made me of the little white dog of the Otto-Ida (and fairy) race, by name Fido. I shall tell you how this is, and you will see how much I am obliged to you for Fido, *upsetting* little thing although he is.

Every morning here's what I do.

(Little Mary, with Fido on her lap, is sitting beside me, and for her diversion I shall make this to rhyme) :—

> 10 A.M., or even before,
> Upstairs comes your little Fido,
>   Barking at my chamber door,
> And if Fido gets no answer,
>   Gets no answer save a snore.
> " Oh ! you are a lazy man, sir,"
>   Fido barks out more and more.

And if still he gets no answer,
  None but silence or a snore,
  Fido pushes up my door.
Little gipsy, mad or tipsy,
  Puffing, snuffing, sneezing, wheezing,
Frisky, like a dog in whisky,
  Up he dances pirouetting
To the centre of the floor,
  Where up on his hind legs getting
Fifteen inches tall and more !
  His raised eyes on a level setting
With the nose that gives the snore.
  Gipsy ! neither mad nor tipsy,
Sober now as judge or Gough,
He says, " Rauf ! "—
  Fido speaks German—
  And this is his little sermon,
Sum and substance of his speech is,
" Rauf ! herauf ! herauf ! rauf ! " which is
  The dogmatics Fido preaches,
Standing surpliced on my floor.
  And if still I give no answer,
None but silence or a snore,
  Pirouettes my little dancer,
Pirouettes mad as before,
Pirouettes across the floor,
  To the clothes I have been wearing,
Clothes that yesterday I wore ;
  Takes them, pulls them, tossing, tearing,
Strews them up and down the floor,
  Coat and vest, and shoe and stocking,
  " Ho ! you dog you, this is shocking !
Auf ! du Hündchen ! rauf ! hör 'auf ! "
  Then, his head on one side cocking,

Wags his tail, and my words mocking,
Barks in answer, "rauf! rauf! rauf!"
   Till at last he beats me fairly,
   I must get up, get up early.
   This is what each morning I do,
   Many thanks to you for Fido!

To Mr. John Smith.

Oxford, 20th May, 1858.

. . . It is past midnight, and the landlord of the
"Mitre" has this moment knocked at my door to say that
I have forgot to put out my light. However, let him knock
as often as he likes I must finish this epistle.

What a pleasant afternoon and evening I have had with
Oxford men, some of whom I knew before, and others whose
acquaintance I have made now. I am glad to find that my
friends are among the first men at this far-famed University.
(Well done, Scotland!) What with architectural, musical,
and literary celebrities, a boat race on the Isis, strolls
through classic ground, visits to distinguished men, and a
splendid evening with Oxonians, who have all been rung into
their rooms at twelve, the time has passed very swiftly, and
I am left alone at midnight with the thought of you across
the Atlantic.

. . . (There's that "Mitre" official ringing his curfew
at my door again. He seems to think me amenable to
university regulations.)

. . . I have been in Bristol for two Sabbaths, with
a stroll through old cathedrals—Glastonbury, Wells, Salisbury, Winchester, and then, too, Isle of Wight and London,
of course. . . . There's that man at the door the third
time saying, "Please, sir, it's half-past one." Good-night.

To the Same.

IRVINE, 18th June, 1858.

. . . You are missing little, perhaps, by your absence, unless it be some grand thunderstorms, the like of which, I suppose, have not before been seen here—not inferior to our famous Alpine one of happy memory. The country has been in a fever of tropical heat, and then it has taken to the cold water cure.

In ecclesiastical affairs the organ question is not stifled,[1] but rather merged into a broader question on the relation of literature and fine art to religion. I wish some wave of genuine revival would visit us from the West. Couldn't you bring some of that home with you? It would go to settle many questions here, that would be swept out of sight in a high current of religious life. Do you think it will tend in the West to the abolition of slavery?

A pleasant excursion into the Highlands in company with his sister, the Misses Smith, and some other friends, brightened the opening week of August.

To MISS AGNES SMITH.

August, 1858.

After leaving you I went by Edinburgh to Melrose and sunned myself in the light of a new and brilliant circle of friends. It was a rendezvous of gifted heads, bright faces, and warm hearts, such as one seldom meets with, and we feasted and sang, reasoned and romanced, strolled in sun-

---

[1] There had that May been no small stir in United Presbyterian circles by the proposal of the congregation of Claremont Church, Glasgow, to introduce an organ, and by the resolution of the Synod forbidding its introduction—a resolution rescinded in 1872.

shine through gardens and orchards and about the old
Abbey, drove to Dryburgh, etc., etc.—quite a carnival of
intellectual and social delight.   But all could not make me
forget the beautiful by-past week, and especially the sunrise
on Ben Lomond and the Sabbath at Glenorchy.   Shall we
not remember these for ever?   May we remember them for
ever without regret excepting the regret that they are gone.
They have placed some green and sunny spots in our
memory.

At Dryburgh Abbey I found a monument to the Erskines,
the fathers of our (Secession) Church, built into a ruined
wall of the Abbey behind the altar.   On one side of it a
slain lamb sculptured in stone, and on the other an inscription which could not, they said, be read, but I found it to
be a " Kurie," as it is called, in old Greek characters, signi-
fying " O Christ, have mercy upon us."

Think of these venerable fathers of all strict Burghers and
Anti-burghers being immortalized in such a popish place,
and with such popish accessories !

To Mr. John Smith.

PLEAN, by BANNOCKBURN, 13th August, 1858.

.   .   .   They have probably written and told you how
much they enjoyed it, especially the quiet Sabbath in beautiful Glenorchy.   I preached in the parish church at request of
the quaint old minister, who said Mr. Scott of Caputh was
his best friend, for he had once tried to get a wife for him.
The precentor had only seven tunes in his stock, and could
sing only four of them.   The congregation numbered about
50, four times the usual number, I believe ; and the collection,
gathered by a ladle, had a corresponding increase.   We had
afternoon worship on the hillside.   I wish you could have

been with us. You and I must go again, when I have promised to preach once more for the old gentleman.

And so, you see, your kind wish about my not losing my holiday has been realized already in happy company. After seeing them off at Greenock, I hurried to Edinburgh, where in a few hours I had to lecture to the Divinity students by appointment of a committee of Synod. From that I went to Melrose, where my friend, Mr. Curle, had gathered a number of brother and sister spirits to meet me, and laid out pleasant plans for our enjoyment. And I am still prolonging my holiday and may do so a week or two longer.

To Miss Agnes Smith.

Greenhill, by Bannockburn, 20th August, 1858.

. . . But I am hardly in a mood for mirth just now, writing in the shadow of a very melancholy event. You remember Willie Smith of Bannockburn, whom you beat some years ago in learning "Bone Pastor," though, by the way, Willie is a first-class Latin scholar now.

Poor Willie! he has been suddenly made fatherless in a very mournful way, Mr. Smith being drowned last Saturday in bathing at Aberdeen. A bold, expert swimmer, as most Orcadians are (Mr. S. was from Orkney), he ventured out too far. The life-boat was put out and came very near him. They saw his earnest, living eyes, looking at them within one or two oars' lengths, but suddenly he sank and disappeared.

A dark piece of tragedy—dark on this side, though very bright no doubt on the other side that he has got to. He has passed through the crystal gate (they say it is perhaps the gentlest entrance) into the eternal sunlight. No doubt of that, for Mr. Smith was a true, godly man. I remember here his Sabbath evening text when he assisted me at the communion—" Precious in the sight of the Lord is the death of His saints."

The casket of the body, though rifled of its jewel by the " angel of the waters," has been searched for, and has at length been found on the Aberdeen coast. Some consolation to the poor widow and Willie that it shall not be tossed as a waif on the ocean, or entombed in what Tennyson has called " the vast and wandering grave." The dews of grief have been glittering on all eyes for miles round Bannockburn, for Mr. Smith was much loved in the neighbourhood. Providentially I have been here, and been able to devote myself to the service of sorrow till relatives from a distance should arrive.

And this is what I referred to as occupying my hands, head, and heart here, and checking playfulness a little; though playfulness, indeed, is always better than peevishness, and laughter admits of being sanctified as well as tears. In truth, I often think a holy laugh—a frank, good-hearted, holy laugh—is a much higher attainment in spiritual life than a holy prayer or tear. Many get the length of the latter—few get so high as the former. I hope you can. God bless your young gladness, and keep your eyes from tears !

To the Same.

IRVINE, 25th August, 1858.

. . . I am back in quiet Irvine again, having arrived a few hours ago. The Mary-mass fair is over last week, and public pleasure, that seems to have got more than usually drunk on the occasion, being somewhat sobered again, is looking forward to some grand festival of archery in Eglinton grounds to-morrow and Friday. Abominable thing that drunkenness, but a very pretty sport the archery, innocent in itself, beautiful in the attitude it develops—not useless in the healthful exercise and pleasant excitement that it gives, and suggestive of romantic old times, so I think I must go and see it. But what a pity that these beautiful sports are so often married to mischief. . . . May we be able to take our pleasure with true gladness. I wonder if beautiful public sports shall ever be quite redeemed from the devil's hands—at the millennium, perhaps !

On getting up into my study and looking out at the north window, the first thing that arrests my attention is the flagstaff erected in front of Hamilfield like a tall, thin mast of a sloop amid the cordage and rigging of your poplar trees, and the house for the quarterdeck. And with what do you think it is surmounted ? A fish—one that looks at this distance like a French prince among fishes—that is, as you know, a dolphin, a queer fish to swim so high ! A silver fish just now in the silver sunshine, a gold fish, no doubt, at golden sunset. But there it turns and veers with the changing wind to all the points of the compass. It will tell me always how the wind blows. Thank you, good fish !

To the Same.

IRVINE, 10th September, 1858.

. . . Pardon the question, Do you think sometimes of joining the church sacramentally ? By and by, but you feel young enough yet ? But you have been placed among the flock at the baptismal well, and I am sure you wish to follow in its " footsteps "—the flock of the Good Shepherd, that " hears His voice " and " He calleth them all by name." He has called you by name, as He called Mary by name at the empty sepulchre, and you have said, Rabboni, Master.

Out of our Sabbath class I have seen, with much joy, one and another go forth, through the gate of decision for Christ, perhaps to teach a little Sabbath class. May not the day come when you, too, with your better education, and perhaps your higher gifts, shall be a shepherdess with some little flock of lambs at the well. I must not say more about that here, but only this : Be brave, be good, be true, and be sure that the great future (veiled as it is) will rise up and bless you ! . . .

Talitha Cumi.

Maiden to my twelfth year come,
 I had read in Scripture story
Of a damsel cold and dumb,
 Wakened by the Lord of Glory ;
And it seemed to me he spoke,
 And His living word thrilled through me,
Till in me new life awoke,
 As He said, Talitha Cumi !

I had to my chamber gone,
 Eyes all swollen and red with weeping,
For my heart felt like a stone,
 And my life a dream in sleeping ;
Jesus in my chamber stood,
 Jesus stretched His hands unto me—
Hands all pierced and dropping blood,
 As He said, Talitha Cumi !

Friends and neighbours gathered in,
 Made no small ado and weeping,
Dead I was, yes, dead to sin,
 Dead, but I was only sleeping ;
For Thy word renewed me, Lord.
 Freed from the disease that slew me,

And to pious friends restored,
　Crown'd with Thy Talitha Cumi.

Now with lamp I watch and wait
　For my Lord's returning to me ;
Should I slumber when 'tis late,
　Let that word rouse and renew me ;
And when long laid in the tomb,
　Long forgot by those who knew me,
Thou wilt not forget to come,
　Come with Thy Talitha Cumi.

It was probably at the close of some unusually bright day when he had been brimful of mirth, which in its overflow had made his companions glad, that the undertone of sadness which ran through all the music of his life found expression thus :—

Man is Born unto Trouble.

Whatever is not made human
　Is, while it lives, quite glad ;
But man, that is born of woman,
　His days are few and sad.

The tiny insect in gladness
　Its little lifetime plays ;
But man that is born to sadness
　Goes darkly all his days.

The jaded hack has his stable,
　The hunted fox his den ;
But nothing on earth is able
　To give true rest to men.

The eagle has her high eyrie,
    The lark her lowly bed ;
But the Son of Man, when weary,
    Had nowhere to lay His head.

Toward the close of this year a great calamity
befell an old and valued friend   John Logan, son of
the St. Ninian's manse, and brother of the Sheriff, had
become more and more associated with Mr. Robertson ; and Mrs. Logan, the memory of whose brightness will ever linger in the hearts of those who
had the privilege of knowing her, was one of his
dearest friends.   Amid the shadows of the winter
a commercial crisis involved Mr. Logan in difficulties,
and made the years that remained to him, and to his
wife, years of anxiety and struggle.   The following
verses accompanied a letter of sympathy :—

The Serbing Maid.

" DEDICATED (31st Dec., 1858) TO LADY LOGAN.

                                                W. B. R."

Good to Evil said,
    " Evil—might I borrow,
For a serving maid,
    Your dark daughter, Sorrow ? "
" Surely," Evil said,
    " Take her—oh ! my goodness,
A nice serving maid
    Free from every rudeness."

Evil laughed, and quick
    Ran to tell the Devil,

Of this clever trick,
  Played on Good by Evil;
Ne'er more guest will come
  To the house of Goodness,
When this maid comes home,
  With her dreadful rudeness.

Yet in house of Goodness
  Sorrow, altered, grows,
Puts off all her rudeness,
  On soft footstep goes.
Ne'er more word of cursing,
  She is meek and mild,
And she takes to nursing
  Goodness' little child—

Patience; pale and sickly
  Is this child to nurse,
He seems dying quickly,
  Getting worse and worse.
Till she, strange drink giving,
  Feeds him with her tears,
Then the child gets thriving
  Nobly, for his years.

Lullabies she sings him,
  In most mournful strain,
Nourishment she brings him,
  All in cups of pain;
Nursed, apart and lonely,
  In the darkest rooms,
And she walks him only
  Out among the tombs.

Dressed like him in mourning,
  Blacker every year,
M

With the sole adorning
　Of the jewell'd tear—
Tear, on white face glistening
　In the dim lamp light,
When she sitteth listening
　To his moan all night.

Him for schooling too sick,
　She herself must train,
So she gives him music
　From the sobbing rain,
From the lone wind's sighing,
　From the murm'ring brooks;
And the strewed leaves lying
　Round him, are the books—

Books, which none but Sorrow
　Sibyl-like has read,
Of a green to-morrow
　For the withered dead.
Pictures too, portraying
　Red cross, and white throne,
And a knelt child, praying,
　Lord "Thy will be done."

So through Sorrow's teaching,
　Patience perfect grows,
Till to manhood reaching,
　Forth to war he goes.
Forth, meekly defiant
　Of all danger wild,
Stronger than a giant,
　Gentler than a child.

"Who is this?" cries Evil,
　Coming down this way,

"Who!" thunders the Devil,
  "Friend or foeman, say?"
Com'st to help or harm him,
  Pale-faced warrior—thou,
Mailed with grief-worn armour,
  Plumed with pensive brow?

Down together rushing
  On him so, these twain,
Through meek endurance crushing,
  He has smote and slain.
Thus through endured temptation,
  Blessing springs from curse,
And to Victor Patience
  Sorrow must be nurse.

It was probably the change of fortune that had so unexpectedly come to his friends which impressed him, at this new-year time, with the proverbial uncertainty of the future, and led him to write the following verses which afterwards appeared in an early number of *Good Words*, under the editorship of his friend, Dr. Norman Macleod :—

The Veiled Bride.

Veiled the future comes refusing
  To be seen, like **Isaac's** bride,
Whom the lonely **man** met musing
  In the fields at eventide.

Round him o'er the darkening waste,
  Deeper shades of evening fall;
And behind him in the past,
  Mother Sarah's funeral.

Mother Sarah being dead,
   Cometh then his destiny ;
Veil'd Rebecca he must wed,
   Whatsoe'er her features be.

On he walks in silent prayer,
   Bids the veil'd Rebecca hail !
Doubting not she will prove fair,
   When at length she drops the veil.

When the veil is dropt aside,
   Dropt in Mother Sarah's tent,
Oh ! she is right fair, this bride,
   Whom his loving God has sent !

So then walking 'twixt the two,
   'Twixt the past, with pleasures dead,
And the future veil'd from view,
   The veil'd future *thou* must wed.

Walk, like Isaac, praying God,
   Walk by faith and not by sight,
And tho' darker grows the road,
   Doubt not all will yet come 'right.

Things behind forgetting, hail
   Every future from above !
Doubt not when it drops the veil,
   'Twill be such as thou canst love.

The following, which will again remind our readers
of some of George Herbert's conceits, was sent to his
niece Margaret on her tenth birthday; but it was
written in the album of many another Margaret both
before and after. It belongs to the time of which we
are now writing.

Margaret.

A BIRTHDAY WISH.

Minstrel monks in days of old,
Sang some quaint conceits and pretty,
Of those twelve pearls set in gold,
That make gates into the city.
  Such a gate amongst us set,
  Such a pearl and fairer yet,
  Mayst thou be, pearl Margaret !

Jasper [1] like the earth is green,
Sapphire,[2] azure, like the sky ;
And like fires that glance between,
The pale flamed chalcedony.[3]
  Such like pearl, or fairer yet,
  All pearl beauties in thee met,
  Mayst thou be, pearl Margaret !

Emerald,[4] greener than the spring,
Black sardonyx,[5] red and white ;
Sardius,[6] with its crimson ring,
And the gold flamed crysolite.[7]
  Such like pearl, or fairer yet,
  All pearl beauties in thee met,
  Mayst thou be, pearl Margaret !

Beryl [8] hath tears that sunlight hold,
Topaz [9] flashes dazzling blaze,
And with sprinkled drops of gold
Shines the purple chrysoprase.[10]

[1] Betokens, they say, evergreen faith.
[2] Heavenly mindedness. [3] Humble and earnest prayer.
[4] Great faithfulness. [5] Grief for sin, and purity.
[6] Cross-bearing. [7] Charity. [8] Hope in sorrow. [9] Holiness.
[10] Love or charity amid suffering.

Such like pearl, or fairer yet,
All fair beauties in thee met,
Mayst thou be, pearl Margaret!

Jacinth [1] changing with the sky,
Vies with rose flamed amethyst ; [2]
But what pearl can ever vie,
With young lips no guile has kissed,
And all stars must wane and set,
Where pure eyes dawn, Margaret !

Good, be thou then—more than fair,
    For mere beauty may befool,
Though our hearts to temple prayer
    Go best through "Gate Beautiful."
So to the holy, nearer yet
Through thee, pearl gate 'mongst us set,
    May we come, pearl Margaret !

[1] Adaptation to circumstances.   [2] Spiritual beauty.

CHAPTER X.

Revival and Church-Building.

THE revival of religion in America, to which Mr.
Robertson had referred in his letters to Mr. Smith,
began in the year 1859 to make its influence
felt, first in Ireland, and then in Scotland.   There
were signs of deeper earnestness in the church at
Irvine, which cheered its minister.   He had greater
joy than heretofore in preaching to the eager listeners
who filled the pews, and in conversing with those who
sought his guidance in their spiritual perplexities.
There were no physical manifestations as in Ireland—
no excitement, nothing inconsistent with that Kingdom
of God which cometh not with observation.

Mr. Robertson had special delight in preaching to
the miners in and around the village of Dreghorn
some three miles distant, at meetings arranged by a
Free Church student in the neighbourhood, afterwards
one of the succession of ministers who laboured in the
Wynd Mission of Glasgow, now the Rev. Robert
Howie, of Free St. Mary's, Govan.

His attitude in relation to the " Revival "—his earnest desire to avail himself of every opportunity of good which it brought, and at the same time to guard against the risk of fanaticism which it involved—is illustrated by the following extract from a letter written about this time to one of his elders, who had sent him an account of a meeting addressed by the Rev. Mr. Gebbie of Dunlop.

To Mr. John Wright.

London, Wednesday Night, past 12.

The narrative you relate from his address is a very interesting one, and most profitable for " instruction in righteousness," even the righteousness of God, to those that can make the proper use of it.   Such cases require to be delicately handled, both for the sake of the persons themselves, lest they should be exalted above measure by thinking they have got special revelations, and by having their case set forth for public admiration ; and for the sake of the hearers, lest they should be dissatisfied with the ordinary mode of entering the kingdom, and demand and wait for a sign from heaven, and seek for some other light to guide them than that which shines from the face of Jesus Christ in the mirror of the Word as the glory of the Lord, and which we all are bidden with unveiled face to behold.   Even in respect of real visions and voices, does not the Apostle say that we have a more sure word of prophecy, unto which we do well to take heed as unto a light shining in a dark place.   The visions no doubt were purely subjective, *i.e.*, the product of the imagination, yet under the guidance of God's holy converting Spirit, I trust, who can certainly make the imagination an organ of his converting and sanctifying offices—as well as the intellect—and whose work in that remarkable faculty is probably not sufficiently recognized in our theology. But whether it was the Holy Spirit's work or no remains to be seen by the woman's future conduct. Let us hope it will prove so, and be neither faithless nor credulous.

The only surviving daughter of Mr. Paterson, Corsehill, an Irvine elder, whose farm was near Dreghorn, writes to me : " The meetings were begun in the cottages of the colliers. As the numbers increased they met sometimes in the corner of a field on my father's farm ; and, as the dark autumn evenings came on, in an empty byre on Corsehill homestead, while a mission hall was being put up by Mrs. Mure Macredie of Perceton, in which the mission work was afterwards conducted." "Without doubt," my correspondent adds, "the whole neighbourhood got an impetus to 'higher life.'"

I remember a letter which Mr. Robertson wrote to me at the time, but which unfortunately has not been preserved. He described the crowds of eager faces seen in chiaroscuro in the cattle stalls, and likened the scene to the adoration of the Magi, on which subject I had been preaching at Irvine some time before.

Mrs. M'Cunn remembers his once bidding her remark "how religious feeling glorified and refined the roughest natures ; and he illustrated this by his experience in a mining village in Ayrshire, where during a religious revival the women grew to look like Madonnas, and both men and women sung like

angels.   Of course it could not last, but it was
wonderful how the spiritual light transformed the
material man."

In the midst of his hard, hopeful work, the tidings
reached him that his brother Robert was dying, and
he at once went to him.   Robert was one of the most
richly gifted of the family to which he belonged.   He
had completed his studies for the ministry, and revealed to those who heard him remarkable power as
a preacher, in which a measure of William's imagination was combined with James's intensity and direct-
ness.   Shrinking modesty kept him from taking
license, and he contented himself with working as a
city missionary under Dr. Eadie in Glasgow, till his
health gave way.   He died on 13th November, 1859.

To His Father.

IRVINE, November, 1859.

I heard you say by the grave that "this was a dark
passage, but there was light at the other end."

Let us not be impatient for the light coming too soon.   We
shall all meet in it I hope by and by, and surely we should
thank God for having lifted the darkness off our dear Robert's
eyes !   A more lamb-like, Christ-like sufferer I never saw ;
and as I stood by his breathless form at midnight and closed
his weary eyes, I thought he looked like a picture of "the
dead Christ."   And as I brought it home in the train, I had
no doubt that shining ones were watching at the head and
feet in the dark van, and the funeral was largely attended,
if our eyes could have seen them in that dim drizzly yesterday.

Was he not about the same age with the dying Saviour? and buried on a Friday too? I hope the third day (when this may reach you) will have brought much balm of comfort and sweet spices, and rolled away any stony doubt that may be lying about the door of the sepulchre, "for now is Christ risen from the dead."

To His Younger Sister.

IRVINE, 7th Dec., 1859.

Do you think Andrew could get some other for Thursday first for evening service in Auchenbowie School, and let me off for a week or two? Almost every day I am getting some new inquirers, and don't like to turn them off for want of time, or because I am going from home. One must be as little absent from the farm as possible when the fields are white, or whitening, to the harvest.

To Rev. William Blair, Dunblane.

IRVINE, 10th January, 1860.

It is now high time to acknowledge your letter received some time in the course of last year. Let me hope that you have had . . . a safe crossing from the old year to the new, and a pleasant landing on the shore of '60, and ten joyous days journey up through the undiscovered land.

Concerning revivals, there is a decided movement of "the kingdom that cometh not with observation" among us. It gives one more work than one can well manage, preaching every second night at least, and holding private meetings daily. But it is blessed work, and even in present results has a thousand times more than its reward. . . .

Mrs. Risk, whose death called forth the letter from which the following extracts are made, was a kinswoman, sister of the Rev. Dr. William Bruce, Edinburgh :—

To Provost Risk, Dumbarton.

15th Feb., 1860.

. . . The pure and quiet stream that flowed so gently and so long in the shadow of death has dropped now into the eternal ocean.   But you must be glad for her sake that her sufferings are for ever over, and the weary night watch of sickness replaced with the joy unspeakable of serving Him day and night in His temple.   For what were her sufferings but a preparation for a more exceeding weight of glory, realized now, when the days of preparation are accomplished, and at the midnight cry the chamber of the body has been thrown open, ahd the sainted spirit gone forth in her beauty to meet the Lord ?   The weeping of survivors in the valleys has been answered by the shoutings of the blessed on the hills above us, and the funeral here was but a dark shadow of a shining procession in the heavens.

We have been very busy here of late, both sowing and reaping in revival.   I am afraid it is now passing by —that it has " come to pass " as all things do—as death and funeral with you have come not to stay, but come to pass. So our revival too, and yet I think the Phenomenal has not passed without leaving a deep deposit of the Eternal Real among us.   .   .   .

Another of the frequently recurring family bereavements came in the midst of his labours.   His eldest brother, Andrew, died on 27th February, 1860.

To Mr. John Smith.

Greenhill, Bannockburn, 3rd March, 1860.

The shadow of death has darkened again over our house, but with great mixture of heavenly light.   I have just lost one of the best of brothers, the eldest, Andrew. He has been carried off by cramp-spasms that have been assailing him periodically for some time, and that have struck the heart at last. He died suddenly, but very peacefully, and death has hardly changed his pleasant look.

To the REV. JAMES M'OWAN, M.A.

GREENHILL, Saturday.

The shadow of death has had little darkness in it to Andrew. How much in *it* to comfort us, as well as in that life which it transfigured and carried up on high. Though these cramp-spasms made short work when they got to the heart of mortal life, they could not touch the higher life, but only released it. I think the Lord has been here, and our brother has not died. Let us not say "departed"; perhaps he is nearer than ever, and may be with you to-morrow still.

This private sorrow was ever afterwards linked in his memory with a calamity which took place on the same date, and deeply moved his sympathy. The schooner "Success," of Nantes, was wrecked on Irvine bar on February 27th, and the bodies of her crew of seven were washed ashore. Mr. Robertson was busily occupied during the whole day with the arrangements for their funeral. With characteristic consideration he proposed that, as the men had manifestly belonged to the Roman Catholic communion, they should be buried according to the rites of their Church, urging the plea that if those who loved them ever came to learn where they lay, it would be a comfort to them to know that the last offices for their dead had been rendered in the form they deemed most sacred. His proposal met with opposition, and only served to stir up bitterness. He had at length to yield, and content himself with making, in the funeral service, as large use of the " office for the dead," as was possible for a Protestant minister.

When he returned home from the contention, weary and worried in spirit because of the perversity that could let sectarian exclusiveness assert itself in presence of a mystery of human sorrow, he threw himself into an easy chair by the study fire, and in the dusk of the February evening fell asleep. The chair, made by an Auchenbowie joiner, was of so comfortable a shape, that each member of the Greenhill family, on leaving home to set up house for himself, took one of the same pattern with him. As he lay in that chair he had a most vivid dream. His brother, Andrew, seemed to come into the room, and, as he rose to meet him, he thought there was a far-off look on his face, on which, too, he saw lines of pain. And then he awoke. The dream dwelt on his mind; and when next morning, as he sat at breakfast, he saw a messenger from Auchenbowie coming up to the manse, he was sure that he was the bringer of heavy tidings. He learned that at the very hour, the night before, at which he had awakened from his dream, Andrew died in the chair of the same pattern as that in which he had been sleeping.

When a monument was erected to mark the grave

of the seven strangers, Mr. Robertson furnished the
following verses which are carved on the stone:—

Epitaph in Irvine Churchyard.

Seven dead the sea gave to the shore,
   To wrap beneath the sod,
Till they and we shall stand before
   The judgment seat of God.

Their names, their lives, their faith unknown,
   These dumb dead here arrive;
But what's hid now shall then be shown,
   When here they stand alive.

Sail on! dark coffined fleet of seven!
   On to revealing day;
And may we make the harbour Heaven,
   Not lost nor cast away.

As might have been expected, in the case of one
whose eloquent preaching was heard in so many
places, frequent overtures were made to Mr. Robertson
to induce him to accept charges in one or other of the
great cities. Whenever he could, he took measures to
prevent a formal invitation. But he was not always
successful. In 1861 two "calls" came to him from
Glasgow—one from the congregation of Regent Place,
and the other from his old friends of Shamrock Street
Church, whose pulpit was vacant, through the death
of the minister who had accepted the charge Mr.
Robertson declined ten years before. His speech in
dealing with the Regent Place call was brief; but he

seemed to feel that the Shamrock Street people who, after an interval of ten years, had not forgotten him, were entitled to a full statement of his reasons for a second refusal. The pleadings in the Presbytery, which met on 11th June, 1861, were memorable. The Irvine commissioners put forth all their strength, and one of them, a plain, homely elder, made a speech at which all who heard it wondered, because of its spiritual insight and its nobility of tone. A member of Presbytery came to Mr. Robertson when the proceedings were over, and asked who that remarkable elder was. " He's a man who lives in communion with God and makes *shoon*," was the characteristic reply.

In his speech Mr. Robertson told how he had become bound up with his people.

"Where is the household in that Irvine church into which, some time or other, during these seventeen years—into whose inmost heart of love the angel of joy, or the stronger angel of grief, has not admitted me? . . . Do city brethren rightly apprehend the close relationship between a country pastor and his people? Child of their childless, father of their orphans, brother of them all; entering into all their household joys and griefs in the most homely and familiar way; interested in the father's work and wages, in the children's education, in the son's going to sea, in the daughter's going out to service, in the grandfather's ailments, in the very baby's frolics, and in the mother's earnest prayers and keen heart-wrestlings for them all. He lives in them and he lets them live in him, and seeks to interpenetrate their common life with his own more sacred life; and their sorrows, and their troubles, and their triumphs, are reproduced on Sabbath in the pulpit; and the moans of their suffering, and the music of their joy, and the questions of their inner life return upon them through his Sabbath prayers and sermons, idealized, corrected, sublimated in the light of the Cross and of eternity—he is one with them and they with him identified. Was not this something different from preaching two discourses eloquently to a crowded city audience upon the Sabbath, and losing sight of them, as one must do, in a great measure, amid the roar and bustle of the following week? .   .   .

An elder, a commissioner from Irvine, has gone to the heart of my reason for wishing to remain—has spoken of blessed revivals that have been changing not so much the face as the heart of my church of late, bringing in among us a great increase of spiritual life, and making all things new. I may almost say that the church has been born again within the last few years. Veils have been rent from the faces of the sleepers, and dead eyes awakened to the visions of the Eternal Real. The church that could hardly be built outward has I believe been building upward. I could tell of souls awakened, of souls saved, of souls sanctified, and of sanctified souls ascending triumphant to glory. I am no enthusiast and have no sympathy with the parading of the holiest secrets of men's hearts before all eyes, but there are secrets there of the kingdom that cometh not with observation, which will come out when the books are opened —and there lies the deepest reason of my attachment to my present charge. Why should I forsake a work that God seems to be blessing, and has blessed? .   .   .

Some worldly people may give me credit for making a sacrifice. They know nothing of the lofty spiritual regions in which such questions are discussed. To them it is a mere question of a lower or higher position, of a less or greater salary; therefore I crave leave to say the question

N

in this form has never been present to my mind, and I will
not take credit for making sacrifice when I do not feel in
my heart that I am doing anything of the kind. Some
Christian Epicureans seem to think that the way of duty is
always that which is lighted with the silver and golden
lamps, while Christian Stoics think it is that which is marked
with the most numerous crosses and the sharpest thorns.
For my part I believe that it is neither, or that it may be
either, but that it is always that on which the Spirit of the
Lord leads, whose prayer-sought guidance I seek to follow,
undeterred alike by the splendour on the one side, or the
comparative obscurity on the other.   .   .   .

The good people of Irvine were so delighted with
their pastor's resolution to remain with them that they
felt bound to give substantial expression to their joy.
Ten years before, his refusal of the first call from
Shamrock Street Church had been signalized by the
building of a manse ; and now the second refusal
led to the resolution to build a new church. Not
the congregation only, but the whole community
interested themselves in the project of providing a
sanctuary more in harmony with the sermons of the
poet-preacher and the services which he conducted,
than the old kirk in the Cotton Row. When it was
known that the site on which Mr. Robertson wished
the church to be erected was on the hill Mizar, overlooking the river, in line with the Established Church
to the south and the Free Church to the north, the
proprietors of the ground, though the chief of them was
a prominent member of the Established Church, came

forward and asked to be permitted to present it as a free gift.

After competitive plans had been examined, the work was entrusted to Mr. F. T. Pilkington, Edinburgh, in whom Mr. Robertson found an artist who entered with enthusiasm into all his ideas with regard to ecclesiastical architecture, and the possibility of adapting it to the purposes of Presbyterian worship. The church, which was built in the Venetian Gothic style with variegated colour in the stone, is cruciform, the adaptation to Presbyterian worship being obtained by treating three members of the cross, the chancel and the two transepts, as apses, so that the sitters in all parts of the building can see the pulpit. As the site chosen was on the summit of a rising ground sloping down towards the west, a most effective western façade overlooking the river was secured by the underbuilding, in the form of an arcade, on which the gable, pierced by a fine St. Catherine's window, rests. The tower and spire are at the north-western corner. The roof is supported by four pillars at the corners of the transepts. The platform-pulpit occupies the whole of the chancel, separated from the rest of the building by a stone balustrade, on which are *bas reliefs* representing the Last Supper, the baptism of our Lord, and the marriage at Cana of Galilee, with figures of the four evangelists in niches between.

To Miss Crum, Auldhouse.

Irvine, 18th Nov., 1861.

There is *work* enough and *word* enough to keep any one from being miserable, and if these two are not enough, then there is weeping enough. For "into each life some rain must fall" to keep it green, since constant sunshine would be wearisome and withering—

> " Prithee weep, May Lilian !
>   Gaiety without eclipse
> Wearieth me, May Lilian."

Miss Brown, I hear, has been with you. I hope she has not carried you off with her. Some faint design she had of coming here on Saturday last. I wish she had come, and you too, for indeed I do not at any time remember a finer Sabbath day altogether than yesterday was—with the grace within the church and the glory outside. I mean the glory of the fine blue winter day; and at dusk, what a glory ! The dim earth lying between golden moonrise and flaming sunset—like "the one at the head and the other at the feet"—or like those shining, burning ones on either side the mystic ark, that continually do cry " Holy, Holy, Holy, the whole earth is full of Thy glory."

You know the glory of our winter sunsets here. I wonder if they are really finer on Sabbath evenings, if Nature too has a Sunday dress, and shows her jewellery and silks in going home from church, as they say too that birds and timid little hares are not so frightened for us on Sabbaths. But I suppose it is the outcome of the deeper sense of peace and sense of glory in ourselves. Let us be in the Spirit on the Lord's day, and we too, in our way, shall get the Apocalypse.

IRVINE, 21st November, 1861.

What a tunnel of clouds and darkness Miss Brown would have to travel through ! May it brighten and calm for you ere to-morrow—for how it has changed since I wrote. These three days so royally dark, fit for the burial of a hundred kings, and it rains over the sands and the water-reaches, out to the misty sea, the wind roaring down the chimneys like a score of sweeps. Isabella comes up smiling and pokes my study fire, and the fire irons ring like a peal of bells.

To His Younger Sister.

IRVINE, 27th June, 1862.

In my last note I told you of a trip to England, and now I am going to Holland. Mr. Henderson of Park, the Christian Crœsus, has asked Dr. Robson and me to go over and visit the Dutch churches there, and we mean to start on Monday night or Tuesday morning, and stay a fortnight or so among the Low people. The arrangement has been come to rather suddenly, and of course I have some packing and preparing to do ere going to the Mynheers. I wish I could come and see you on the way, but this I doubt will not be possible.

Please tell father, and ask him if he has any word to Amsterdam. It is very kind of Mr. H., who of course pays travelling expenses and handsomely. It is not a Synodical deputation, but a private embassage. In fact Mr. H. just wants I suppose to give Dr. Robson and me a trip. Thank you, good Mr. H. Our church is now laid out and well begun.

The Rev. William France of Paisley, was added to the travelling party, and the trip was thoroughly enjoyed.

To His Younger Sister.

ARNHEIM, 11th July, 1862.

If you have not forgot your geography you may know that the Rhine divides hereabout, that one of its branches becomes the Yssel, and running through Gelderland and Overyssel falls into the Zuider Zee. From the shores of that Zuider Zee up the banks of that Yssel, we have come to-day by diligence, and are tabernacling here over-night, in the prospect of going up the Rhine to Bonn to-morrow, and spending the Sabbath there. I think of setting out again for Irvine. We have finished, as far as visitation is concerned, the work we came out for, that is inquiring into the state of the Dutch Secession Church. The duty has taken us to Amsterdam, Utrecht, Leyden, Hague, and a great many places besides; but especially to a pretty little town called Kampen, on the border of Friesland, where the professor and students are, where we had to hold forth in the church on Sabbath last, where we had a grand meeting with the heads of the church yesterday—a most singular mixture of Christianity and coffee, prayers and pipes, all the ministers smoking from the beginning of the meeting at four to the end of it at half-past ten—and where we wound up with a supper after that at Professor Brummelkamp's, when I did my best in the way of speaking Dutch to his daughters Kate and Jenny.

Dr. Robson and Mr. France are excellent travelling companions, and though they neither speak Dutch nor German, English is spoken 100 for 1 to what it was when I was on the Continent first.

On his return from Holland, Mr. Robertson found the church building so far advanced that arrangements had to be made at once for laying the foundation stone. At the request of the building committee, the pastor himself performed the ceremony on August 26th, 1862. He was supported by a goodly number of his ministerial and other friends, and by a large assembly of the townspeople, including the Magistrates and Council of the ancient burgh, who, preceded by their halberdiers, formed a picturesque feature in the procession from the King's Arms Inn to the site of the new church on the Mizar Hill. The scene there on a lovely autumn afternoon, with the river and the dunes in the foreground and Arran in the distance, was very striking ; and Mr. Robertson seemed to speak under the influence of his surroundings :—

. . . In laying the foundation stone of even an ordinary dwelling-house, much interest will naturally gather round it. We think on to the time when the building shall be finished, and human life astir beneath its roof; the drama of domestic life begun within its walls, with marriages crossing its threshold, birth cradled in its chambers, and funerals departing from its doors ; with mother nursing the children, and father returning from his work at eventide, and sons and daughters growing up, and old age sitting in the chimney corner, and all together eating, drinking, sleeping, waking, mourning, and rejoicing, in that mingled play of human life upon the household stage, on which the curtain rises at the cradle and drops in heavy folds around the tomb. Forecasting all this, as we naturally do, what wonder if an interest gathers round the laying the foundation stone even of an ordinary house ! But how much more around the laying of the foundation stone of a new church—a church ! a House of the Lord, as my learned friends know that that is the literal meaning of the word—a house devoted, dedicated, set apart to God—a house to stand among the other houses of the town like a Christian among other men, or a Sabbath among other days—a church ! in which, when once it shall be opened, shall come and go the scenes of the divinest drama of our human life : with marriages—yes, marriages, we trust, of souls, when " He that hath the bride is the Bridegroom, and the friend of the Bridegroom that standeth and heareth him shall rejoice greatly because of the Bridegroom's voice;" of births—yes, births, we trust, of souls, when "it of Zion shall be said, this man and that man was born in her;" and where, too, holy grief shall sit, within these walls, bemoaning her dead, till He who is the Resurrection and the Life shall come to her and say, "Weep not," and bid her dead arise. A church where, Sabbath after Sabbath, penitence shall weep, prayer supplicate, praise sing, and preaching sound the silver trumpet of the Gospel; and, somewhere thereabout, babes shall be brought for baptism; and where, too, season after season, gathering in from the surrounding town and neighbourhood, souls dressed in white shall sit together at the table of the Holy Supper, where God's own presence shall look down, and where the mystic ladder shall be placed, with its ascending and descending angels, and where the worshippers, awaking from their earthly dreams into a higher life, shall cry, " This is none other than the house of God, and it is the gate of heaven." Surely the laying of the foundation stone of such an edifice as this ought to be done with great solemnity. We do not lay it with masonic honours, we do not lay it with great pomp, parade, and pageantry, with rattling drum and ringing clarion and salvos of thundering artillery, as they may lay the foundation stone of a new college or a palace, a senate house or an exchange; but in far simpler, and, I think, far sublimer style, we lay it with simple song and speech and prayer—earnest dedicative prayer to God. . . .

I am told that when our spire is built it will be a signal seen far out at sea; and if, perhaps, we put an illuminated clock in it, ship-masters say that it will be a very excellent beacon light, to guide ships into harbour. However that may be, I trust the church itself will be a lighthouse in a dark and dangerous sea, and that the congregation, as the peaceful family within, doing all things without murmurings and disputings, will shine as lights in the world, holding forth the Word of Life, that immortal souls, tossed to and fro upon the dark and angry waters, may not suffer shipwreck and go down with all their precious treasures to the depths of everlasting woe. . . .

And now, on this beautiful site, we would lift up our eyes to those heavens and say unto Him who has brought us hitherto, Master, it is good for us to be here, let us build! And now unto Him that loved us and washed us from our sins in His blood, and hath made us kings and priests to God, even the Father, to worship Him both in the earthly and heavenly temple, both in the God's house made with hands, and in the house of God not made with hands; to Him by whom the handling of the mallet and the trowel and other offices of masonry and carpentry are numbered with the arts and sacrifices of His holy priesthood; to Him who has instructed us to lay the rule, and square, and compasses, and other symbols of our skill and industry upon His altar, to find their consecration there; to Him who wrought with His own hands at Nazareth, and wreathed, in doing so, a crown of glory round the sweating brow of manual toil; to Him from whom comes forth the skill to plan, the power to execute, the patience to toil on, and the reward, and without whom nothing is strong, nothing is beautiful, nothing prospers—to Him do we commit this work which we this day so auspiciously begin: for except the Lord build the house, they labour in vain that build it.   For He shall build the temple of the Lord, and He shall bear the glory.

To MISS CRUM, Auldhouse.

IRVINE, 17th November, 186?.

There is something about a friend's appearance which the memory cannot carry away, but which the photograph succeeds in fixing and retaining and reproducing to the eye in the distance—something that, like the perfume of the flower, refuses to be carried away from it—or like the sunshine in the Norse legend, which the "lassie" strives in vain to catch in her apron and carry into her dark house.   Thanks to this photographic art which enables us to catch and to keep it, and to you for the gift of your nice little picture.

I suppose this photographic art must prove the ruin of mere likeness—mere imitative portrait-painting—as the sun-pictures must always be mathematically more correct than the exactest that your empiricists, that work by rule of thumb, can ever make.

But the function of the high class, the ideal portrait painter, I take it, is to paint us not so much as we are, but rather as we ought to be—to enter, by the force of his genius (I say it reverently) into the chamber of divine creation— and, in virtue of his sympathy with God's own creating power, find out the perfect individual types that each of us ought to realize (and may yet realize in a more favourable future—I hope we will), and paint us *that*.   And this is what the sun can never do, with all respect to that most useful luminary who has our annual dinner to cook at his great solar fire, and who, I daresay, was never meant to excel, in their own walk of art, our good pre-Raphaelites.

How much I would thank the painter who would paint me as I ought to be.   Would he not be, in his own language, a preacher of righteousness? I sometimes think I get a glimpse of it myself—immeasurably far away, I know. Well, I am glad to have you pictured as you are, for, I daresay, you come as near to what you ought to be as most people, and none the less, I hope, for my afflicting you with this epistolary transcendentalism.

I ought to have sent you the enclosed sooner, as you did me the compliment to ask for it, but some days were consumed in having to write to Moffat for a fresh supply.

Then, too, I got Edward Irving to read as soon as I could after seeing you, and have (though not yet all) been reading it accordingly.

Addison tells of two friends—sentimental enough truly—who, being parted, had agreed to look each night at the moon at eight o'clock precisely, that they might have the pleasure of thinking that they were both at the same time looking at the same object. I can scarcely ask you to do this, because, for one thing, the moon is not visible just now at eight o'clock, and, for another, although uniform time is much better delivered from Greenwich through the empire than it was in the days of the *Spectator*, yet through lunar changes such a pleasure could not survive a month. But seriously, it has enhanced the pleasure of reading Mrs. Oliphant to think how your thoughts are or have been journeying in the same track. Pleasure? Strange mixed pleasure, for is he not a prince among Prince Edwards? How colossal in all his movements all the way from the "wooden cradle" to the old cathedral crypt, after his being carried up in the whirlwind! As true a son as ever was of our dark mother "Tragedy with sceptred pall!" But what a real child of God was he not after all? Did you ever read such another journal as that of his to the Kirkcaldy Isabella? I could almost pray for that man's simple-hearted faith, though it should be at the cost of his dark destiny.

Dark ! only on this side doubtless.   The aeronaut emerges into dazzling sunshine immediately when he has pierced through the black cloud—" It may be we shall reach the golden shore and see the great Achilles."   I should like to know what you think of him after having seen him to " the crypt."   Will you not make another pilgrimage to that crypt for his sake ?   I shall the first time I am again in Glasgow.

In this winter of 1862-3 Mr. Robertson prepared his lecture on Luther.   It was first delivered in the Abbey of Paisley for the benefit of Paisley Infirmary. Even there, where he was hampered by a pulpit and by the restraints which the sacred associations of the ancient building put upon him, it produced a deep impression.   But when familiarity made him inde-pendent of the manuscript, when he had the free scope of a platform for its delivery, when there was nothing to hinder the fullest outflow of his humour, or to make the heartiest response on the part of the audience unseemly, the power of the lecture was owned by all who heard it.   His famili-arity with Germany and with German modes of life gave reality to his pictures.   His intense doctrinal convictions, which were in entire accord with the leading positions of the Reformation theology, gave earnestness of tone ; while his sympathy with the broad humanity of the German reformer, with his love of music and of laughter, made the lecture bright with ringing mirth.   It seldom occupied less than two hours, but there was never any sense of weariness, even on the part of sterner auditors, who were disposed to condemn it as a histrionic display. They were carried away spite of themselves, as the lecturer played upon his audience as on a many-stringed instrument, now thrilling them with pathos, and now convulsing them with laughter ; now hushing them to breathless silence, and now awaking the echoes with tumultuous applause.

The manuscript had many adventures. It was often amissing, and only came to light again after anxious search. Mr. Kirkwood writes :—

There is an incident in connection with the delivery of this lecture in Troon which is illustrative of the doctor's character. A few days after it, he wrote saying that Martin had taken flight, and could by no means be found. He hoped he had not made his long migration. He drove over with a friend (the doctor was fond of driving with his friends instead of taking the train), still saying Martin had not come back to his breeding place. Search was made in the house and church, and at last he was found nestling under a pew beneath the spot where the platform had been raised. It was a narrow escape, for had the manuscript remained a little longer where it was, it might have been tossed by an ignorant hand into the vestry fire.

On Tuesday, 29th December, 1863, the new church was opened for public worship by Mr. Robertson's old friend and fellow-student, Dr. Cairns of Berwick, now Principal Cairns of Edinburgh, and on the following Sabbath the minister was assisted by another old friend and fellow-student, Dr. Alexander MacEwen, of Claremont Church, Glasgow, and by his brother, Mr.

Robertson of Newington. He conducted the afternoon service himself. The lesson which he read was
the record of Jacob's dream, and in commenting on
it he told the German legend of the Lost Church.
His text was from the Apocalypse—"And the four
beasts said, Amen"—the idea of the sermon being
that the throne bearers, the ideals of all excellence,
human and divine, the upholders of the holiness of
God, were satisfied in Christ. He thus spoke at the
close—

I am glad to say that we have been enabled, by the help
of God, and through the liberality of others as well as yourselves, to rear so far an edifice that is not only meant for the
accommodation of the worshippers, however excellently that
has been attained, but that is also meant, through the
language of the architectural art that makes the "very
stones cry out," to utter something of that homage and that
honour we render to the worthy Lamb that was slain, whom
we proclaim as King, not only of the good and true, but also
of the beautiful ; and who, we believe, does not disdain the
worship rendered Him through the art of the Bezaleel, or
Aholiab the artificer, or the Asaph the harmonist, or the
Aaron the orator. I am glad to-day that here upon this hill
on this sea shore, we have been raising a protest in stone
against that notion which has been so prevalent amongst us,
that while our business, our pleasure, our domestic love and
joy, may dwell in ceiled houses, any sort of house, however
mean, is good enough for worshipping God in—against that
unhappy divorce of truth and goodness from beauty, which,
upon the part of our noble Covenanting and Seceding fore-
fathers, was indeed a matter of stern duty, conscience, and
necessity, but upon the part of us, their children, seems to

be no longer so. We place this house, then, at the feet of Jesus ; to Him we devote it, and it is enough for us if He shall be pleased to accept of it. We seek to link it on to that grand orchestral anthem that is rising to Him through the very stones themselves, from every creature in heaven and in earth, and under the earth and in the sea.

The building so auspiciously opened was named " Trinity Church ; " and the minister thus vindicated the departure from Presbyterian usage :—

It is better than the " Burgher Kirk ; " better than calling it by the name of the minister, as is so often done, as if the minister was some Roman saint, or rather some sort of shopkeeper who displays his ecclesiastical wares on his pulpit-counter Sabbath after Sabbath to church-going customers,—a theory of the ministry which I entirely repudiate ; better too than calling it after St. Paul, or St. Peter, or St. James, or any other of " the glorious company of the Apostles ; " and much better than calling it after Augustine, or Ambrose, or any Roman saint, or any Presbyterian saint either, such as Knox, Erskine, or Gillespie. I cannot admire the consistency of those who refuse to call their churches by the names of any of the Apostles and yet name them after their own Presbyterian saints and fathers. We get rid of all that by getting away from men's names altogether, and calling it Trinity Church. We enter the church through the gate of baptism in the name of the Trinity, and are dismissed every Sabbath by the benediction in the name of the Trinity; and we worship God the Father, through Christ the Son, in and by the Holy Spirit.

CHAPTER XI.

The Closing Years of his Erbine Ministry.

THE new church brought to Mr. Robertson an added
joy in his ministry. It was a delight to him to
conduct divine service and preach the gospel in a
building which to some extent realized his ideal of a
place of Christian worship. There are lines in St.
Aldhelm's version of the 84th Psalm which were then
often on his lips :—

> " Lord, Thy minsters to me are
> Courts of honour passing fair,
> And my soul doth love right well
> There to be and there to dwell."

His delight in the new church was not the less, that
the structure as designed, remained to the end of his life
unfinished. It resembled the better, on that account,
the great cathedrals, and was a fitter type of the
spiritual house which "groweth into a holy temple in
the Lord." His interest was kept alive by schemes for
completing the design and adding fitting adornments

Members of the congregation contributed painted windows for the principal lights in the chancel and north transept, while the St. Catherine's window in the west gable was the gift of Mr. J. H. Young of Glasgow.

He took special interest in the filling of the principal window in the south transept, which was contributed, two years after the church opening, by Mr. and Mrs. David M'Cowan of Glasgow, as a memorial of their nephew, Melville Walker, whose early death called forth Mr. Robertson's brotherly sympathy, and thus deepened and hallowed their friendship with him.

He threw his whole heart into their project, and took counsel with the architect, Mr. Pilkington, and with Mr. Heath Wilson, under whose supervision the windows of Glasgow Cathedral had just been filled with Munich glass. The idea which he wished to have expressed was, Mothers representing the leading types of the human race bringing their children to Christ. After long delay, which often called forth from Mr. Robertson, in his voluminous correspondence on the subject, such words as, "Germans are slow," "No word yet from these slow Munichers," a design was furnished and admirably carried out by a firm of Munich artists. It is the opinion of competent judges that no better specimen of German glass is to be found in Scotland. Mr. Robertson gave repeated warnings against the danger of "vulgarizing angels into Bavarian peasants sausage-fed," and we find in his letters many such sentences as this, which reveals how truly earnest he was that the gift of his friends should serve the highest ends: " I hope, wish, pray that our artist in Munich may be guided by Him who inspired Bezaleel and Aholiab of old to carve the cherubim, that he may be enabled to put much of divine truth and heavenly beauty and childish innocence and sweetness into the pictured window, which is to preach in its own way comfort to Rachels weeping for their children, and the Evangel of Him who said, Suffer the little children and forbid them not to come unto Me."

One interesting feature of the window is that the representative of the Caucasian type among the children brought to Christ is a striking likeness of the child in whose memory it was erected. With reference to the window, and to a monument as to the design of which Mr. M'Cowan had consulted him, he writes of date 30th August, 1865 :—" I hope and am sure you will never have cause to regret laying the hands of your grief and generosity on the head of stones and glass and ordaining them in their own way to preach. May the monument tend to comfort you also through instructing others."

Some time later, the spire of the church was built with the aid of friends beyond the congregation, who sought thus to testify their regard for one who served not his own flock only, but the whole Church.

The following reminiscences of her childhood, furnished by Miss Maxwell of " The Cottage," which stands on the Kilwinning road, next door neighbour to the manse, refer to the time of which we have been writing :—

I can give you some small idea of what **Dr. Robertson** was to us in our childhood. Though in these days we esteemed him great, because we were told he was, it only seemed to us that he was quite unlike other men in his ways, his home, his sayings, and doings. His utter disregard for his dinner hour struck us as strange, and one of the great desires we had respecting him was that he would spend more time over his meals. His student ways we did not understand, and when he would receive us, his early morning visitors, and begin tales of Greek mythology, we, knowing that he had not yet breakfasted, were in despair. We could not enjoy the stories, feeling that he was breaking some unwritten code by which breakfast was made an early and first duty of the day, and so our pity for Cassiopeia weeping over the untimely fate of her sisters was mingled with compassion for the narrator. Or it might be he would tell in his own imaginative way the allegory of Orion,—of how that mighty giant after freeing Chios from all evils was imprisoned, and made blind by the old king Ænopian ; but when the spring returned the giant escaped, and the bright beams of the sun restored his sight, and he wandered again, his sword by his side, free and life-giving, over the vine-clad hills, only again to be crushed and imprisoned when the time of vintage was fully come. Sometimes, however, our visit was passed almost in silence, till perhaps he would seat himself at the organ and play on and on, till his childish audience wearied and non-comprehending, would stray softly out of the drawing-room window, leaving him playing dreamily to himself, till summoned by some one to the sterner duties of the day. Or it might be, if one went in alone towards evening, he would speak of the things of the kingdom of

God with mystic language and far-away look, till the listener felt that like Moses of old he had gone up into the mount, and the child only was left below.

To Mrs. Maxwell.

RAVENSBROOK, IRVINE, 14th February, 1865.

You may be sure that in my hermitage by the unseen brook Cherith I do not cross my arms in daily and nightly supplication without enfolding you all in them ; and may I say again, dear sister, like John Newton to his friend, "When you are with the King and getting good for yourself, speak a word for me." I must quote more—the words are truly beautiful—" I have reason to think you see him oftener and have nearer access to Him than myself. Yet I am not wholly without His notice. He supplies all my wants, and I live under his protection. My enemies see His royal arms over my door and dare not enter."

Should you find any leisure to write me, please to say how the classes are getting on, and the singing of "Brief Life," etc., and whatever you may be sure will be interesting to a loving Uncle Ecclesiastical. I hope the Good Shepherd, dividing the flock with the crook—the cross—has already put your lambs all on the right, as the blessed who shall inherit the kingdom.

> "And now we fight the battle,
>   But then —— "

You say you are in the thick of the battle. I suppose we must be somewhere while here. But let us keep a brave heart and clear armour. What beautiful armour for a Christian lady that "armour of light," "having on the breastplate of righteousness." I was talking of that at our prayer meeting an hour since. It was suggested by going into my study late last night. The windows were open—shutters not to ; but as I looked out into the moonlight I saw there was a fine defence of snow round the house ; for no robber would venture to come and leave his footmarks there. Think of the Angel of Snow defending our houses, *i.e.*, pure, white, new fallen snow, for if the snow is trampled on and turned into slush it's no longer of use that way. It is only in its purity that it is a guard and a defence.

About Mrs. S———. She sadly longs to hear the music of your footstep on the stair ; but the weather is so severe, and I am afraid she will never hear it till she hear it on the golden stair of a very different house, where she may be able to distinguish it among all others, and sure to welcome it. Is not this what is meant by "making to yourselves friends of (by means of) the mammon of unrighteousness, that when ye fail they may receive you into everlasting habitations."

11th May, 1865.

Poor Mrs. S——— died yesterday morning. Not for some time had I seen her, having been two Sundays in England since Easter, and on making inquiry to-day I found her dead. I hope she has now got up those golden stairs, at the foot of which she has so long lain, and on which too she is to listen for other footsteps coming—coming to Him who said "I was sick and ye visited me." Shall we not believe that there has been a visit of angels in that little dark untidy garret in the Town-end ? Yes, coming down the golden ladder of that sky-lit, campceiled garret room (where sits that tiny child on her wee stool before the fire, into which her little face gazes silently) to carry up the soul of the dying, poor mother—though the visit must have been in the darkness and silence of night, for in the morning the neighbours say they found her dead.

We have already referred to the pleasure Mr.

Robertson had in the near neighbourhood of his kinsman and co-presbyter, Dr. Bruce of Newmilns. That venerable pastor's jubilee fell in July, 1865, and we are indebted to his son-in-law and colleague, Mr. Alston, now of Carluke, for this account of the services by which it was celebrated :—

Dr. Robertson was in the early years of his ministry a frequent visitor at Newmilns, often officiating for Dr. Bruce; and the people listened with equal wonder and delight to the eloquence of the young preacher. These visits were the more frequent and the more relished because of the name which he bore, William Bruce, a name which indicated that he stood to the venerable minister of the congregation " in a relationship," as he himself used to say, " too near to be disputed, and too dear to be disowned." When Dr. Bruce's jubilee was celebrated in 1865, an immense gathering of members of the congregation and friends of the aged minister from far and near came together—a gathering all the greater that " Robertson of Irvine," was announced as the preacher. The text which he gave out was Matthew xi. 6—" And blessed is he, whosoever shall not be offended in Me." As the sermon went on the congregation were at a loss to see where the preacher would find the point of transition to the jubilee, but the link was found. At the close he suddenly lowered his voice to its deepest tones, and said—" John the Baptist is not the only John of whom we read in Scripture. There is another John, of different character and history from his : for while the Baptist was a preacher stern, majestic, terrible, this other John was gentle, amiable, mild ; and while the Baptist was cut off in the midtime of his days, this other John lived to see his jubilee, and beyond it too. If in present times, among our fathers and brethren in the ministry, there is one rather than another upon whom the mantle of the beloved John has fallen, it is he whose happy jubilee to-day we celebrate, whose praise for sweetest gentleness of holy life is in all the churches."

The sermon spoken of by Mr. Alston was first preached in Wellington Street Church, Glasgow, on a Christmas day, to the Society of the Sons of Ministers of the United Presbyterian Church. The audience which assembled to hear it was one of the most remarkable ever brought together in the western city. It comprised not only representatives of all the churches, but a goodly number from the debatable land, where neither presbyter nor bishop has sway. Mingling with the intelligent merchants, who have long been the strength of the Church of the Erskines, and many of whom are sons of the manse, were representatives of the University, and of the faculties of law and medicine. Here and there, Bohemian-looking men of the pen and pencil, who sat as if they were little accustomed to the restraints of a church pew, were rubbing clothes with famous preachers, who had come to see whether this country minister was a reed shaken by the wind, or perchance a prophet. All were alike hushed to silence as soon as the deep, rich voice was heard announcing and reading the opening Psalm. The new book of that Christmas season was a volume by Longfellow, and it was remarked that the echo of the poet's verse could be heard in all the devotional services of the day. When the text was announced—" Blessed is he whosoever shall not be offended in Me," it was at once linked on to the occasion by the opening sentence:

" These words were first spoken of a minister's son—of John, the son of Zacharias, minister of the Hebrew sanctuary, whose quiet manse lay far from the bustle of the city in the hill country of Judah." Then followed a picture of the manse, with father Zacharias, and mother Elizabeth, and their kindly hospitalities when friends came to visit them.   It was evident that he had made a study for his picture in some country manse, at Newmilns, or elsewhere.   He then spoke of how the minister's son, coming forth from the retirement of the manse into the midst of the great world, is specially liable to be offended in Christ ; and set forth four reasons why John might have been offended, on each point turning the lessons of the Baptist's life to account in view of the intellectual and spiritual perplexities of the time.

In the spring of 1866, Mr. Robertson had a delightful excursion as the guest of Mr. Samuel Stitt of Liverpool.   They went by way of Tours, Bordeaux, Pau, Montpelier, and the Riviera to Florence.   His letters home were brief and hurried, but they reveal thorough enjoyment of the holiday.

To His Younger Sister.

Irvine, 7th August, 1866.

. . . I am paying the penalty of my spring tour by having to work on without holiday in the summer months, and since I was at Greenhill I have not been a Sabbath away, so that I have not got back again to see you.

Did they tell you the tragedy of poor Oscar?   He never

lifted his head after his wickedness in slaughtering the hens. I spoke to him without beating him, and showed him one of his victims, bidding him "just look at that," and he turned away in sore compunction and distress, and died, I believe, of a dog's broken heart. The shame was too much for him ; for he was a respectable dog, not to say a minister's, and had always borne a blameless reputation, at least since the days of sowing his wild oats in his youth, when he is suspected of having slain at least one sheep.

Prince of dog-fanciers, Rab ! Did you hear how ill he has been, and I am afraid still is. Miss Brown has written to tell me.

I am asked for this and the next month to open more churches than there are Sabbaths in them. One offer I have accepted which will bring me your way next month at least, if not before. By this post I decline another invitation to come and lecture this next session to the Stirling School of Arts. It's such a queer place, Stirling, though I like it too. But it's close on post hour, and this is the seventh epistle I have written to-day. My best of elders, William Cunningham, is dying—I shall miss him most of all.

To the Same.

IRVINE, January 16th, 1867.

What extraordinarily cold weather. But I like it, and try to keep myself warm doing a good deal of out-door work in visiting, which had got sadly behind. Then I come in at ten or eleven, and read till three or four in the cheery, well-warmed dining-room where, Isabella being absent, I allow myself ane quiet smoke. What volumes I have gone through, Whately's Life (by his daughter), High Church Essays, Venice (Mrs. Hall's), Savonarola (Villari), Italian Monks, Gardenhurst, etc., any of which almost I could send, as some of them I have bought from MacLehose.

I have a long letter from Curwen (sol-fa) asking me to help him for some lectures he has to deliver at the Glasgow Andersonian. You will be pleased with the way our music is getting on here. The Sabbath evening choir sings Litany, Benedictus, Te Deum, etc.

I am getting a good name for staying close at home, refusing every invitation to go out right and left, only some long-made engagements are coming on that I cannot escape.

One of the long-made engagements that he could not escape was to preach in London. Professor Roberts of St. Andrews, then in London, gives us the following reminiscences of his visit :—

" Robertson of Irvine," as the great preacher was familiarly and affectionately called, came up from Scotland on one occasion to assist me at the communion when I was minister of the Presbyterian Church, St. John's Wood, London. It was a truly memorable visit. The date was, I think, July, 1867, but though twenty years have thus passed away since then, I still have a very vivid recollection of the wealth of imagery, and weight of thought, which distinguished the pulpit utterances of Robertson. He might have been compared to a man with a bag of diamonds in his hand, and scattering them at will among those around him. The series of rich poetical thoughts which crowded one upon the other, as he spoke, seemed inexhaustible, and fairly entranced his audience. The sermon which I heard him deliver far exceeded the ordinary length, but regret that it was finished, mingled with admiration of its beauty and power when it came to a close. A chime as of silver bells seemed still to linger on the ear.

Two things especially cling to my mind in connection with that visit of Dr. Robertson. One is the very striking way in which he commenced the service. He began as usual by reading four verses of a metrical psalm. The psalm he chose was the seventy-third from the twenty-third to the twenty-sixth verse. That is an extremely rich and beautiful passage, but every Scotch minister must have felt how awkwardly it opens with the prosaic and almost grotesque line—"Nevertheless continually." Yet Robertson taught me to love the line by the few simple remarks which, ere reading farther, he made upon it. "Nevertheless," he said, "that is always the utterance of the faith of the Christian. He feels his unworthiness in the sight of God, *nevertheless* he must come into the Divine presence; he is guilty and polluted, *nevertheless* provision has been made for his pardon and purification; he is weak and helpless, *nevertheless* through Christ he can do all things." Thus he showed, in the most striking way, what a suggestive expression was that apparently strange and uncouth "nevertheless," as always indicating the up-springing of hope in the heart, and as containing an expression of unfaltering confidence in God.

The other thing I remember so vividly is that Robertson told me, after the service, that he hesitated long as to the text from which he should that day preach. He said he was very much inclined to base his discourse on these words in Rev. v. 14, "And the four beasts said, Amen." He changed his mind, however, almost at the last moment, and took another text. He held that the Apocalypse was constructed on something like the lines of a Greek drama; and, he added, "All this is in favour of your view as to the habitual use of Greek by the Jews of Palestine in the time of Christ, for no one, whose mind was not familiar with the Greek drama, could have written the Apocalypse."

On the return journey from London he made, in company with an Irvine artist, an excursion into Cowper's country, and thus wrote to a young friend at school, whom he had visited when in the metropolis :—

OLNEY, 13th July, 1867.

From the Wolverton station my *compagnon de voyage* and I had to drive through nine miles of moonlight to this Olney, and it was so late when we arrived that it became this morning ere I could (not remember, but) redeem my promise to send you another note.

This one must be of the briefest as, if I do not overtake this post, which goes within ten minutes ! they tell me there is no other from this for thirty-six hours.

From the windows of the Bull Hotel we see out through the triangular market place (a great elm in the centre) to what was Cowper's Olney house, and have just been sitting in the room where Lady Austin (who had been shopping at the draper's opposite, and had been asked in to tea) told him the diverting history of John Gilpin ; and we have been pacing the hall where the tame hares played about. On the way through the garden to the summer house where he wrote " Truth," whom did we get a glimpse of but " yon cottager that sits," etc. I now understand the mystery of " pillows and bobbins," and as I thought you might like to see a bit of the lace that " she " makes, I send the accompanying. And indeed it must do for the rest of the letter for the waiter says, Instantly—or too late.

On the same date he wrote to his sister :—

We have been along to Weston too, and through the scenery so graphically described in *The Sofa*. Likewise in John Newton's church and the pew where Cowper used to sit. How like Olney is to Irvine, Mackinlay says, and so it is.

To the same young friend to whom he wrote from Olney, this birthday letter was sent :—

RAVENSBROOK, IRVINE, 19th September, 1867.

I wrote you a little note yesterday conveying the birthday wish that you might never grow old. Shall I tell you how to keep from growing old? Most young ladies would like to know, and oldish people like papa and me don't like to feel that they are growing old. . If ever you come to the like age (it will be a long time of course) you may feel the same. It is a good feeling too, it " also cometh forth from the Lord of Hosts." It is designed to lead us to the fountain of perpetual youth.

Well, in our bodies we can't keep from growing old. They are part of the material universe (the vesture of the spirit) that is all destined to decay and wax old. The very sun himself is growing old, poor Sol! And the moon walking in her brightness, poor Luna! and the stars, Lady Venus, and Cassiopeia, and all the rest of them that are starring it in the nightly drawing-room upstairs, are growing old. And mother earth of ours has long since passed her teens, according to the last return in the census of the planets, and the geological register, though not so old, perhaps, as the wise men that are descended (they say) from monkeys would make her—yet she is, no doubt, a very venerable lady, an old grandmother Gaia! And the stars (I am told) have a tendency to group themselves into clusters, which star-clusters are just like the disc of some great sunflower or daisy, and the time must come (though my arithmetic cannot count when) at which the floral giants of the sky must bow their heads and shed their golden stars, like flower dust on a windy day. Yea (says the Word that is more lasting than them all) they shall all wax old as doth a garment. And Lady ——— too, with her pretty face and rounded form, and lightsome step, and graceful attitude, and sparkling eye, must go a far, far shorter journey the same road to old age and decay! What a vain little old woman you will make, won't you, when you are a great-grandmother, whoever lives to see it. No help for it! You must come to the " end of days," and "the years without pleasure," if you live long enough, as finely described in Ecclesiastes xii., where you are earnestly besought before-hand to "remember now thy Creator in the days of thy youth," and then—the silver cord is loosed, and the golden bowl broken at last. For there is no road to perfect beauty of outward form but through the black door, and the dark, underground valley, and the gate of resurrection, which shall open and lead into the city of the angels, where ———, too, will walk among them clothed in white!

But while you cannot in the body, in the spirit you may keep from ever growing old. But for this it needs to be born again. You " must be born again," Christ says. Don't think this is not needed for the like of you. You know the little daughter of Jairus needs the Lord's awaking, just as well as the young man whose funeral is at the city gates, or the Lazarus that has been rotting four days in his grave. Some of the dead are very beautiful, " before decay's effacing fingers have swept the lines where beauty lingers." " But they are dead all the same. And so too with the dead in trespasses and sins." That is the birthday that is kept in heaven with joy in the presence of the angels of God, when one is born again. For if you are, then you will have a life that never more can die, and never more grow old, and so I hope that on her birthday, this 19th September, when "the fields are white unto the harvest," a certain Scottish maiden with her pitcher on her shoulder is going alone to the well, the well where Jesus sits, thirsting as He always does for our salvation, and singing as she goes, "Just as I am," and asking of Him, and getting the living water. And what a gift on your birthday from Him! He died for love that He might give it you, and it will be in you as "a well of water springing up to everlasting life."

And then by being always humble, you will be always young. Humility is a "little child." This is Christ's picture of it. But Pride is old, as old as that old serpent, the devil. If you indulge in pride you'll make the pretty face of your soul old and wrinkled in no time. And Faith too is "a little child," and makes you, and keeps you, always young; and Hope is young, and Love is young, and Joy is young, and Generosity is young. The graces are all young, but sin is an ugly old hag. And so I hope you will be dressed afresh to-day in the beauties of holiness, and baptized afresh into the dew of youth, and this, my dear ——— is my birthday wish for you.

On the 24th December, 1867, his father died.

To Mrs. Maxwell.

GREENHILL, BANNOCKBURN, 28th December, 1867.

You would not be ashamed, dear Mrs. Maxwell, to call me brother had you known what a noble father I had. I wish you had seen him, if it had only been for an hour. In the reverend old man—a disciple that Jesus loved—sitting cheerfully in the apocalyptic lights of a serene and holy age, you would have seen what, with your sympathy with all that is true and good, you could never have forgotten till you see him, as you will, with your own honoured and beloved father in the circle of the spirits of just men made perfect.

At the great age, I find, of 87, he has been numbered with the immortals, has renewed his youth as the eagles.

At noon he died. " The path of the just is as the forenoon sunlight " that shines in fine crescendo of the light to mid-day, and has no afternoon declension to the west, but dawns and rises on the horizon of another and a higher sphere. So he died at noon. The chariots of Israel ! Our fathers, where are they? We know well where they are, yet let us not seek them, but rather Him, " the Lord God of our fathers." May He be the Lord God of their children after them.

Isabella is quietly sad; but neither she nor any of us is without great comfort. ONE " who lived and died " is here in the still darkness, with a lamp in His hand that " turns the shadow of death into the morning."

Kindest remembrances to my good brother, and all love to the dear children—those at home, and dear daughters that are away, and yet always near.

After our dark pilgrimage on Monday to St. Ninians (on the road the everlasting light), I hope to get back to see you all well on some early day of the new year.

To MISS HELEN RANKIN (afterwards MRS. BATTISCOMBE).

IRVINE, 21st January, 1868.

The shadow of death, as you know, has fallen of late on all the movements of my hands and heart. I have had scores of letters of sympathy, but truly, I think, the last is the sweetest of all. God bless you for a sweet comforter ! and make you " a succourer of many and of me also," filling you evermore with His grace, with the comfort of His Holy Ghost in your young, guileless heart, which I pray may be ever free from sorrow of its own.

Had you known my father (one of the grandest men, I

think, God ever made) you would not disdain to let me call you, as I sometimes wish to do, my sister Helen !

The telegraphic message of his death met me going out to our "service" on Christmas Eve. But I went on with it—children's carols, church decked with evergreens, and so forth—and went through with it, without either betraying the disturbing thought, or being able for a moment to forget it. Strange what good hypocrites we can become when there is need for it. Nor were the old man's death and the young child's birth felt after all to be at variance ; and, though the mistletoe of my last Christmas was changed into cypress, there were still voices singing the "Abide with me." My sisters have been with me for a week, but are yesterday returned to the fatherless house.

Let me thank you truly for your kind letter. It is not only the words that it contains, and that are indeed " good words," but a certain delicate aroma that it breathes, that you must have shed into it unconsciously from a heart-shaped alabaster box of yours—as, indeed, you would, and could not help doing, in writing to any one, but which it is not every one that might so readily perceive or so richly prize as I do.

To MISS AMY MAXWELL (returning from School).

IRVINE, 1st July, 1868.

What joy the return of our two young princesses of the West End—that everybody rejoices to hear are coming—must make in The Cottage, where the Misses have been so sadly missed ; though pretty large, and with a good margin of lawn and garden ground, and many hearts, none of which is small, but all capable of holding many firkins of joy apiece, it will yet not be able to contain all the joy that the return of these daughters of The Cottage will give, so that it

P

must overflow the dyke between us and flood my house with its brightness also.

So we will give you hearty welcome home. *Todie* will bark, and *Oscar* over the wall will answer him, and the trees will wave, and all of us will be glad.

Only, as every rose, they say, has its thorn and every sunbeam its shadow, so this bright home-coming of yours brings to me the shadow that it shall cut off the opportunity that I have so long had, and so shabbily neglected, of writing a little letter to " dear Amy " at school. Well, if I had written you always when I thought about you, I should long ago have ruined your purse with the postages; and as I was going to write you every day that I forgot you, I never wrote to you at all.

To Miss Crum, Thornliebank.

IRVINE, 6th August, 1868.

Your welcome letter reached me yesterday morning when setting out on a pic-nic with some 200 children and their teachers, belonging to our Trinity Church Sunday school— their mid-summer festival, and I thought I should go and enjoy it with them—a brave little army of tiny forms and feet and faces, marching through fields and woods to find the "Sangreal" in the enchanted castle of happiness—a castle in the air as it is to most of us; yet they seemed to find it in a green field, where we encamped, and with music, sports, and sweetmeats, laid siege to it for several hours, and having won as much joy as their little hearts could hold, returned triumphant at sunset, all with palms in their hands and crowns (none of them broken) on their heads. And so I left this for a while and read your letter in a shady nook of summer and quiet corner of the kingdom of green leaves.

During all his ministry, Mr. Robertson took a deep

interest in the improvement not only, as we have seen, of the singing, but of the other parts of public worship as well. His prayers were always carefully arranged and expressed in chaste and well-chosen language. In the later years, when in the new church he had more harmonious surroundings, he bestowed yet greater pains on the conduct of the devotions. He sought to give unity to each service of worship by making one dominant thought run through it, from the opening psalm to the closing benediction, the thought developing and expanding as the service proceeded. So far from having any sympathy with those who would prescribe a liturgy, he claimed even greater freedom than is common in our Scottish churches. He revived old customs that have fallen into disuse, such as "prefacing" the opening psalm with such comment as helped the people to sing it more intelligently, and giving a running exposition of the chapters read.

Mrs. M'Cunn thus recalls his conversations on this subject after his retirement :—

Delightful as was his talk about Italian art and mediæval belief, and vivid and picturesque as were his stories of Scotch history, there is nothing that remains so delightfully in my memory as his occasional references to his early ministry and life at Irvine. He told me once about a Christmas service, possibly the first, when he had gone up into the pulpit, and had begun with ὁ λογος ἐγένετο σάρξ, and again *Das Wort ward Fleisch*, and again the Latin equivalent (which I have forgotten), and then paused and said—"But all this is an unknown tongue to us," and then clear and full and triumphantly he gave out, "The Word was made flesh and dwelt among us." And then he went on to show how it was only by becoming flesh, by speaking to us in our own human language, that God could make Himself known to us. How wise was his attitude of mind towards all the innovations which this earnest, cultured, restless generation wants to introduce into our dear old "National Zion." "When the spirit in the people gets too full and rich for the old forms let them make new ones, but let the inner feeling be there first." In connection with this, he told us how he had explained the nature of the Litany to his people, and had bidden them respond to such of the petitions as they felt came home to them ; and how, at an evening service in the gathering twilight, he had stood up before them and given out each petition, and how full and spontaneous and heartfelt the response had swelled out— "We beseech Thee to hear us, good Lord."

Another valued correspondent (Miss Margaret Nairn, niece of his friend Dr. Ker), has preserved notes of his conversations in his later years, and thus writes :—

He was firmly attached to the principles of his own denomination, and used to say, "There is no doubt that we are in the right." Yet his breadth enabled him to take in the good of other churches, just as his keen discernment showed him their weaknesses. He complained of the practice in the English Church of repeating the psalms in alternate verses, and described to us the true meaning of the old antiphone, in which each verse of the psalm naturally divides itself into two parts, the second either an answer to, or a deepening of, the other ; whereas the modern system is meaningless, and merely a degeneration of the old. He often condemned what he characterized as *Ape-iscopacy*—the servile imitation in our churches of the mere externals of the Episcopal mode of worship, by those who forget that the outward form should always be an expression of the spirit within, and not the controller of it. While appreciating the beauties of the English Prayer-book, he would say, "I could never be fettered by a liturgy."

As might have been expected, the changes introduced into the forms of worship in Trinity Church, though they were strictly on Presbyterian lines, were spoken of as "innovations," and caused some anxiety to persons of the "straiter sect." A good lady, belonging to another communion, once remonstrated with Mr. Robertson. She said—"I hear you are introducing some dreadful innovations into your church service." "Indeed," he replied, "what innovations have we introduced?" "Oh," she said, "I hear that you read the commandments at the communion." "Is that all you have heard of?" was his reply, "we have introduced a far greater innovation than that." "What is it?" said the good lady in some alarm. "We try to keep them," he replied.

He used to tell gleefully of the caution of his old beadle, Andrew, who was aware that suspicions were abroad as to the decorations and services in the church. Dr. Robert Buchanan had come to preach at an anniversary, and in the interval of worship was going over the building, while Mr. Robertson was busy in the vestry with his afternoon sermon. Dr. Buchanan called Andrew, to ask him some questions about the *bas reliefs* in front of the pulpit; but Andrew, afraid lest the great **Free Church** leader meant to make some sinister use of the information sought, became dry and uncommunicative. " I canna lay't aff to ye, sir ; ye'll need to ask himsel', " was all that could be got from him.

The Christmas service to which Mrs. M'Cunn refers was the innocent occasion of no small stir. It had been the custom from the time of his ordination to celebrate the anniversary of the event by a congregational soiree. But Mr. Robertson grew weary of the annual gathering with its inevitable personal references; and, as he had been ordained at Christmas time, it occurred to him to substitute for the soiree a service of worship which took its complexion from the season of the year. It came to be held regularly on Christmas Eve. He encouraged the young people to give expression to their joy by decorating the church with flowers and evergreens, and great pains were taken by himself and by the choir to make the service beautiful and harmonious. The children, with their hymns and carols, had, as was meet, a special place in the celebration, and they and their elders alike looked forward to it as one of the brightest and happiest nights in all the year. This had gone on for several seasons, and no objection had been taken or offence dreamed of, till a report of the 1868 celebration, written by a friendly hand, gave a detailed account of the service, which was simple enough, with its alternation of hymns, prayers, readings of the Scriptures, and addresses. But the singing of the *Adeste Fideles* (at least under its Latin name), the *Te Deum*, Christmas carols, and the anthem, " In the Beginning," and the repetition of the Creed and Lord's Prayer, with responsive "Amens" from the choir, had a more alarming appearance twenty years ago than they would have now. It was not wonderful that Mr. Robertson had letters from leading ministers of his Church asking with some concern what these things meant, or that an article in the denominational *Magazine* should sound a note of alarm. With perhaps more kindness than discretion the Presbytery of Kilmarnock took the matter in hand, and rebuked the *Magazine* for its unconstitutional attack on their brother. Of course the *Magazine* must have its reply, and the matter threatened at one time to assume the proportions of a "controversy"; but counsels of peace prevailed, and the Christmas Eve celebrations went on from year to year undisturbed. In his vindication before the Presbytery, Mr. Robertson took the ground that the "ritualism" which alarmists feared had its essence not in a beautiful service, but in sacramentarian doctrine, and that its inroads could be most effectually resisted by making our non-ritualistic worship as beautiful as possible.

"Rome and Ritual," he argued, shall be most effectively put down by taking out of them anything that may be good in them and using it ourselves. If they sing well, let us not, therefore, sit dumb and put our fingers in our ears or act "the howling wilderness," but let us try and sing all the better.   Ulysses' way of resisting the singing of the sirens, when he had himself bound to the mast and the ears of his sailors stopped with wax, ordering them on no account to let him loose, however urgently he might entreat them, when the sirens were singing as the ships sailed by, was not accounted so good as Orpheus' way when he took his lyre aboard and sung to it aloud hymns of praise, and so drowned the singing of the sirens.

To Mr. David M‘Cowan.

IRVINE, 7th January, 1869.

Your wine comes from the vintage of the grapes of Eshcol. I know before ever tasting it : for you live in that region, do you not ?—on the border of the land of promise ; so that a present from your stores has the aroma of "a field and a garden that the Lord has blessed."   May He bless you and yours more and more !   May the new year of '69 be full of happy days for you !—365 in a row, like the water-pots at the marriage at Cana—each of them holding a good deal, say two or three firkins apiece, and all of them filled to the brim with the water of gladness ; or if any of them should be filled with the water of grief, you know One who can turn that water into wine.

Some of us who have been over 40 years in the pilgrimage ought to be thinking of crossing the river by and by.   How many of our caravan of pilgrims have gone on before us, to enter and search out the promised land, but they have not returned to tell us what it is like.

I am glad you liked our Christmas service.   Your presence would have enriched it.   It was almost wholly devotional. I hope there is a new spirit of worship awakening amongst us, requiring new forms to hold it all, new wine requiring new bottles, otherwise the old bottles would be more than enough.

You may guess that I have been writing the above after midnight when very sleepy, having returned late from weary country walking, where I have had two days of pastoral visitation this week, so that I can hardly spell, not to say write legibly.

On reading over the allusion to Cana above, your gift of wine sets me to try a rhyme—New Year, '69.

Water into Wine.

Like water-pots at Cana stand
　　Behind us stony years,
That have been filled at Christ's command
　　With grievous rain of tears.

Some fewer firkins, others more,
　　These stony urns contain;
Not into every year could pour
　　An equal fall of rain.

But firkins two or three apiece,
　　That fill them to the brim;
When all are filled so, rain will cease,
　　Waiting the word from Him.

The word comes, " Draw out now and bear "—
　　When—miracle divine !
They draw and bear to banquet, where
　　The water now is wine.

The best wine first, the last the worst—
　　Man's feasts are ordered so;
They run to waste, pall on the taste,
　　From bad to worse they go.

Joy loses joy in course of years,
　　And is quite lost when past;

But rain of tears such vintage bears
    As yields the good wine last.

And as Lord Christ in vineyard still
    Makes yearly wine from rain,
So His first miracle He will,
    Returning, work again.

When, His own marriage being come,
    He, seated by her side,
Shall order to the banquet-room
    The new wine for His bride.

And her cup-bearer, Memory,
    From urns of ancient years,
Shall fetch those choicest draughts that be,
    The wine that once was tears.

Which, if it were good, I would dedicate to you.   Excuse
first copy.   So with both rhyme and reason, I am, your
much obliged, W. B. R.

In the spring of 1869, the Senate of the University
of Glasgow, in which his friend Dr. Caird had become
professor of theology, conferred on him the degree of
Doctor of Divinity.   The honour was the more
appreciated that it was given at the same time to one
of his most valued friends, Walter Smith.

A powerful sermon that he prepared in these closing
years of his active ministry, was from the text Exodus
xxxiv. 29—"And Moses wist not that the skin of his
face shone." The main idea of the sermon was rendered
into verse thus :—

Unconscious Beauty.

Unconscious beauty is most rare,
  Unconscious art most true ;
The noblest works of artists are
  Those they unconscious do.

Who is the artist high ?   The wife,
  That her true mission knows,
To mould the poetry of life
  Out of its hard dull prose.

She never may have learnt the art
  Of song, or sketch, at school ;
But all the same, out of her heart
  Shall well the beautiful.

The mere arrangement of a room
  Shall equal genius show
With works of Masters old, by whom
  The art lived long ago.

Give her a table, a few chairs,
  Some books, perhaps—no more,
With these few notes, she'll play off airs
  That Handel could not score.

The simplest forms of household toil
  Shall grow beneath her touch
To pictures—Raphaël in oil
  Or fresco made not such.

The true poetic gleam is there,
  The Orphic rhythm and ring ;
She makes the stones clasp hands in prayer,
  And cloistered silence sing.

The mystic beauty shed abroad
　　On all her work and way;
It is the beauty of her God,
　　Upon her night and day.

For God's own life within her beats,
　　And thrills from heart to face;
Her little life, His life repeats
　　Responsive, "grace for grace."

Oh ! daughter of Almighty God,
　　Thy birth and rank are high !
Thou art a Princess of the Blood— .
　　Seed royal of the sky !

And Priestess to the world around,
　　With white unsandalled feet;
Where'er thou walk'st is holy ground,
　　Where souls with God shall meet.

Let every work of household toil
　　In Lord Christ's name be done,
And the anointing holy oil
　　O'er all thy raiment run.

Till virtue from the very hem
　　Of thy white robe shall flow,
To make men touch with awe, and them
　　That touch be healed so.

Priestess of God ! let every breath
　　In prayer and praise arise;
Thy life the daily offering, death
　　Thy evening sacrifice.

To Mrs. Maxwell.

IRVINE, 8th July, 1870.

. . . We had a lovely "Service of Song." Nothing was awanting except yourselves. It passed like a pleasant midsummer night's dream, but has left, I hope, deep spiritual devotional impressions, and brought us nearer to the Holiest of all.

His letters toward the end of 1870 show that the cloud which was to descend on his life at the beginning of the following year, was already casting its shadow over him. In one of these he writes to a friend in Glasgow, who, with his two sisters, was mourning the death of their father, which had followed at a brief interval the death of their mother :—

IRVINE, 15th December, 1870.

I should have come in to see you ere now—you and your dear sisters in their fresh affliction ; but have brought home from London a weight of cold, on throat and voice, which I am not permitted, by going out, to run the risk of increasing. . . .

Of all the homes on earth the home where Christ most loved to visit and to tabernacle over-night, was that of a brother and two sisters, orphans too. . . . He usually came at the darkening, and when the night was darkest and the rain heaviest, was surest to come. " Behold He stands at the door and knocks !" Which of the three shall be the first to hear His voice and open the door? I am sure that all your torn hearts lie open more than ever, broken open by bereavement, to Him. May He enter them farther than ever with his softest and sweetest blessing of peace. . . .

You will recognize the enclosed.

Thy will be done.

'Twas with a garden time began—
The garden whence God drave the man,
'Tis with a garden time shall close—
The garden to which Christ brings those
That with Himself shall first have been
In that Gethsemane between,
That on the road from Eden lies,
When journeying to Paradise.

In Eden garden first man put,
When eating of forbidden fruit,
His own will 'gainst the will Divine,
He said, My will be done, not Thine.
In garden next, Gethsemane,
Has Christ redeemed the will, when He
His own will did to God's resign,
He said, Thy will be done not mine.

There is a garden third above
Where will is so absorbed in love,
That there, Thy will be done is said,
But mention none of ours is made.
O Garden fair from heaven descend,
That, as at first so in the end, .
God's will and man's will may be one,
Even so on earth Thy will be done.

To Mr. David M‘Cowan.

IRVINE, 19th December, 1870.

From London, after too much speaking, I brought home
such a weight of cold on chest and voice as made it harder
work to get through my communion and other services,

and left me no time to write (so as I wished to do) last week.

And so you are motherless. I know what it is, and can the rather sympathize with you. It is one of the few sorrows that are not less in reality than in anticipation. How often we fear without cause when we enter into the cloud. When once we are in, it is not, after all, so dark as we expected. But this can hardly be said of the cloud that stoops in mother's death and funeral. What love so strong and true and faithful as that of a mother to her son? "Can a woman forget her child and not compassionate her son?" And so what grief should bow down more heavily than that of one that mourneth for his mother? But if nature has put special emphasis on this grief, grace, for you, has put special emphasis on the consolation. For how thankful you must be that you had such a mother, and that you had her so long; and that she has "come to her grave in a good old age, like a shock of corn in his season;" and that, since all of us, sooner or later, as the wise woman said, "must needs die," she has been so long spared, to make her ripe for the sickle and meet for the inheritance, in the mellow lights of the autumn of life—and the ties that bound her to the world so gradually and imperceptibly loosened in advancing life, in order to her closer walk with God in the light at eventide, that, for her, death, when it came, should come as kindly and gently as might be, and with much of its bitterness already past. She had her work, her life-day's work, and many a good work upon Christ, I am sure, like the Mary who did what she could; and her work being done, and well done, and the night coming on, she went to her rest. "So giveth He His beloved sleep."

How often, earlier than you remember, has she hushed you to sleep in the cradle, and in the arms of the Good Shepherd of your youth; and now you have seen her laid to sleep in the dust, and in the arms of the Shepherd of her good old age, who was with her in crossing the dark valley to the heavenly fold, in crossing the Bridge of Sighs into the heavenly palaces ; and who is with her both above and beneath, for above she is with Christ in Paradise, and beneath she is "asleep in Jesus"—blessed sleep.   She is not dead but sleeping, and sleeping at the foot of the mystic ladder with the ascending and descending angels, till the morning break and she awake and say, This dreadful place also is the house of God.   It is the gate of heaven.

I have often wished to see again that cheerful, venerable face and form, that I remember so well coming through our church, and the beautiful stained light of your memorial window, on her way to that other church where we see no more through a glass darkly.   As she was *your* mother, I could not help feeling drawn to her almost as if she were my own.   .   .   .

How rapidly our younger friends and elder, our Melvilles and our mothers, from behind us and from before, are gathering there, and brothers too from our side.   Earth is growing poorer for us year by year, more and more treasure laying up for us in heaven.   We shall find them all again if we do not lose the way ourselves.   God grant that we may not. May he give us the orphan's promised guidance home— "When father and mother forsake me then the Lord will take me up."   "This God is our God for ever and ever. He will be our guide, even He, unto death."

"As one whom his mother comforteth," so God comforteth those He has made motherless.   They weaned us in our infancy from the "milk for babes," not to starve us, but to lead us up to stronger meat, from a lower to a higher kind of nourishment ; and so when He takes them themselves away, He weans us from the earthly to the heavenly, from the creature to Himself.   A man may be born again when

he is getting old. A man may be weaned again when he is getting old. Children at the weaning are said to be fretful and fractious ; but as children so weaned of their mother, when the mother's breast, so full of the milk of tenderness and love to the last—when the mother herself is taken away, we should "behave ourselves with quiet spirit and mild." I have just been thinking that something like that must be meant by Psalm cxxxi. 2.

Yes, we are getting older, and are now advanced to the front rank of the march and the battle of life, and face to face with the last enemy, the generation of fathers and mothers, that stood before us and between, being cut down. Let us be more glad at it than sorry. The night is further spent; the day is all the nearer at hand, "For we are saved by hope." Blessed changes that bring us near the unchanging !—partings that bring us near the meeting to part no more.

CHAPTER XII.

The Valley of the Shadow of Death.

THE cold with which Dr. Robertson returned from
London in the close of 1870, and to which reference is
made in the letters at the end of the preceding chapter,
proved severe and persistent.   But his unwillingness
to acknowledge himself disabled, or to disappoint any
one whom he had promised to serve, led him to disregard it.   During a severe January, he not only did his
own work, but kept every engagement he had made,
and even undertook additional duty.   He went to one
of the coldest upland districts of Ayrshire and delivered his lecture on Luther ; he consented to take
the place of a co-presbyter, who was ill, in presiding
at an ordination service in Cumnock, twenty-four
miles from Irvine, and in his hurry to catch the train
forgot to take either top-coat or plaid ; he returned to
the same place a week later to attend the funeral of
an old friend ; and he went to Paisley and spoke for
an hour to a crowded evening meeting.   No one who
heard him that night, when his rich sonorous voice

filled the hall, could have dreamed that he was suffering from a pleurisy of some weeks' standing. But so it was, and when the meeting was over the re-action came. He spent a sleepless night, but in the morning concealed his illness, and was allowed to walk to the station. He often said that he thought he would have died before he reached it.

When he returned home, his indomitable spirit had to yield and the doctor was called in. The gravity of the case was soon sufficiently apparent, and one of the most experienced practitioners in the county was called to consult with his young medical attendant, Dr. Dunlop. A week later, on Friday, February 17th, Professor George Buchanan was summoned in haste to operate for the removal of water from the chest. The operation brought him instant relief, and though his weakness was extreme he was full of gladness. On the day following he said that before Dr. Buchanan came it was only a question of hours, and that he was not greatly moved at the prospect of death; "but that," he added, "may have been partly due to the assurance I had that Buchanan would be able to relieve me." "Once too," he said, "I felt the joy of the thought of awakening to hear the blowing of the golden trumpets on the grand Easter morning."

On Sunday he told me that when he had finished his last service in London one of Dr. Edmond's elders said to him, "What a grand voice you have!" He replied, "It is a peculiarity of my voice that the longer I speak it gets into the better order. But," he continued, "when I had said that, something came over me, and I added, 'I must not be too proud of my voice, we cannot tell what may come to it.' Now, God knows I have never been proud, or boasted of my ministry. I have never felt that I had anything to be proud of, but wouldn't it be an awful thing if it should be found that my ministry, like my voice, had hollowness beneath it?"

When his brother was conducting evening prayer in the dining-room, I sat by William's bedside. He asked me if I had heard the Trinity bells. I said I had, and asked if he had been able to hear them. He wished he had. This led him to speak of his work and the possibility of his being taken from it. He said it was sad to think of leaving it half done, and feared that he had been able to go only a little way in what he believed to be the special work he had been called to do, viz., the solution of the question as to the true relation between religion and the fine arts—and that, if he were to die then, all that he had done in that direction would be lost, as there was no one to take up his work where he had left it and carry it on. He added, "one of the greatest comforts I have, lying here, is to remember the singing in our church."

On the following day he asked me to read Paul Gerhardt's hymn, "O sacred head once wounded." When I had done so and prayed at his request, he sent me to ask his sister to play on the organ, the music of the hymn I had been reading, and to follow

it with Luther's hymn—"a grand bracing hymn," he
called it. When the music ceased, I went up to his
room and saw that he had been deeply moved.
He said, "I have come through the deepest depths,
but nothing has ever really moved me, till I heard
the first few notes of that passion chorale. They
fairly dissolved me into tears." He went on to say,
"It is by the greatest of all composers, Sebastian
Bach," and then, in words I cannot reproduce, proceeded to give an analysis of the music, in which
he found a representation of the mystery of redemption
—"twisted harmonies resolved," and "seeming confusion rising into order and passing into strains of
triumph."

Then days of uncertainty passed. Now he would
be bright and cheerful, and anon weary and depressed.
A week after the day on which he heard the passion
chorale, he was greatly distressed, till a change of
posture gave him temporary relief, and he said, "I
feel as if I were in the old world again." Then after
a pause, "It is good to be here, but to depart and be
with Christ is far better." Reference was made to his
sermon on that "Strait betwixt two." "Yes," he said,
"I have often preached it, and on the text, 'For
to me to live is Christ, and to die is gain;' I believed
every word of that sermon. On looking back on my
ministry, I cannot charge myself with having ever
uttered a word from the pulpit which I did not believe,
and I never spoke what was frivolous. If I were to
express in one word what has been the great aim of

my ministry, it would be this—to lead all the human race to cry, 'O Lamb of God, who takest away the sin of the world, have mercy upon us.' I never cared to reckon up conversions by arithmetic, I have been willing to do my work and to leave the results of it to God."

On the whole he seemed to be losing ground. As there was a complication requiring surgical aid, Professor Buchanan, with the most ungrudging kind- ness, travelled to Irvine every other day to see him. On one of these visits he pronounced that the case seemed hopeless, and that the end could not be dis- tant. After he had gone, Dr. Robertson sent for me, and when I went into the room he said, "So I have got my doom." He asked me to sit by him, and pro- ceeded with perfect calmness to set his house in order, giving me charges about his sister, about his manu- scripts, about everything that it was needful to arrange for. He then passed on to speak of his hope for the future, and with deepest humility, confessed his un- faltering confidence in Christ, and asked me to pray. When I had risen from prayer, he said, with a smile that reminded me of the old days of his health and gladness—"Well, we have got all that arranged, but I'm not going to die a bit. I am determined to cheat Buchanan yet!"

And he set himself resolutely to do battle with the grim adversary who had seemed so near his victory. On the morning of the day when Professor Buchanan was next expected, he asked me if I would go to meet him ; and then after a pause, " Do you think it right to tell a man that he is certainly dying ? " and went on to say that he entirely disapproved of doing so, that it was apt to demoralize, and that preparation for death, made in the panic produced by such an announcement was valueless. I understood him to mean that I was to ask Dr. Buchanan not to say anything further to discourage him in the hard fight for life he was resolved to make.

It was a hard fight indeed, and lasted through weary weeks. A second operation was needed; bronchitis began in the hitherto sound lung, and on account of a persistent east wind refused to yield to treatment. For a second time hope seemed to fail, till one evening Dr. Dunlop said, as he left the sick room, " There are signs of mending to-night." Leading me to the front door, he bade me listen to the sound of the sea in the bay, and said, " We never have that sound with an east wind. The wind has changed into the west, and already I can detect relief in his chest." When I told Robertson what the doctor had said, he was greatly interested, and spoke of the wind that bloweth where it listeth, the emblem of the great Divine healing power.

From that evening he began to recover. It was a toilsome journey up from the depths to which he had gone down, but he made it patiently and with growing cheerfulness. As he himself put it, he had said " I shall not die but live," and he reckoned that the work given him to do was to recover strength. By the beginning of May he was able to change his room, and by the end of that month he could walk with help into the study.

In July he was removed to Pitlochrie, and in September migrated to Brighton, attracted to that special southern resort by the fact that his former co-presbyter, Dr. Hamilton, was a Presbyterian minister there. But a further migration was necessary, and at the end of October he and his sister, Isabella, went to Mentone, where arrangements were made for their spending the winter, the necessary funds being provided by the spontaneous liberality of the members of his congregation.

To that congregation he wrote, in his enforced exile, a succession of pastoral letters, which were printed for private circulation. From these, extracts will be made as our narrative proceeds.

To His Congregation.

MENTONE, FRANCE, 2nd January, 1872.

. . . I could not longer delay writing, being moved to it partly by the feeling of returning health, which grows stronger upon me than hitherto, and seems to promise a complete recovery, and comfortable return to my beloved friends and work, so soon, at least, as the winter is past and the rain and snow over and gone, and sooner, I hope, than you seem to expect ; and partly have I been moved by the return of another new year, and the sacred and touching memories it brings along with it. For round that cape, at the turn of the year, when we have doubled the lowest point of winter, and set sail back toward summer, how many ships of memory come floating, freighted with most precious remembrance of the living and the dead ! The opening of our new church, the opening of my ministry among you in the old one, the issues of that ministry to you and me, in *Time*, whose accounts are not yet closed, and to so many in *Eternity*, whose books of life are shut and sealed till the judgment be set and the books opened. So many to whom I was ordained pastor, have gone on before us to the everlasting habitation ! I knew not when my life was trembling in the balance—when I was down at the dark cypress gates and seemed to have glimpses of those within—I knew not whether I belonged more to them or to you—whether more white hands beckoned me to go on, or to stay. But by God's good pleasure I continue to this day with the surviving church, and greet you now across the distance with the salutation of "A Happy New Year." If I am still spared to return to you, as I hope soon, dear brethren, shall I not have to preach to you, more earnestly and affectionately than before, the same old blessed truth as it is in Jesus, which only shows the brighter and shines the more through affliction, as fine gold tried in the fire? Meantime I can always be present with you in spirit in the holy hours of Sabbath worship; and how often, on other days of the week, I find myself still visiting about among the homes of the church, and especially where, as I understand, sickness and sorrow have been seeking admittance for that Healer of the heart who stands at the door and knocks ; and where death has been wreathing a crown of glory round the hoary head, and making young life and loveliness immortal, and gathering to the Good Shepherd dear little infant lambs, some of whom, though of my own flock, I have never seen, but we shall see them in the land that is "bright, bright as day." . . .

The following letter was written to a young minister about to be ordained at Dollar. He was the son of one of the Irvine elders; and, being the first whom Robertson baptized, he had received, in accordance with Scottish custom, the minister's name.

To the REV. W. B. R. WILSON.

MENTONE, FRANCE, 17th Jan., 1872.

. . . Rare delight it would have been to me to have reached forth again the same hand stretched over you in infancy, together with those of other brethren, over your down-bowed head, when you were kneeling to receive the ordination of the Presbytery. But this is not permitted me; only in spirit can I from this distance be present with you. But present or absent no one will pray more earnestly than he who, so many years ago, baptized you with water, that now, for all the purposes and offices of His holy ministry, One who is infinitely greater than us all would baptize you with the Holy Ghost and with fire!

I am glad that you have chosen Dollar, Dollar having first had the wisdom to choose you. "The lines," I should say, "have fallen to you in pleasant places"—in a country town far enough, yet not too far, from the cities. I used to think (when looking at it through the eyes of childish romance from the heights above Bannockburn) that the garden of Scotland, not to say of Eden, lay somewhere along the sunny side of the Ochils to Dollar eastward, and that the flocks in summer evenings on those hills were tended by the veritable "shepherds of the Delectable Mountains."

. . . I have always counted Dollar about the choicest of the little towns that nestle in the shelter of that north wall of hills. A slumbrous, academical air, too, seemed to me (as in our own quiet Irvine) to overlie the town, which is of a more classical build than its neighbours to the right and left. This atmosphere must be more congenial to a thoughtful mind than the rush and roar of cities. Of course I do not mean that you will ever "take things easy" in your ministry. You have too much of earnestness, of faithfulness, of hard work in you ever to turn Castle Campbell into a Castle of Indolence, or become a lotus eater on the banks of the Devon. Some may tell you to take warning from me and not work too hard. I say nothing of the sort. I would work harder than ever if I had opportunity, only I would balance and divide my work more wisely. I would dread far less the rebuke to a rash servant who has "a zeal" for work "not according to knowledge," than the doom of the wicked and slothful one. . . .

His residence at Mentone was brightened by the presence there of his old friends, Mrs. Walter Crum of Thornliebank and her daughter, Miss Crum, with (for a time) her son-in-law and his wife, Dr. and Mrs. Watson of Largs.

To Miss Crum.

GRAND HOTEL, MENTONE [Spring of 1872].

After you left us on Sunday (perhaps because of your leaving, for you brought much sunshine with you, if you did not take it away), I caught a little cold, the worst of which, the only bad effect indeed, is that it has prevented my coming to you yesterday and also to-day. For, besides inquiring for you all, I would like to learn what you may have heard of the farewell of Dr. Macleod Campbell. The life of such a man has been eloquent, though his death may have been dumb. But, perhaps, it was permitted to him to "go on and talk" to his beloved daughters as Elijah to Elisha, till the chariot and horses came, and even then, as he took his seat and dropped his mantle, and began to see and hear the things "unutterable" "God hath prepared for them that love Him," to go on repeating with the lips of a new life, "God is love." To him, in any case, death cannot have been death, but only the shadow of life, as suffering is the shadow of God's hand, as darkness and doubt (of which we spoke) are—are they not?—"the shadow of His wing." If only the angel of His presence shall carry the children home in His bosom, may it not be best for them, and make them cling closer to Himself, that they be haunted with doubts and dreads, and made to sob their very hearts out upon His breast, covered not crushed, hidden not harmed by the "shadow of His wing." "What *I* do (should it not be enough for us that it is *He* that does it?) thou knowest not now, but thou shalt know hereafter." The thing must be done and suffered, like Peter's feet-washing, before it is explained. From the height of that "Hereafter," side by side with Himself, another friend is looking back now! A landscape is best seen, looking in the same direction with the sun. May we too climb to see it so! "Then shall we know;" for this life, broken off from its immortal whole, has no meaning—like a fragment broken off from a statue—like a few bars cut out of the best piece of music. For the anthem, in its movement through the earthly bars, is full of minor passages and discords imperfectly resolved; but to him who hears it further on, these shall only bring in, with a richer harmony of all chords on the original key, the chorus and refrain of "God is love." And well for him that can seize (as Dr. Campbell did) on that governing key and keep it in sight and recognize its presence, though unheard, all through the music, through the most shattering discords and departures out of it. He has found that which gives it all a unity and meaning and interprets to his heart (if it should not be to his understanding, in technical terms of flats and sharps), what seems to others mere chaos and confusion of noise ; and if he too lose it for a little while, though never altogether, shall not this only bring it back more grandly, more sonorously, when it returns—when the golden morning breaks with a chorus of all voices singing, " God is love ! "

I must not write more, lest I write you a letter—a pleasure which is still forbidden fruit to me in this garden of idleness. I only wanted to enclose you the lines I will add on the other side, and though when reduced to writing they may seem little worth enough, yet the thought I am sure is a good one and true, and if they please you, that is something.

The lines accompanying this letter were the following :—

Chiaroscuro.

The superstitious darkness take
    To be of all things head and chief,
And ignorance the mother make
    Of all devotion and belief.

To sceptics truth is what is plain,
    What they can clearly see all round ;
They make their little three-inch brain
    Gauge of all mysteries profound.

But not the dark, but not the clear,
    Can be the measure of the true ;
Nor night, nor noon, is given us here,
    But chiaroscuro 'twixt the two ;

Which to the good is dawn of heaven
That brightens to the perfect light,
But to the bad a dusk of even
That darkens to eternal night.

To His Congregation.

MENTONE, 15th March, 1872.

.   .   .   And this Mentone is a very excellent con
valescent home—a harbour for disabled vessels, most
commodious to winter in.   Walled all round on three
sides—west, north, and east—by a double range of mountains, through which no valley cuts a passage for the wind,
it is effectually screened, in God's kind providence, from all
western mistrals, northern glacials, and eastern Euroclydons,
such as that which wrecked the ship of Alexandria which had
St. Paul aboard.   The space thus enclosed—a semi-circular
or crescent area, some seven miles in diameter, with the
old Mentone town built along a ridge in the centre, and
dividing the bay into two—is, in truth, a large natural
greenery, with a purely southern exposure, on whose broad
south wall, sloping from the grey mountains down to the
blue sea, are spread in tropical luxuriance, and more than
tropical variety, the flowers and the trees.   .   .   .
Amid such trees of Oriental mould and of Judean growth,
rich and fragrant with Scriptural and sacred associations, as
I wander in this genial climate seeking health and finding
it, one can scarcely fail to hear the voice of the Lord God
walking among the trees in the garden ; and if sometimes
it seems to chide and say, " What dost thou here, standing
all day idle, for there is a vineyard to be cultivated elsewhere, and barren fig trees in it too, perhaps ?" yet oftener
I seem to hear the voice speaking good, comfortable words,
and saying, " I, the Lord, do keep it ; I will water it every

moment, lest any hurt it! I will keep it night and day;"
and " Rest thou in the Lord; wait patiently for His time
for thy returning. Do not fret." . . .

The following verses were given to Mrs. Watson
and Miss Crum at Mentone :—

" Et Darkens ere the Dawning."

It darkens ere the dawning
   More than in all the night,
Earth's shadows stretch an awning
   Across the doors of light;
O'er the horizon nearest
   Lie balanced light and shade,
And when the light is clearest
   The dark is darkest made.

It darkens to the dying,
   As ne'er in life before,
The shadows blackest lying
   About the heavenly door;
The heavenly light sheds glances
   On pilgrims' eyes afar,
But he finds who advances
   How dark the shadows are.

" No light" from lamp or casement.
   " No light " here can you see,
Dear child! what sore amazement
   Of darkness fell on thee,
That holy autumn morning,
   Till dawn of glory pours
Round thy white brow, adorning
   Another morn than ours !

Our light's a veil that hides us,
  And hides all from our sight.
It none the less divides us
  Although the veil be white ;
And what, when life is ending,
  When heart and eye-sight fail,
Is darkness but the rending
  Of this dividing veil?

Not so, through veils, God sees us,
  But by immediate sight,
And those in heaven with Jesus
  See too, in God's own light ;
"Know as they're known," asunder
  Is every veil withdrawn,
And now they cease to wonder
  It darkened ere the dawn.

Returning to God.

"They have forsaken me."
"All is vanity."
"When he came to himself he said, I will arise and go to my Father.'

To Thee my God returning,
  I to myself came first,
And found within me burning
  Such quenchless fire of thirst,
That I must seek Thee rather
  Than perish, thirsting so :
Then said I, "To my Father
  I will arise and go."

Away from Thee, the fountain
  Of living waters deep,
I hewed me in the mountain
  A cistern, rain to keep ;

The cloud came, and I caught her,
   And her moist garments wrung,
Yet found no drop of water
   To cool my parched tongue.

Blest are the discontented
   That evermore desire!
Blest are the souls tormented
   In that ascending fire:
From God himself asunder
   They cannot long remain,
For nothing else and under
   Can ever heal their pain.

CHAPTER XIII.

Hope Deferred.

As the spring of 1872 advanced it became evident that the hope of returning to work in May, by which Dr. Robertson had been upborne during the long winter, was not to be fulfilled. Acting under the advice of Dr. Drummond, then practising in Nice, he escaped from the heat of the Riviera to Lake Como. In the Villa Serbelloni at Bellagio, he spent the earlier half of summer, finding in the change of scene and in the marvellous beauty of his new surroundings, some measure of solace from the disappointment which came to him when he was forbidden to return to Scotland.

The following extracts from a rhyming letter, written to the sister of his friend, Dr. John Brown, introduce us to the surroundings amid which he now found himself, and reveal the thoughts, graver and more gay, which were passing through his mind :—

To Miss Brown.

My dear friend and Isabella's,
Though I'm not yet quite so well as
   I expected by this time,
Here I write *at length* a letter,
And the tandem may run better
   In the leathery trace of rhyme.

   .   .   .   .

Now the omnibus *adagio*
Climbs the steep above Bellagio,
Starting at good trotting pace
From the steamboat landing place
To a stiffer slope of hill, a
Short way past Frizzoni Villa ;
Turning then by north to east,
Past the church where the old priest,
In his black skull cap and surtout,
Looks with his great dark eyes at you,
Taking for his health of body
(If not also of his soul)
Not a go or two of toddy,
Like priests nearer to the pole,
But (much better on the whole)
Evening exercise, *al fresco*,
Walking to and fro before
The old church's romanesque (oh
What a poor style !) west front door ;
Square flat, with round windows o'er,
'Neath his Campanile bells,
That hang like inverted wells,
With their round mouths gaping down
On the little red-tiled town,—
Ready each with iron tongue,

From the brazen larynx hung,
Vibrating when it is swung,
Noisy torrents forth to pour,
Every half or quarter hour,
To baptize the district round,
And to shield it so from evil,
From the Turk and from the devil,
Who, as monarch of the air,
Made them to put bells up there,—
Four bells in a turret square,
And one deep-toned great bell under,
Rolling its baptized thunder
With the lighter sprinkling chimes,
Ringing at all sorts of times,
To dislodge the fiend unholy.
See ! the ringers mount the stair ;
Ring them softly, ring them slowly !
Ring them faster, ring them freely !
From the old square Campanile.

But the devil and his works
Being little worse than the Turks,
That is—brave old Paynim (oh no !)—
They are infidels that swear
Now-a-days by Döllinger,
'Gainst the blessed Pio Nono.
So 'gainst Protestants like us,
Rumbling past in the omnibus,
Each mouth must needs wag its tongue
To dissolve the baneful spell
That our presence carries.   Well,
Anyway, the bells are ringing,
Oh, how sweet in the evening air !
Strokes for the hour, and chimes for prayer,

Six for the time, and a sweet-toned chime,
Prettily called an Angelus.

Ring out under the great blue dome,
Answer from Trinity bells at home.
Up and out of your prayer-house small,
Up to the roof and out over the wall.
Up to the roof must Saint Peter go,
Praying while dinner's cooked below ;
There shall he learn to slay and eat
Out of the great four-cornered sheet ;
There shall he see each party wall,
Builded so high with stones so small—
Builded by his sect, and by all,
Topple and crumble, and crash and fall.
Then from the roof of his church at Rome,
Shall he stretch his hands forth meeting
Ours, that shall return the greeting.
Each shall find the dome too small—
Roman Saint Peter and London Saint Paul.
Only the world with dome of air
Can assemble all to prayer,
By the church bells ringing there—
Silver bells for the days in white,
Sombre golden bells for the night,
Like the four in the turret square,
Crosswise and lengthwise—two a pair,
Bright and dark, and dark and bright,
Or alternate in straight row,
That across the year doth go,
One for the day and one for the night ;
Day from day its answer bringing,
Night unto night its echo ringing,
David heard them sounding so,
Some three thousand years ago ;

And, still rung by unseen hands,
They are telling throughout all lands,
(Blessed is he that understands)
Men should lift up hands in prayer,
Holy, and always, and everywhere,
" For Heaven will hear if men will call
As the blue sky bendeth over all."

From the high and narrow street,
Where the two sides almost meet,
Narrower lanes and wider go,
Crosswise to the lake below—
Lanes that lengthen out the more
As you leave the line of shore,
Lengthening from the angle sharp,
Like the strings upon a harp,
To that low lane steep and stony,
Which, if you have missed your seat,
You must climb with weary feet,
To the gates of Serbelloni.

A big portress keeps the key,
On a little salary.
She, or else her youthful mate
(She ran off with him of late),
Always, or by turns, must wait,
To enclose or shut the gate.
And to keep well free of starving,
As their salary's not great,
They sell wood ('tis olive) carving,
Done by his young henpecked hands.
The bazaar-like table stands
Up a few steps near the arches,
Covered with its wooden gold,
Of which they make double profit,

Since, if you buy any of it,
Both the wood and you are sold !
Then at tinkle, tinkle small,
Scarcely heard, if heard at all,
Forth, like grenadier, she marches,
Should'ring the great iron key ;
As Saint Peter's wife, when he
Otherwise engaged may be,
Hears the tinkling silver bell,
Whose dear sound he knows so well,
Clink, clink, in the money box,
To pay up the ransom high
Of poor souls in Purgatory.

He sends her forth, and she unlocks
(For poor scorched souls, in a trice)
The cool gates of Paradise.
But not for heretics like us,
Come straight up from earthly ice,
With our wickedness and vice
Not burnt out of us, and so,
Thinking in our robes of snow
Through the blessed gates to go,
Whether in a Free Church fly,
With its blinded windows high,
Or, with open windows thus,
In a Broad Church omnibus.

Broad Church !   I confess that I
Am a Broad Churchman ; and why
" Broad " may not be also " High "
In artistic culture, and
Sound and orthodox withal,
Thoroughly " Evangelical,"
I can never understand.

I have no faith in the juggling tricks
Practised by Roman Catholics,
Who "hocus pocus" the holy bread,
And kindle fires beneath the dead,
Which, whatever the grate may hold,
Yield good ashes of silver and gold
From the flames outside painted red.

I don't believe in pardons sold,
And salvation by wafers made
Every morning at mass, and laid
All by the priest on the people's lips,
Betwixt his thumb and his finger's tips,
Like sixpences made and with sixpences paid ;
And the poor soul, having paid the fees,
Passes, with one or two of these
Stuck 'twixt his marble close-pressed lips,
On through the dark detective grave,
Where they unmask the priest as a knave,
Whose design was neither to save
The poor man's soul nor his sixpences.

I do not believe in those who mix
Tinsel with gold and truth with tricks,
In the Church of the Roman Catholics ;
But I do believe in one Living, Broad,
Holy, Catholic Church of God,
Where there is neither bond nor free,
Primate nor priest nor plain U.P.,
Open prayer nor liturgy ;
But in the Church they all are one,
Who one Father, through one Son,
By one Spirit, seek in prayer,
And, as brothers of one Brother,
Worship *Him*, and love each other :

And it matters nothing where,
Whether in a barn of bricks
Or a cloistered aisle with a crucifix,
If only, under the dome of love,
Wide as the blue heavens above,
Ring the bells, and the bells reply—
" Earth is Broad, and Heaven is High,
In the Church of the Holy Trinity."

Think ye not when the bells are rung
And the grand " Venite " sung
In the temple courts below,
Thousands all in white shall spring
Out from the cloistered shades, to sing
" Exultemus Domino " ?
Think you not when the trumpet's thunder,
Shatt'ring, rends all tombs asunder,
That from vaulted crypt, from under
Chancel aisle and minster floor,
Pav'd with broken tombstones o'er ;
From beneath the crosses seen
Planted thick on the churchyard green ;
From beneath the ruins hoary
Of old monastery and cell,
Where last morn the matin bell
Found the sleepless saint still slowly,
Through profoundest melancholy,
Toiling after peace and holy
Conquest over sin and hell,
Where the softened morning-ringing
Drew the crowd of pilgrims, singing,
Up the hill with its seven stations,
To the cross, 'twixt walls of stone
Frescoed o'er with gospel story,
And the Christ, in golden glory,

As Redeemer of the nations,
Sitting, crowned upon a throne,
Worshipped in this mute evangel
By long lines of saint and angel,
Out of which there always rose a
Gentle " Mater Dolorosa " :
Pictures preached when priests were dumb,
And the singing pilgrims come,
" Veni, Redemptor Gentium " !
While the listening veiled maiden,
With some early sorrow laden,
Looks up through her lattice lonely,
Looks, I hope, to " Jesus only ":
Now they sleep in the vaults below,
And the bells are silenced long ago—
Think you not, when the shatt'ring thunder,
Rending sepulchres asunder,
Brings up all things hidden under,
That from their old buried places,
From their dark forgotten slumber,
Multitudes that none can number,
Visions of sweet angel faces,
Bearing on their furrows traces
Of sore weeping, forms still clasping
White hands as of old, but grasping
Now a golden lyre between,
And a victor's palm branch green—
Think you not that crowds on crowds,
Faces white, in golden clouds
Shall float up into the light,
To Jerusalem the Golden,
To that dear loved Lamb in white,
Whose red cross they long had pressed,
In unutterable sadness,

To their bruised and throbbing breast,
Finding peace, but never gladness,
For the much rain in the night,
And because their eyes were holden
That they could not see Him right ?

Now they do, and, thank God, never
Shall they cease to see Him more,
As they spread alongst the river,
On the green and golden shore,
And in widening circles round ;
Whilst from Horeb caves afar,
Those that have been fretting ever
That so few are faithful found,
Shall look forth amazed to see
What vast multitudes there are
That have never bowed the knee
Unto Baal on Romish ground,
Nor have even like them (so sound)
Bowed to Baals of Bigotry,
And the Moloch, Reprobation,
And impossible Salvation—
Made so by divine decree,
Save to those few, two or three,
Who believe in their creation
To the peerage, and the station
Of church aristocracy.

But these are after thoughts, and not
Being uttered on the spot,
For this, and another reason,
That they come 'twixt bits of laughter
Both before, and also after,
As things serious shouldn't do,

You may think them out of season,
And I rather think so too !
.   .   .   .   .   .

Out now on the terrace bold,
Ere the day melts down its gold,
Orange rocks above the trees
And pale yellow cottages,
Sprinkled over fell and wold—
The dark purple of the hills,
Broken with white crests of snow,
And red granite bands below,
Over which the silver rills
And white tumbling cascades flow,
Shading thro' breadths of tender green,
Over which soft sunlights low
With a clear soft brightness go,
To the white line of the lake,
Where small crested ripples break
Under walls of rocks and trees,
Saffron villages between,
With white churches high o'er these,
Up black cypressed terraces.
The upward slopes, inverted, seem
Mirrored in the crystal green,
Where, like huge unweildy boat,
The dark mountains seem to float
On aërial depths, that go
Fathomless down to the skies below,
And in sharp-cut outlines show
Jagged points and winding bays,
Round the green lake now ablaze, ·
Like the jasper sea in the holy dream,
With softened tinted lights that gleam
With white sails of tiny barks,

Flitting betwixt lights and darks,
All with scarlet awning hung
O'er some would-be mermaid young,
That with graceful hands doth steer,
To her singing gondolier,
In to the black shade in shore,
From the clear enamelled lake,
With bright fairy streaks that break
The mosaic picture wrought,
Delicate as maiden thought,
That doth softly come and go
As it listeth, to and fro,
Toned down in its tinting so,
One scarce knows what it has been ;
Or like colours I have seen
Glancing betwixt lights and darks
On the church walls of Saint Mark's ;
Or the necks of the doves that flock
Thither by the minster clock
Daily at the stroke of two,
To be fed there—thousands do—
And, alighted in the square,
In the shades and sunlights there,
Gleam in every rainbow hue ;
While their softly murmured coo,
Which in thousands they repeat,
Floats in wavelets to your feet,
As you walk in the piazza,
And with that soft murmur adds a
Likeness more unto the lake,
Where the waves mere ripples make
That so softly shoreward break.

· — · — · — · — · ; — · — ·

The letter from which extracts are now to be

given is a continuation of one begun in pencil at
Serbelloni.

To the Rev. James Brown.

St. Moritz, Ober Engadine, 29th July, 1872.

Having got thus far in the footpath of a pencil note, I
lost my way and stuck, instead of getting out at last, as now,
into the king's highway of pen and ink. The fact is I have
not been quite so well, and the above, which I send as I
began it, was written in bed, to which I was shut down for
a few days, and where I did not get opportunity to finish it.
I did not care to write you, either, till I could say that I was
quite better, and this I can now truly say, but not till now.
Somehow, when I was finishing (as I did abruptly) that
letter you were rehearsing in the vestry on the congregational meeting night, some not very pleasant symptoms
returned upon me. But as Isabella had to go to Milan to
get some preparation made for a longer tack of this Continental life, of course I went too, and enjoyed it very well,
and thought myself all right again (only the heat was dreadful). But Dr. Drummond, on his way to this St. Moritz,
found me in Milan quite unexpectedly, and sent me, sooner
perhaps than I otherwise would, back to Serbelloni, to
which he followed in another day himself, with his family;
and then he sent me to bed for a good while, whence, as I
said, I began the above by stealth, Isabella always keeping
most loving, faithful, and stern watch lest I should show
any symptoms of that distemper of which I have been too
well cured—the *Cacoethes scribendi.* Then as soon as I
was able to be well up again, Dr. Drummond found it was
too hot for us all at Bellagio, and had us off to this St.
Moritz on Friday fortnight. I reached it lively enough
(who would not be enlivened by such wonderful scenery,
though otherwise three-quarters dead), yet groaning a little

by the way. But if Bellagio was too hot, this is certainly cold enough. No wonder I had difficulty in breathing. The doctor himself and several others complained of the same. As for me, I was, the next day after, dismissed to bed and smothered up in a snowstorm of pillows and bed-clothes, that has now thawed and melted down, and I have again got my head above water.

But enough, and more than enough of *meeself* (as I may say after Dr. W. A., seeing the me is a "W. B."). An English clergyman was telling me a little ago he had gone to Glasgow to hear, and did hear the two greatest men to his view in it, viz., Dr. Anderson and Dr. Macleod. Alas, Norman ! Your character of him is very just. Except your miniature and Dr. W. Smith's prayer, I have seen nothing about him, except also a newspaper extract of sermons and of Strahan's (is'nt it good ?) in the *Contemporary*. And I suppose Glasgow goes on much the same without him ; and there is not a laugh the less, that his broad genial laughter is gone out. . . .

They don't need to salt beef here. It is preserved through being dried in the mountain air, and in that sense I also, that is the flesh of me, may get *cured*. . . . The hope of getting home for a few weeks has been almost wholly driven out of me, by the weight of your arguments on the other side, and by the falling (though but a few degrees) of the mercury in the barometer of my health, which, how-ever, is on the rise again, steadily I hope, and the index now pointing at "set fair." Where to migrate to as the cold weather comes back I have left entirely an open question. Only it might be over-doing the Nice and Mentone district to return there for the winter. One drowsy six months, I should say, is enough of that, for all medical as well as other (*e.g.*, mental improvement and economical) purposes. Living here is rather high, as beseems an elevation of 6,000 feet, covered with silver snow and sunshine by day, and golden Alpine after-glow and stars by night, that make the skies look very blue ! . . . As I write this in a clinical position, Dr. Drummond comes in and surprises me at it. He has ordered me to shut up, and will allow me to write no letter, except a love letter. So I have told him this is one, and so it is.

One at least of the difficulties in the way of a continued residence abroad was removed by the liberality of Dr. Robertson's friends. As soon as it was known that he could not return to duty in the summer of 1872, consultation took place among them ; and, during the meetings of the Synod in Edinburgh in May, some gentlemen met at dinner, on the invitation of Sir Peter Coats, and it was then formally resolved to present Dr. Robertson with a testimonial. So heartily was the matter gone into, that, before the guests had left the table, the sum of £1,050 had been promised by five subscribers. Before the autumn was far advanced, Mr. David M'Cowan was able to write to Dr. Robertson a letter, from which two paragraphs are here given, with extracts from Dr. Robertson's reply :—

GLASGOW, 27th August, 1872.

It is no breach of confidence to tell you that at the meeting referred to, all those present were of opinion that it would be quite unworthy to offer you less than £4,000. The result has shown that they did not miscalculate the feelings and the wishes of others with whom they had afterwards necessarily to enter into communication. For it is now my privilege to inform you that the gifts with which they have been intrusted, and of which I have now formally to ask your acceptance, amount to five thousand guineas.

It is also my good fortune to be able to assure you, that nothing of the kind could possibly have been prosecuted with more comfort and less ado. The preliminary circular usual on such occasions was entirely avoided. Every one was more ready with his gift than another, and thus to testify his warm interest in one whom so many regard, and with whom, in his affliction, they deeply sympathize. If any error was committed at all, it was in not giving a wider circle an opportunity of sharing in a deed which has given so much delight to those who performed it.

To Mr. David M'Cowan.

ST. MORITZ, ENGADINE, 13th September, 1872.

Most thankfully do I hereby acknowledge receipt of yours of the 27th ultimo, announcing to me the completed "ingathering" of a singularly rich testimonial of love and sympathy, amounting to five thousand guineas, and of which, in the name of the committee and subscribers, you " formally " ask my acceptance.

It is a golden harvest that has been ripening, it seems, under your skilful cultivation, during these last summer months, and which you have now reaped and garnered for me in the autumn of the year (and the autumn of my life), to make provision against what winter I may yet be spared to see.

In formally accepting of the testimonial, which you have, in such kind and beautiful words, presented—as now, across the distance that divides us, I do accept of it, with this right hand, into which, as I write, all my heart is throbbing— I feel (as you have done in asking my acceptance) that

S

mere formal words cannot utter all that is meant betwixt us. "New wine" needs "new bottles"; and as, when one is quite full, you cannot empty it by turning it suddenly over, so I have been sitting, with your letter in my hands, for I shall not say how long, not knowing at all what answer to make. It has marked an epoch in my life that I had never expected to see—an "Ebenezer" and memorial pillar on this side that long "bridge of sighs" over which, in my sickness and exile, I have been travelling, and to which, as to other mercies which you also entreat for me, God in His great goodness has spared me, and, by a way that I know not, softly and gently guided me on.

I need hardly say that the value of the gift, in itself so high, is greatly enhanced by the friendship—to me so precious—and loving sympathy, so deep and widely spread, of which it is the symbol and the proof. Had it come to me by inheritance, or even by honest toil, I could not have prized it so highly as when coming, as it does, not from the cold hands of legal right, but from the warm heart of Christian love. To me more precious than all honey-combs of golden treasure on earth is, of course, or ought to be, that "good name that is better than great riches," which you encourage me to seek after and strive to maintain, by writing it out—small enough in my case as it is—in such large letters of silver and gold. But not less precious is the pleasure, or, as I must say, the pride, of numbering among friends of mine such and so many truly Christian gentlemen —not only "righteous" men that "do justly," but "good" men that do much more. They have wrought a "good work" on one of the lowliest of the members of that Body whose Head is in heaven—that Church which is in earth and heaven both—down with whose feet on earth, in the dust, I have meantime been cast, torn, wayworn, and weary, and you have come and bound up the wounds and bathed them and anointed them with kindness, and I do pray that I may be so counted one of His, that He may say unto you, " You have done it unto Me."

It was decided that Dr. Robertson should spend his second winter of exile in Florence. His medical advisers believed that the *tramontane* and other climatic drawbacks on the banks of the Arno, would be more than counterbalanced by the mental enjoyment which so earnest a lover of sacred art would find in the city of Giotto and Michel Angelo.

To His Congregation.

FLORENCE, ITALY, 14th November, 1872.

From Switzerland we have been driven southward, before the darkening winter, into Italy, and (not without prospect of being presently driven by the cold still further south) are at present in Tuscany, in the beautiful vale of the Arno—in Florence, the city of Savonarola—the prison of the Madiais— the fountain of modern Italian literature and art. . . . How differently Protestants are treated now in Italy from what they were used to in the Madiais' times. Not only Florence, Rome itself has emptied its convents by hundreds of the monks of the crucifix, and opened its gates to the ministers of the Cross. . . . About all this I hope to bring you home some full, correct, and interesting information, as well as concerning a church in the highest inhabited valley in Europe, the Grison Church (Protestant) in the Engadine, with which this summer I have become acquainted, which has been hidden (not a few of God's " hidden ones," I hope, amongst them) for centuries in the rock cliffs of the Alps beneath the glaciers—speaking an unknown tongue, unintelligible to all foreigners, and themselves to the rest of Christendom next to utterly unknown. . . .

FLORENCE, 31st December, 1873.

How many New-Years' themes have we thought upon together, as we walked and talked together down the five-and-twenty years and more. I can recall some of them, such as, "The changes of time working out the unchanging purposes of the Eternal;" "The mystery of this dark-bright life—its monotony, its misery, its majesty and meanness in contrast;" "The scripture solution of 'What is our life';" "The danger of missing the end God made us for;" "The question in profit and loss for the ledger on New-Year's Day, 'What shall it profit,' etc.;" "The shortness of the time, and the evanescence of the world" (how all things "come to pass"), and learning thence the fleeting nature of the phenomenal (objects of sight), and abiding nature of the real (objects of faith); "The acceptable year, and the closed book;" "The new man—making all things new," etc., etc.

Did not our hearts burn within us as He talked with us by the way, and opened to us the scriptures on our new-year Sabbath journey through a quarter of a century, till the shadows of evening began to gather round, and we besought him to

> "Abide with us when night is nigh,
> For without Thee we dare not die."

For evermore, I trust, the end of our conversation was (and yet shall be, please God) Jesus Christ—"the same yesterday, and to-day, and for ever." . . .

I well remember some faces in my audience in Irvine that shone with a beautiful light (though they wist not they were shining so), when, once, after trying (in vain, of course) to picture heaven, I paused and said, "There is only one preacher can show you what heaven is like; *he can*—his name is Death "—faces, ah ! shining now with a still sweeter lustre—on the mount, and in the vision of God—then they saw through a glass darkly, but *now* face to face. . . .

Spite of his continued bodily weakness, Dr. Robertson entered, even during his first winter's residence in Florence, on the congenial study of the history and art of the city, and ere the winter was ended had been recognized as one of the most competent guides to the churches and galleries. It was a great joy to him when any old friends, travelling in Italy, halted in Florence, and gave him the opportunity of making their stay there for ever memorable to them, by his unwearied attentions, and by the light, in which he enabled them, at every turn, to see what would have been hidden from them if they had wandered aimlessly, as so many travellers do, from church to church and from gallery to gallery. But he did not confine his attention to former friends. Many noted travellers sought and obtained introductions, and none who did so, failed to acknowledge the charm of his presence and discourse. To some of these, especially to younger members of the parties, their meeting with him marked an era in their intellectual and spiritual history. I have before me many letters in which the warmest testimony is borne to the enduring value of his teaching in the cloisters of Maria Novello and San Marco, and his other favourite haunts. Extracts from some of these, with rough notes of his talk will be given in a subsequent chapter.

As the spring advanced he made some excursions among the ancient cities of Tuscany. He visited Perugia and Assisi, the latter deeply interesting to him from its connection with St. Francis ; and made his first acquaintance with the Etruscan tombs, into the dark recesses of which it was his delight, on subsequent visits to Italy, to penetrate.

When the time for leaving Italy had arrived, it was a sore disappointment to Dr. Robertson that he was pronounced still unfit for work ; but though his homecoming, on June 24th, 1873, was not such as he had fondly hoped it would be, yet he came in great spirits. He was unable to preach, but his summer residence in Irvine was of much service to the congregation. As far as strength permitted he visited the people in their homes, in no case failing to go to those whom in their sorrows he had from the distance yearned to see, or to those who, in protracted sickness, had wearily watched for his coming. Nor did he fail, in the course of his visitation, to find, as of old, humorous incidents which served to lighten what, from its very nature, was necessarily a trying duty. He went to see one old man who had something on his mind which he could not unburden to any other than his minister. When they were alone the trouble was revealed. Some months before, being very weary, he had said his evening prayer without taking off his night-cap. The irreverent omission had weighed heavily on his conscience and he had failed to find comfort. It would have been easy of course to make light of the scrupulousness which magnified so slight a fault. But Dr. Robertson was wise enough to see that this expedient would not meet the case before him, and so he replied, "There are two ways of expressing reverence. We in the west uncover our heads, but eastern nations uncover their feet, as Moses, you remember, was bidden take off his shoes, for the place whereon he stood was holy ground. Both actions mean the same thing. They signify the shortening of the person in token of self-abasement before God. Now, if your feet were bare, there was no need that you should also uncover your head ; and I presume you had not on your shoes ? " " No," said the old man, rising up in bed with a sigh of relief, " No ; *nor my stockins neather.*" " Ah then," said the minister, "it is all right." " Oh, sir," was the reply, "I'm sae glad ; I was quite sure that when ye cam' back ye wud be able to pit it a' richt someway."

As the autumn advanced it became evident that an early migration was essential, if he was not to lose what he had gained, and, at the end of October, he started for Florence. A fondly cherished project, which was the subject of many letters to his friend, Mr. M'Cowan, that they should together visit Egypt and Palestine, could not be carried out. With the exception of the time devoted to a brief visit to Naples and Rome, he and his elder sister spent the winter in Florence.

To Rev. James Brown.

FLORENCE, 16th April, 1874.

. . . So here I am in Florence with prospect only of small excursions about till it is time to return home. . . . Meantime Florence is flooded with visitors who find me out, and, with the other friends I have made here, drag me, perhaps rather much, into the churches and galleries, and for the rest occupy my time, so that at nights I don't feel up to much study or letter-writing. And yet some of the friends I would not miss on any account. . . . To mention no other, Mrs. Oliphant has come out under commission from Macmillan to gather materials for a book on Dante, Angelo, and my friend Savonarola. I have been showing her over the haunts of "these three men"—the first three—during three days of this week.

18th April, 1874.

To-day I have been attending (among other wheres) at the Greek (Russian) Church, which holds its sittings, or rather its standings and prostrations (for they do not sit in their worship at all), in a hall in the court of our Palazzo, and have tried to interpret the service (which has much beauty in it) by a very little knowledge of Slavonic, by the help of Stanley (Eastern Church) and other books, and by that sympathy with Christianity in all its shapes and phases, which you will not condemn in me as too broad. The priest is rather a favourite friend of mine, and very pleasant men the deacon and reader. . . .

As the time for again returning to Scotland approached, a medical examination revealed the fact that Dr. Robertson was not yet fit for work, and that a further rest of at least two years was essential. At the same time intelligence from Irvine made it plain that, though the arrangements for temporary supply of the pulpit, first by Mr. James Orr, B.D. (now Dr. Orr of Hawick), and then by Mr. Matthew Muir Dickie, B.D., afterwards of Haddington, had been most satisfactory, it would not be wise, in view of the best interests of the congregation, that it should remain longer without a settled pastor. In these circumstances it was arranged that the necessary steps should be taken for the election of a colleague and successor, who should have the whole responsibility for work.

His fellow-student, the Rev. Dr. MacEwen, of Claremont Church, Glasgow, who had been his steadfast friend all through the years of their ministry, and who had gone to see him at the crisis of his illness—on the day on which Professor Buchanan performed the first operation—had himself fallen ill and been laid aside from duty. A revival of strength, which, alas, proved temporary, had enabled him to resume work.

To the Rev. Alex. MacEwen, D.D.

IRVINE, 29th October, 1874.

How glad I am to hear that you have returned to your work in perfect health and strength for the winter. Long may they be given you to be devoted to the great aim of life which you are still so steadily, so faithfully, so triumphantly pursuing !

As for me, I am still lagging behind with broken wind,

though not with broken will and purpose. Some day ere very long I hope to find myself as strong for work as ever or (as I am always somewhat *waik*, let us say) stronger.

I have dipped in the Jordan, and my flesh has come again as a little child's. I wish I could return like a lion from the swellings !..

How shall I forget the kindly light of your dark beaming eye that shone on me like a lamp when I seemed about to enter the dark doors ! Its powerful, eloquent, silent sympathy—there is nothing I remember more constantly, and had I died then I would have carried the remembrance far into other worlds.

The hope that he would be able to take part in the ordination of a colleague and successor, before again going abroad, kept Dr. Robertson in Scotland till the winter of 1874-5 had set in with full severity. Partly the risk of travelling in time of hard frost, and partly anxiety about the health of his elder sister, detained him still longer, till it ended in his spending the winter at home. During the earlier months he struggled as best he could to do visitation work at Irvine, but toward spring he was compelled to seek perfect rest at Bridge of Allan, which had become the home of his younger sister.

The summer which followed was shadowed by much sorrow. His sister's illness caused him increasing anxiety, and his old friend Dr. MacEwen was struck down in the mid-time of his days.

To Mrs. MacEwen.

Irvine, Wednesday, 9th June, 1875.

.   .   .   What noble work through grace he has been honoured to do. It seems quite impossible to see how his place is ever to be filled. The whole Church may well sympathize with you in your affliction, for her own grief is not unlike that of the widow and fatherless!

And what a warm, true, faithful, generous, friend he was, as I by many proofs well know, and—in the shadow of death that recalls them (as night recalls the stars), though they were never out of mind—most vividly remember. To me, from old acquaintanceship in early years, he stood a faithful friend in long-tried truth; and through the intimacy that I had with him—and that was never broken—from his great wealth of intellect, of learning, of Christian experience, my own life, I always felt was greatly enriched. I never knew any one like him for breadth and balance of character —for that exquisite symmetry and fulness of life that consti-tutes (on lower or on loftier scale) the "perfect" man—and his scale of life was a lofty one. His very presence gave a sense of power. I never knew which more to admire in him—the manly strength or the womanly tenderness, the sage gravity or the child-like cheerfulness, the classic dignity or the romantic geniality, the meditative or the active, the intensely devotional or the intensely practical. What was most to be admired was the union of the two in one har-monious whole of life, complete all round. It was no doubt this completeness or integrity of character—covering human life in all its breadth, and Christian experience in all its variety—which, with the lofty aims that he was ever steadily and strenuously pursuing, made him such a power for good in the Church and the community, and such a successful leader and king of men.   .   .   .

Another sorrow fell on him in the illness and death of one who had been, by her Christian character and her good works, a strength to the congregation.

To Mr. David M'Cowan.

Irvine, 26th August, 1875.

. . . Our loving and beloved Mrs. Brown is still with us, but "wearying, wearying," as she said to-night, "to be home." How sublimely simple her faith is—without all fear or doubt—not trusting to swim ashore on any raft of doctrine, or system of orthodoxy, or even on separate Scripture texts and promises, "boards and broken pieces of the ship," still less, least of all, not at all on any works or merits of her own, but clinging to the hand of "Jesus only," who has come to her over the waters of death, and bids her come to Him—to Him who gives the weary rest. "O Lamb of God, I come." She cannot be long outside the harbour, one would think. May she have an abundant entrance. As I left the house to-night late in the darkness under the trees, it was not difficult to imagine that the shining ones were waiting about the doors.

To Miss Kay, Cornhill, Biggar.

Irvine, 3rd September, 1875.

How I wish you had been with us here on the evening of the 1st inst., when, after the funeral on that day of that admirable Christian lady—one of the loveliest of God's daughters—whose death, as you know, drew me back and detained me here last week, there was held in the church one of our sweetest and holiest services of worship— what some might (ritualistically) call a choral funeral service

—what Dr. Begg would profanely call a mass or requiem—
but which the Apostle Paul would call a speaking to one
another, or "teaching and admonishing one another in
psalms, and hymns, and spiritual songs," and the record
of which is written in God's book of remembrance for us, I
trust, as those that fear the Lord, and speak often one to
another, so that we need not be ashamed of it when the
Judgment is set and the books are opened.

It began with a prayer for the presence of One who had
Himself been seen by many walking that day in the midst of
the mourners—the High Priest in white, the King invisible,
the Christ of sympathy, the Christ of tears—beseeching Him,
constraining Him to abide with us when it was towards
evening, and show His face, when the face of another dear
friend was hid away in the darkness and dust.

Then from the choir gallery floated a strain of tender
music, "When our heads are bowed with woe," so purely,
softly, touchingly sung (or rather only breathed), that
at the very first "Jesu, Son of Mary," most of the congregation stood in tears.   Then followed a prayer for the widowed
and motherless, the sons and daughters of sorrow, to Him
who knoweth our frame, and remembereth that we are dust.

The music next described the ravages of death because of
sin from Psalm xc., sung by selected voices to Felton's exquisite chant in C minor.   The succeeding prayer carried
down the confession of sorrow to the confession of sin, its
root, and gave thanks for the written Word that endures
when all flesh is grass, but most especially for the incarnate
personal Word, that by His cross and passion, death and
burial, has opened the heavenly kingdom, and abolished
death.

Then was read Romans v. 12 to the end, showing
the contrast between our ruin and redemption; how the
latter is not only even so as, but much more than, the

former—death is not only conquered, but swallowed up in
victory.   The discourse that followed took this for its text,
and rose by help of Scripture reading, prayer and song from
the depths of darkness and the grave to the heights of light
and life eternal—appropriate music being sung at the successive ascending stages, culminating in the anthem of
Resurrection, 1 Cor. xv. 51.   Among the rest we sang the
hymn "Thou art my hiding-place," which our friend was
fond of singing alone to her instrumental accompaniment.
The voices nearly broke down through emotion in the last
verse, yet gave the last words firmly.

In closing the service we showed how faith (child-like faith
in a personal Saviour such as hers was—not in mere doctrines,
still less in any Shibboleth) took outcome in works of charity.
The story of Dorcas was read, and the lady's beautiful work
in the society of that name referred to ; and the patience
which in her had its perfect work—perfecting, sculpture-
like, with the chisel of anguish, with the gravure of pain, the
beautiful white statue of character.   Finally her favourite
hymn was sung, and it sounded, in the very beauty of the
singing, like a voice from Heaven of one who being dead yet
speaketh—" Art thou weary, art thou languid, art thou sore
distrest?"   .

But I should not try to describe what, in its musical parts
at least, and in its effects as a whole, is not to be described.
It was not, as it was not meant to be, a thing of shreds
and patches, but a garment rather, woven from the top
throughout.   I hope we were landed on a higher reach of
the spiritual life nearer to God than when the service was
begun.

If I am spared I mean to pay still more attention to the
matter of public worship, in which it seems to me there lies
great undeveloped power for good.   I wish you would help
me with some of your sweet, good thoughts, fresh from the

pure heart of a Christian young lady, who lives near to the Holy of holies, and hears the angels sing.

The protracted anxiety with regard to the settlement of a colleague was at length, after several disappointments, set at rest for the time by the ordination of Mr. George K. Heughan on February 18th, 1876.

CHAPTER XIV.

In and around Florence.

THE first use Dr. Robertson made of the entire free-dom from responsibility for work which the ordination of his colleague gave him, was to return to his haunts in Florence. The state of his sister Isabella's health was such that she could not accompany him, but his younger sister went as his companion. They reached Florence towards the end of February. His sister stayed till May, but he lingered on in Italy and the Engadine till the close of the summer of 1877. He had thus good opportunity, of which he failed not to avail himself, for continuing his favourite studies; and he was as willing as before to pour out his treasures for the instruction of such sojourners like himself, or passing travellers, as sought his guidance through the churches and galleries.

In February, 1876, I had occasion to be in Florence with some travelling companions. In prospect of our journey, I wrote to Dr. Robertson to ask him what we should specially see. He most kindly arranged so to

time his arrival as to meet us, and we were led by
him to the churches and loggias which he liked best
to expound. I could not hope to convey any
idea of the brilliant talk, anon full of deepest earnestness, and anon rippling with humour, to which we
listened day after day; but fortunately some rough
jottings, with which he furnished Miss Florence Sellar
when she went to Italy in 1882, have been preserved.
They conduct us only half way round the Church of
Santa Maria Novella, which was generally the first to
which he took his friends. Written hurriedly, and
at a distance from the scene, they are necessarily far
inferior to his talk; but they at least indicate the
themes of that talk.

NOTES—JOTTINGS FOR FLORENCE LA BELLA.

The Chiesa Santa Maria Novella—a Dominican church,
called in other days " Angelo's Bride," but which, now at
least, has no beauty. It has been spoiled by restoration.
But Angelo had little sense of beauty. Terrible power his !
The Italian Romanesque at best is poor compared with our
Gothic minsters. It yielded the church walls, in large flat
spaces, as panels to the painter. It has no sense of growth
from within—the German *Werden*—but puts on beauty
from without, like a priest that saves you by putting wafer
on your lips and oil on your forehead, and holy water on
your finger ends. Even Giotto's Campanile and the
cathedral are only veneered with marble. Their poetry in
stone is somewhat shelly (I don't mean Percy Bysshe, poor
youth, whose thoughts are often as deep as the sea—your
Gulf of Spezia that drowned him). They are perfect ac-

T

cording to rule, perhaps,—squares, circles, finite forms,
touching the righteousness that is in the law of Euclid—
blameless, but just therefore not to be compared with that
art whose essence is incompleteness, and which struggles
through that to the infinite beyond.

The façade of the Santa Maria Novella is an unhappy
mixture of Gothic forms in the under part and Greek above.
The effect is disagreeable. It is surmounted by a triangular
gable wall that has no corresponding roof behind, and
therefore faces the public with a lie on its forehead, a false
face—a mark of the Beast which, however, is not confined to
Roman Catholics and Italy.

Ship-a-hoy! In a stone panel of the façade, to the right,
you look up and see the ship a-sail that brought home to
the Rucellai their dyes from the Levant. They were the
Orcellarii, great drysalters of Florence, who shipped the
Orchis dye from the east, which helped to found chapels in
the church, and to give suppers in the Rucellai gardens;
you pass them by the way coming in the directest road from
your hotel.

Inside the church—passing the beggar, who will think
you the sweetest, saintliest young heretic (which you are, all
the same) if you give him a *soldo* or two—there is let into
the entrance wall, beneath Giotto's crucifix and the fine old
stained glass rose window, a fresco by Masaccio, taken
from the dividing screen of the church. It represents the
Trinity—the *Père Eternel* above, Christ on the cross, and
the Holy Spirit as a dove between. On the other side of
the door there is a fresco of the school of Giotto, representing the Annunciation, the virgin having the type of face
afterwards worked out by Fra Angelico, the white ground in
this fresco contrasting with the black in Masaccio's. Both
have been restored from under the shroud of whitewash
which has been the means of preserving what it threat-

ened to destroy, as the snow does the fruitening earth in winter.

The Trinity is a frequent subject, interesting in the theology of art, the balance of the three Persons in the different pictures depending on the religious sentiments of the painter and the time. Giotto, for example, in a picture in the Certosa, gives prominence to the loving Father; Albertinelli (picture in Academia), to the crucified Son, the doctrine of the atonement being in his time deemed more important than the doctrine of the Fatherhood of God. The Holy Ghost, from whom the beautiful, the tender, the motherly, the womanly had passed over into the Virgin Mary, since the formulating of the Athanasian creed, has come down through the Middle Ages, and appears in the pictures ὡσεὶ περιστεράν, " in form as a dove," proceeding from the Father and the Son, says our western creed, but the eastern denies the " Filioque." Singular that the Greek Church had a conference with the Roman here, when, in 1439, this fresco, touching the great difference betwixt them, must (if by Masaccio), have been before their eyes. They had been driven by the plague from Ferrara down here, where the Patriarch Josephus died. His monument is round the corner of the Rucellai transept.

In looking up the nave, mark how the arches overhead narrow and how the floor is raised toward the high altar and the choir, a trick of architectural perspective to make the church seem longer than it is. Dominican churches were seldom " cumbered with columns," as the country beadle said of our noble Glasgow Cathedral. All free space possible was left for the crowding audiences that came to hear the Lenten and other sermons of the *Frati Predicatori*, who were the Dominicans. Of these, Savonarola (Fra or Frate Girolamo) was one, though he did not preach here, but in San Lorenzo, in the Duomo, in his own San Marco.

But he came sometimes, for in one sermon, speaking of fine
art as the handmaid of devotion, he bids you go and take
your stand (please do) at the corner of the Rucellai transept,
and look down through the vista and entanglement of
columns in the beautiful light of the stained glass windows.
You don't see much in it, neither do I ; but Savonarola saw
it with other eyes and in other light than ours. From where
you are standing, from where he stood, he could see and
you can see—the one to the right, the other in the far
transept before you—the two sepulchral chapels of the Strozzi
family. It was a daughter of this ducal house, driven from
Florence by the rival Medicis, and exiled in Ferrara, that
gave the great disappointment to the then young medical
student. It turned the whole current of his life, and drove
it in a different direction, all the fiercer for having been
checked and resisted, all the stronger in its struggling for
having been suppressed. He wrote hymns on the vanity of
the world, as the manner of men crossed in love is, went
sighing through the woods and saw visions of angels, and
finally renounced his profession and prospects, entered the
convent, and with relentless determination threw himself
with a terrible earnestness into the work God had given
him to do. He never mentioned her, never even seemed
to remember her, but none the less had she dissolved into
his being and permeated all his life ; none the less did the
love of her, did the hatred of her, stir him like the alternate
strokes of a powerful engine, that might have driven him on
to madness had they not driven him on to the divine madness of a monk that gave up all, even his own soul, for
God. Do you wonder that he saw a beauty others cannot
see in those aisles of the Santa Maria Novella, which,
in themselves, were not very much richer in beauty
then than they are to-day? Our æsthetic judgments are
often the products of very subtle involutions of feeling

that are not easy to analyze. But this does not seem very difficult.

She had said haughtily, that a noble Strozzi could not stoop to alliance with a base Savonarola. He had answered as proudly and retired. Impudent girl ! Vain, conceited thing ! And yet I praise you, Signorina. I thank you, I bless you, proud daughter of the Strozzi. Many thousands do. For had you taken him, he might have had, would have had, to trot about all his days, like his father before him, dispensing drugs and water-gruels in Ferrara, instead of shaking Florence with his thunder, and all Italy, all Europe ; and marching on, how grandly, to the bravest noblest martyrdom, of which for many centuries, to the eternal shame of Rome and Florence too, the Church of the true God has had to boast.

Now double cape-corner bound for the Madonna, and as you do so, see, beside the Patriarch's monument, the sharp-featured bust of the good Antonino, like an old Anti-burgher or Covenanter looking down—Archbishop of Florence in the days of Fra Angelico, whose bosom friend he was. He did not save souls, as Carlyle, the scorner, would say, by putting on a shovel hat and short apron; but he saved men's lives as he could in the time of the famine and plague, driving about, on foot, through the street and the by-road, to the sick and the poor, the plague-stricken and starving, a donkey laden with bread and wine for the sacrament of holy charity, the needs of daily life. Kiss your hand to him, lady, *i.e.*, (Saxon) *Laif-day*, bread-giver to the poor; you shall meet him again in San Marco.

And now ascend over the tomb of the Rucellai to the feet of the Madonna. You may glance, on her right, at the Bugiardini—assisted, they say, by his master, the terrible Angelo—in the St. Catherine and the wheel of her martyrdom (you know the legend, though I would like to tell it to you

in my own way some time) : and on the Madonna's left, look
only at Rossellini's Villana, lying in her blessed white marble
slumber, and the angels drawing aside the drapery to let you
see.   Rossellini is a favourite sculptor of the second class.
You will see him at his best, not here, but in the Vallom-
brosan series in the Bargello, and specially the death of John
Gualbert in a chapel of San Miniato, in the monument of a
cardinal slumbering in saintly purity—unutterable depths of
peace in the white marble.   These Christian sculptors, even
of the second class, could deal with death as no Greek
sculptor ever could, and you know why.   This blessed
Villana was a very gay young lady, who, on coming home one
morning from a midnight dance and masquerade, and looking in the mirror, saw the devil.   She shrieked and got the
mirror changed, but still——.   Of course, it ends in her
becoming a holy nun and dying in the odour of sanctity.
Much truth in the legend, as in that of the St. Catherine and
so many others ; though the truth is more in the fiction than
the fact.   I know some wise good people insist on separat-
ing the fact from the fiction, and throwing the latter away.
But that may be the best of it, most likely is.   They remind
me of the ladies of England, who, when tea was first brought
to this country, infused it, and then poured off the dusky
brown water and ate the leaves with butter !

Ave Maria ! CIMABUE'S MADONNA. Colossal. Mary
enthroned, with child on knee, three angels on either side—
picture on panel, *in tempera*, on gold ground.   The mother
Eve of a new world of art, the mother of all living Madonnas
since.   Hitherto they had been dead, as the dogmas of a
lifeless abstract creed, being in fact, and meant to be, not at
all beautiful pictures, even if they could have painted them,
full of human tenderness, of womanly grace, of mother's
love, but only a sort of hieroglyphic symbol of the Church's
dogma — formulated A.D. 430, with anathemas against

Nestorius—that Mary was "the Mother of God." The hard, stiff, dry, dark Byzantine pictures would serve their purpose better than others of a more pleasing kind, and so they had been repeated, mechanically to order, from age to age, in the Church's orthodox *ateliers*, under strict censorship of the priests. Any deviation, in the smallest iota, from the established type, would have seemed to the Church as heretical and censurable as the slightest deviation from the Westminster Confession to Dr. Begg, or the sound of an organ or chant of a psalm to Kidston of Ferniegair. Any smile on the face, any tear on the cheek, any yearning in the lips, or the light of the eyes, might have laid the innovating artist under terror of excommunication by bell, book, and candle. You see how Cimabue, partly perhaps from fear of the priests, partly from want of power to go further, partly from the instinct of conservatism that was in him as an aristocrat (see his portrait in the group on the east wall of the adjoining Spanish Chapel), still clings to the archaic type, with low forehead, long Greek nose, narrow slit eyes, small mouth and chin, passionless expression, stiff attitude, etc., etc., though there is a beginning of breadth and freedom in the drapery, and a breathing of life and beauty, womanly, motherly, human, in the Madonna, and still more, after its kind, in the child, and most of all, I think, in the angels, which did not come so much perhaps within the surveillance and rigid rubric of the priests. Giotto, the shepherd boy, that ugly little plebeian urchin, in whom the noble and generous Cimabue has found a genius beyond his own—he and his followers will carry the reform and rebellion against the stiff old orthodoxy further, till, two centuries later, it perfects itself and perishes in Raphael, and in Andrea del Sarto, who impudently puts the portrait of his own lovely, wicked wife in the sanctissima Madonna.

How it fell to Cimabue to inaugurate the change of

treatment and create a new era in art, it occurs to me suddenly to ask.   Let me think a moment.   Had he not a rare
mother of his own, like all other sons and daughters of
genius, the divinest children of the race, and may not the
remembrance of her from earliest childhood—of a mother's
kisses—have haunted and inspired him?   A most kindly
uncle he had also, prior of the Dominican convent, in this
same Santa Maria Novella, who kept school and had his
nephew for a pupil.   If you look into the great cloister
passing out that way to opposite the railway station, you
may see the schoolboys playing still as they did 600
years ago, when Cimabue was scholar there.   His good
noble uncle did not check, or scold, or beat him, when he
would make studies of angels' heads and Madonnas' faces
on the margin of his grammatical exercises, but encouraged
him, though the art of the painter then, which was merely
mechanical, was scarcely thought fit for a gentleman.   And
by his influence with the Church, may he not have smoothed
the artist's way, through all risk of giving offence to the
orthodox in breaking away from the old tradition of
ecclesiastical art, and making a quite *nova* Madonna, a
quite new Mary, for the church of the Santa Maria Novella?

And then even the common people's ideal of the Madonna
must have grown into something quite different from what
the old, hard, dark pictures of her represented.   For as her
Son has grown sorrowful and angry down the centuries—the
face of Jesus Christ, that in the Catacombs (3rd century),
and still in the mosaics of Ravenna (5th and 6th), wears the
benign aspect of the beautiful young Shepherd feeding his
flock, or carrying the lamb on his shoulder, darkening into
the face of the Judge, returning to take vengeance on men
who had crucified him, the " Rex tremendæ majestatis " of
the " Dies Iræ " which was even then uttering its wail
through the convents and cathedrals, announcing the day

of judgment as a day of wrath and terror to the Church herself—the Virgin Mother becomes more and more the Intercessor, who is to save them from the terrible wrath of the Lamb.

In another series of pictures of the Madonna—solitary, from the house of John Mark, where last in the New Testament we see her with the others praying—from the Catacombs, where she appears as the *Orante* with arms outstretched in supplication—from the mosaics of the 7th century (you will see one in San Marco) in which she bends her arms as if in supplication more earnest, on her way to the judgment seat to arrest the wrath of her Son, as in the Campo Santo fresco of the 14th century and the Sistine Chapel of the 16th—as she travels on to the judgment to become the Saviour from Christ himself, and instead of Him, there gathered round her more and more the grace, the beauty, the sweetness of the motherly, the tender, the sympathetic, the pitiful; and when the picture of Cimabue, though not belonging to this series, shows her for the first time, and suddenly, invested with so much of this, what wonder if they welcome it with shouts and songs. It answers to their own ideal and desire, and they carry it in triumph, and with Hosanna singing (as the ark of old was carried in procession to the temple) to its shrine in the Rucellai Chapel of the Santa Maria Novella, and there it has rested for six centuries before the eyes of Florence, and generation after generation has come to look at it, and passed on to the darkness, and still there it is.

> " Art is long, but life is fleeting."

" These are the immortals," said the monk to Wordsworth, " we are the shadows that pass by and look at them."

Here the jottings, which were to have been continued to guide his friend to all the art treasures of

Florence, come to an end.   From the Rucellai Chapel,
with its famous Madonna, he led our party to the chapel
of Filippo Strozzi, where he described to us his burial
there "with great pomp on a Saturday afternoon at
dusk."   Then he took us into the apse behind the
high altar, frescoed by Ghirlandajo, and through the
chapel with Brunelleschi's cross — "made to show
Donatello how he should have done it,"—into the
Strozzi Chapel at the end of the south transept,
where he dwelt lovingly on Orcagna's "Judgment"
and "Heaven," specially asking us to note in the
"Heaven" "the cataract of beautiful faces on either
side."

Passing out of the church into the Green Cloister,
we entered the Spanish Chapel.   Here I am indebted
to Mr. Robert Caird, who was intimately associated
with Dr. Robertson in many of his Florentine researches.   He writes :—

The Spanish Chapel was built early in the 14th century
by a Florentine merchant, Buonamico di Lapo Guidalotto,
with the aid of the prior, and decorated with frescoes by
painters of the early Tuscan school, contemporaries or immediate successors of Cimabue, and among them, notably,
Simone Martini of Siena, assisted, perhaps, by his nephew,
Lippo Memmi, and Taddeo Gaddi, the favourite pupil
and follower of the immortal Giotto.   The chapel takes its
name from the Spanish residents of Florence of the time of
Cosimo de' Medici.   They secured it for their services
after its abandonment as the chapter-room of the Dominican
order.   But its whole interest is in the frescoes, the interpretation of which was an unfailing source of delight to Dr.

Robertson. Here he came ever and again, alone or accompanied by troops of friends, to study or expound—with that matchless eloquence and rare gift of arousing attention and of exciting enthusiastic interest, which worked like a spell upon the dullest and least imaginative of his hearers—that wondrous scheme of philosophy and of church history, reverently and beautifully depicted in soft *tempera* tones, which the centuries have but enhanced, upon its lofty walls and high-pitched, vaulted roof.

The scheme of the frescoes is given in Ruskin's "Vaulted Book," in the series of "Mornings in Florence"; and elsewhere, writing of the Church militant wall, Ruskin says of the group of infidels and heretics, "which, with the Paradise above, I hold one of the grandest things in Italy." And Dr. Robertson's improvisations, full of finest poetry and quaintest imagery, as interludes to forcible dramatic portraiture of leading figures, would have been, if only they had been recorded and preserved, as valuable to literature as the frescoes themselves are to art.

Those who were privileged to hear him in the Spanish Chapel, as in San Marco, when his sympathies with his subject were fairly aroused, will understand how hopeless it is to attempt to reproduce the flow of description, now penetrating into the obscurest corners of forgotten lore, now placing the most seemingly incongruous incidents into juxtaposition, and with sudden humour startling us into laughter, mixed with awe at the new-born truth; ever and anon throwing his own intense individuality into the personalities he was describing, with an overwhelming histrionic power giving movement to the placid scenes the early Tuscan painters had recorded at the bidding of their ecclesiastical patrons.

So far did he sometimes carry this illusion, that, on one occasion, in the chapel of San Lorenzo, after speaking in the person of Michel Angelo's Lorenzo, he was asked how he knew what he was describing. "Oh," he answered, "of course I know; I was living then; I knew Lorenzo well." His power of losing himself in the character he was personating was unrivalled, and this is the more remarkable, in that he never lost his strong Doric, least of all in moments of creative excitement.

In the afternoon of the day on which we visited Santa Maria Novella we drove to the Certosa in the Val d'Ema. There we listened to the story of the founding of the order of the Monks of Silence after the death of Raymond, which the stained glass in the corridor illustrates; and with the memory of the weird tale, so effectively told, filling our minds, we drove back to Florence in the rich evening light.

Next day we were taken first to San Lorenzo, where in the sacristy we had a wonderful exposition of Michel Angelo's famous monuments to the Medici —the helmeted Julian, whom Robertson named *Il Penseroso*, sitting in dark melancholy thought over the Evening and Morning, on his right and left; and on the opposite wall, Lorenzo, the representative of the *Allegro* side of life—the epicurean, with the Night and Day, right and left, at his feet. On the wall, at right angles to both, there is a Virgin and Child— placed there, Robertson believed, because the mystery of the Holy Incarnation is the one solution of the contradictions of life, in which alone the harmony of its sadness and its gladness is revealed.

From San Lorenzo we passed to the Annunziata,

and in the afternoon we went to the Misericordia, and saw the brotherhood assemble in their every-day raiment, and come out from the vestry in their long black robes and masks. They knelt, and their chaplain having read the brief prayer, that has been read there day by day for many centuries, they took up their litter and went to carry a sick child to the hospital. Passing to the Santa Maria Nuova we found they had already arrived and handed over their charge to the sisterhood, and were kneeling picturesquely, hooded and in black, around a bed at which a priest was administering extreme unction. We then heard the story of the founding of the order 600 years ago by Luca Borsi, that it might give useful employment to the lounging, swearing woolporters of the city. It now embraces in its membership some 2000 of the first citizens of Florence, who, on duty in detachments, are bound to various works of charity, prominent among which is the one we had just seen performed—the carrying sick people to the hospital.

Regarding the Annunziata a correspondent writes:—

We were lingering over Andrea del Sarto's frescoes. Dr. Robertson was pointing out the freshness of the colouring, the beauty of the forms, and the perfect life-like rendering of the flesh, when he turned suddenly round, in that quick way of his, and said: "But it is the flesh and blood that shall not inherit the Kingdom."

Next day was devoted to San Marco, of which the same correspondent says :—

We first wandered into the refectory, and, sitting

opposite Fra Angelico's great fresco of the Crucifixion, had a long desultory talk about the painter and his prayerful work; then the spring sunshine lured us into the court of the cloisters.

The first thing that caught Dr. Robertson's eye was the window of Savonarola's cell, and he suddenly seemed to become oblivious of us and of the present, and, transporting himself into the 15th century, carried on a dialogue between Savonarola and a messenger from Lorenzo de Medici.

He gave a most wonderful *resumé* of the life of Lorenzo. The messenger relating his good works, charities, patronage of art, support of the convent, etc., etc. Savonarola reproaching him with selfish motives, family pride, want of sincerity, depriving the Florentines of their liberty, and most bitterly with trying to bribe him by putting gold into the treasury of San Marco.

Interview upon interview was represented.   One time Savonarola was commanded to come into the presence of Lorenzo, and dark suggestions made of the power of the latter as "Head of the Family;" another time he was forbidden.   But neither threats nor coaxing could move the monk from his cold, stern, disapprobation.   He was a very John the Baptist in his courageous denunciations.   At last, there came the rumour that Lorenzo was stricken with illness likely to prove fatal.   Then Savonarola lends a pitying ear to the account of a troubled conscience, and hints of obedience to the demands of his confessor, and so, unable to resist the appeal of the dying man, he goes to hear Lorenzo's confession.

I shall never forget the dramatic power of that scene. The spirit and appreciation of character with which the dialogue was carried on, and the power our friend possessed of transporting, not only himself, but his audience, into the midst of the scenes he so vividly represented.

Dr. Robertson accompanied us to Venice, where he was our guide to the Doge's palace, St. Mark's, and the other churches. From Venice we went to Milan, where we saw the Carnival procession from the balcony of our hotel on the Corso. When the rest of us were entering into the mirth, catching and throwing back the *confetti* aimed at us, he was busy taking notes. He read me afterwards what he had written. In his pencilled scrawl he had drawn a vivid picture of the shifting, many-coloured panorama that had been passing and re-passing before our eyes. He said he made a point of making a study from every such scene; his notes would be of service when he wrote his projected book on Italy!

We spent the Sunday at Milan. There was no service in English, and so we went in the forenoon to see Leonardo da Vinci's "Last Supper," in the refectory of the convent of Santa Maria delle Grazie. He made the visit a real service of worship. Arranging seats for us opposite the great painting, he sat down with his chair slightly turned round, so that we could hear him, and told us the history of the painting, explaining the reason of its decay, as contrasted with a perfectly preserved fresco on the opposite wall. Leonardo da Vinci could not work in fresco, which does not admit of alteration, but must be done by one who can realize his ideal at once. The great painter, especially in painting the Christ, could not work so, but must be always striving after the highest. He had, therefore, the wall prepared by some process that

he might work in oil; but the preparation was to a
large extent a failure, and hence the picture has
become blurred and blotted.   But he told us how it
suffered further from the monks, who, desiring to have
a door by which their dinner could be brought in more
directly, and in better season, from the kitchen, had
cut away the feet of the Christ—the " blessed feet " he
called them ; and still more from the profane French
soldiers quartered in the convent, who had stabled
their horses in the refectory, and had shown their
contempt for religion by making the head of the
Christ a target for pistol practice.   He then passed on
to analyze the picture and to explain its groupings, till
he concentrated attention on the central figure, and
then it could be truly said that " he preached unto us
Jesus."   I found to my surprise when we rose to go
that he had spoken for an hour.   It was a memorable
hour, and all of us felt when it was over, that we had
been brought nearer to Him, whom the painter had
sought to glorify.   Some years later, he wrote to his
friend Mr. Kirkwood, who had been visiting Italy :—

I hear you thought Da Vinci's face of the Christ the best,
indeed the only one.   So do I.   Its very disfigurement
enhances its beauty, partly by remanding it back into that
region of the indistinct, bordering on the unseen, through
which and which alone divine spiritual beauty can look out
on you.

In the afternoon we went to the cathedral.   It was
the first Sunday in Lent, according to the Ambrosian

calendar. I do not know whether the service was one peculiar to the Ambrosian ritual, but it was certainly most impressive. Cloud and rain were alternating with gleams of sunshine, that sent great shafts of light through the wilderness of marble columns. The officiating clergy and choristers left the chancel and marched in procession round the church, with united voice pouring out as they walked some common words of confession or supplication, which ever and again changed into song. We had been separated as the service proceeded. When I rejoined Robertson I found him in tears. He took me by the hand and said that nothing had ever moved him more deeply than the act of worship we had just witnessed.

Next day he took us to the church of S. Ambrogio —the former cathedral—the actual church of St. Ambrose, rebuilt bit by bit, but so that its identity had been preserved. He told us, with enthusiasm lighting up his face, the familiar story of how the good bishop had caused the doors to be shut in the face of the Emperor Theodosius, when, after the massacre of Thessalonica, he came with pomp to worship in the cathedral.

In these years a succession of sore bereavements fell on his brother James. At the close of 1874, his wife died, and now in March, 1876, his third daughter was suddenly taken from him, the first of three who passed away within little more than twelve months.

To Mr. David M'Cowan.

17 Corso Vittorio Emmanuele,
Florence, 30th March, 1876.

You would sympathize keenly with James in his most affecting and overwhelming bereavement which has put our dear Eliza into the white circle of the blessed, and all the rest of us into the black company of mourners. To me she was very loving and very dear, as I baptized her and claimed her in some sort as more my own, and had her—in her bright and most delightsome youth, that had the dew of the holy morning so freshly and fully on it—more, by permission, at Irvine, than any of the rest. . . . I am thankful that James is so strong and well comforted, as I see from his cheerful and brave way of writing me, when I could hardly have expected that he would write at all. I had telegraphed to say that we would come home directly if he wished it in the least, but he kindly writes to arrest our proposed return; and Jessie and I stay on in this beautiful Italy, where I am getting great good, both outward and inward, more than ever. . . . We mean to go in a few days to Siena to take there two weeks, or it may be three. The old city is a mine of wealth in those peculiar treasures of church history, with which I am almost (not foolishly, I hope) making haste to be rich; and as only the hand of the diligent maketh so, I don't mean (my health being ever so good) to stand in the celebrated market-places, in which the wise faces of some score of centuries look down—to loiter about and stand there all the day idle. Then, too, it is a centre from which explorers can radiate on radiant days into the mysterious, old Etruscan tombs, with their mysterious handwriting on the wall, which no Daniel has yet come to interpret, and which it is by no means likely that a disabled, strolling, U.P. minister will; but which, nevertheless, I would like to see on its own table of stone, and not in mere painted and photographed copies, and that not in the blinding light of any 19th century museum, but in its own appropriate dark light in those funereal vaults and extraordinary chambers of imagery, in which lie buried a dead language, and a race of "men dead long ago." Dead but not lost, let us hope, like the language, not lost beyond hope as the language itself, in another sense, is not. How intensely interesting to trace their belief in immortality beyond the grave (if not in expiation itself, and the pardon of guilt, through the sacrifice of One whom they sought, groping after Him in the darkness as the Desire of all nations, if haply they might find Him, but yet could not see) as told in the handwriting and pictures on the wall, along which rides the Rider on the pale horse, attended by the Furies to punish the impenitent and wicked, and by the beautiful angels, called the Lassas, to carry the good to their reward. These show the works of the law written in their hearts—the law by which they have been judged, and shall be judged, and may it not be that it shall be more tolerable in the end for them than for some of ourselves, and that the nation of the lost Etruria from their ancestral tombs shall rise up in the judgment against us. . . .

Before going to Siena, Dr. Robertson and his sister went to Orvieto. His object in going there was to investigate the Etruscan tombs in the neighbourhood. But though the visit extended to three days, he never got beyond the cathedral, so charmed was he with its wonderful façade, and with Luca Signorelli's frescoes of the "Last Judgment" that have immortalized his name, and Fra Angelico's matchless " Prophetarum

Laudabilis," (with angels sitting round) in pyramidal group in the chapel of San Brizio.

From Orvieto they passed to Chiusi, which does not offer much attraction to the student either of architecture or painting.   On their arrival they found the town in commotion.   A great procession was about to start to the shrine of some saint in the neighbourhood. It was headed by archbishops and bishops, who were followed by white vestured priests and a long line of students gathered from all the colleges in the locality. As the procession, which extended to half a mile, wended its way along the country road leading from the city to the shrine, the peasants in the fields left their work and coming to the hedges by the way-side knelt down to receive the blessing of their spiritual fathers.   But when the wail of the *Miserere Mei* rose from the multitude of voices, a responsive chord was struck, and Dr. Robertson impulsively hurried forward till he reached the part of the procession in which the priests were marching.   Falling into their ranks, and laying hold of one side of the book borne by a venerable ecclesiastic, he began to join in the chant, and soon his voice could be discerned rising rich and clear above all the others.   So engrossed was he with his singing, that, in going down some steps toward the tomb, he stumbled and fell.   There was great excitement among the priests lest their new and unexpected companion had hurt himself.   They kindly helped to raise him, and the one by whose side he had been walking gave him his arm.   Thus supported he walked back to Chiusi in earnest conversation. He told his sister that he had never had a more intensely interesting talk.

Next day they set out for what is supposed to be the tomb of Lars Porsena. It had rained for three days and the road was all but impassable. No horse could go, but nothing daunted, Dr. Robertson hired a cart drawn by oxen. The patient beasts of burden plodded through the mud which was of the appearance and consistency of mortar. They sank near to the thighs at every step, and as they drew out their legs it was with a sound resembling a pistol shot. Progress was in these circumstances necessarily slow, and, though the tomb was only a few miles distant, twelve hours, from eight in the morning till eight at night, were spent on the expedition. But even the time passed on the way did not seem long. They were attended by about a dozen children, who, attracted by the *soldi* with which Dr. Robertson never failed to provide himself, crowded into the cart and delighted him with their prattle.

From Chiusi they proceeded to Siena.

To Mr. David M'Cowan.

SIENA, 15th April, 1876.

Here we are in Siena, . . . and since we have come here, as it is what they call Holy Week, the richest in the year for the sort of study I am pursuing, I have been almost every hour of the day running out into the churches to watch the "offices," which throng after each other in thick and almost ceaseless succession at this time, and if possible to gather

some light from the present to reflect upon the history of the
past and to help me to expound it. How terribly the Church
of Rome has fallen, even, it seems to me, since the days of
Luther and the Reformation ! Much every way, but chiefly in
the way of Mariolatry. I think I told you that the Virgin
retires more out of sight through Lent, and on till Easter,
holding only a subordinate place as the " dolorous mother "
standing by the cross—the season being devoted more
exclusively to the passion, death and resurrection of our
" Jesus only." But, as Siena is a city specially dedicated
from of old to the Virgin, and as yesterday was Good Friday,
two churches and two hours were devoted to her worship,
in commemoration of her in the character of the mother
with the sword in her heart. It is the first time I have
witnessed anything so humbling, even in the Romish Church.
Artistically it was not attractive, but most repulsive. The
singing was (no organ) execrable—bad enough I believe to
please Dr. Begg—worse than the shouting of colliers in the
singing school of discord at Auchenbowie, which I remember
from my childhood, and entirely different from the exquisite
passion music we had heard in the cathedral in the morning,
where for hours there was never the smallest allusion to that
Virgin, but to the suffering Saviour only. I came home
thinking of Paul at Athens, whose spirit was stirred within
him when he saw the city wholly given to idolatry, and
wondering whether I could not open a station here as Dr.
Ker did at San Remo.

The following fragment of a letter, which probably
never reached its destination, has been found among
Dr. Robertson's papers :—

TOGNAZZI, 19 VIA BANDINI,
SIENA, TOSCANA, [April, 1876].

Tognazzi is the name of our landlord, from whom we

have hired a very nice lodging of four rooms, with windows
that look (like those in Bunyan's Chamber of Peace) toward
the sunrise, away over gardens that are all ablaze with the
blossoms, and fragrant with the incense of the early summer,
and that stretch out to the old city wall, flanked with its
antique towers and pierced with its old-world gates, which
are still closed and guarded every night at sundown, after
the ringing of the Ave Maria bell.   Over all this we lodge
high enough to see away for miles over the Tuscan uplands,
that rise around us, mound above mound and mile above
mile, like the waves of a billowy sea, suddenly stiffened
into brown earth and limestone rock, and bearing on their
crests clumps of grey olives and black cypresses, and
whitening villas on the green knolls here and there.   To
one who is a lover, as I happen to be, of mediæval history,
and all history on its pious and poetic side, the region is full
of rich, romantic interest.   Along the reaches of green hill,
moorland, and morass, that stretch from this, eastward, away
to the heights of Assisi, came St. Francis, half a millennium
ago, like a bridegroom fresh from his marriage with his
bride, called Poverty, strong in faith, and singing his hymns,
and seeing his visions, and dreaming his dreams, and
preaching to the beasts and birds when the people would
not hear him—followed by his troop of friars of Order
Grey—awaking, all along these Tuscan uplands, a new life of
sincere, if also superstitious devotion, which has been the
fountain of not a little that was best and most beautiful in
the life and art and literature of the succeeding golden era
of Dante and Giotto and St. Louis ; and which, flowing north-
ward with the Arno and southward with the Tiber, watered,
like the rivers of Paradise, the sunny slopes of Italy, running especially through those broad and beautiful gardens
of the city of Florence, in the Val d'Arno, like the first of
those rivers of Paradise that " compasseth the whole land

of Havilah where there is gold." Siena itself is, next to
Florence, the richest among the cities of Italy in treasures
of mediæval art; and though Florence is richer in its
inheritance of pictures and other possessions, Siena is
rarer in its peculiar appearance as a typical city of the
Middle Ages, having better preserved its antiquity, and more
effectually resisted the raid of ruinous reform.

At the end of April tidings came of the sudden,
though not unexpected death of Mr. James Robertson's
eldest daughter, Mary, the wife of his colleague and
successor, the Rev. John Young, and that the shadows
of a fourth bereavement were already falling on his
path, in the serious illness of his youngest daughter,
Jessie.   These sorrows, as well as the state of
Isabella's health, interrupted Dr. Robertson's studies
at Siena, and made it necessary for his younger sister
to return home in May, leaving him alone at Florence.

To His Younger Sister.

VALLOMBROSA, 9th June, 1876.

 . . . Sad tidings do pursue you into the hermitage, and
find you out.   For the stunning news of the death of Dr.
Eadie (whom, of all men, I knew so well and liked so
much) I had almost looked in your letter, and in a paper
that came to Mr. M'Dougall along with it; as yesterday
I had seen a paper of Friday last which sounded the death
warning very distinctly, and I could not forget how, when I
went to bid him farewell last winter, he told me his eyesight
was failing, and how it might be the shadow of the coming
darkness when no man can work.   What work he has done
since those old days, you cannot remember, when he came

with his red cheeks and leonine playfulness to Greenhill, and rather, I thought, took a fancy for me, of which I was extremely proud, and which he never lost, no more than I my affection for him and great admiration in many ways. And now his extraordinary amount of work is done, and none of us has done his work so laboriously, done so wonderfully much, and done it so willingly and so well. . . .

I have made some interesting and instructive explorations in the old historic home of John Gualbert of the 11th century. I have had a talk with the monks, and more than one interview in the church and outside with the queer organist —the Guido ; though I have now made out for certain that Guido the musical, of Arezzo, never was a monk of Vallombrosa at all, though the guide books and other books (all modern) say so. I have got hold of the old chronicles and legends, and find that the modern tradition is a mistake.

To His Niece in Glasgow.

FLORENCE, June 21st, 1876.

Can you find for me in the Bible a text like this, " I am miserable unless I hold a spade." *Sum misero (sic) nisi tenerem ligonem* is the Latin original, inscribed beneath a great fresco of the early part of the 13th century, just discovered at Cortona. The director of the Royal Gallery here—a great friend of mine—was told by the priests that it was taken from Scripture. He said I knew Scripture much better than they did, and he would ask me. I said there was no such text in canonical Scripture, nor apocryphal either as far as I knew. He called in the head clerk, who said the priests held that if not in the text of the Vulgate, it was in some of the multitudinous annotations, which are all the same. There is more of the inscription, but partly obliterated, and the rest not yet understood. The picture is one of Paradise, with Adam using a spade and hoe, and Eve spinning,—a rare old piece of Scripture illustration. It lies very much in my way of study which I am pursuing as hot as I can ; for in this Paradise of climates, in the Vale of the Arno and the City of Flowers, it is not good to be idle— " I am miserable unless I hold a spade."

To Mr. David M'Cowan.

FLORENCE, 21st June, 1876.

Sister Jessie—my epistle general to the brethren, whom the post hour having arrived, I charged with messages of remembrance, folded up with regret and despatched with sorrow—would tell you, among other things, in what comfortable circumstances and excellent health and good keeping she had left me. It has been my hap all my life to fall in, outside of my own family, with good, kind friends, . . . and specially, somehow, with good landladies, at college and hall, in Germany and in Irvine. And certainly my Mother Smith here, the present mistress of the robes and queen of the kitchen to my U.P. self is, if the last in office, not the least in worth. She leaves me no room at all to think of what I shall eat or drink, or even wherewithal I shall be clothed, as with invisible and silent hands the refection is put upon the parlour table, and the suit of fresh apparel in the bed and dressing chamber, as regular as need is, and as punctual as clockwork, in the Palazzo here, as in the famous child's story (if I remember rightly) of the Palace of Beauty and the Beast. And what a cook she is, old Mother Smith, and cooks are, for dyspeptic patients at least, the best of doctors ; and how cheerful when you like to talk to her, which, however, I do not always do, for, to tell the truth, she is about as deaf as a door nail.

But her husband, Mr. Smith, my groom, you understand (if

I had a horse), has ears as keen as a hedgehog, and bristles as sharp too, towards any one who would dare in any way to annoy " the Doctor," which however nobody does, so that the hedgehog in him has a sinecure, and only the graceful and lordly finds development, as it does to perfection, when with his tall, erect, well-dressed figure of six feet and upwards, unbent by the weight of 76 years, he waits at table, as has happened once or twice in a way this winter, in the presence of illustrious strangers, and as will happen again when you come certainly. And then Clarinda, the maid-of-all-work, vies with them both in the ministry of service, and has begun to think and ask a good deal about that New Testament I have given her to read.

Since Jessie left I have been a week at Vallombrosa (known to all English readers through Milton); and from old books, pictures, legends, and localities have been reading up the remarkable romantic life, and, such as it was, the Christian life of the 12th century. I have seen and talked with the last of the old race of monks, for after they die the order is extinct, for the monasteries, in Italy at least, are in this way undergoing suppression and getting stamped out; and glad I am to have seen the last of them ere they wholly disappear. A remarkable race those Vallombrosa monks, as well as the neighbouring hermits of Camaldoli, stretching in unbroken line with their historical records across eight centuries. They are now replaced in the monastery (into a corner of which the few remaining monks are retired) by a college of fast young lads of no religion to speak of, who sing their convivial songs, and drink their *vino*, and rattle their glasses, and shout their *vivas* in the open-air at sundown, when the chanting of the vesper used to be heard to the sound of the organ, played by a rare white haired old Maestro, now heard no more floating through the pine woods at evening when the Ave Maria bell is ringing

and the westering sun goes down in distant sea behind
Florence, that is visible with its glittering domes and spires
and towers far down the valley, till the owl comes out and
hoots its mocking litany to the moon—"tu-whit, tu-whoo."
It may be a change for the better—we shall see.   But what
a noble movement this young Italy would be if it were only
evangelized and Christian !

To His Younger Sister.

Florence, 21st June, 1876.

Two nights since we drove up to the top of Fiesole,
through labyrinths of gardens and orchards, all ablaze with
blossoms, and cool with green and burning with golden
fruit—the bud, the blossom, the young, the middle-sized,
the old, ripe fruit—all contemporaneous, you understand,
on the same tree.   We stopped to mark it, particularly on
the terrace of the old wayside abbey of San Marco, on which
Lorenzo the magnificent used to stroll arm in arm with the
Prince di Mirandola, when he came down from his Fiesolan
villa, or across from Careggi, to visit the young Phœnix and
wonder at once of the fashionable and literary world, when
studying hard in search of the truth as it is in Jesus in the
monastic cloister there, with its red-tiled, conical roof, and
sweet-toned bells, and great black hedge of yews (fronting
the fantastic but beautifully chequered marble façade of the
11th century), to screen him from the southern sun, and
throw a deeper tone of shadow and dejection into his pensive musings on the mystery of human life, when he went
out at eventide to meditate.   I seemed to see him, with his
open, eager face and streaming hair (as pictured in the gallery
of the Uffizi), pacing the large lozenge-shaped cloister of
Michelozzi, under its beautifully vaulted arcades, and out
upon the long, open loggia that runs eastward to possible

glimpses of daybreak over the dark pinewoods of Vallombrosa—see him wringing his hands, as if seeking, and in
vain, to wash them from the guilt of some great murder of
the innocent and tragedy of wrong in which he is obviously
conscious of having had a part, and asking, in deep
undertone of calm passion, " Where is the place of
wisdom ? " and with Pilate, " What is truth ? " The
vaults of Michelozzi overhead give no echo or reply, but
rather seem by their groined arches to wring their white
hands also, and look up. Still more silent is the great
vault of heaven over all, into whose depths of illimitable
space (from the tower of Galileo, which you can see from
here across Val d'Arno) the telescope had not yet plunged,
to sound the fathomless abyss, or read off the handwriting
of mystery inscribed on the black wall of the night.

CHAPTER XV.

In the Engadine.

DRIVEN at last from Tuscany by the heat, Dr. Robertson set out, in the end of June, for the Engadine, accompanied by Dr. Young of Florence and his family.

TO HIS YOUNGER SISTER.

TOBLACH, TYROL, 5th July, 1876.

We have come out of the Dolomites, most extraordinary mountain ranges, which are not to be described in one letter, nor in all the letters of the alphabet, however skilfully put together; and being now within reach of railway at this outlandish Tyrolese village of Toblach, which you will hardly find in the map, we hope to-morrow to ask for letters at the post office of that Bozana or Botzen, the name of which I sent you. . . . We have changed our route, and go by Meran and Martinsbrück to the lower, and by that to St. Moritz in the upper, Engadine. . . . You must know that in doing the Dolomites we have at the same time been doing what they call "Titian's country," and studying, among other things, the relation of landscape painting, which Titian is absurdly said to have invented, to that painter's personal history and his character as an artist and a man. . . . How I wish you were with us. It is as good in its way as Siena, Orvieto, or Chiusi, though very different. . . .

. . . Süss is the Grison village (not to be confounded with the Zutz, in the Upper Engadine) where the Albula pass from Chur falls, about two thirds down, into the singular lofty valley that runs down from St. Moritz and the Maloya to Schulz-Tarasp and St. Martinsbrück. I have been up and down the valley now, and four years ago more than once, and am trying to study it chiefly from an ecclesiastico-historical point of view; and when this great work of mine is published you will see that Süss is the centre from which, after a great "disputation," in which the leading Swiss Church gladiators were engaged in the church under the shadow of whose old tower I am writing, the Reformation radiated up and down the glen, and through the passes that converge upon the Engadine.

The leading figure in the picture is a certain Ulrich Campill, or Campbell (very Scotch-like, isn't it?), who was minister of the church in these times here, and who, for the admirable and earnest sketches he has given of this and other crises of the Grison life in Church and State, has been called the father of Rhetian history. The Rhetians are the Rasenæ or Etruscans after their expulsion from Italy, the centre column of these refugees hailing from Clusium or Chiusi (of cart and oxen memory), which gives a remarkable enhancement to the interest of my researches here, as you will understand.

Anna Campbell, wife of Ulrich, was a brave woman. A flood came roaring down the Engadine from the melting of

200 glaciers, carrying some twenty bridges along with it, when over the bridge of wood that in the narrow gorge separated the town from the manse, Anna dared for her husband's sake to cross, and, the two side piers being just then swept away, she was left standing in the raging flood and storm, alone on the midmost. They heard her clear musical voice singing out, "*In tuas manus*" ("Into Thy hands," etc.), when, suddenly remembering that she had the keys of the cupboard at her girdle, and the bairns would need their supper, she stopped her prayer, and shouted, "There's the keys, weans!" and threw them ashore, disappearing the same moment down the ravine.

The family of the heroine and the grand old reformed historian are still here, in the third or fourth, or somewhere between that and the thousandth generation of them "that love God and keep His commandments." They do so in a manner most distinctly pronounced, and are a Christian family of as Puritan, or even old Seceder, a type as you might ever wish to see. To be sure they are only brewers. However, they brew very good beer. It is with them I am lodging now, or rather with an uncle of the family, who is a sugar-baker, returned with some winnings to his native Engadine, and whose wife is a most motherly body as I have ever known.

My chamber is a nice square box of pine wood, red and fresh and fragrant as cedar, with three windows looking out over the snow and far up the glens. The embroidered curtain and wash-stand linen are of unspotted whiteness, and the bed, with its "laced" pillow and golden and scarlet eider down coverlet, is as soft and fresh and pure as snow. Dr. George Buchanan saw it in passing, and strongly recommended me to take it instead of any room in the hotel. However, the Frau Flüghi modestly declines to cook dinner good enough for the *Engländer* and for that I have to go to the Inn, *i.e.*, not the river so called, the rushing of which as I write is (as your Allan water used to be) in my ears, but the *Schweizerhof.*

The Campbells are almost next door, and the widowed mother, a lady-like woman of the old noble family of the Plantas, in her deep mourning (her husband died in spring) and with her swimming eyes, clings to me, since she knows who I am, in a most kindly and earnest manner for consolation; and she seems so like some of my old widows of the Bridgegate or the Halfway. It is singular to see how sorrow and comfort repeat themselves in precisely the same moods and the same words in Swiss and Scotch, in the Engadine and in Irvine ! How she pores over the old family Bible, with its record of their marriage and the baptism of their children, written by *his* own hand, each entry with a prayer, and a beautiful one, by which he being dead yet speaketh. I can read it pretty well with her in the Romaunsch, though she, belonging to the educated classes, speaks German as well (or if not " as well," at least " also"). One of her sons, a bold young chamois hunter of twenty-four, volunteers to be my guide on any excursion longer or shorter into the valleys ; and he has already to-day had me to the ruins of the castle that guarded the pass, and to the treasure chamber of old books and MSS. of *the* Campill of the Campills, the father of Rhetian history and of *him.*

Dr. George Buchanan I have mentioned. You know how he came to be here? You have heard, perhaps, of the sudden death at Schulz-Tarasp of Mr. James Blair.[1] He had suffered, but not much, from inflammation in the throat. It suppurated and burst inwards, suffocating him almost immediately. Mr. A. B. M'Grigor, from Glasgow, a friend of his, had notice by telegraph from Scotland of Mr. Blair's

[1] C.E., of Edinburgh—a member of one of the principal families in Irvine, and brother-in-law to Dr. George Buchanan.

death two days after it had occurred. Mrs. M'Grigor and he set out next morning (Saturday), taking me along with them.

We found on our arrival that the funeral, which in the Grison must take place, not so quick as in Florence, but still within forty-eight hours, had been arrested by a telegram from Patrick Blair, Sheriff-Substitute, Inverness, who was already on the way to Schulz to take the body home for burial. We found it—embalmed in a leaden coffin, with a glazed casement over the face, and this again in a wooden shell, all garlanded with wreaths of Alpine roses and edelweiss—in a low chamber, hard by the church, down the steep, stony street of the village, at the gate of the gardens of the Belvidere, from which the wreaths had been gathered (in a garden there was a sepulchre). The chamber was not much unlike to some of those Etruscan tombs we visited, but dry, and neat, and clean, and dimly lighted through white-screened, low, square windows, and hung, all over the tables and other furniture, with simple white ; the only variety being a pair or two of branching candlesticks, whether only for use in case the friends should come to see him by night, I do not know, or whether also to symbolize the resurrection, when the life of the shrouded sleeper, like the flame of the white extinguished candle, would be rekindled. Both, perhaps. But the Commune of Schulz is intensely Protestant, the rather, perhaps, that their next neighbours of Tarasp are just as Romish.

Partly from this, and partly from a democratic feeling that would know no difference between rich and poor—but chiefly from the smallness of their beautiful churchyard, a little green knoll, rising precipitately on the banks of the Inn, which cannot be extended, and is scarcely large enough for themselves, though the graves are obliterated every five-and-twenty years—no grave stones are permitted, and still less any more lasting monuments to the dead. And so when the Sheriff arrived on Tuesday night, and Dr. George with him, and resolved, all the more on finding me there, to have James buried in Schulz, it became a somewhat difficult negotiation with the Commune to get leave, not only to have him buried, but to get a monument erected to him in the Schulz-Friedhof. . . .

However, it was managed, and at eleven on Wednesday the bell began to toll, inviting all the Schulzers to the funeral. They consider themselves as brothers of one family, into which the dead stranger had been adopted. How the doors and windows were darkened with the crowd! I began with the English service for the dead, and at the lesson from 1st Corinthians broke off into the Scotch service of free prayer. Then I conducted the service for the rest in German till the bell resumed tolling, and the coffin was borne out and up to the churchyard shoulder-high by the Mayor and Council, the leading men of the Commune. A good many English ladies also walked among the mourners. At the grave, when the bell again ceased tolling, the English service was resumed,. and at the end of this the Grison pastor had a prayer in Romaunsch, concluding with the benediction, which I translated into English.

It was a beautiful quiet day, and the whole scene of this burial among the mountains was singularly impressive, as you can more easily fancy than I can describe. The *Musik Direktor* of Stuttgart was present, and has described it in a beautiful prelude, which he composed, he said, immediately, like one inspired. He wanted to accompany the service on the organ in the church, but found the instrument execrable.

Professor Buchanan gives us a characteristic glimpse of Dr. Robertson at home in one of his favourite haunts :—

On the day following the funeral, Sheriff Blair and I, along with Dr. Robertson and Mr. John D. Campbell, drove up the valley to St. Moritz.   Dr. Robertson was at his best. What a wonderful companion in such a place !   Every spot seemed familiar to him, and he went on with anecdotes of the people, the place, its history and its traditions, as if he had lived in it all his life.   Two or three hours after starting, we stayed about half an hour to rest the horses in the shade. Dr. Robertson said, " I wish to take you, and especially Mr. John Campbell, to call at a house I know in this village." We went to the door, which was standing open, and Robertson called out some name, knocking at the same time. Presently a young woman came out and shook hands with the Doctor, and welcomed us in.   It was the meeting place of a club of riflemen, formerly of crossbow-men, still called the Crossbow Club.   Presently the brother came in and shook hands with Dr. Robertson, who introduced him to us, and specially to Mr. Campbell, saying, " This also is a Mr. John Campbell."   Of course we laughed at what we thought Robertson's joke, but he asked the young man to bring down from his cupboard a parchment diploma of membership of the club, when, sure enough, we read his name, Giovanni Campobello.

Writing of the Engadine, in 1884, Dr. Robertson says :—

My good pastor down the valley I could never find at home.   He had always gone, like Elijah's Baal, to the hunting.   He was an accomplished musician, and had his church choir admirably trained, to something very different from the howling wilderness of psalmody that prevails in some other mountain glens.   As among ourselves, the elderly people complain that the young ministry is not so rich in the doctrines of free grace and orthodox theology as

the good old men were wont to be, and they take refuge in
singing strongly pronounced evangelical hymns, which the
tuneful pastor and his jaunty choir have dropped from their
church hymn book. Such is that "*Su-su mein cœur*" (Up,
up, my heart).

Engadine Hymn.

Up, up, my heart !
No more give way to sadness;
　But know thou art
Redeemed to life and gladness.
　The secret, God long hid
In dark evangels,
　Now comes abroad
With trumpets of the angels.

　The hidden morn,
With which time long went mother,
　At last is born ;
O Christ ! Thou, and no other
　Com'st us to save,
From sin and dark disgraces,
　And through Thy grave
Show us sweet holy faces.

　In Bethlehem, see
One born of woman lowly,
　Meek Virgin she,
In shadow of the Holy.
　But Him, oh tell !
Who towers in grandeur lonely ?
　Earth, Heaven, and Hell
Make answer, "Jesus only."

Both God and man,
Unutterable wonder !
  In person one,
In nature still asunder.
  Of our flesh, God
Disrobeth Himself never ;
  And men, by blood,
His brothers are for ever.

  Who with sore pain
Death on the cross hath tasted,
  Our foes hath slain,
And their black kingdom wasted.
  The while He lay,
Bound in the grave's dark prison,
  Till the third day,
Behold the Conqueror risen !

  Him high Heaven holds,
With hands all pierced and bleeding,
  Which now He folds
For sinners interceding ;
  And shields us so
From Satan's fierce assaulting,
  When pilgrims go
Upon their journey halting.

  Up then, my heart !
To Thee, my Jesus only,
  Till when I part
On my last journey lonely,
  Safe from all harms,
Thy blood shall shield me dying,
  Till in Thine arms
I wake to find me lying.

This in the Romaunsch I heard sung, to a simple mountain
air, by my landlady, as she sat knitting in her wainscoted
parlour, waiting the return of her children from school, and
her goats from the meadow. The foremost goat which bears
the bell, rings it over the lower sash of the little wicket in
the great half-moon house-door. She rises still singing, and
opens to her flock of goats, wondering the while whether a
door might not be opened to some other goats, though their
creed was not orthodox, if they brought home udders well
filled with sweet milk! The goats, having been well behaved, get their reward in salt ; and the children, having just
come home, ride on their backs across the floor before
tumbling them down to the lower regions of the cellar. All
this I overhear, sitting in Madame's deliciously-scented red
pine chamber up the ladder, that conducts to the hay-loft on
the right hand, and this best room on the left, through whose
little white curtained western window, I have seen the goats
and the children cross the village bridge over the river Inn,
and climb the ascent to Madame Flüghi's, that stands, a
stately house, hard by the belfred church where the choir
sings. Under its shadow in the green mound, looking across
the Inn every moonlight night from the hay-loft, I saw the
ghost of a poor soul that had moved his neighbour's land-
mark in his life time, carrying it back after his death,
and doomed to carry it with sighs and groans, that sounded
like the wind among the pines and snow, to all eternity.
There too sounded the voice of the shepherd who had
neglected to give his flock their salt, and had come back to
call them, but they never came.

In this green churchyard by the mountains old Planta de
Sadour had just been buried. An aged branch of the old
Planta tree, and representative of the family, he had wished
to bequeath to me, as much as he could convey in words, of
his antiquarian lore, but took ill on the day I arrived, and I

saw him first in his shroud. I was at the funeral feast, which began early in the morning, and reminded me strongly of the feasts I had seen pictured on the walls of Etrurian sepulchres, as for instance at Chiusi, the ancient Clusium, after which the next place up the valley seems to have derived its name of Clus. On the open street the coffin was placed, and the burial service read by the hunting pastor, in gown and cap, in presence of the Commune, in front of the door, that rose above a flight of steps, and carried the inscription on its lintel—

> " Planta has this house restored,
>   Let all who enter praise the Lord."

At ten that night the timid "Messiner" or sexton seemed more nervous than usual in ringing the church bell. His wife who was braver than her husband, like the wife of Manoah, had to stand on the steeple stair with a lantern in her hand, while he ascended to ring the bell. At twelve he began to call the hours—a timid night watch—beginning as usual under my window with a simple chant of a minor third—C the reciting and A the final note as thus :—

> " *In mann da* | *Dieu*
>   *Hat dat das dodesh in mann da* | *Dieu.*"

Miss Robertson has furnished the following note :—

In the summer of 1884, a young woman in the neighbourhood of Westfield was dying of consumption. William was much interested in her case and he visited her frequently during the last weeks of her life. On the evening of the last visit, I remember meeting him on his return, when he was standing at the gate under the pines, listening to the weird and melancholy music overhead, which seemed to have in it that night a deeper wail than usual. "She is still alive," he said, "but evidently unconscious, though she wakened up when I repeated the closing lines of the Engadine hymn—the last she will ever hear on earth. When it comes to midnight—for that's the time she'll go— we must sing that hymn;" and so when the midnight hour came, in the dimly-lighted room, and to the solemn tones of the organ, we sang softly as in the presence of death—

> " Up then, my heart !
> To Thee, my Jesus only,
>   Till when I part
> On my last journey lonely,
>   Safe from all harms,
> Thy blood shall shield me dying,
>   Till in Thine arms
> I wake to find me lying."

" I think she will be across now," he said, and we parted for the night.

When we came down in the morning, the news were awaiting us that she had passed away.

To Miss T. Melville-Lee, the friend to whom the letter about the hymn was written, I am indebted for an interesting account of Dr. Robertson's Engadine life, from which some extracts are given :—

I was very young when I made the acquaintance of Dr. Robertson, nearly ten years ago. I had gone with my mother for a first journey abroad, and we met at the Kulm Hotel, St. Moritz, Engadine. I well recall the evening of our first meeting. A friend had introduced him to my mother, and they fell into a long talk on the history of the Middle Ages. I listened, watching the play of light and humour over his well-cut features, and liking his deep musical voice with its delicate Scotch accent and the expressive roll of the letter " *r.*"

He would tell us in our afternoon walks of Engadine
history and legends; and on a very cold afternoon, when the
trees were covered with light snow, and the winter seemed
fairly to have begun, he took us to call on the village pastor
and to see the village school.   He talked to the children in
Romaunsch, and they seemed quite at home with him.   " In
Süss " he said " I gathered some of the children from the
streets, and had them in to say, or sing, and I wrote down, as
I could, their playful rhymes of the Mary-may-tanza (dance)
and Zingar (Gipsy) ring class and I tried to tell them stories—
among others, some of their own country, but found myself
forestalled by their excellent primary school-books, which tell
the story in little snatches of clear continuous narrative for
simple reading lessons, in the German language, which these
children must be taught to enable them to mix with the rest
of the world."   He showed us some of these reading books
with the story of Winkelried, William Tell, etc., and we
stayed to watch the sturdy dark-eyed children making pot
hooks and hangers in their copy books.

In the late autumn evenings, Dr. Robertson would invite us into his salon to sit round his warm stove, and
among the books piled on chairs and floor, while he made
out routes for our Italian tour and told us the history of places
and men, to illuminate our way, until he should join us himself.   To those who had not the privilege of hearing that
voice, I can never hope to convey the charm of his conversation.   His knowledge of languages and his extraordinary
memory enabled him to select the exact words he wanted, and
he was beyond this, gifted by nature with a peculiar grace
and aptitude of speech.   Above all his great gifts, shone his
kindliness, and his tender insight into the feelings of others.
He had an irresistible desire to give them some of his own
joy, in nature, art, literature, or any other thing through
which pleasure could possibly reach them.

There was in the hotel a strange German gentleman who avoided every one, and was in consequence generally shunned, and his habits and form of dress were so singular and unpleasing that no one felt inclined to interfere with him. He paced alone outside the hotel, and appeared only at meal times when he ate voraciously and complained of the dishes. He was known as a woman-hater, and had been heard to speak of us (the harmless ladies of the hotel circle), as "vultures." His lonely life attracted the ready sympathy of Dr. Robertson, who would sit with him of an evening, in the cold little smoking room, and draw him into conversation. Singular and unlikable as he was, Dr. Robertson's kindliness penetrated the crust of suspicion gathered by a life of mistake and disappointment. To him, this solitary man confided the story of his life, and how it was that he had come to regard all women as "vultures"! Whether Dr. Robertson was able to shake his opinion I cannot say, but a few weeks after, Dr. Robertson disappeared from the *table-d'hôte*, and soon after the strange German disappeared too. On inquiry we learned that Dr. Robertson was ill, having been affected by the sudden cold. He was with us again in a few days making light of his illness, but he told us of the devotion of his strange friend, who had asked to sit up with him at night, and had nursed him by day, bringing his meals to eat in his room, and waiting on him with persistent faithfulness.

The extract which follows, addressed to the son of his old friend, in answer to a request that he should contribute a sketch of Dr. MacEwen for a memorial volume, illustrates that inability to put his thoughts into writing, which was so disappointing to the many friends who listened to Dr. Robertson's conversation.

To Mr. Alexander R. MacEwen, M.A. (Oxon.).

St. Moritz, Friday, October, 1876.

. . . I was willing to try and write something or
other (though it should never, or only in an indirect manner,
be made use of) if I could, because you wished it; but the
state of my health and the shortness of the time totally
prevent me. The table in my room, on which your papers
lie, I have haunted as a moth haunts the candle. Briskly I
went at it, resolved to conquer the feeling of illness by the
force of will, and to write in spite of it; and I did so, but
had to pay the penalty. Some fragmentary notes I wrote
for a beginning, but since doing so I have not even been
able to transcribe them.

An undated fragment found among his papers,
which evidently, from the handwriting, belongs to this
period, reveals that the difficulty of writing was
with him not a temporary result of illness, but had
its root in the peculiar constitution of his mind :—

Through what hidden ways, I say, the mind works, and
how rapidly too, not by going from thought to thought, as
speech must do, like a policeman with a lantern by night
from door to door, but by glances—swift, lightning-like
glances—that take them all in simultaneously and abreast.
For what a mystery our thinking is, and what a small, a very
small percentage speech is on that untold wealth of thought
that flashes through the mind sometimes in a single moment !
Words are only as the successive drop-drop-droppings from
a cistern that holds an ocean all at once. You can never
say the hundredth part of what you want to say, nor perhaps
the thousandth part of what you think, if you think to
any purpose and with any power. Behind the words

behind the speech, behind the broadest, freest, most abundant eloquence, there always lies a vast infinity of thoughts unuttered and things unspeakable—a firmament on firmament of brilliant thought, it may be, that ascends, like Paul, into the third heaven; and words are at the most and best, like Paul on his return. They are as the stars on the dark and silent face of the midnight sky—those little punctured pinholes (as a child would say)—those "gimlet holes to let the glory through." Where it is so difficult as one finds it, to write letters—to write anything as one would—it may be speech is somewhat easier, because in public speaking a necessity is laid upon you to be always saying something; for if you halt a single moment, staggering beneath the weight of great thought that oppresses you, you are lost, you are undone, and you know it; and so you run on determinedly, and all visions of angels will not attract you when you're running in terror for your life. But with writing it is different, unless you happen to be writing for a newspaper or a periodical, which must be out immediately, or writing with the wolf of hunger and the printer's devils at your heels. To every little opening of the mouth, to every little scribble on paper that you make and tell in word, a hundred or a thousand thoughts are crowding, crying all, all, "Let us out," and you can only let out one at once.

CHAPTER XVI.

Again in Italy and at Home.

It was arranged that Mr. James Robertson of Newington should, for the sake of the health of his youngest daughter, Jessie, spend the winter of 1876-7 at San Remo, and take charge of the Presbyterian station which had been opened there some years before by Dr. John Ker. When, therefore, Dr. Robertson was compelled by the cold to leave the Engadine at the end of October, he bent his steps in the direction of the Riviera, instead of going at once to Florence.

To His Younger Sister.

Hotel de Londres, San Remo, 7th November, 1876.

Day after day on my journey down I carried the thought of you, and the desire and purpose of writing you, past every station and post office on the way. There was Chiavenna, which Isabella will remember, where I climbed the castle rock and made a fresh unsuccessful search for asbestos. Then Cadenabbia, where I stayed four days, but did not cross to our old haunt at Bellagio. Then

Como, where, being All Souls' Day, some acres of cemetery were lighted up at dusk, under the full moonshine, with lamps in the royal Italian colours, red, green, and white—a Dantesque way of projecting the politics of one world into the picture and prospect of another. Then Milan, where I revisited the cathedral and Cenacolo and St. Ambrose, of course, and foregathered with some friends, with whom I visited the Certosa, and from that came all alone to the historical old town of Pavia. . . .

Thanks for your notes on my clothes, with which I will provide myself fully under Mrs. Smith's instructions. Mrs. S. packed into my trunk a great treasure of bobbins, and buttons, and worsted, and work-bags, and pin-cushions, and needles, and thread, and all, which have been of infinite service to me—not that I ever made the smallest use of them, but they made my trunk look furnished-like; and Jessie has just got some of them away to mend my stocking-holes, and other holes in my coat. In the shoulder of my dress coat there was one which showed the lining, but I mended it in the Engadine with ink.

The friend who has furnished us with an account of the Engadine, again writes :—

On a bright, cold morning, when all the trees were covered with heavy rime we left St. Moritz. Two nights later we were in Milan. . . . There Dr. Robertson joined us next day, arriving at some late hour at night when I had gone to bed, having mistaken the train and gone out of his way to please some strangers by taking them to see a ruined castle. "Nevertheless, I am here to be your Greatheart in your pilgrimage," he said, cheerily, when he came down to breakfast; and I had not been many hours with him in Milan before I realized that he was there indeed! From him I learned to understand and admire the purity and harmony and Christian symbolism of the early Gothic. "The arch," he said, " is like the hands put up in prayer ; the roof is like alternative singing of the *decani* and *cantores* in the choir, as the voices cut each other in the arch. Gothic architecture, specially in its early days, is pure, severe, and noble. The lofty shaft, the spring of the arch, and the high-pitched roof it dared to conceive and produce, are full of aspiration and unwavering faith. In the architecture of the philosophic Greeks we have a different style. Their buildings are strong and full of exquisite decoration and proportion, but complete in themselves, bearing up the heavy weight of mind and thought, of present and future, alone in symmetrical completion ; while the Gothic would say, ' Look upward. Not here ! '

" But Gothic architecture has never flourished in perfection on the southern side of the Alps. It belongs to Germany, England, North France, and to lands of cold and severity, as the name implies, where the gabled roof is built to throw off the storm, and trees asssume a pyramidal shape for the same reason. As you cross the Alps, and near the southern sun, the roof becomes flatter, and the trees spread out their branches almost in level bars, like the stone-pines and palm-trees of Italy. You will see the round Romanesque arch prevails most widely through Italy, that which you would call in England, Norman, though it has not the same ornamentation."

We parted with him at the Pavia station, after one day at the Certosa, with hope of meeting again at Florence. A strange picturesque figure he looked, as he stood at the window of the railway carriage in Inverness cloak, his wild, grey hair thrown back under a soft, grey felt hat.

His niece so far rallied that he was able to leave her about the beginning of December, and spend a month at Florence, where he was found once more in his old haunts, followed by eager listeners.　Early in January he returned to San Remo, taking with him as far as Pisa a party of his Florence friends, one of whom testifies that the day they spent there "was a day never to be forgotten."　He was in his most brilliant mood, his earnest expositions of the frescoes in the Campo Santo being ever and again lighted up with flashes of humour, as when, pointing to the figure representing a soul in the "Last Judgment"—a little naked figure drawn upwards by an angel, and downwards by a devil, he said, "The black fellow has the law of gravitation on his side."

The following lines were the outcome of that visit to Pisa :—

The "Campo Santo."

In the Campo Santo, Pisa,
Every passing tourist sees a
Cloistered square of holy mould,
Brought from Palestine of old—
From the garden—from the clay—
From the place where Jesus lay.

Pious thought of those old Pisans,
Which, for this, and other reasons,
Moved them, at great cost and toil,
To fetch home the holy soil,
Fifty ship loads, shipped at Acre;
The good templar knights the while,
Seaward from the holy city,
When crusaders fought to take her,
Guarding transport troops that came a
Quick route overland by Rama,

Camels, mules, and loaded waggons,
Guarding from those flying dragons,
Moslem horsemen, bent on war,
Hovering round them near and far,
With glitt'ring shield and scimitar.

All those ship loads through the seas,
Brought by Pisan galleys strong,
Priests aboard on bended knees
Chanting holy prayer and song,
While the sailor to the breeze
Spreads the sail, and sings with these,
Now an *Ave*, now a *Canto*,
Till at length the port is made,
And the holy earth all laid
In the Pisan Campo Santo.

Then for very joy they weep,
Thinking, when they die, to sleep
Safely in that very clay,
In which blessed Jesus lay.
Blessed rest for the Pisans weary!
Tho' the night be dark and dreary,
With the cold ground for their bed,
And the stony pillow underhead,
Yet, in the dream of death below,
Angels in white may come and go,—
As in the marble, where one sees a
Jacob's dream by John of Pisa,—
Till in the morning dawn they hear,
Maybe with somewhat less of fear,
Maybe with somewhat less dismay,
Because they are clad in the holy clay,
Ringing loud, and shrill, and clear,
The trump of the " Dies Iræ."

As for me this Easter morn,
Since I have seen the buried corn,
To its tomb so lately borne,
Rise as the Christ rose from the dead,
Lifting high its living head,
Over the dry and blackened mould,
Under which, in damp and cold,
It did lie but yesterday,—
Now I know that all the clay,
Through all fields and gardens spread,
Weaving the garments for the dead,—
All the earth and all the mould,
In all churchyards new and old,
Has been blessed and sanctified,
Through the grave of the Christ that died,—
Blest as truly from His lips,
As the holy earth in the Pisan ships;
And whether at Palestine or Pisa,
Or wherever else one sees a
Grave—Hark ! " Come !" the angels say,
" See the place where Jesus lay."

TO MR. WILLIAM M'CALL, Irvine.

SAN REMO, 20th January, 1877.

You ask me if I am writing a book, or what I am doing ;
and I have written the answer in a general way in a little
playful song—in a solution of weak rhyme. *Eviva* is the
refrain of many Italian songs. I shall tell you more particularly afterwards, when I write you also in answer to your
inquiries about music.

Eviva.

I heard all the birds, in the days of spring,
Twitter and chatter, and whistle and sing,

But the earth in these days gave no fruit,
Nor till harvest time when the birds were mute ;
And then came the reaper and vintager out,
And brought home the corn and wine with a shout—
                                        Eviva.

In days of old, when I was young,
Flowed silver speech from a fluent tongue,
But now I keep silence, as I ought,
And the silence gives me golden thought ;
And whether by speech or by pictured book,
For something or other ere long you may look—
                                        Eviva.

The gay young summer, in whites and greens,
Is never an end, but is only a means
To that higher end which the autumn brings,
When sweating brow'd labour feasts with kings,
And the year is crown'd with a golden crown,
And all heaven's paths drop fatness down—
                                        Eviva.

So those who prefer their youth to their age
Must be making a backward pilgrimage ;
When things go right, the beginning's not ill,
But the end, says the wise man, is better still,
And fools they must be, who prefer the past,
When the Banquet of Life gives the good wine last—
                                        Eviva.

His niece died on April 22nd. Some time after he
returned to Florence, and in the early summer took up
his quarters at the Villa Mozzi near Fiesole, placed
at his disposal by the proprietor, the Cav. Guglielmo
Spence, an English artist almost Italianized. with

whom Dr. Robertson was on terms of friendly cordiality.

To Mr. William M'Call, Irvine.

Villa Mozzi, Fiesole, June, 1877.

You have heard of the sorrows of successive bereavement in which my brother, "deep calling unto deep," has been plunged, and in which, in its last gulf, I myself got more involved, through presence and sight and sympathy, than I could have counted on. She was a lovely, holy child that, with much desire and longing, and without a moment's doubt or misgiving, went to join her sisters and mother in the white circle of the blessed, and "Jesus in the midst." Her father, terribly broken down at the beginning, behaved himself at the end, to our wonder and admiration, in the grand dignity and composure of a truly Christian grief; and out of that last depth and baptism of grief he, I trust, and all of us, have come, in white raiment and spirit, more subdued and quiet and mild, yet also brave, for the joy that is set every day and hour, and more especially through darker days more nearly and more clearly, before us.

Mr. Caird thus describes the Villa Mozzi :—

The villa is situated about halfway between San Domenico and Fiesole, rather nearer the latter, on the slope of the steep hill, a spur of the Apennines. The view is one of the most enchanting imaginable. Looking south-west, about two hundred feet below, Florence lies on either side of the silver Arno, rearing aloft her domes and spires in the keen Tuscan air—such a dream of beauty as is scarcely to be equalled on earth. The whole country is dotted with fair villas in sumptuous gardens, with dark, sharp-pointed cypresses breaking the lines of mulberries, bearing festoons of vines at regular

intervals in the golden grain fields.   The horizon is bounded
by tier upon tier of terraced hills melting into dim distance,
enclosing a land consecrated by memories of patriots, poets,
philosophers, and painters such as no other portion of the
world can boast.   No fitter setting surely could be found for
the central figure of your memoir.   And no one could enjoy
more fully the natural beauties spread before his gaze.   The
villa was built by Cosimo "pater patriae," and completed
by his son, Lorenzo il Magnifico.   Here the Florentine
Academy, the group of *littérateurs* who brought about, under
the fostering of the Medici, the ever famous revival of letters,
held their meetings.   Here Pico della Mirandola, Angelo
Poliziano, and Marsilio Ficino perfected those translations of
and disquisitions on the Platonic writings, which have borne
such abundant fruit in all subsequent ages.

The rooms of the Villa are furnished in the style of the
period, the *quattro-cento*, and it needs no great effort of imagination to transport oneself back to the 15th century, when
the famous Academy under the leadership of the brilliant,
scholarly, if licentious, Lorenzo, held converse on the eternal
verities of the Platonic dialogues under the ilex groves of
the villa garden.   The dome of the cathedral rears itself
side by side with the Campanile now as then ; the spires of
Santa Croce and of Santa Maria Novella cleave the silent
air not otherwise than four hundred years ago.   Nothing is
changed.

Here Dr. Robertson spent several weeks, living as surely
in the sacred past of several centuries ago as if he too had
been one of that famous band—forgetting sometimes that he
was not.

He occupied the bedroom which bears the name of
Marsilio Ficino, the celebrated translator of Plato.

His days were spent in wandering about Fiesole, exploring
the remains of Etruscan and Roman architecture with which

the neighbourhood abounds, and in excursions in the Val
d'Arno, in search of unearthed art treasures, in the company
of a few belated English students. His evenings were in-
terminable, and often prolonged themselves into the next day.

The associations with which the Villa abounded impelled
him to a closer study of the lives of the great men who had
made it famous, and he used to wander night after night
from room to room book in hand, apostrophizing and in-
terrogating their long dead but immortal inmates. Here
too he was in touch with his ideal martyr, Fra Girolamo
Savonarola, the contemporary and counterpoise of the
Academy. And from him to Luther, his great rival, and the
subject of Dr. Robertson's greatest essay, was but a short
step. A correspondent writes how one night in the Villa
Mozzi, long after the great bell of the Duomo of Florence
had sent its midnight tollings booming through the heavy
air of the campagna, and the whole world was sunk in
slumbers, Dr. Robertson worked back from the heroes of
the Pagan revival through Savonarola to the founder of Pro-
testantism, and told how the idea of the lecture on Luther
had first taken form in his mind. Unconsciously he drew
himself up ; invisible audiences started up before him, and
with all the old unction and emphasis he gave again the
never to be forgotten scene of the birth of the great
Reformer.

To Miss T. Melville-Lee.

At Midnight, from the top of Fiesole,
19-20th June, 1877.

As I write at midnight in a high open loggia of the old
" Villa Medici " at Fiesole, the noiseless moon is "walking
in brightness through the heavens,"

"The moon, whose orb
Through optic glass the Tuscan artist views
At evening, from the top of Fesolé,"

making me think less of Galileo and his telescope than of a certain hour of prayer, as you may understand. Midnight here will scarcely be eleven with you, for the shadow on the great sun dial, which is the earth itself, moves slowly westward, so that the light lingers with you after it has left us. But to us shall it not return the sooner in the morning? Even as the light of life will be shining, no doubt, on your face, still young, when that of your old friend is lying under the darkness; through this, after all, shall he not come the sooner, and before you, to the sunrise, and the angels of the everlasting dawn coming to meet him, through the cypresses of death. For so I have sometimes thought of a morning, when looking at daybreak from my chamber in the east. It was the same that was occupied, 400 years ago, by Pico, the Prince of Mirandola, and, like the chamber of peace in the " Pilgrim's Progress," it has its casement opening to the sunrise, and from it you can look along the black avenue of cypresses that stretch aslant the hill side, between the house and the highway.

Down such an avenue our Fra Giovanni of Fiesole may have seen the shining ones walking, with the rainbow hues of the morning on their white dewy wings, when he caught them and imprisoned them in the tower and the temple of the marvellous, till he let them out again to walk, as they still do, along the cloisters of San Marco. The abbey of San Domenico, where he (Fra Angelico) saw the vision of his youth, lies deep under, but not far from our south windows, and the terrace on which they open. You will see that I am living, as I meant to do, at the " Villa Medici"; they call it " Villa Mozzi," and also " Villa Spence," but " Medici " is the true name, by which I find it called in the old books, and which I have been urging Mr. Spence to restore. Here Lorenzo, the Magnificent, gathered around him the chosen spirits (and, especially, the seven stars) of the Platonic Academy. They had their rooms along the corridor, upstairs ; I have the whole range of them, and indeed, of the whole house, and when driven from one (say Pico's, by the heat) may retire into the next, which is Poliziano's, and which is cooler, and then into the next, which is Ficino's, and so on to the last, which was Leo's (the 10th). There I have put my books, and established my study. It opens on the western loggia, in which I write by the golden olive lamp light, in the delicious moonlight, and midnight coolness *al fresco*, and flash of fire-flies, and serenade of nightingales, and slumberous rustle of the trees, that sweeten and perfume the air, and in all the witchery of a soft, clear, balmy, Tuscan summer night. I look down through open arches upon the city of Florence, like a wilderness of stars, almost like a running river of fire, in the Val d'Arno, and upwards to where (speaking learnedly, as becomes the classic spot) Diana is mounting the sky to the haunt of the Great Bear, and Cassiopeia, in her low arm-chair, in the north, looking up sulkily, and forward down the Val d'Arno, and over the Carrara Mountains, Westward Ho !—to home—and all that is dearest to me still on earth (delightful, though it be, this Italy), and upward—reverently—above things visible, above all moons and firmaments of stars, to seek and see the face of the Unseen, the splendour of the King Invisible, before whose face the earth and the heavens shall flee away, but yet before whom in the very holiest of all, I hope to stand in Christ, and see you stand dressed in spotless white ! " The Lord bless thee and keep thee ! Oh, that Thou wouldst bless her indeed ! and keep her from evil that it may not grieve her. The Lord lift upon thee the light of His countenance, and give thee peace ! "

During this visit to Florence, Dr. Robertson was

commissioned by his friend Dr. Young of Kelly to purchase pictures of the old masters for a collection he was trying to form. The following fragment of a letter refers to this commission :—

Such as it is, my loving appreciation of fine art is that of the mere child (the baby, if you please)—who gazes on fine pictures with open eyes of wonder and delight, which one does not care to analyze, and that is the more genuine, and even more precious perhaps as an æsthetical judgment, that it is unsophisticated and unconscious, though, I daresay, I could give good reasons enough for my likings and dislikings if need were—rather than that of the expert, the connoisseur, the professional critic, the picture dealer, on whose province I have no right, and still less than no desire, to intrude. To the educated eye, that can read off at a glance whole pages of pictorial scripture, and go into microscopic technical details, I can make no pretensions. But there is another eye which does not necessarily make a pair with that, and yet may see in its own way as keenly and as far—the eye, sometimes called " the single eye," into which conscience enters, which sees in the "true light that lighteth every man that cometh into the world," and which distinguishes between good and bad painting, by distinguishing between moral good and evil. I do not mean to say I am a Purist (though I confess I do prefer that school), but I do mean to say, and you will not misunderstand me when I say what I say with all reverence, that I have seen some pictured Christs—for instance, yon Da Vinci at Milan— containing so much of the real Christ—so much of Him that is holy, Him that is true—of the divinely sad and the unutterably beautiful—that it would have seemed to me a sort of sacrilege to speak of buying and selling them ; it would have reminded me most uncomfortably of the bargain between Judas and the High Priests to have proposed to value them at so many pieces of silver, it matters not how many. I would rather, if it were possible, that the buyers and sellers should be driven from temples of fine art. Of course, that is impossible, but it may help to explain to you how I don't much care to be mixed up in the traffic of sacred pictures.

Dr. Robertson's return home was, as on a former occasion, hastened by tidings of trouble in Trinity Church. The letters he received cost him much anxious thought. The spirit in which he answered them may be gathered from the following fragment :—

To MR. JOHN WRIGHT, Irvine.

TRENT, AUSTRIAN TYROL, 18th July, 1877.

.   .   .   You must know that we older men are apt to be impatient of a younger, even though it should be a more excellent ministry ; and to think it not nearly so good as what we ourselves used to enjoy or exercise. And just the longer and the more deeply we have been interested in the true welfare of the church, just the more tempted are we to be suspicious of change that after all is not real change, of ways that are new ways, but have still the old direction, of music that seems new music, but has still the old ring. We are tempted to lament that the old stage-coach has been replaced by the less poetic railway, though the latter brings us to our destination as surely and more quickly after all. I speak for myself. I know I am liable to this temptation as I grow older, and I pray against it. It is so natural. "No man when he hath tasted old wine straightway desireth new, for he saith, the old is better." But the new wine may turn out the better wine in the end, if it come of a better vintage and be not checked and spoiled in the fermenting. Of course it must always be the true "wine of the kingdom." All else is vinegar and gall to those that have their senses exercised to discern between good and evil. But what if the good wine of the covenant itself be sometimes mistaken by us, as we grow old, for vinegar. You remember my own young sermons, in the old Cotton Row—weak enough truly. I am ashamed to think of them. But they had new ways of thought and speech for the time ; and you who were young, as I was, sympathized with me. How I remember you then in that front gallery, looking so critical, yet so kind ! But the old orthodox—how they listened to know if this new music had the old evangelical ring. It had, and they discerned it, and forgave the new thinking for the sake of the old gospel ; and finally accepted it themselves and broadened and rose with us into a wider and higher, but still more distinctly pronounced, evangelism. Never through Trinity pulpit may any other be heard than the voice of the Good Shepherd, which the children of the Truth shall recognize ! But may He not utter that voice through new disguises, just to prove and try us older men, whether we can recognize it under all disguises, as, if we are the children of the Truth, we shall be able to do? "The voice of my Beloved !" Should I not know it under all change and all disguise? "Jesus saith unto her, Mary. She saith to Him, Rabboni, Master." The voice of the Good Shepherd that calleth His sheep by name. They know Him and they follow Him ; and a stranger will they not follow, for they know not the voice of strangers.

To Mr. William M'Call, Irvine.

Cologne, 2nd August, 1877.

Here I am, looking out on the Cologne minster, on the last Continental stage, as I hope, of my journey homeward,

as to-morrow I go on without more halt to London, unless
something unexpected detain me.   .   .   .

I would have kept up to time, and am not very much behind it, as indicated in my programme, had I not been
detained first in Trent, by some things I was finding out
about the grand Council held there of old; and second in
Munich, where I lost two days. Lost, did I say? What
days of gain they were. On each of them I saw Dr. Döllinger, and, though I had no introduction to him, dined with
this great man at his own invitation, and had long conversations alone—a privilege, they tell me, he does not accord to
one among a thousand that wait on him, being very difficult
of access, and much shut up in his study and himself.

Dr. Robertson often spoke of the extreme cordiality
with which Dr. Döllinger received him. He met him
at the University and introduced himself by simply
presenting his card. Döllinger then asked him to
dinner. The conversation became so earnest that
when dinner was brought in they did not heed it, and
hardly ate at all. The housekeeper came in again and
again, and looked pathetically at the untasted food.

Dr. Robertson's love for the Trinity Church, to which
he returned from his wanderings, made a gift which
came to him at the close of 1877 specially valuable.

To MISS TAYLOR, Edinburgh.

IRVINE, 15th December, 1877.

By the hands of his young Reverence Monsignore, the
latest abbot-elect of Kilwinning,[1] I have been put in posses-

---

[1] Miss Taylor's brother had just been elected minister of the United
Presbyterian Church of Kilwinning. The family to which they belonged
was connected with Mr. James Robertson's congregation in Newington.

sion of your Eccellenza's charming picture of the interior—
apse and south transept of our Trinity Church.   .   .   .

In your dream-like picture I seem to myself again to
enter that pulpit, and see, rising around me, many faces
of the living and the dead, all agleam with the light of
devotion, and, by the prayers, by the preaching, by the
music, by the ladder of art and grace around them, climbing
up through the half-opened gate called Beautiful, to glimpses
of the temple of God opened in Heaven, and the King in
His beauty in the land afar off.   How often, in the bright
midsummer mornings—how often in the dark December days
—breakings of the dawn above all dawn have seemed to fall
upon us there !   And that very light you seem to me to have
caught and put somehow into your picture.   It is not
that rose-coloured light I mean that you have caught from
the tinted transept window and made to blossom out so
richly in the sculptured Caen stone ; not that, but a " light
that never was on sea or land," and which must have fallen
on the picture and spread itself from some mystic lamp in
the temple of your brain, where there is a shrine, I believe,
and sanctuary (is there not ?) to the Holiest of All, that has
His presence chamber in your inmost heart within ; and
with that light you will always, I hope, mix your colours.

Another cause which rendered Dr. Robertson's
home-coming urgent in the autumn of 1877 was the
state of his sister Isabella's health.   The illness which
had hindered her from accompanying him when he
went abroad eighteen months before, had taken a new
development, involving severe pain, under which her
strength gradually failed, till, on December 22nd, 1877,
she passed away.

To the Rev. James Brown.

Bridge of Allan, Sunday, 23rd December, 1877.

For our dear Isabella the mystery is now all ended. She sees no more through a glass darkly. The light dawned of "the other morn than ours," yesterday evening at half-past five

How often she went timidly to church, shrinking back from it in great and true humility. To-day she is gone up to church, humble as ever, self-condemned as a very publican praying in the temple; and yet, or should I not say, and therefore, she is presented faultless in the presence of the throne.

The sweetest singer in our church choir, I know not if there is a sweeter singer in the upper choir to-day. I wonder if her song makes any mention, James, of your name and mine. I am afraid they are not too well known there. But that is a selfish remark. How utterly unselfish she was, and how self-sacrificing in her sisterly affection. Her love to me was wonderful, and her whole life intensely beautiful, as you had eyes to see; though hung about with strange curtains of shadow, which the poor child could not understand. They are all withdrawn now.

I never knew any other that brought Christ so near to me as she did. She was so like Him in gentle innocence, and sorest suffering, and agony of quiet, exhaustless love. All my saddest hours, and truly gladdest hours, are bound up with her, and the shortest day, which has torn her from us, has proved the very darkest in my life. And yet how thankful we should be, and are, that there have been granted her, with Jessie here at the Bridge, such a light at evening time, such a sweetening and brightening of her last days when the mental powers, which could be obscured, but could not be hid, and when the moral loveliness, that could not even be obscured, shone out as bright, or brighter, than ever.

To Mrs. Watson, Largs.

Bridge of Allan, 3rd January, 1878.

Nothing in my life, that has been darkened with many bereavements, has touched me like the loss of this sweetest and gentlest of sisters, the companion and crown for many years of my otherwise lonely life, and the mysterious depth of whose self-sacrificing love to me especially (you saw something of that in Mentone), none, save God, who Himself endowed her with it, knows.

That you, with your quick, sympathetic discernment of whatsoever things are lovely, should have seen a rare loveliness in her I do not wonder. Even to others, to all with whom she came into contact, she wore a beauty of character of the most refined and delicate grace and texture, rendered transparent by the holy light within. . . . For several weeks her great sufferings from spinal paralysis, that had been growing on her for years, made her sick-room a very Gethsemane of trial; but the strengthening angel was with her in the agony, and the Christ of the Gethsemane was in her; and, through her pain, her love to us all broke forth continually, and her song, "Nearer, my God, to Thee," and her prayer, "Thy will be done." . . . To the last her attitude was that of one saying, "Though I cannot keep hold on Him, He will (will He not?) keep me;" and so she fell asleep in His arms, not a cry or struggle at the end; no wrestling with the angel of death in the night. She knew His name of Love, and he blessed her there, and the morning broke.

It was at the hour of evening sacrifice, on a clear winter night, and presently she was beyond the stars, and the "Brother born for adversity" healing all the wounds of sorrow of her gentle spirit, with leaves from the Tree of Life, that is in the midst of the Paradise of God. Everything goes to comfort us concerning her who is asleep, and as you have been sympathizing with us in the sorrow, I have written that you may also in the consolation.

The breathless form, still beautiful, was laid away in darkness underground beneath the fresh-fallen snow on Thursday last in the old churchyard of St. Ninians, and there with the stone for her pillow she sleeps, as she has done every night for long, long years at home or abroad, beneath the ascending and descending angels, at the gate of heaven, till the day dawn. May we all meet in gladness there! And shall we not at all remember Mentone in that reunion? Shall there not stand distinguished in the group your admirable mother, of whom Isabella used to speak so very often as one of the queenliest of ladies she had ever met? Must they not have met again? . . .

At the close of January Dr. Robertson and his only surviving sister left for the south. They took lodgings in London in the neighbourhood of the British Museum, where he continued the archæological studies he had entered on in Italy. At the beginning of March they returned to Tuscany that he might resume his investigations among the Etruscan cities, which had been interrupted in 1876. Florence was their headquarters, but the greater part of their time was spent in other places. They revisited Orvieto. Thence they passed to San Gemignano, whither he went in search of mediæval music, which to this day is sung in the churches of that old town in much of its original purity. He got what he wanted through the clever little daughter of their landlord Giusti, a tiny child of nine, possessing that wonderful musical power which is not rare among Italian children. She entertained them for hours by singing the entire round of Festa music for the year. Many of the airs were taken down as she sang them ; and in his enthusiasm a translation of each church hymn was to be made on the spot ! The only one actually accomplished was the " Stabat Mater." He had translated it hurriedly when at Siena two years before, but was dissatisfied with his work. Under the inspiration of the music he heard at San Gemignano the following version was produced :—

Stabat Mater.

Stands the dolorous mother weeping,
By the cross her vigil keeping,
Where her Son was crucified.
> Stabat Mater dolorosa,
> Juxta crucem lacrymosa,
> Dum pendebat Filius.

Where her drooping eyelids languish
O'er Him, and the sword of anguish
Pierces through the Mother's side,
> Stabat Mater, etc.

Veil'd she stands in grief unspoken,
How much more is Thy heart broken.
Oh, Jesu Maria thou !
> Stabat Mater, etc.

Hers of ours was anguish double,
Grief for sin, and Mother's trouble
Met and mingled both in one.
> Stabat Mater, etc.

Both to life and death she brought Him,
And in double anguish sought Him
As her Saviour and her Son.
>> Stabat Mater, etc.

Oh ! Thou Son of Man, our Brother,
A frail woman was Thy Mother,
And Thy Father is our God !
>> Stabat Mater, etc.

Help us, like to her who bore Thee,
Deeply mourning, to adore Thee,
Who hast saved us by Thy blood.
>> Stabat Mater, etc.

Help us through Thy Cross to borrow
Double strength of love and sorrow,
Like to her who called Thee Son.
>> Stabat Mater, etc.

Till rich Heaven repay all losses,
And the crowns repay the crosses,
When the victory is won.
>> Stabat Mater, etc.

From San Gemignano they went to Siena, *en route* for Volterra. His companion writes :—

To reach this latter town had long been a dream to him, and he resolved to get at it in the most adventurous way possible. To go by train was too commonplace to be thought of; so a *calèche* was hired, and through the Maremma we drove thirty-six miles in pouring rain, which, at the rate of Italian driving, took, including rests, sixteen hours at least. At 2 A.M., and thoroughly drenched, we reached the summit of the hill on which stands the old walled town. I have

never yet been able to discover how we drove through the
Maremma in going from Siena to Volterra, but we *did* it.

In answer to some questions about the route, Miss
Robertson writes again :—

I do not wonder that you thought the order of our
journey in 1878 like the wanderings of the children of Israel.
It was one of the charms of that tour that our movements
were so erratic. We never knew when we went to a railway
station where we were going ; and, even after the tickets
were secured, the appearance of the most casual friend going
in the opposite direction, or the passing suggestion of a railway guard, would suddenly change our course. When the
tickets could be exchanged it was all right, but when they
couldn't, that made no difference ! The new impulse had to
be followed ; and so you need not wonder at our driving
through the Maremma in going from Siena to Volterra, of
which, however, I think you are a little incredulous.

The visit to Volterra was partly lost in its purpose
by a dense fog in which we found the town enveloped, and
which we were told on arriving might last for weeks. We
tried to grope our way to the Museum, but it wouldn't do.
It was as black as night, and there was nothing for it but
staying within doors, where we sat for three days by a dim
rushlight, reading aloud or taking notes from Dennis, Taylor,
or Mrs. Hamilton' Gray, his favourite writers on Etruria,
when now and then some passage would give rise to a flow
of talk that would last for hours. In this way the dark days
passed very pleasantly till, on the morning we had resolved
to leave, the curtain rose, revealing in the bright sunlight
the most wonderful magnificence of scenery that the eye
could look upon. It was like a new creation. He was wild
with delight, sang like a boy, and ran, as he did in his

student days, with his hat off! Often afterwards he used to
speak of this as the finest surprise of the kind he had ever
experienced. We did not leave that day or the next, but
the time was now too short and the heat too great (it was
the middle of May) to attempt anything below the mere
surface; and so the two days were spent in lingering about
the Etruscan Walls—the chief glory of Volterra—with their
lofty gateways and arches, and especially the magnificent
" Porta all'arco," with its three dark mysterious heads that
have been frowning dismally for centuries, and that he used to
study with a sort of silent reverence as above all else the most
incontestably old and purely Etruscan. Then the " Balze,"
" that frightful Balze," as he used to call it, " black in the
shadow of its own depth," had a weird attraction for him—
all the more, perhaps, that only a few weeks before an old
church had been carried down into the gulf by a landslip,
leaving only the gable on the awful edge to tell the tale. I
remember walking with him round the walls by moonlight
till we came to this spot. We felt as if hanging in mid-air
between two great immensities. He struck up " God's
bright temple in the skies, night is opening slowly." We
sang it through, on to " Star lamps now are lit with fire,
heaven's broad dome revealing," when we heard the patter-
ing of little feet behind us. It was a party of children
attracted by the singing, who had come out to hear what was
going on. Nervously remembering the landslip, he ran to
meet them, and implored them to go back, which, however,
they were very slow to do, and it was not till they were
blessed with a shower of centimes that they yielded to his
entreaties.

The Church of Santa Chiara, the Convent of " La Badia,"
" The Grotta de' Marmini," were merely touched, when,
pressed by the extreme heat which had set in, we had to
retrace our steps to Siena and Florence, and thence home.

It was in Florence, and while the music he had
heard in the Cathedral at Siena was still ringing in his
ears, that he wrote the verses founded on the Song of
the Well in Numbers xxi. 17, 18 :—

" Spring up, oh Well."

As when pilgrims faint and weary,
 Where the sandy billows swell,
Sing across the desert dreary,
    " Spring up, oh well,"
Lo the Church, the Royal Daughter,
 Brought in wilderness to dwell,
Sings in search of living water,
    " Spring up, oh well."

Lo ! while yet the song is singing,
 Breaks the living water through,
Like the tears of earth upspringing
 From her eyes of deepest blue.
Thus in streams it runs and rushes,
 As the choral voices swell,
Till full out the fountain gushes,
    " Spring up, oh well."

Sing it softly, sing it slowly,
 Sing it with the morning bell,
Singing " Holy, Holy, Holy,"
    " Spring up, oh well."
Quick the singing, quick the springing,
 Quick the welling waters flow,
Through the weary deserts dreary,
 Sounds of mirth and gladness go.

Hark ! the voice of many waters
   Breaking through the desert dumb ;
Come ye, come ye, sons and daughters,
   Every one that thirsteth, "Come !"
All, for all the fountain springing,
   And let him that heareth tell
How he hears the pilgrims singing,
        "Spring up, oh well."

Still for God our souls are weary
   In this dry and thirsty land,
Till beyond the desert dreary,
   When beneath the palms we stand,
We shall hear behind us ringing
   Soft and low the funeral knell,
And before bright angels singing
        "Spring up, oh well."

The following letter was written in October, 1885, in answer to a question as to the origin of the music to which he had set these verses :—

To Mrs. Hannay.

The "Music from Trent" belongs, I believe, to the old hymn, "Veni, Redemptor Gentium," and renders in its lively movement and melody the gladness of that "blessed hope," which was almost quenched in the Romish Church in the Dark Ages—in the awful darkness of the "Dies Iræ," a hymn of the 13th century, adopted by the Council of Trent, at its final severance from the Reformation in the 16th century, into the dismal office for the dead. But still the hope, "lively and joyful," lived on in the songs of the children among which I found it, and in the child-like hidden ones that carry in their hands, through all ages, the box of Pandora, with the Hope that never can be crushed or driven out, though all the other graces are. So still it goes sing- ing in the same Church, like sweet voices and sunlight, breaking through the awful black thunder of the " Missa pro defunctis "; but it needed the Reformation to give us a hallelujah chorus !

The song in Numbers may be the survival of an old incan- tation to water, such as are found among the ancient Chaldeans and others (I have found them among the Etruscans too). It was a talk on this in the *Archæologist* that suggested to me this song. The popular air may have been in " Holy Song of the Pilgrims," as German old *Volkslieder* have been used in chorales, *e.g.*, " Oh, Haupt voll Blut," etc., or the grand theme of that grandest of devout oratorios, Bach's Passion Music, or the " Jonath-Elim- Rehokim." I suppose it is hopeless to find the old music or to like it if we did.

On their homeward journey Dr. Robertson and his sister came by way of San Remo that they might visit the grave that had been dug there a year before. They lingered at Avignon and Vaucluse, where they listened to the music of the stream beside which Petrarch wrote his sonnets.

In Paris they found their way on the Sunday morn- ing to the Scotch Church, which then worshipped in the Oratoire, and were surprised and delighted as they entered to recognize the familiar voice of Princi- pal Cairns in the service. Dr. Robertson was induced to preach in the afternoon, though he was furnished with neither notes nor clerical garb.

This hurried visit, in the spring and early summer of 1878, was his farewell to Florence and Italy. He left his books behind him in the hope that he would ere long return to resume his studies, and, if possible, write his long projected book; but he never went again, and the book was never written.

CHAPTER XVII.

At Bridge of Allan.

THE summer of 1878 was Dr. Robertson's last summer
in the manse at Irvine. Many things had contributed
to prepare him for the final severance from the home
which had been the scene of so much joy and
sorrow. Irvine had changed, and changed for the
worse. Great chemical works had been established
down by the harbour, which had darkened the air, and
filled the quiet streets with unfamiliar faces, and sometimes with uproarious crowds. One by one the friends
who were associated with him in the work of the
church had been passing away during his years of
absence, and it was not wonderful if he was sometimes
moved to say—-

> " ——the days darken round me, and the years,
> Among new men, strange faces, other minds."

But most of all were the ties that bound him to
Irvine as a home loosened by the troubles which had
come into the congregation, and which, in the autumn
of 1878, ended in the resignation of his colleague, and

in a schism in the membership. He had most earnestly striven to act as a mediator between contending parties, and, while faithfully seeking what he believed to be for the highest interests of the church, not to identify himself with either. But it was inevitable that those who were disappointed with the result of the contention should cast the blame on him; and he had much to bear from some whom he had implicitly trusted as his friends.

In these circumstances he proposed a new arrangement with his congregation, by which he should give up the manse and be entirely relieved from the responsibility of the pastorate, while still retaining the position of senior minister. This arrangement was effected in November, 1878.

It was while the troubles were distressing his sensitive nature that he wrote the following verses which, like the Psalms of the David of whom he sung, acquire peculiar interest when read in the light of the circumstances in which they had their origin.

"Jonath-Elim-Rehokim."

PSALM LVI.

"Jonath-Elim-Rehokim,"
  Dove of the Terebinth Tree,
Bearing the sorrow that stroke him,
  Bearing it silently.

So did the David heart-broken.
  How could he tell it in Gath?

All the hard things had been spoken
    Against him by friends in wrath.

Driven from home among strangers,
    Wand'ring with wildered brain ;
Ne'er did he 'mid the new dangers
    Of the old wrong complain.

Only when grief grew violent,
    Then his good harp took he,
And played the old air of the silent
    Dove of the Terebinth Tree.

Wild through the strings went his fingers,
    Dashing out wrath 'gainst his foes ;
Over his friends the strain lingers,
    Never a word against those.

How would the Philistines glory
    O'er him, had David showed
The sin, and the shame, and the story
    Of wrong in the house of God.

Much they had done to provoke him,
    Never a word said he,
" Jonath-Elim-Rehokim,"
    Dove of the Terebinth Tree.

In the midst of the troubles Mr. Kirkwood
asked him to attend the celebration of his semi-
jubilee at Troon. But he was in no mood, neither
had he strength for such a celebration. He writes :—

If you will excuse me for this time, I think I may safely
promise, if I am spared, to come without fail to your next
jubilee—that is, the Jubilee the Golden. May you live to

see it, as you are more likely to do than I am, though, indeed, I may do so too, if I attain to the days of my father and fathers in the days of their pilgrimage. They were not ministers, however, nor Dunfermline weavers, like one who was expounding the Scripture concerning Methuselah, and observed that "if he had worked in *Dumfarlin* at a damask *wabb*, he would not have lived so long." It was a story of my old friend Dr. Macfarlane, and now he too is gone, and how many? Our fathers, where are they? Why, I, and you also in your turn, my young friend, not long hence will become the fathers ourselves.

Early in December he was gratified by the announcement conveyed to him by the son of his old friend Dr. MacEwen that the students of the United Presbyterian College had elected him to the honorary presidency of their Theological and Literary Society. He had some difficulty in accepting the office, as, though it involved only the delivery of an inaugural address, he was afraid to commit himself even to that. But ultimately his reluctance was overcome, and his tenure of office was the beginning of very pleasant relations between him and the students, to whom from time to time he gave lectures and addresses. The leisure and freedom which his more complete retirement brought left him freer than he had heretofore been (at least at home) to follow out, in correspondence and otherwise, trains of thought on subjects which had always deeply interested him.

To Dr. John Muir.

Bridge of Allan, December, 1878.

From one like you any letter were an honour, and such a letter as that of yours of the 10th brought me special delight. The gift of books it carried in its train takes from the giver a value greater than its own, which is not small. Especially your own valuable little volume of latest translations, for which I thank you, I have read and re-read with much profit and delight. . . .

To me, a novice, standing outside the gates of the temple of Sanskrit literature, it is delightful to hear them open to the sound of music ; and should I ever penetrate, as I wish —though it can only be a very, very little way—towards the interior into the far depths and darkness of which you of all men have *con amore* and successfully plunged, I shall never forget how your metrical translations drew me in. On that debatable ground on which you join issue (though not entirely) with Dr. Lorimer I am too much under the influence *Tames* (doesn't that mean darkness ?) to give an opinion. But all my sympathies as a minister of the New Testament run strongly in favour of your view as differing from his It seems to me a much grander tribute to the truth and testi-mony to the divine origin of Scripture that it should, than, on the contrary, that it should not, be found, in part at least, and broken syllables, written on the sibylline leaves strewn beforehand through the nations and the centuries, and on the lips of earnest men seeking and groping in the darkness after God. The height of the divinity of Scripture and of Christ Himself is expounded to me by the breadth of their humanity, as you measure the height of a tower by the distance to which it throws the breadth of shadow at its base. *He* is not the less Divine that He had human ances-try, and *they* are not the less Divine, that teachings, which they perhaps accept rather than originate, and stamp with the imprimatur of their Divine authority as the only reliable revelation and only rule of faith and practice, have worked up their way into the light (truth springs from earth) through the spirit that is in man, and the "inspiration of the Almighty that giveth him understanding."

Some may think that, in a literary point of view, you are robbing the Scriptures of their claim to originality, but I am not aware that Scripture puts in any such claim for itself as a literary production, any more than as a manual of geology or astronomy, or other of the sciences; and though some masters of the German school would press that also into the service of their apologetics, and I would not refuse it all due weight, yet surely it were a pity to vindicate the literary originality of Scripture, if it could only be done at the expense of the love of God Himself, who by His wisdom has been teaching men of all nations and ages, and irradiating them here and there at least with flashes in the darkness more or less vivid—more or less conscious—of that " True Light that coming into the world enlighteneth every man." . . . I wish I had eyes like yours for reading off those Greek and Sanskrit legends on the altar with the inscription, ἀγνώστῳ θεῷ.

For certain reasons, you may know, I take most interest, perhaps, in those that emerge in the artistic form of the myth, which is a richer vehicle of truth, carrying with it life and passion too, than the dogma—mediating indeed between that and real life, and mediating between human aspiration and Divine fulfilment. I hope it is quite lawful for a good U.P. minister to behold with delight the fulfilling of the finest aspirations of the Greek drama and the myth, in Christ, for whose coming I always seem to hear the tragic chorus passionately shouting, and who by His cross and passion has unbound Prometheus from his rock of misery

that " by His stripes he might be healed," and comforted the
melancholy Glaucus bewailing his immortality, and slain the
dragon that guarded the golden fruit of the Hesperides, and
put the Furies to sleep beneath the altar; so that the ship is
sailing through the sculptured seas and painted ocean of the
catacombs toward the desired haven, and the song of the
sirens is resisted, not by Ulysses stopping the ears of his
sailors with wax, but by Orpheus taking his lyre and chanting the praises of the immortal gods !

The Gellert myth, well told in Æsop, and by Southey and
many others, is found in the Hetopadesa, where the dog that
does the service and is slain is replaced by an anteater.
The essence of the myth, through its variety of shapes, is
not the mere fact of the slaughter of the innocent, and not
at all the sentiment of substitution in the sacrifice, nor of submission of a lower to a higher will, but it is the sentiment of
strong regret at having slain the innocent, when He was
bravely and nobly risking his life in our behalf.   How
powerfully this feeling works in softening the heart and
moulding the character is well known.   In the moral dyna-
mics of atonement it was to take a leading place, and this
has been foreshadowed in the myth.   I well remember how
the story thrilled me in my childhood, touching as it did the
most sensitive chord perhaps in the whole emotional nature,
the same that vibrates afterwards, when come to sterner years,
in agonies of unutterable tenderness, when, in presence of
the holy mystery of the Passion, the soul makes conscious
transition from the lower to the higher life—" They look on
Him whom they have pierced, and mourn for Him and are
in bitterness."   May not the myth be as a schoolmaster to
bring men to Christ ?   May not the whole of the grand
" Passion Music " be found overhead, if we only had the
ears to hear it, in mythic snatches of old Orphic and
Vedic melodies, that have come singing to us up the

centuries, of a "Lamb slain from the foundation of the world."

But if it is too much to say that the mysteries of our holy religion were even dimly foreshown to thoughtful men of old, it cannot be too much to say that its moralities were. And if any man shall have his faith shaken by your showing him that some even of the highest moral teachings of the Scripture have been anticipated, perhaps it is time that his faith were shaken, that he may shift it from the Book to the Person. He may yet have to learn that God is greater than the Scripture, as "he that buildeth the house is greater than the house." The Divine has not been made verses, but "made flesh," crucified, dead, risen again; and if he shall have chosen to speak to others outside the Church, why should we limit the Holy One of Israel? Why should not the Spirit that came down in the mighty rushing wind of Pentecost be in His movements free and uncontrolled— "the Spirit that like wind doth blow, as it listeth to and fro?"

To the Rev. James Brown, D.D.

BRIDGE OF ALLAN, December, 1878.

. . . But when the frost is breaking up, let us ask whither is the thaw to carry us?—the question you asked or quoted one night so thoughtfully at Paisley, with the poker in your hand to let go smash at the fire. Here the literal frost has broken up, and large blocks of ice have come tumbling down the Allan water. On one of them, I am told, were perched two ducks that no doubt said to each other (in the duck tongue, whatever that might be)— "We have got liberty, but where do you think we are going to? I don't know." Not such a pity perhaps of ducks, for even when carried out to depths, and the ice melted, they might fly or swim or waddle somehow to the shore. But

2 A

after the ducks came, for all the world, a calf! on another
iceberg, carried down by the spate in the river, standing
helpless enough, poor beast, yet rather seeming to enjoy it.
" Liberty! Bey-y ! Where are we going to? Bey ! Bey !"
To the bottom, sure enough. He was drowned in the mill
lade.   Poor calf! Your leaders of thought may be ζῷα
living creatures, with the wings of eagles (or angels), by
which they can lift themselves out of the depths and whirl-
pools even when swept down into them. But what is to
come of the herd that follows them? They have no power
to extricate themselves from the perils by water. They are
safest, and only safe, within the orthodox enclosure, fenced
in by the standards. Mere *oxen* that become *heterodoxen*
are in a bad way; and when I see any of them (and there
are now-a-days so many) following the leaders of thought,
sailing down the modern stream of tendency, I rather pity
them. . . . I have much in me of the "ancient mariner"
that is haunted with a passion for the sea. So that we may
say to each other, as I heard two Ayrshire boors, one
summer morning aboard the Arran steamer, say—" Y'ill
be gaun for a sail the day?"   " Ou, aye " (long embarrassing
pause, then). " Y'ill be gaun for a sail yersel'?"   "Ou,
aye." " Weel, there's naething wrang i' that." No, there's
"naething wrang" in that; but yet there may be something
perilous if, though the steering be good, and the sails well
set, and the watch well kept, and all that all right, there
should yet come a time when the ship, the Church, should
leave behind her, on her voyage across the ages, and lose
sight of, the great red light of Calvary, and shining lamp of
the Holy Sepulchre of Him who was delivered for our
offences, and raised again for our justification. . . . If
these be lost sight of, what lights are to be sighted next?
Were it not better to strike sail in the darkness and cast
anchor astern, and wait for the day? No, you say, and I

say with you; sail on; the lights are not only stationary, though they are also stationary—not only earthly, though they are also earthly. They are heavenly stars that travel with you all the night. Even so, and therefore let us not lose sight of them, never till the day dawn, never till the lights of the first coming are swallowed up in the light of the second, as stars in the morning. They are but "broken lights of Thee," even these stars; but till we see Thee as Thou art, we shall be guided by the light of them nearer to Thee through the dark and through the sea, lest, losing sight of them, we fall among the shallows or the breakers, and make shipwreck of our faith!

Yet another great sorrow fell on him in the early summer of 1879 in the sudden death of Mr. James Robertson of Newington. It was a touching coincidence that the days of mourning for his brother had to be spent in the bustle of removing from the Irvine manse, with his life in which that brother had been so much bound up.

To Mr. David M'Cowan.

IRVINE, 17th June, 1879.

I have quite enough to do up to the latest minute here in the troublous task of flitting, with which Jessie and I are greatly exercised, ere setting forth, like Abram, on my pilgrimage, with something of his faith, I hope. . .

The service on Friday night was exquisitely tender and comforting. Mr. Taylor's text was, "Enoch walked with God," etc., and his descriptive sketch of one at whose feet he had sat, and whom he loved as a father, was truly admirable and appreciative; while the singing of the hymns, and especially the anthem, "I heard a voice from Heaven,"

by our choir, every one of whom felt deeply what they were
singing, was very striking, and brought us very near those
above. The communion service on Sabbath was specially
solemn and refreshing. The people are more clinging and
affectionate to me than ever, and their mourning for James
and tribute of true affection for his memory, who was more
than worthy of it all, have touched me very much.

A few days after the date of this letter, he went,
with his friend and kinsman, Dr. William Bruce of
Edinburgh, on a tour among the English Cathedrals.
Ely, Peterborough, Lincoln, Norwich, and Oxford
were visited. He then took lodgings in London for
some weeks' study in the British Museum.

To the REV. WILLIAM BRUCE, D.D.

LONDON, July, 1879.

And so you got safely and comfortably home, I calculate,
in your Pullman car, in the *cool—i.e.*, the nightcap—of a
summer day, to receive the warm greetings that awaited you
from your son and daughter and sister, to all whom you
forgot to give my loving remembrances, but to whom, as
you refreshed yourself after your journey with potations of
nothing hotter than hot water, you laid off such glowing
descriptions of our cathedral excursion and steeplechase,
that they could not choose but wish that when we " next
do ride " they " may be there to see."

You must come again once I settle down in that old
cathedral town, Ely, where still the churchmen sing, like
the four-and-twenty white birds set before the king—*i.e.,*
Canute—" *Merten singen manches binnen Ely,*" etc. But
better at Lincoln, better even than in the Temple, where, on
Sabbath, I sat in the front barristers' bench, and could see

over the white shoulders of the tenors and basses to the music, followed by a most excellent sermon; but not better than at Westminster, where, in the anthem of evening service after the funeral of Lord Lawrence, the most wonderful effect I ever heard was produced by the singing of invisible youths in the organ loft, or triforium (it might be the vox humana stop—but I think not—of the organ), representing, in most ethereal, dream-like music, the " voice from heaven," before the choristers below took up the theme and repeated it; while the echo music returned and died away in swell and fall, in light and shade, along the fretted roof. Sentimental, no doubt, but very tender and beautiful all the same.

TO MISS JANET BRUCE.

LONDON, 27th July, 1879.

The trip, not a dance, but rather a slow and easy movement—*adagio*, not *andante*—through the cathedrals was truly delightful, made so to me by the radiance of your father's company, as well as the blaze of beauty and flashes of genius that broke upon us from the old stones, that still utter the living speech of " men dead long ago," down the long arched aisles of the centuries, with the music and the white singing boys.

Dr. Robertson returned from the south to preside, on August 5th, at the ordination of Mr. William S. Dickie of Aberdeen, whom the congregation of Trinity had unanimously chosen to be his colleague. Though he had no longer his home in Irvine, his intercourse with Mr. Dickie, and his joy in the returning prosperity which came to the congregation did much to brighten the closing years of the senior pastor's life.

In the later autumn he preached for the first time
in connection with the Presbyterian service begun in
Cambridge.   In the cultured audience that on a
succession of visits crowded to hear him, and in the
fellowship he enjoyed alike with dons and undergraduates of the famous University, he found a new
stimulus to work.

To Mr. (now Sir) George B. Bruce.

Bridge of Allan, 22nd August, 1879.

.   .   .   If you have still in reserve for me one or two,
any two, Sabbaths in October, I hope to be able to occupy
them and execute the office of a prophet as best I can to
the service of your church in that old pleasant city of
renown.   I cannot do the work you require in the style of
my noble friend "The Graham"; but perhaps he may
gather a greater audience in his two Sabbaths than I may be
able to disperse in mine.   And if you are willing to risk it,
so am I.   My health and strength and freshness, I am
thankful to say, have been in great, if not yet in perfect,
measure restored to me ; and most thankfully will I lay the
first-fruits of what I hope will be the "latter harvest of my
life," on the altar of your young Cambridge Church.   I have
been reaping sheaves of it already, and find myself taking, in
some sort, more kindly and eagerly than ever to the work,
after long worship of silence and schooling of sorrow ; and
the harvest that my latter years (if years they be) shall yield,
may not be the less plentiful for the long period of the
"latter rain" that has preceded it.   Heavy rain, too, from
dark clouds of bereavement—clouds that have received so
many out of our sight.   Of my nearest and dearest relatives, six have of late been taken, and the nearest and

dearest sister and brother taken last. But through all, thank God, my own health has not been broken down again, and after all it seems built up about as fresh and strong as ever. . . .

I would be delighted to accept of your kind invitation to be your guest in London, and run down on the Saturday to Cambridge. But I have a great fancy to stay in Cambridge as much as I can, for there are some studies I am pursuing that have sent me there already this very summer, and made me resolve on returning if I could soon, little thinking of the opportunity you should offer of my doing so.

To Mr. David M'Cowan.

LONDON, 29th October, 1879.

The second Sabbath I have stood I think still better than the first. As far at least as appearance went it was very successful. In the evening all standing room was taken up both inside the door and in the corridors without. This fusion of Town and Gown is quite a novelty, I believe, in Cambridge. The *élite* of what they call good society, I was told, that would never think of entering a Nonconformist chapel, found in Presbytery, I suppose, a middle ground between the Episcopalian exclusive sheepfold and the Dissenting open common; and University men of different grades, but chiefly undergraduates, I believe, in their gowns --some of them crowding up the platform steps, or occupying whole benches together—gave the audience the most learned appearance of any I have ever addressed; while shopkeepers, tradespeople, and servants were mixed up with the rest—a pleasant sight, but rare, if not unique, in Cambridge. . . .

I don't like to appear as what I am not—a partizan of Presbytery or anything else, but don't object to preach to

thoughtful young men on the ground of our common
Christianity, or common humanity even; and the Presbyterian
door seems to be the only one by which I could get at them;
while it seems right and dutiful to provide for our own—and
especially for those of our own house—to provide services of
which they may, if they wish, avail themselves, as they are
now at liberty, as University men, to do.

In 1879, I was appointed editor of the *Missionary
Record* of the United Presbyterian Church, and applied
to Dr. Robertson to contribute something to my earlier
numbers. The claims of friendship proved stronger
than ambition, or than the importunity of "able
editors" of more important periodicals, and he sent
three contributions in verse. For the January (1880)
number he sent this fragment :—

New Mercies.

> Each day of days the last !
> The archangel's trumpet blast
> Is every moment blowing,
> And earth to ashes going ;
> And were to ashes gone :
> But, sitting on the Throne,
> He saith—whose name is True—
> Lo ! I make all things new !

For the February number he sent a hymn, which
gives expression to much of his most earnest, most
characteristic thought : —

Hymn to the Holy Ghost.

ROM. VIII. 26, 27; EPH. III. 19-21.

When joys are joys that words transcend,
   When griefs have shut the heart;
When we, who at the altar bend,
   Can only pray in part;
When angels, both of joy and grief,
   Strike priests at prayer-time dumb,
'Tis then, with Thy Divine relief,
   Thou, Comforter, dost come!

When we with words of Scripture pray,
   And do not, cannot know
The meaning full of what we say,
   In praying Scripture so,—
By Thee, in meaning full before
   The Throne, the prayer is brought,
Whence we receive exceeding more
   Than we have asked or thought.

When joys are joys unspeakable,
   That rise all thought above,
And earnest souls with rapture fill
   In the silent heavens of love;—
As babe soft mother's arms upraise,
   Thou, Dove! on Thy white wings
Dost bear us up, on God to gaze!—
   Far down the angel sings!

And when our griefs deep buried lie
   Beneath all utterance dumb;
Into that silent agony
   Thou with Thy help dost come!

Then, with the unutterable groans,
　　Is intercession given,
That makes above all trumpet-tones
　　Our silence heard in Heaven.

Oh ! Holy Ghost, the Comforter !
　　All speed to help us make ;
Our hearts with griefs they cannot bear
　　With very joys they break ;
Blind yearnings after God, dumb cries
　　That ne'er their aim could reach,
Didst Thou not give their blindness eyes,
　　And make their silence speech.

In sending the hymn, he wrote as follows :—

To the Rev. James Brown, D.D.

Bridge of Allan, 16th January, 1880.

The hymn is expository (as well as devotional) of Romans
viii. 26 and 27, also Ephesians iii. 19-21. "When we with
words of Scripture pray," as *e.g.*, when your *Record* readers
pray, "Thy Kingdom come," who knows what all is meant
by that petition as Christ did when he put it into the prayer
for all ages? or what two that join in praying agree (agree
they must to some extent, according to the rubric, "If two
of you shall agree," etc.), but what two agree, not only in
meaning all that Christ meant, and that the inspired words
themselves mean, but that agree in meaning exactly the same
thing?—some inclining, more like your great master of old,
Dr. Anderson, to millenarian views, and some like
"meeself"! more to orthodoxy (which is the theology of
common sense). And then the amount of misconception,
or at least of imperfect intellectual conception, in the views

of all of us, it would be impossible to calculate or analyze. It is quite impossible that the prayer should be answered, *i.e.*, in Scripture language, " heard," according to our variety of views, with all their falsehood and imperfection. But then I take it, if the prayer be sincere and the feeling true, and the worshipper praying in the Spirit and through Christ the Truth, and that not in the words which man's wisdom teacheth, then these words have not only come to us inspired, but they return from us inspired as well, "the Holy Ghost interpreting them into their full significance, in presence of the Throne,"—a phrase of deep meaning I picked up at the feet of Dr. Duncan of Mid-Calder many, many years ago; so that our prayer, "Thy Kingdom come, Thy will be done on earth," or whatever else it be, is heard, not according to the meaning we put, but according to the meaning *He* puts upon it ; and this in virtue of His Intercession, one function of which is, I should say, Interpretation. We receive " exceeding abundantly above all we ask or think, according to the power that worketh in us," " For He that searcheth the heart knoweth what is the mind of the Spirit, because He maketh intercession for the saints according to the will of God." Whatever be the meaning of these verses, and, of course, they are more for δοξα than δογμα, for feeling than formula, for mystical longings than mechanical logic (excuse my old trick of alliteration), it is clear to me that part of that meaning is what I have given in stanza two. If doctrinally they do not mean that, I do not see what else or other they can mean at all. But if you do not think so, or if you do not think that this is the interpretation that is, or that would be, commonly received, perhaps you might strike out the second stanza altogether. If you thought that a hymn in your *Record* should not contain anything which, however true and Scriptural, and however much to be insisted on in sermon and expository lecture, is yet not truth already so familiar as to have entered fully into our Christian life and consciousness, or according to the Scripture as commonly but ignorantly understood, the bridge would stand without this arch, and the train of thought and sentiment and song (such as it is) pass even fluently over ; but it would certainly be not so complete and satisfactory without it, and I daresay you will let it stand.

As for the rest, the love that passeth knowledge, the joys and sorrows that transcend not only the bounds of utterance, but even of self-consciousness, if there are any of your readers that know nothing of all this, the deepest worship of silence, which, of all acts of worship and means of grace, brings us nearest to God, nearest to the Unseen and Eternal Real, excepting only the silence of death itself—which is indeed only the last act of that worship, and last means of that grace—it may be well for such to know, and these lines may help to show them, that a religion that can be measured in its length and breadth by words, that cannot go beyond drawing near to God with the mouth and honouring Him with the lip, is a false and fair and hollow-hearted thing after all ; and that only through the silence of the unutterable, or even of the unthinkable, or even of the unconscious in communion with God, can we become prepared for the trying silence that shall be, when utter darkness opens our eyes in the stillness of the dead.

I am not writing a scholium on the passages, still less a eulogium on my verses, nor an apology for them either ; but somehow since I have begun, the words flow on, and I know you are to have a Sabbath of rest, so that you will have patience to spell and time even to read them.

A longer poem, entitled " Table Triplets," appeared in April. It was an expansion of verses written at an earlier date.

We give the first part :—

Table Triplets.

Year by year the Man Divine,
Where the southern sunlights shine,
Turns the water into wine.

Year by year He makes the corn,
Underground in spring-time borne,
Rise with Him on Easter morn.

Whence, ere one year's store is spent,
Bread and wine afresh are sent
For the next year's Sacrament,

And, like Abram, life is fed,
Coming Victor o'er the dead,
With the High Priest's wine and bread.

Priest of God, and Prince of Peace,
How the bread and wine increase
In thy hands and never cease !

Down the ages, feeding all,
Olden men and children small,
In a world-wide banquet hall,

Spread with tapestry, flower'd and green,
Underneath a dome-like screen,
Blue with golden stars between.

Guests in thousands come and go,
And Thou, walking to and fro,
From Thy pierced hand feed'st them so !

Oh, Thou Cup-bearer Divine,
What a bitter draught was Thine,
Ere Thou brought'st us this sweet wine !

Thou wast crown'd with thorns, that Thou
Mightst twine roses round the brow,
Of Thy guests at table now.

Thou wast broken 'mongst the dead,
That our hunger might be fed
Day by day with daily bread.

Whence in things both great and small,
Life becomes transfigured all
To a high church festival.

Not with host to be adored,
But with every poor man's board
Counted holy to the Lord.

To Mr. Andrew T. Taylor.

Bridge of Allan, 3rd February, 1880.

I had a great admiration of your lovely sister, Aggie.
Nothing pleased me more than to have her come along in
the summer days and sit, as she sometimes did, for an hour
or two at the organ, which she enjoyed—filling the house
(though we might be in different rooms), flooding it with a
sense of her gentle presence, and with a music, tender,
devotional, modest, graceful, like herself, and in which her
spirit seemed to melt away—with a joy that was more akin
to tears than laughter. And the music has passed away,
and the minstrel; but we shall hear it again—on a ten-
stringed harp touched by the finger of that little hand—where

there shall be no more crying, but only the remembrance and echo that shall haunt the *Gloria in excelsis* up to the highest ranges, as a shadow often enriches the brilliancy. I remember to have said to her she ought to be very good, and so she was, for it seemed to me that the angels in singing often called her by name, άγιος ! when singing to the Holy : and she smiled, I daresay at my pedantry, which had much truth in it, nevertheless.

Forgive me if I think that before all angels she would look out for her dear old minister,[1] and before both, and before all, for *Him* whom her heart loved above all, and with whom she *is*—and it is far better.

A slight affection of the throat kept Dr. Robertson from preaching anywhere during the first three months of 1880 ; but he was able to fulfil an engagement to preach again at Cambridge on three Sundays in April.

To Mr. David M'Cowan.

CAMBRIDGE, 22nd April, 1880.

I have had great pleasure in my fresh mission here, having found myself quite equal to it, as I had hoped by higher help to be. The assembly in the evening would have doubly filled the usual place of meeting; but I prudently and firmly resisted all proposals of migration to the larger hall, which is said to be difficult to speak in.

You must come and see this Cambridge with me ere very long. My acquaintance with University men is broadening as much and as pleasantly as ever I could desire.

[1] Mr. Robertson of Newington.

CAMBRIDGE, 13th May, 1880.

I went by invitation on Monday last as a guest to the great annual feast of St. John's. All the heads of college, and greater lights were met to eat and drink; and such splendour of dishes, of dresses, of drinking vessels of silver and gold, was surely never seen since Belshazzar's feast, or since the last St. John's one. I extended my acquaintance with professors and other dons in the Combination Room, where after dinner a magnificent banquet of wine was served up. . . . Some of the younger clergy are very earnest inquirers as to how best to preach and do their Master's work, and, if possible, save souls; and are not unwilling to take instruction even from an ecclesiastical Ishmaelite. A knot of them had me yesterday to dine and discourse with them; and they say others would want me if I would give them the opportunity.

A visit to Bournemouth as the guest of his old friend, Mr. Stitt of Liverpool, followed his Cambridge service.

In July he went with Mr. M'Cowan to Conishead Priory, and in August, accompanied Dr. Young of Kelly, whom he used playfully to name "The Lord of the Oils," on a cruise among the Hebrides.

TO HIS SISTER.

ON BOARD THE "NYANZA" (YACHT),
OFF SKYE, 10th August, 1880.

We have had some odd experiences, which I cannot at present detail. On the evening we sailed from Tobermory,

Mull, tacking N.W., through the darkening and through the sea, between Rum and Eigg to Loch Scavaig, where there is no harbour, and we had to cast anchor in the Sound of Soa and wait for the day. But by day no sun, as by night neither moon nor stars appeared; according to the normal weather of the Hebrides, only clouds drifting in the wind, and rain, rain, rain. However, through a cleft of the storm, we climbed through a cleft of the rock, up to the most dreary loch known in Britain, if not in the world, a weird mountain tarn, three miles round. The yachtsmen of the "Nyanza" carried up the dingy, or smallest boat, and launched it on the green lake, and didn't we all—that is Professor and Mrs. Thomson, Dr. Young and myself—row over into the awful shadow of the precipices on the other side? The Lake Averno at Naples—the way to the *Inferno* of Horace, Virgil, and Dante, is as the lake in St. James' Park to this. No leaf or blade of grass, or any living thing, or sound of any smallest bit of stone broken off from the hard, black iron mass of rock, rising in jagged peaks, cleaving the mists, and making the dreariest gloom you ever saw. Only the "Balze," at Volterra, equals it, in its own way, for dreariness. After two days out on the wild sea, with the white breakers gleaming along cavernous rocky shores, where landing is impracticable, we returned to Tobermory and shipped Dr. Angus Smith. But the latter has left us, not without reckoning the sailing somewhat risky, as we have ventured through a narrow passage from Isle Oronsay to this, in which tides and currents meet in a most extraordinary manner, and with the wind against us, trying the skill of our skipper. After hurrying us here into the straits under the tower of Saucy Mary who threw a chain across the chasm and levied toll of passing ships, he cannot bring us out. He has tried it twice and each time has been on the point of wreckage on the lighthouse rocks. So here we are—shut in where King Haco of Norway lay with his ships, on his voyage over to the battle of Largs, in 1293, when he came to grief; and a storm has come on, and if it don't mend, we shall have to row ashore and get down by some other conveyance to Oban.

A friend passing in his steam yacht took Dr. Robertson on board and landed him in Iona.

To His Sister.

IONA, 3rd September, 1880.

Here I am still in Iona, which, though one has to rough it a very little sometimes, is full of attraction, instruction, and delight—and work too, in which I have been somewhat abounding. Last Sabbath I preached in the Free Church. Blacklock, the minister, was away in Mull, and there was no other service in the island, so I got the bell rung, and gathered an audience of the islanders and summer visitors —among whom there are a good many artists from London and Edinburgh, every one of whom seemed to come at the call of said bell. In the evening I had a service on the western shore, on the beautiful green knoll, where the angels met and walked with St. Columba, artistically a most effective picture—hill and sea and sunset, and an ample theatre of earnest faces and varied costumes. Herd- man and Adam (Scottish Academicians) said it was the most striking they had ever seen, and spiritually, they said, and all said, and I felt, it was peculiarly impressive.

Mr. Payne, rector of Reading, prayed like a prince with God at the close, and his girlish daughter, Mary, led off the hymn, which the children all caught up—the older people too deeply moved, some of them to sing (except in an occa- sional *staccato* bass)—and which floated over the green pastures and the delectable mountains, up the reaches of yellow corn that shone like streets of gold in the weird, wonderful sunset, like a " chorus angelorum" carrying home the blessed " Safe in the arms of Jesus." For that was the hymn sung after the sermon on the " Rainbow round about the Throne," which I adapted, and which adapted itself to the scene in outward nature and worship *al fresco*, with its John in Patmos, and the vision of the elders sitting round, and the angels in the back ground. An infant's funeral, that two days before, with much sympathy from all, had moved from a Highland hut along the street of the dead to the latest little grave in Reilig Oran—the " tombs of the kings," made me start the service from Romans v. 12, and intertwine it with allusions to the "great salvation of the dead children." I read also (as I did at the Bridge) the " Sennacherib " psalm, hearing the waters of the ocean close behind me, that could not rise any more than " sin " or the "wrath of man " could, above the water-mark. Through King Hezekiah's sickness, I glanced at Columba's that was not unto death, when, by the prayers of the Church, the angels sent for him were arrested on the red granite rocks of Mull, over the Sound, where he saw them standing in white.

But what singing on Saturday last from Lambeth's choir, especially when, on a green mound in the " royal city of the silent dead," they stood and sung Spohr's " Blessed are the departed." It was Mrs. Lambeth's selection—so she told me —and with fine taste and Christian charity she chose it, to sing it there on the graves of autumn, of royalty, and of priesthood, Columbans, Culdees, and Roman Catholics. To me and all who heard it, it was the perfection, the *ne plus ultra* of sacred singing, in this world at least. Lambeth thought himself they had never done better. After singing again in the cathedral, he begged me to go with him to Staffa, which I did. I can give you no idea of the extraordinary effect of the pure voices piercing the thunder of the waves, and breaking, clear and sweet, through the pauses between, and ringing resonances, harmony perfectly correct, so unlike the artificial ; and from the natural organ of basaltic columns (you remember the Baptistery at Pisa?), dying away in retiring waves up under the darkening arched vault of the grand cathedral, the "house of God not made with hands." Why were you not here? To-night I go to preach at the lighthouse station to a most interesting colony, of dozens or scores of people, families of the keepers, boatmen, and others. Then the great lighthouse itself—Dhu Heartach —I have visited, a great adventure, which I have not time now to describe.

The memory of the scene in Iona on that Sunday evening at the Angel's Hill dwelt lovingly in Mr. Herdman's memory. He delighted to describe it as only an artist could, and had promised to write his description for these pages ; but alas! he was called away before the promise was fulfilled.

CHAPTER XVIII.

At Westfield.

WHEN Dr. Robertson gave up the Irvine manse he stored his furniture and books in Glasgow, and went to live with his sister at Bridge of Allan. But early in 1881 he established for himself a new home. His friend Dr. Young of Kelly put in order, and leased to him on easy terms, the mansion of the little estate of Westfield, in Midlothian, which he had acquired for the sake of its oil-yielding mineral. The place suited Robertson's taste. The house was old and quaint, with ample wall space for his pictures and book-cases, and with endless rooms—opening off other rooms—where he could stow away the vast collection of books and prints he had gathered in his wanderings. The Calder woods shut him in pleasantly from the sounds of the busy world, which yet was not inconveniently distant. Ten minutes' walk eastward, down an avenue arched with trees, brought him to Newpark station on the Caledonian Railway, whence the run to Edinburgh was only half an hour, and the run to Glasgow a little more than an hour. In the opposite direction, two and a half miles distant, lay the post-town of West Calder, where also there is a railway station with frequent trains to both cities. He used to describe his new abode in some such terms as these : " My sylvan hermitage, my cell in the forest, my Bettws-y-Coed, or cloister in the woods, to which I have retired from the world, only emerging now and then, like a Dominican of the *Frati Predicatori*, to preach." To make the place yet more to his mind he put a verandah with creeping plants in front of his study windows ; and to remind him of his beloved Florence he had a copy made in painted glass for the lobby door, of a favourite window in the Duomo, which represents the arrival at Emmaus, with the legend below in Greek and English, " Abide with us: for it is toward evening, and the day is far spent."

The legend was appropriate. One of the chief recommendations of the house to him was that it offered space for the exercise of an unstinted hospitality. Even before the rooms were in order he had begun to write to his friends begging them to come and visit him ; and they were not slow to respond to his invitations. Often the situation was such as he describes in the following extract from a letter to a friend who had offered a visit :—

I expect ere the week closes as many as eight into my ark, which, with myself and the servants and Kaiser fill the vessel so that not even a dove could be taken in at the window. So soon as they come and I know from them when the flood (which I expect to be a pleasant one) is likely to be over, the waters down and dry land up again, I will immediately let you know.

The " Kaiser " referred to in this extract was, from the summer of 1883 onward, a notable inmate of the new home. He was a St. Bernard of splendid proportions and of great intelligence, in whose company, in the house and in his walks among the woods, Dr. Robertson had much delight. Kaiser's formidable appearance was in itself a protection against unlawful intruders ; but there were some even of the invited guests, who, when they were approaching the house, thought of the great beast not without tremor.

In addition to those who made longer visits there were some who occasionally came from Edinburgh to spend the day. To these also he gave lordly welcome, and by his brilliant talk and genial kindness made their days at Westfield for ever memorable.

Miss Florence Sellar was one of those welcome visitors. She tells how, on their arrival at Newpark, she and her friend, Miss Annie Macleod, daughter of Dr. Norman Macleod, " were always met by him, and latterly by him and his imperial companion, Kaiser." " How benignant," she adds, " was his hospitality, how he tried to show one in every way that one's presence was a pleasure to him ; how he filled up every minute, pacing up and down that muddy little platform till the very last moment, bringing out of his storehouse things new and old." Extracts have already been given, at their appropriate places, from the reminiscences of his conversation furnished by Miss Sellar. The following may here be added :—

Since I heard from you I have been living over mentally many of the wonderful talks, or rather listenings, one had with him. What a wonderful stream of talk it was, often almost rhythmic in cadence and touching so many and apparently unconnected points, and yet always bringing out the underlying relation of one to the other. How fascinating it was, how unforgettable, how utterly impossible to reproduce ! If I were to meet you I know we could remind each other of many an exquisite saying and beautiful fanciful analogy and sudden swift glance into the heart of things. Till I met him I never fully realized that communion of saints in which he habitually lived, touching Francis of Assisi with the one hand, and " precious Master Peden " with the other—not straining analogies, nor generalizing philosophically on the religious temperament and experience in all ages, but understanding the humanity and the holiness of each by reason of the brotherliness of his own rich nature, and his love of the Master whom they also loved. Can you or any biographer make those who did not know him ever realize that wonderfully graphic power he had in talking about men and women long dead, till you seemed to know them, and all their loving and hating and sinning and repenting, until, indeed, you felt just as if you were clasping hands across the centuries ?

I should like to recall some few of the things he said. This was a beautiful and simple piece of advice he gave to me on my first going to Italy and into the presence of the old masters—" Stand before them and ask them that great question which century is asking century, ' What think ye of Christ ? ' "

I remember his telling me a great deal about the old

mediæval idea of the redemption of the whole earth through the body of Christ having lain in the earth, the belief which lies obscured in the Festival of the Corpus Christi. I thought of that when I saw how at Ravenna the early Church used animals and plants as the glad symbols of redemption. Then you remember how he contrasted the joyful sense of redemption in the early Church with the terrible vision of judgment which came into art after the end of the 10th century, " when the Dies Iræ was sending its wail through Christendom." Then Christ appeared only as the Judge, "very stern and terrible"; and all the tender attributes of God, " the motherliness," and yearning mercy, passed over to the Madonna.

I remember one year, when I was much taken up with the history of the religious struggle in Scotland, getting him to talk of those times. I remember his giving us a sermon of Richard Cameron's, in which he calls the "Shaw Heid" to witness of the offer of salvation made to the people that day ; and I remember the way his face lit up as he told of Hugh Mackail, "the young San Lorenzo of the Scottish Covenant." He had as much love and sympathy for those grim, stern men, with their passionate religion and flashes of tenderness, as for the perfect sweetness of his own St. Francis.

I used to like the quaint, homely way in which he used illustrations to help simple, perplexed faith. In the early days of his ministry many were the schemes of salvation by which conscientious people tried to solve the question that has wounded so many tender souls, "Who then can be saved ? " One lad, an apprentice, at last found comfort in the thought that all should be saved who believed in universal redemption. But then his master, a kind, honest, upright man, did not believe in any such loose and uncovenanted scheme; and could he, the lad, think that this want of belief was to exclude his master? It was very perplexing. "Well," said Dr. Robertson, "suppose you were in a boat with seven more men and the boat was upset, and the hand of a deliverer was stretched out to save you, would you first ask, Do you mean to save us all or only some of us? Would you not rather grasp and keep hold of the saving hand?"

How quaintly and beautifully he used the Scriptures to illustrate events in one's own life. Talking of his dear friend Dr. John Muir, and his difficulty in accepting the Church view of the Divinity of Christ, while honouring Him and loving Him with all his heart, he said, "But I tell him he is just the wise man from the east, laying down his wealth of learning at the Saviour's feet."

This is one text I always associate with Dr. Robertson— "In Him was life, and the life was the light of men." "The life was the light, not the light was life." That was all his comment, but it was sufficient.

One or two stray thoughts were always recurring in his talk and being variously applied. One was, "When any system is logically complete, reject it ; it must be false." Another perpetually recurring idea was, "All truth is the combination of two opposing truths ; " and growing out of this was the suggestion that if you crystallized one part of the truth in your creed, the other part remained in solution in your life. "No people," he would say, "were such absolute predestinarians as the Scotch Covenanters in their creed ; none were so determined on their own way in their lives."

Miss Macleod has, in a letter to her friend, furnished some reminiscences :—

Was it not a day between winter and spring when you first took me with you to West Calder to see him? I remember my first sight of him when the train stopped, and you said, "There he is," and I looked out of the window and

saw some one standing, not very tall, with a long loose over-
coat, rather long grey hair, and a face with a radiant
light in it—the peaceful look that those people have who are
in love with things outside of themselves.   Is there not a
text, "In Thy light we shall see light"?   That was what
happened with him.   He had an atmosphere of love about
him, and beside him you saw all the beauty of heaven and
earth, and loved both along with him.

He only spoke about the things he loved, and there
seemed to be no end to them.   The store was inexhaustible.
A characteristic which struck me in his conversation was his
sense of continuity, which was a passion with him.   It was
as if he swept over continents and through centuries, picking
up one fact here and another there to illustrate his subject,
and vivifying everything he touched so that you felt as if he
had lived in that very place and time, and could tell you
every detail connected with it—what the country was like,
and how the people looked, and what they said and felt.

I remember once, when we were speaking about music,
he said the best music was national, coming from the heart
of the people.   Then a great musician, some Handel or
Haydn, took this air and clothed and embodied it in his
own harmonies.   And it lived on, changed perhaps in
rhythm, but the old notes still there.   Then the people had
it again, and it passed into some popular song, and children
sang it in the street.   And then he sang some airs, and traced
their history in this way.   He had no doubt, he said, that
David chose national airs for the words of his psalms.   There
was the psalm, for instance, he composed when he was a
prisoner in the power of Achish and feigned to be mad.
And what a beautiful air he had chosen for it—"The
Dove of the Terebinth tree."[1]   That name surely belonged to
an air he had known or heard the country people in his own

[1] See page 363.

home singing. It would come back to him now when he was in trouble.

He had the power of genius to make you see by a word or gesture a whole scene, so that when you think of his stories you at once see a succession of vivid pictures. What delighted me in these stories was the marvellous insight they showed into human nature. He knew what it was possible for men and women to be and do. He expected the best. But he understood too the hundred subtle modifying influences that exist. He saw all round the position so to speak, and made you see it too by little touches of tender, loving humour. It was this power of realizing the smallest details, as well as the great whole, which made any advice he gave so sane and human, and at the same time so ennobling.

Another Westfield visitor was the Rev. John Haddin, whose notes of Dr. Robertson's conversation have already been quoted. Some additional items —in which the attempt is made to reproduce his own words—are worthy to be preserved. Mr. Haddin, the contemporary of his elder brother, and his own friend since boyhood, often drew him out to speak of himself—a subject which he never chose spontaneously:—

The course in preaching is to be unconscious of all mental action. When attention is given to this the power of impression is lost. An illustration occurred lately. When preaching at Dollar on the fulness of joy with which the soul might be filled when contemplating salvation, I remarked that it began with one step, as a round in a ladder, and proceeded to another and still another, until lost in rapture. So was it with sorrow for the loss of the soul. There was one degree of sorrow, then another and another, until the soul was overwhelmed with grief and remorse. Mr. Wilson afterwards told me my face changed with every step of the feeling, and the impression produced was great. At Cambridge, afterwards, remembering the circumstances, I repeated the passage, but, from the recollection being present to my mind, the passage fell flat, and no emotion was produced.

There was a young lady residing with me, a fine musician. After she played some hymns admirably I took her aside, and said that, while she played well, there was no thought of God in her service. Afterwards she wrote to me that my words had gone home to her heart, and proved the turning point of her life.

When in company and contact with persons holding different religious views from my own, I always act on the principle that I may be wrong, and hold myself ready to consider their statements.

In all greatness or great men there is sadness. ('This,' says Mr. Haddin, 'was his reply to some observations made by me as we gazed on the portrait of Cardinal Newman.')

An English lady, who was staying with us in Irvine, said, "Why do Scotch people call water 'watter'?" I replied, "Do you not know that when men began to build boats they were at first coracles, small vessels hollowed out of the trunks of trees. Then they rose to small boats, with which they skirted the shores of the ocean. Then they rose to large ships, with which they traversed at will the whole sea. At last a man sprang up in Greenock called James Watt, who invented the steamship. That was a wonderful invention, quite mastering the ocean, rendering it the complete servant of man. And so now we in Scotland call it 'watt-er'."

Yet another of his Westfield visitors, Miss Margaret

Nairn, has given me notes of his conversation, on which I have already drawn.   She writes—

One of his views was, that the highest art, music and architecture, in the Roman Catholic Church received a death-blow at the Reformation from which they never recovered.   The finest sacred music we find either in the Roman Catholic Church before, or in the Protestant Church after, Luther's time.   For example, the Gregorian chants on the one hand, the oratorios and passion music on the other.   For Haydn's " Creation," he affirmed, was not an oratorio, but an opera ; and Mozart's " Masses" were but waltzes, lacking the dignity of religious worship.   In architecture, all the grandest Gothic piles were built before the 15th century.   Painting and sculpture too reached their height in Raphael and Michel Angelo.

Bach was his favourite composer ; the violin his favourite instrument.   He once said how beautiful it was that the book of Revelation spoke only of stringed instruments in heaven.   His opinion was that the nearer a man came into sympathy with his instrument, the more music he brought forth.   Thus the human voice surpasses all instruments, because coming nearest to the man himself.

His life, he used to say, had increased year by year in happiness.   Along with the most intense power of suffering, he had an infinite capacity for enjoyment.   He had the gift of extracting humour out of the very absence of it in others, and had many a story to tell in connection with this.   On one occasion he told an old man in his congregation singularly devoid of the humorous faculty the story of the baker brushing against the sweep, and the latter turning round to him with the words, " You dirty fellow, see what a mess you've made of me."   After a pause the old man said, " Weel, sir, I think it should jist hae been the ither way, for it was the sweep that wad dirty the baker." "But don't you see," said Dr. Robertson, "that that's the point of the story?" "Point o' the story," replied he, "it's jist clean nonsense a'thegither."

His handwriting was notorious for its indistinctness. Some one, speaking of this failing which he had in common with two of his regular correspondents, Dr. Graham and Mr. Stitt, said, "How can you three understand each other's letters?" "Oh," said he, "we correspond on the basis of mutual illegibility!"

Once when the snow was on the ground he remarked on the fine contrast of colours in that verse, "She is not afraid of the snow for her household, for all her household are clothed in scarlet."

Most of his Sundays for a considerable time after his removal to Westfield were spent on duty. In March, 1881, he preached before the University of Glasgow, and in the following May he fulfilled a third engagement at Cambridge, where, in addition to conducting the Church services, he delivered his lectures on "Luther," and on "Poetry and Fine Art."

The friend to whom the following letter, found among Dr. Robertson's papers, is addressed writes— "I find on looking back among my notes for 1881, indications of a charming three days with Robertson at West Calder, Saturday, Sunday, and Monday, April 16-18. This letter, which I never received, must, though there is a discrepancy in date, refer to this visit, for I find in the skeleton record, on which I shall some day endeavour to put flesh, 'His brilliant conversation—Music, Art, Italy. Read, by

request, some of my volume to him, which had then
just appeared.'"

To Professor Nichol, LL.D.

WESTFIELD, April, 1881.

In the beginning of this week I have been whirled away
from home, returning however in brave good time for meeting you at West Calder had you come yesterday. Equally
convenient will it be, and a rare delight to have you, as you
kindly say, on Friday, the 16th, to stay over Sunday as the
stranger that is within my gates, when I shall do no manner
of work—not preaching anywhere that day ; and, except for
"going together to the kirk" with me (if you like it) at noon,
you shall rest (for the rest) and read me, won't you?—while I
listen in reverent silence—such snatches of the genuine old
Orphic melody, that has come singing down the ages through
the darkness and the depths, as break from your lips (when
the fountain of the deep in you is broken up) fitfully, in
songs of "Lethe" and "Revelation, Immortality, and God."
They are prayer and song and sermon—sighing, singing,
seeing—all in one; and make the hour that hears them holy,
and the place none other than the "house of God."   How
glad I am to hear you singing so, a non-professional upon
the sacred harp. I wish I could preach as you sing, drawing
souls upward—UP.   Pardon the terrible paronomasia, but
really and truly I sometimes console myself for the indignity
of the denominational name by reflecting that U.P. preachers
and U.P. poets must be always the best—that all good
preaching and all good poetry is U.P.   The spirit of a man
goeth upward ; and if you face round upon him from a pulpit
or a platform above, and hurl down dogmas in the teeth of
him, you will crush his aspirations and break his ascent,
and prevent him from climbing with you and after you, up

through the darkness, up through the silence, to catch glimpses beyond of the vision your eye has seen, to catch echoes beyond of the voices your ear has heard. The greatest of all teachers was lifted up upon a cross that He might draw all men unto Him, and it is then when we in our measure are lifted up upon a cross of suffering, of mental agony, or moral grief, or other great anguish, that we are most powerful to draw others after us upward. For the sorrow at once opens our eyes to see the God above us, and our hearts to sympathize with fellow-sufferers beneath. Only the crucified can ascend and draw men up along with him. Only in the form of the cross does hope climb upwards, like the bird with outstretched wings. Only in the likeness of the Crucified with hands outstretched in agony, with thorn-crowned brow and drooping head and languid eyes and pallid cheek, with pierced heart and pierced hands and feet all stained with blood, do the Cowpers, and the Gerhards, and the Chattertons, and the mighty poets in their misery dead, draw souls after them ; and the Christ-like singer in the darkness on the cross—crying, "My God, My God, why hast Thou forsaken Me ?", and, through the darkness of desertion, the darkness of death, the darkness of dreadful doubt sometimes whether there be any God at all, struggling, yearning, looking for the light of God—shall draw men heavenward far more surely, far more resistlessly than any dogmatist from platform or pulpit delivering down to them a system of theology, and driving it home with logical arguments, and laying it down all cut and square. And he knows all about it and is quite sure that he is right and every one who differs from him wrong.

To Miss Janet Bruce.

WESTFIELD, 19th April, 1881.

You shouldn't flirt away all the evening and leave your poor old grandfather to the mercies of a moment at "the eleventh hour." However I forgive you, for that moment is momentous as showing, though only in a momentary glimpse, a picture of no moment, as the best pictures painted by genius are. That is they do not represent the real and finite in any given special passing moment; but through that little casement of a moment show the ideal . . . Eccola! You have often seen a Madonna and Child of Raphael's —*Buonissimo.* I saw a Madonna and Child just now going down the avenue under the cypress and yew. She looked somewhat sad, as if her child were sick. No wonder ! She is wedded, it may be said, to sorrow, for she is the wife of the *grieve*, and her little boy's name is Lamb—which was indeed his father's before him, so that is not very surprising. But now these real Madonnas go down the avenues of life, and pass away under the yew and cypress, down into the darkness and the nothingness and out of sight and out of mind ; but Raphael's Madonna lives on because it represents, as near as possible perhaps to man, the ideal Madonna, that is perpetually incarnating itself in the real, the everlasting that is perpetually looking forth through the casement of time and of the finite, perpetually robing itself in fresh attire that waxes old and perishes and passes away, while this remaineth—as the picture of your face remains in a clear, running stream, though the stream itself is changing by the water running on.

To Dr. Angus Smith, Manchester.

Westfield, 26th April, 1881.

. . . Would you add to your other kindness that of coming to visit me here, as you promised to do? You see how—through favour of our modern Prometheus,[1] that has brought light, not down from the bright and sunny heaven above, but (much more wonderful) from the dark depths of the black pit beneath; and by his "wonderful lamp," has built or rebuilt quite a palace of a place here in its own way —I have come for the time into possession of a house to which I can now invite you.

In the autumn of 1881, he revisited Iona, taking with him his sister and some friends from Bridge of Allan. He had arranged with his landlord of the year before, that a boat with rowers should join the steamer at Iona and go on with it to Staffa, to take the party back. When the steamer called at Iona the weather was threatening, and the boat provided seemed hardly fit for a heavy sea, but it was hurriedly resolved to proceed. When Staffa was reached the aspect of the sky and sea was not reassuring; but the steamer was allowed to go, and then there was no choice, except either to camp on the shelterless island, or face the peril of the voyage back. The latter alternative was chosen; but it was soon found that progress in the direction of Iona was all but impossible. Hours passed and they seemed to come no nearer to their destination. The storm increased and it was

[1] Dr. Young of Kelly.

resolved to go before the wind in the direction of
the island of Gometra, where it was known shelter
could be had in the house of the proprietor. The
situation was sufficiently serious. Now and again the
waves broke over the little craft, thoroughly drench-
ing the passengers and giving them hard work to bale
out the water and keep afloat. They were seven in
number, and one of them tells that all that weary day
the words from the epitaph in Irvine churchyard would
keep sounding in her ears, " Sail on, dark coffined fleet
of seven."

At last at midnight, when they had been on the sea
for nine hours, they made the island, and a two miles
walk brought them, dripping and bedraggled as they
were, to the laird's house. Word had gone on before
them, and they found the house lighted up on their
approach. But the host did not appear, and they
were received by the servants in silence and with
solemn funereal faces, which were yet further elongated,
when Robertson, thinking thereby to win the greater
favour, as Highlanders have a proverbial reverence for
the clergy, introduced himself, and one after another
of the gentlemen of the party as "the Rev."! They
learned afterwards that Highland reverence for the
clergy is so mixed with superstition, that a company
who have escaped the sea are reckoned specially
"uncanny," if they number among them any of the
clerical profession.

But though thus received in grim silence, which was
unbroken to the end, they got such hospitality as the

house could furnish—a late supper, and some hours
of rest, if not of sleep. By some means, next morning, a life-boat was procured, embarking in which,
they again faced the unabated storm, and made for
Staffa, which they reached in time for the steamer
that, on alternate days, calls there first. They thus
at last reached Iona in safety. Robertson was accustomed to make light of the danger, and to dwell
rather on the humorous incidents of the stormy voyage. He told with great glee how, on questioning the
boatmen, as they were nearing Staffa, whether they
could in any way account for the sudden storm, they,
resolute adherents of the "constitutional party" in the
Free Church, connected it with the "heresies" of
Professor Robertson Smith, and the "temporizings"
of Principal Rainy. When the travellers went on
board the steamer, the first passenger they saw—
indeed, almost the only one who had ventured to face
the storm—was the learned Principal, who was all
unconscious of the thaumaturgic power with which he
is credited in the "Highlands and Islands," that are
under his special care. After his return to Westfield,
Dr. Robertson wrote to his sister : " I would not for a
great deal have missed that romantic Highland vigil
in the house of the invisible chieftain, M'Lean, nor
the jolly life-boat, nor even the other boat, now that
it is all over and no one is a bit the worse for it."

To Mr. William M'Call, Irvine.

Westfield, 15th August, 1881.

. . . I am vowing a vow of total abstinence from preaching for some time. Thus I can say to any one who asks me, as the Auchenbowie collier said to his minister, who was scolding him for not attending church, "Weel, sir, if I dinna gang to your kirk, I dinna gang by't." I had forgotten this story till reminded of it by the landlady of the "Great Western," at Oban, who said she had heard me tell it in Dr. Knox's, years and years ago; and for the sake of that and other old memories refused to accept any payment of hotel-bill either for myself or my party of five. I said she was as bad as Mr. MacLehose, who had made me free of his fine circulating library for many long years. Sometimes I have far too many books out and keep them far too long; and if he sends word hinting to send them back, I say if he gives me any more of his impudence I will leave him!

A movement begun that autumn, chiefly among the younger ministers, for the improvement of the devotional services of the Church, greatly interested him.

To His Sister.

Westfield, Friday.

. . . I will stand faithfully by them, and lend them all the help I can. You know how I think many late "improvements" no improvements at all, and some that are wanted still less so, especially the light jaunty style of singing, and the liturgical bonds which some would impose. Our Presbyterian worship, if kept free and well instructed and guided, is capable of development into the purest form of church worship, even among the Scotch, and among the so-called "vulgar," but withal honest and manly U.P.'s. I hope to convince them that many innovations reached, or indicated as desirable, are not improvements, and that if they get upon the wrong lines the old fogies may easily checkmate them, and ought to. Even a worship ideally the best may not be the best for our Church as yet, or for a long while. There were ninety ministers present, the younger U.P. ministers that seemed the very flower of our Church. If the movement, which is a very healthful one if rightly inspired and instructed and managed, should go astray, I should not hold myself guiltless if I had not done my best to keep it on the right lines. It is in keeping with the spirit of the age and must succeed ; and those who are out of sympathy with it, and keep aloof from it, or set themselves against it, must make up their minds to be defeated, for better or for worse. Best to help to guide it right if one can. Some may, strangely enough, think it a fault for ministers and members of the Church to associate for the purpose of consulting, and showing one another how best, according to the Scriptures and the freedom the Church allows, to worship God. They are not sure of their own ground, and don't want to see such questions raised. But they are raised in spite of them, and wise it is to let us deal with them and dispose of them as wisely as we can, and great good will come of it.

A lady whom he had known and loved as a child and to whom he had once written a birthday letter,[1] having become a mother, wrote to tell him of the death of one of her children. He wrote in reply :—

[1] See page 221.

It was touchingly kind of you to remember in your sorrow to write me, when you could scarcely see to do so in "the shadow of death," when your beautiful baby could have scarcely crossed the threshold accompanied by the songs of a thousand churches, assembled just then, when the bells had ceased to ring.   The little pilgrim has come to Zion with songs, and joined the children in the streets and in the temple, that sing their Hosannas, or rather their Hallelujahs to the children's King and Saviour, as they wave their little palm branches glittering with the dew of their immortal youth.

And she has strewed her beautiful little garment in the way.   If so beautiful in death how beautiful will it be in resurrection.   You will have it folded up and laid aside in the wardrobe of the grave to-morrow, and I will come and join you in your sadness, or rather in your sure and certain hope.

She has taken higher rank in heaven as one of Christ's redeemed from earth, than if she had been created all at once a holy angel in heaven ; and through the shadow of death and mystery of pain, and the mother's tears and kisses, and the "Blood of the Lamb," has passed up all unconsciously but yet most safely to the highest heavens, where

> " Babes thither caught from mother's breast
> Claim right to sing above the rest,
> Because they found the happy shore
> They neither saw nor sought before."

And now you will always see a sweet face looking down, and a dear little voice singing overhead and calling you to "come up hither"—and it will do you good, and we shall all meet beyond the shadows and be very happy together, and not forget the little crib, that with the beautiful child suffering so softly did not look at all like a death-bed, as you said; and you thought it so strange, till you remembered that death is abolished, and for the "Babe in Christ" not so much—not at all—the hearse and the funeral, but the chariot and the angels come!

I thank God you are so calm in "Christ's own Peace," and comforted as one whom a mother comforteth. Your note I have answered by return of post somewhat hurriedly. —I am, my dear child, yours in sorrow.

To Mr. George Brown, Irvine.

Westfield, 22nd February, 1882.

. . . The spring is breaking with great sweetness and beauty, and I am making a new garden toward the sunrise to meet it—planting a garden eastward in Eden, though there is no prospect whatever of an Eve! Nor can I afford to have a man to till the ground!

The late Mr. Robert Herdman, R.S.A., whose friendship Dr. Robertson had made during his month's residence in Iona in 1881, had asked leave to make a study of his head for a picture of St. Columba.

To Mr. Robert Herdman, R.S.A.

Westfield, 2nd March, 1882.

My Dear Raphael,—In what costume should I come? The surtout or swallow-tail would hardly be worn by the "saints" of the Holy Isle in the 6th century. Perhaps an *ulster* would be more suggestive of their Irish descent. Should I shorten my hair, or let it flow in its weird, grey dishevelment—which nobody likes—and I suppose I must

cut it. Should I shear my grisly beard and accept the
irregular tonsure of the monks of the Hebrides?

If I had that pretty child (Mary Payne) who led the
hymns at my feet[1] it would make me look twenty years
older.   But no women, still less pretty children, and no
cows (I don't say no calves) were permitted in I-Colm-kill
during my old residence there.—Your affectionate humble
servant, COLUMBA.

To the REV. JOHN KIRKWOOD.

WESTFIELD, 1st May, 1882.

How miserably I have behaved! Your letter will be a
week old to-morrow. I must baptize it with tears. . . .
At present, and for some time, I am under a vow, from
which there is no absolviter, to preach no anniversary, or any
such-like service, on any account, any occasion, any solicitation whatever. "The sweep of July" that you offer me
must be a very idle fellow, for there are few smockacles or
little reek that month. A preacher at Bridge of Allan spoke
grandly of "taking the sweep of the universe." Old John
M'Robie, sitting by me, asked what he meant by that. I
said, "Surely you know who *he* is, the black sweep of the
universe!"

To MISS FLORENCE SELLAR.

WESTFIELD, 6th May, 1882.

You shall have to begin hearing from me, in the occasional audience you may be kind enough to grant,[2] by an
act of pardon to the old man of delay that is in me (wretched
old man!).

---

[1] On the Angels' Hill, Iona. See p. 386.

[2] Miss Sellar had gone to Florence, and Dr. Robertson had undertaken to send to her some jottings to guide her through the churches
and galleries. See page 289.

I have been imprisoned, you must know, for debt since you left—debt to Duty—an inexorable creditor that agreed to take no *composition*, but has shut me up in jail till it was paid; and when, through the black iron bars, I heard your musical voice, like the singing of the minstrel Blondel, outside the fortress in which Richard was immured, I knew the refrain well, but was sad I could not render it immediately.

Forgive the unavoidable delay—which I will not enlarge a single moment by pausing, even so long, to explain. Nor will I stay to thank you here—as I do most heartily—for your kind mention of the ancient mariner, that might well and deservedly have been forgotten, to the ladies De Quincey. The day of my acquaintance with them, of which, though slight, I was very proud, seemed to be broken off; but, through you, the dawn seems to return at the sunset, and "the evening and the morning make the day." . . .

Daylight is only a veil—though a white veil—and mortal life a veil; but when the veil of light and veil of life shall be withdrawn, shall not "night teach us knowledge"? Shall we not see into the higher heaven beyond the stars—shall we not see each other face to face, with only God between? And God is light, and in that Light, dissolved comes every sorrow—that holy light of God, of which the light of genius is but the dim and distant reflection : and blessed are the pure in heart for they shall see God, and see each other, and see all things in that light of God. For them that light is *sown*, the Scripture says, still under ground and buried, or only springing like the corn in May, but it shall break and blossom into spreading harvest in due season.

"Be patient." "Behold the husbandman waiteth for the harvest." A few things I may be able to teach you, in virtue of my education to that ministry, through long experience and ordination to it in the black robes of sorrow, and with the hand of God laid sometimes heavily enough upon my head. But it is little, it is nothing, I can teach you as other teachers can, and specially the Teacher Darkness and the Teacher Death.

At this point he had paused in his writing. Before he was able to resume it, his and his correspondent's dear friend, Dr. John Brown, died. He then added this fragment of a postscript to the unfinished letter, and wrote the letter which follows it :—

Teacher Death ! Little I thought in writing then of what should next follow. Pausing here to make for you ere continuing. . . .

To the Same.

WESTFIELD, 15th May, 1882.

The shadow of death—thick, dark, heavy—has fallen betwixt us, and I could hardly see to write the latter part of what I have sent,[1] and none of which in the darkened light you may see or care to read.

That dear, dear friend in whose name I had the joy of meeting you first, scarcely a month ago, has passed beyond the shadows into the Light of God. Now he sees no more through a glass darkly, but face to face. On Saturday he sickened ; on Sunday sat a little in the drawing-room ; on Monday seemed a little better ; but sank through Tuesday and Wednesday ; and peacefully on Thursday morning— when the sweet May sunlight was breaking over his beloved Arthur's Seat and Holyrood, up the leafy Princes Street Gardens—the white angels came. "The Master came and called for him ; " and dearest Dr. John Brown had " another morn than ours."

[1] The Jottings on Florence.

No clouds! no broken lights! in his last hours, such as he might have dreaded, for the clouds were just beginning to return after the rain—only very little clouds like a man's hand, but they pointed, after such a sweet long reach of sunlight, to a deeper, blacker gulf and storm of darkness than ever, through which to struggle in the end on to the Light. But the Cloud of Death that over-shadowed him was a "bright cloud," bright with the Presence that would not leave him forsaken; and without the slightest fear he "entered the cloud" and passed, Christ-like, into the beautiful Transfiguration on the Mount of God!

Serene and clear the eventide, the light at evening of a day of such shining—mingled and alternate light and dark—of brightness that outshone the sun, and far outshone us all in intellectual splendour and in holy purity, and gloom that brought him sometimes very near the dark forsaken agony. The Heavens were really opened over him and the vision came and went in that quiet chamber, quite near the tread of common footsteps, and the roar of traffic on the railway and the streets, when it was little thought how close at hand the open gate had been, and scenes of meeting between the shining welcomes and the sad farewells!

He said with unutterable love, dumb in its very depth— simply, "Oh Isabella!" Again "Alexander, you will pray for me"—sometimes, "My trust is in Christ, I cling to Him alone, no more, no more, perfect peace;" then, with that sweet smile of his, you never saw on any other face so beautiful, he fell asleep; and still it lingers on his face, that looks in its white stillness upwards—like a holy dream.

Be glad with me that it has been so with him in the end. I cannot write you more just now, but will do so after the funeral to-morrow. They are wonderfully cheerful in the house of mourning—"The Lord will not forsake his own."

To The Same.

On Tuesday we had the brightest sunlights this summer as yet had brought us ; and shortly after noon, and slowly and sadly, from Rutland Street to the New Calton Cemetery, passed the dark procession of mourners in hundreds to the burial of all that was mortal of one of the greatest, most gifted, most genial, most gentle—I will add with emphasis, most godly of men.

Crowds came to see the funeral pass by. "What went they out for to see?" "A reed shaken with the wind?" Nay, but a prophet, and more than a prophet, and one of the kindliest of woman born. A "Bruised Reed" indeed, but yielding sweeter music, through its having been bruised, in the hands of the Good Shepherd that does not break the bruised reed, but refits it and retunes it, to the utterance of harmonies that could never come so rich from the lips that had never quivered, from the soul that had never suffered, from the reed that had not been "bruised."

How many more than were drawn by the funeral to the streets and the cemetery, have been drawn by the sweet sad life, silently, and by the literary labours of love as well— nearer to the True, and Good and Holy—nearer to the Heaven where with the pure in heart he now sees God.

All along the line of the "dark march" of the shadow of death, that had fallen into the sunlights of Princes Street— on every ledge, terrace and balcony available, there seemed to stand some group of ladies in mourning, many with tears upon their faces and white flowers in their hands.

But for him the heaven had been opened ere the grave was opened, and as we passed along one seemed to lose sight of the dark pageantry of death and funeral, and to see the chariots and horses of fire. Your Master (mine also, like Elisha's) has been taken from us. He walked with God, not drove in a coach and six, like some blustering Christians, but walked like Isaac at eventide—like William Cowper at Olney—like Enoch; and like Enoch, is not, for God has taken him. Let us seek after the God who has taken him, rather than himself. Where is the Lord God of John Brown!

The burial was fitly made in the precincts of the ancestral Holyrood rather than in Dean Cemetery or the Grange, in the early summer, with breaking of new life and blossomings around us, breathing sure and certain hope of resurrection —a sepulchre in a garden, the garden of the early summer, in which the Christ who is risen had himself been laid.

A lark went singing up the clear blue sky, showering down gushes of melody on the mourners, that stood silent and uncovered round the opened grave. I wish you had heard it (true to the kindred points of heaven and home). I think in some sort you always will have to hear a voice from above calling you to sweetness, to make your life a lark-like melody.

> " Be good, sweet maid, . . .
> And so make Life, Death, and that vast For Ever,
> One grand sweet song."

The following fragment seems to have been written at a later date in the same year :—

" Rab and His Friends " was the first remarkable work of one of my oldest, dearest friends, whose funeral darkened the sunlight of a May morning in the early summer of this year. His last visit to the country was paid here but three weeks before, and the light of joy that shone round his wonderfully beautiful head and countenance seemed to us like the " glory " round a saintly brow, and to have less in it of earth and more of heaven. Descended from that shep-

herd lad that led his sheep and read his Greek upon the hill-
sides in the Highlands, without grammar or dictionary, or
other teaching than the "inspiration of the Almighty, which
giveth man understanding," and which has taught him ever
since to read in the same way the hieroglyphic and arrowheaded handwriting on the wall—the same whom the stiff
Seceders, that refused to fraternize with George Whitfield,
would have interdicted from the pulpit because he was
suspected of having eaten, through a fresh temptation of
the serpent, of the tree of knowledge, and of being much
occupied, like the "Faustus" or the builder of Cologne
Cathedral, with the evil one—this last, the greatest of the
gifted race of the Browns, inherited, both by his father's
and his mother's side, both gift and grace, and was indeed
truly a noble man of God, with all his rich, rare humour
sanctified through the holy life that was in him. He had to
struggle up through depths of darkness and moods of even
the forsaken agony, in striking contrast with alternate moods
of mirth and playfulness, like Cowper of Olney, now hidden
by the curtains of sorrow, and now riding a merry race with
John Gilpin, till it came all right in the end, when he had a
sweet and beautiful and saintly death beneath the opened
heavens, and passed away with shining face into the joy
unspeakable—the Light that is inaccessible, in which there
is no darkness at all.

At the United Presbyterian Synod of 1882, Dr.
John Ker had, in connection with the sanctioning of a
"Children's Hymnal," entered a protest against the
growing tendency to use hymns to the exclusion of
the Psalms in worship. The speech was delivered
immediately after Dr. Brown's funeral, and Dr. Robertson, who had sauntered into the Synod Hall, happened

to hear it. The following letter manifestly refers to that speech :—

To the Rev. Dr. John Ker.

WESTFIELD.

. . . It was a pity to banish the Psalms! What human hymn to be compared with the Old 100! But I am afraid you are behind the age, Doctor, not knowing that now-a-days David is counted (among the U.P.'s) nothing to Dunlop, or Jeduthun to Jacque of Auchterarder. (A kingly man, though, is this Jacque, whom I much love and admire, and he does play the fiddle well, and he can write no ordinary commonplaces—witness his "Sweep's Apprentice.") The hymns now in fashion must seem very feeble "milk for babes"—spoon-meat—to those who in their very childhood were fed on the strong meat of "Now Israel may say," "In Judah's land," "God is our Refuge," etc., sung to the Old 124, Martyrs, and Stroudwater, "compared with which Italian trills are tame." But that was ere we learned "Piety" or got into the "Desert."[1] Do you remember them in our college days? No doubt the weird wail of Coleshill at an old sacrament was very barbarous, compared with the mild prettiness of Bonar and Ira Sankey! But somehow I am barbarous enough to prefer it with "Why art thou cast down?" or "O thou, my soul!" The grand march of an old Scotch tune, with all its native wildness, or of its more harmonious cousin german, the chorale, is far finer than the waltzing devotion of 12th masses, and the light tripping gallopade of a metrical chant. Even the "Seed we bury in the earth" of my lamented Dr. Bruce, how trifling it sounds at any funeral, even at his own, com-

---

[1] The names of two most unecclesiastical psalm tunes that were popular in Scotland in the early half of this century.

pared with the solemn dead march of the 90th Psalm, or truly
dirge-like 102nd or 103rd—"Such pity," etc.   Or, if hymn
they will have, why not take the inspired hymn included in
that same chapter, "Death is swallowed up, O Death," etc.,
which is a burst of thanksgiving to God who giveth the victory, and not a mere dialectical discussion.   In very many
cases I believe a little argument will be enough to show that
the old is better, and if the new is better, by all means let us
have it.   What is wanted is rather revival than reform, and
when the spirit of devotion wells up like a flood, all little
dilettante teacups will be swept away soon enough, and
broader, deeper vessels called for, to hold the overflow.
" Stay me with *flagons*, for I am sick of love."   .   .   .

TO DR. ANGUS SMITH, Manchester.

WESTFIELD, 20th October, 1882.

.   .   .   The Union Jack reminds me of the gross
wrong done by Sir Garnet to our Highlanders.   Brave
fellows ! that have won every battle—Tel-el-Kebir, like
the rest—for your lubberly English.   I like the signboard
on a northern public-house—a Highlander with kilt
and claymore, and underneath inscribed, " The Battle
of Waterloo."   Much nearer the truth than Sir Garnet's
despatches.   A young friend, lieutenant in the Black
Watch, has come home wounded, though recovering, to
Edinburgh.   He was among the first within the fort, dashed
on to Arabi's tent, and has brought home his slippers.
They are of golden leather, like those of the King in the
Canticles, whose dress, I take it, is described, and not his
person only, when, among the rest, it is said, " His legs are
as pillars of marble set upon sockets of fine gold."
Why should they say " England," and not " Scotland "
rather, which is the royal land, the ancient cradle of the

kings. "Great Britain" would do, but it does not include Ireland, and Paddy Garnet would kick. "United Kingdom" is a *thing*, and won't do. I propose "United People" of Great Britain and Ireland, which would speedily, of course, become U.P.!!

Give my warmest regards to Miss Smith, with thanks meantime for her kind letter, which gave me great delight, and which I will answer without delay when I have time to write legibly, and not in that fiery haste in which I am going to melt down a pile of letters harder to liquidate than hers. I hope all goes well with your laboratory and its fiery trials. Why do we say *wiry* from *wire*, *miry* from *mire*, *spicy* from *spice*, and not *firy* from *fire*? Can the *fier* be the French (and Italian *fieri*, wild beasts) from which comes *fierce*? Or can the one word have passed into the other as being nearly related, like the den of lions at Babylon and the fiery furnace? Do you know, I told a scorner lately that it was now discovered from the "Bricks" that the *Mene, Mene* of Belshazzar was nothing but the *Menu* of the feast hung on the wall! The unutterable blockhead was so ready to believe it that I had to tell him it was only a guess !

To Miss Florence Sellar.

Westfield, 1st November, 1882.

I wonder if I shall be able to survive Saturday, if you really will come and bring Miss Annie with you. They say, *Vedi Napoli e poi muori.*

You will find here some sheets of a letter on Ravenna that grew upon my hands too large, and not too legible, as from the first it was too late for overtaking you in Italy—to send.

How delicately I am reminded on this day of "All Saints" of two of the very noblest of them [1] by you and your charm-

---

[1] Dr. John Brown and Dr. Norman Macleod.

ing young friend. It sounds like sweet music in a dream, in a requiem.

The following extracts are from the "letter on Ravenna" begun to be written in answer to a series of questions which Miss Sellar had sent to him from the ancient city :—

What eyes you must have to have read off so quickly, so correctly, so much of the mysterious old Ravenna and its handwriting on the wall. I have received with much delight your "Shorter Catechism"; but would rather have been with you. I believe that into the heart and meaning of that fine Christian archaic work I should have seen more keenly, more correctly, through your young, open eyes, and more quickly, than through the old, half-shut, spectacled eyes of laborious microscopic criticism. You remember how the old magician in the eastern tale goes in search of the innocent, pure-eyed child, who alone can open to him the treasure chamber, and how he finds her by putting his ear to the ground and listening till he distinguishes the whisper of her footstep amid the heavy clatter of a thousand others on the streets of a city a hundred miles away. . . .

I will not forget how you carried the thought of me in some sort even through those visions of beauty and wonder floating round you in Ravenna—the saints and martyrs on their mural march across the centuries, back to the cradle, forward to the throne; and the Good Shepherd feeding his flock in pastures green in the shadow of death, in the darkness of the sepulchre, brightened like the night with stars of gold shining with all variety of richest colour, like the plumage of the Bird of Immortality, like the Rainbow of the Heavens around the Throne, which is the meaning and interpretation of that gorgeous blaze of interwoven light and colour with which the very flooring of the house of death is tapestried, with which its walls and ceilings are all draped and hung. It is the " Mene, Mene, Tekel," written in brilliantly illuminated letters—the doom of death in the Divine handwriting on his palace walls. It is still more the heavenly apocalypse of beauty, rising in rich raiment at the sound of the trumpet, putting on her beautiful garments and ascending in robes of triumph from the tomb, when this corruptible shall put on incorruption, and this mortal shall put on immortality. And then, in the midst, sits calmly and quietly, in His own divinest peace, the Good Great Shepherd of the sheep brought again from the dead by the blood of the everlasting covenant—which is indicated by the cross He carries on His shoulder—and gently and tenderly He feeds His sheep out of His pierced hand ; and one of them licks His hand, as it were with a tongue that almost seems to speak, and does speak in the dumb, eloquent language of symbol, and, speaking, says : " Yea, though I walk through the valley of the shadow of death, I will fear no evil."

The following letter was written in answer to an invitation to dine with the " B.B." (Blackie Brotherhood) Club in Edinburgh :—

To Mr. Robert Herdman, R.S.A.

WESTFIELD, 9th December, 1882.

MY DEAR R——,—No not " Raphael"—Herdman is far better, for it is *Bonus Pastor*—when Raphael, I suppose, is only *Rapha*, a giant, *El*, to God.

To speak in colour, but not loud, the kingly autumn has laid aside his golden crown, and the old priestly winter put on his white mitre—how grandly this year!—to lead in to the Sacred Festivals. A merry Christmas I wish you!! and secular as well—Salisbury's that was, Gladstone's that is to be—and, better than either, social feastings of select clubs, like (though there is none other like) the B.B.!

Why do men feast most in winter time? Is it some idea of chiaroscuro or Rembrandtesque interior lights intensified by contrast with the outer darkness—the compress of shadow. Midsummer makes us mildly happy in Iona? Midwinter merry—in the city? We shall see.

Of course to your invitation I say Amen, so let it B.B. The Professor's drawing and your own (as well in solicitation as in sepia), each singly is very powerful, and both together quite resistless: especially when I am touched already with the magnet of a strong attraction to you both, which all this polar weather will not deflect from its proper current (*i.e.*, the 28th current).

We are now here shut in with miles of snow, two feet in depth at least, all round. My postman, who is not so swift as Job's, has accomplished half a mile in two hours, and at the end is exhausted of all the pith (which was never much) that is in him. Back with the letters *he* can't go; *il povero*. I send a ploughman; and the snow plough is out, making its furrows for the seed of the just and the evil doers also, of whom in this neighbourhood there are a good few.

What a wonderful man our Professor is—rare old brave hero! I should not wonder if he went next to Africa and outdid Livingstone, and founded a Chair somewhere, and climbed up and sat in the chair of Cassiopeia. Long may he live!

To Mr. Robert MacLehose.

Westfield, 22nd January, 1883.

. . . Clerk Maxwell's Life, for which I specially thank you, I have almost devoured. With much of Garnett's part of the work I was already familiar, as he had showed it me very fully in Cambridge, where I made his intimate acquaintance, and found him a great power for good in University circles and town society, and in the movements of our own Church there. The unaffected deep religious tone that runs especially through his part of the Memoir, as it did through the whole life of Clerk Maxwell, is strikingly at discord with that optimistic Epicureanism that laughs and sings its drunken song with devils in Paradise ; and not less with the howling wilderness of pessimistic pain—that bellowing and struggling of the old man in his agony and darkness, without God in the world—which characterize so much of the literature that is the outcome of your modern life. Here are two Masters of Science, Maxwell and Garnett after him, who are actually silly enough to believe themselves guilty sinners, and old-fashioned enough to believe in a redeeming God !

The beautiful prayers and Scriptures read, the beautiful hymns and anthems sung (I never heard finer singing) in Trinity College Chapel at Maxwell's funeral, have some meaning in them after all—for us at least, poor fools, who have the simplicity to believe it—and are not mere wildfire gleams to light us down to the eternal darkness, mere mocking songs sung by the sirens of the gulf that swallows up all life, to lure us down complacently with their delicious sweetness into a depth more fathomless, and silence more profound.

To Miss ———

WESTFIELD, March, 1883.

The movement of your own inner life you have vividly depicted—that yearning after beautiful ideals, that sense of something beautiful and lost, which lies in some measure in all human hearts—the scriptural Eden, the classical Hesperides, the mediæval Christ, the Paradise to the thief on the cross—sad sense of something beautiful and lost, which can never be wholly crushed out of the hearts of the rudest. How strongly it works in your gentle heart, how strong by nature and still more by grace, beneath the guidance of that Holy Spirit, who, in the silent depths of our dumb, unsatisfied longings, which lie too deep for words or even for tears, " maketh intercession with groanings that cannot be uttered." Old Hindu legends tell that the cause of that strange sadness you always feel when listening to the sweetest music, is that it awakens memories of a beautiful music once heard on earth, now heard no more; and how often in pensive twilights, in poetic musings these spring evenings, do you not see the flashing of the golden gates now shut, do you not hear the echoes of the beautiful music that has passed away?

But still strong within you is this yearning—deepened and purified too by the Helper of our infirmities, the Comforter, the Holy Ghost—the longing after the Paradise restored. It is the vision of this, I believe, hidden from the eyes of so many, that haunts you and draws you heavenward, and fills you with these unutterable longings which again seek expression through pictures, through music, through one or other of the gates called Beautiful. It is this yearning of soul that makes the difference between us and the lower creatures. We are never satisfied with what we have, or do, or know, but are always struggling above and beyond. Blessed discontent that will not let us rest short of God Himself! For we were made for Him. This is the meaning of our life ; and there are infinities within us that only the Infinite can fill, eternities that only the Eternal can inhabit, longings and yearnings that God alone can satisfy. That these longings should seek expression in more ways than one does not surprise me. There are, I take it, poetry, the several fine arts—just so many ways of expressing poetry (of course there is prosaic art, more properly called manufacture)—architecture, sculpture, painting, music, eloquence, metrical verses, etc., etc., they are all one, the poetry that is written in any one of these languages, might be translated into any other. "Architecture," says Madame de Staël, "is frozen music ; and music, architecture dissolved into sound." And I suppose that the poetry, or art, or inspiration, or yearning, might utter itself equally well in any of these ways if you had been trained to it, and had the technical skill. To which of them you will most devote yourself must, of course, depend on what you count most congenial to your taste, most serviceable to others, and most pleasing to Him, "whose you are, and whom you serve." Your music, drawing, painting, you must not regard as mere amusements to be lightly given up, but as gifts to be consecrated to the Master, like Mary's alabaster box.

Speaking further on of woman's work amongst the poor, he says :—

We men are rather Boanerges—sons of thunder—storm and earthquake even, but you are rather the still small voice, and your gentleness (like God's own) is your strength. How gently the morning dawn irradiates the world, and the spring comes up the glens, scattering snowdrops and violets. Destruction makes a noise, but reconstruction works in silence. I sometimes think " the woman " is the representative in the family of the third person in the Holy Trinity, the Comforter, the Holy Ghost, who is the fountain of all the beautiful, the tender, the motherly, the womanly—the human family being considered the reflex of the Divine, who said, " Let us make man in our image after our likeness," and then we read, " male and female created He them." Nothing will destroy the worship of the Virgin Mother in the Romish Church, where in their pictures she is blasphemously placed upon the same throne with the Father and the Son, the Holy Spirit, whom she has replaced, only hovering as a dove over her head—nothing, I believe, will dethrone her and destroy her worship but a scriptural understanding of the doctrine of the Holy Spirit as the tender, the motherly, the womanly. It was after the Athanasian Creed was made (and you cannot put love and tenderness into a hard, dogmatic creed) that the personal love and most melting tenderness of the Holy Spirit was lost sight of, and His throne and worship profanely given to Mary. But any holy woman is such as she, a representative on earth of Him; and what a pure consecration does not this thought give to you, my dear young friend, in your office as a comforter, a pleader with souls, as thus the Holy Spirit pleads with them to draw them to Christ. It is not you that speak, but the Holy Spirit that is in you, and this is woman's special mission, in this rough and dark and weary world, by love, by gentleness, by most sisterly tenderness, by whatsoever things are lovely, and through all gates called Beautiful, to draw souls, as the Holy Spirit draws them to the Saviour, to testify, as He does of Him, to take, as He does of the things of Christ, and show them to the soul.

Referring to the foregoing extracts, Miss Robertson writes:—

They are the most characteristic of anything I have received. The last, in which is brought out his favourite idea of the womanly and tender element in the Godhead, called up to mind a conversation I remember hearing between him and our landlady in Siena some eight or nine years ago. She was an enlightened Catholic, and a most warm-hearted Christian woman. The conversation turned on the points of difference between her Church and the Church "Inglese," as she called it. (William carefully avoided the word "Protestant," as it was only associated, at that time, in Siena, with a

low infidel reading room and club in one of the worst parts
of the town.) She was dissatisfied with the mass, had a contempt for the confessional, and even for the priests. She
laughed at purgatory, and denied the worship of images and
saints ; but the Virgin she could not give up. "I have a
"Father," she said, "in God. I have a Brother in my Lord
Jesus. But I need a sister too, and I can only find her in
Mary." Turning to me, she said, "I do not wonder at
the Signore, but how can you do without a woman to help
you?" William pointed her to the 15th chapter of Luke,
with its threefold parable of the Father yearning over His
prodigal child; of the Son, the Shepherd, going after the
lost sheep till he found it; and of the Spirit, the woman
searching for the piece of silver, sweeping the house dili-
gently, and calling on her friends, Rejoice with me. She
listened most eagerly till he had finished, and then said,
"And why did no one ever show me that before? I
have been seeking my God in a woman, and I have found
the woman in my God."

To Mr. William M'Call, Irvine.

Westfield, April 4, 1883.

How much delighted I was with the visits of my two last
days at this time in old Irvine, though they were too hurried
and fatiguing after preaching, and have not been without their
penalties since. The sick received me so kindly, and some
mothers that I had introduced to the communion, and I
hope into the Kingdom itself in their youth, brought their
children round me, as if wishing I could speak to them as I
had done to their mothers before them. And altogether
there was a heart not only of kindness, but of deep spiritual
life beating responsively, which, I somehow think, I never
find quite the same elsewhere. Perhaps I might find it in a

family or two of my brother's Newington Church, where I have renewed acquaintance with the father and mother in the children. You see how bigoted I am growing in my old days, like the Arran elder who said, " Do you think that there be any of the Lord's people out of Arran ? " Well, you understand me. That type of piety which my brother James so well represented, and which I think not the only one, certainly, but at least one of the best, I am delighted to find in so many of my old church, and it draws me back to see them. I must come and "sorn" a longer time upon the good M'Kinlays, and visit more at leisure, if I could only get rid of this thorn in the flesh, this internal stinging that sometimes makes me useless for hours on hours together.

Dr. Young of Kelly died on 13th May, 1883. On the Sunday following his funeral, Dr. Robertson preached at the evening service in Skelmorlie United Presbyterian Church, Dr. Goold of Edinburgh preaching in the forenoon. Mr. Boyd, the minister of the church writes :—

In the course of his sermon Dr. Goold insisted strongly that the doctrine of immortality is taught in the Old Testament, and quoted a number of passages in support of his position. Dr. Robertson had arranged to preach in the evening from the text " Christ hath brought life and immortality to light by the gospel," and the psalms, hymns and anthem had been chosen with this text in view. But after the forenoon service he came to me in anxiety and said, " I must change my subject, if I preach the sermon I intended Dr. Goold will think I am controverting his teaching." All afternoon he was restless, evidently thinking over other sermons, but unable to fix on one. When the hour of even-

ing service had come he told me that he was still undecided.
I replied, "Keep to your subject, the choir cannot now
change the hymns." He consented to do so. It was evident that he had taken the position that immortality was
not clearly taught in the Old Testament. With great tact
he succeeded in avoiding the appearance of contradiction
between him and the morning preacher, by saying in well-
chosen words, which I cannot reproduce, something to this
effect :—"Doubtless there are references to the doctrine of
immortality in the Old Testament, as was so well put before
you in the forenoon. But just as he whose death we are
this day remembering with sorrow, found embedded in the
caverns of the earth the dark substance by which he has
illuminated the homes of rich and poor in many lands, so
did Christ bring to light the doctrine of a future life. The
shale was in the earth long before, but it was Dr. Young
who revealed its illuminating power. Even so the doctrine
of immortality, embedded in Old Testament passages, was
practically unrevealed until He came who brought life and
immortality to light."

I can give you no idea of the beautiful touches by which
Dr. Robertson wrought out the thought I have only indicated ; but so skilfully was it done that I think no one in
the church ever dreamt of anything but completest harmony
between the two preachers.

To His Sister.

LONDON, 22nd June, 1883.

. . . I came round by Manchester where I had a
delightful night with Dr. Angus Smith, going on next day to
Nottingham on a visit to Professor Garnett, of St. John's,
Cambridge, who is great in natural science, joint author with
Lewis Campbell of St. Andrew's, of "A Life of Clerk Max-

well," which is nobly written. He is a manly Christian of the evangelical school. . . .

I have, as yet, seen no one, having been much in the British Museum, and all Wednesday at the Handel Festival, including coming and going from twelve noon to ten at night. Such music! especially the stringed instruments accompanying the voices, as in Madame Albani's "Let the bright Cherubim," etc., and Madame Patey's "Lascia ch' io pianga." I would have gone to-day to "Israel in Egypt," but Lady Craft, with her boy and sister, met me to go and visit *Assur-bani-pal* in the Assyrian Court, though I am no Daniel to read off arrowheaded writing on the wall.

I visited the small but most beautiful of all English cathedrals (Lichfield) on Saturday—heard the evening service, when the Bishop preached, and went afterwards with him into the "palace," and had tea with his noble wife and beautiful children, and long talks on Scottish Art, and other kinds of art. He was specially delighted when I pointed out some new beauties in his own old cathedral, and could tell him that an illumination in the gospels of St. Chad in their library (7th century) was the beautiful work of Celtic artists, reared in Ireland and Iona, and passing to St. Gall in Switzerland, and who had done it in Lindisfarne, in the monastery of St. Cuthbert. Since coming to London I have been able to verify thoroughly in the palæography of the Museum, the correctness of what I said, though much I have learned on the Celtic style at Iona and from the Edinburgh "Antiquarian" and "Joseph Anderson," seems yet unknown to the wise men of the south.

The visit to Lichfield was made in company with his old friend Dr. A. L. Simpson, then of Derby, for whom he preached on two successive Sabbaths.

From allusions in the foregoing and other letters, it

will be seen that Dr. Robertson took a deep interest in Biblical archæology, and specially in the department of the Assyrian antiquities. His periodical residences in London, where he seldom failed to halt, sometimes for weeks, on his way to or from the Continent, and latterly to and from Cambridge, were devoted to study in the British Museum. Principal Cairns has furnished the following memorandum on the subject :—

I only discovered that Dr. Robertson had been studying Assyriology some five years before his death ; but he must have been much longer interested in it. I met him in our college buildings, and something led to his entering on the subject. I then discovered that he had been a member of the Society of Biblical Archæology for a good while, and that when in London he had attended the meetings. He spoke with warm interest of the leading persons whom he there saw and heard. I specially remember the names of Mr. Chad Boscawen and Mr. Pinches. Whether he had been introduced to them or others I cannot tell. He spoke with enthusiasm of the field thus opened up to Biblical research, and of the wonderful interest of the Assyrian remains, even as pieces of literature. He dwelt particularly on the quite unexpected grandeur of the description of the descent of the goddess Ishtar to Hades in connection with the Chaldean epic of the deluge. As I was not then a member of the Society of Biblical Archæology, and as he had obtained the "Transactions" from the beginning, he kindly sent me some eight volumes, stretching from 1872 to 1878. When I saw him repeatedly afterwards, our conversation never ran into the same channel, but I have no doubt that his interest continued to the last.

To His Sister.

On Tuesday night I brought home a noble partner for life in this woodland monastery—a magnificent *chien* of the order of St. Bernard—the chest of a lion, and his bark is thunder. But he is a very mild beast, admirable for the boys to play with, gentle as the gentlest we know, that is their mother. And if submission to a higher will, be the crown of religion, as preached now-a-days by certain " budge doctors of the Stoick fur" (as they are called in Comus, where you acted Sabrina), then Kaiser, that is his name, must be a very good Christian.

Among the friends he made at Cambridge he had a special affection for Mr. and Mrs. T. H. Corry, who were equally drawn to him, and included his name in that of their first-born child. Mr. Corry was drowned while boating on Lough Neagh, and Dr. Robertson received from his young widow a touching note, saying, " My heart is very sore. Send me a word of comfort." That was all. He wrote a long letter from which I can only make some extracts :—

To Mrs. Corry, Cambridge.

So few your words are, even so faintly written, they seem to me almost like silence itself from which they are scarcely removed, that is the silence of a grief that lies too deep for utterance in any words. Only the tears are in your troubled eyes, the fountain of the great deep of sorrow in you being struck, and the "Spirit of Sorrow" "making intercession within you with groanings that cannot be uttered." Divine sorrow! that sympathizes with our human sorrow—grieving not at, but *in* it and *with* it, and that interprets it as a mother the inarticulate cry of suffering of her babe, which *she* quite understands. So that our silence becomes strong supplication, and our dumb grief is heard as powerful prayer in heaven, and draws down comfort from the Father's heart, exceeding abundantly above all that we can ask or think! So may the Holy Ghost the Comforter comfort you, dear daughter of sorrow, in your unutterable grief.

What a difference there is between resting our spirits in their anguish upon mere written words and resting them upon a warm beating bosom. His voice, His hand, must lead you through the gloom—voice that on the cross said, "It is finished," hands that "were pierced with the nails." For even His written words may not comfort you unless spoken by His own living voice—the voice of the Good Shepherd that knows all His flock, and they all know Him, and He calleth them all by name. "Jesus saith unto her, Mary." Precious are His promises—but yet more precious Himself. So may His *Presence* go with you, and then, though you walk in the valley of the shadow (of bereavement dark as death) you will not fear, for He is with you, His rod and His staff (because they are His and held in His own hand) shall comfort you. . . .

The horse (pale horse) and his rider, that appeared suddenly upon the banks, like Pharaoh and his horsemen on the banks of the Red Sea, have themselves been overwhelmed in the water—as theirs were in pursuing the Israelites, who passed through the water unharmed and rose with the morning light upon the farther shore, and shouted "Sing to the Lord—The horse and his rider hath He cast into the sea."

When, on my last little visit, you brought in your little

child to get an old man's blessing (if, like a Simeon in the
temple, I had any to give), I thought of the " young mother
and the Blessed Child ; " and when I saw you with the babe
in your arms, and the young, manly father, with womanly
tenderness bending over you, I thought I had never seen a
fairer picture of pure domestic happiness and love.   And
now the beautiful picture is all shattered, "and your very
heart is broken."   Dearest child, it almost breaks mine even
to think of you so sorely suffering, so strangely tried.

You cannot understand it in the least.   But this you
know, that God's ways of deepest darkness are often His
ways of deepest love—" dark with excess of brightness " to
His dearest, sweetest children, so that sometimes they may
fear to be forsaken altogether, and the most loving and beloved of all cry out—" My God, my God, why hast Thou
forsaken me."   But this you *know* that you have now new
claims on God as your God, new titles to the promises and
to a richer inheritance in God himself as your portion, to
which your sorrow and bereavement have served you heirs
—you and your dear little daughter.   For " a Father of the
fatherless and Judge of the widow is God, our God, in His
holy habitation."

And for the rest you have beautifully indicated what, with
your great eyes of sorrow, dear, dear young friend, you see
the Saviour himself stooping down and writing—over all that
is mysterious and inexplicable now, over the sacred dust of
your dearest beloved in the Borough Cemetery,—writing,
" What I do thou knowest not now, but thou shalt know
hereafter."

Beautiful words of the Lord Jesus for inscription as you
have inscribed them " In memoriam."   For surely He who
saw under the cypress—under the palm tree like the forlorn
bride in her widowhood, under the fig tree like Nathanael
in sorrowful solitary prayer, and you believe that He does

see you *there*—has also said of that great " *Hereafter* " which is to explain all that—*Hereafter* you shall see the heavens opened and the angels ascending and descending on the Son of Man.

To Rev. James Brown, D.D.

WESTFIELD, 5th October, 1883.

. . . You should have come to Dr. Begg's funeral, and seen me by the way. It is the death not of a man, but of a party. A loud man. The inscription he put on his first wife's grave is characteristic, " The Lord shall descend from heaven with a shout." He did strive and cry. May he rest in peace !

When the Luther celebrations, toward the close of 1883, were approaching, Dr. Robertson resolved to yield to a desire, which had often been in his mind during his years of wandering, to revisit Germany. He was prevented going to the festival in September, but he set all engagements aside that he might be in Eisleben on the 10th November, the 400th anniversary of the Reformer's birth.

To Mr. William M'Call, Irvine.

HALLE, 21st November, 1883.

Mine old eyes and ears have been almost worn and weary with the continual sights and sounds, shows and songs, all on the key of Luther. There seems a great revival of real evangelical religion since I was here forty years ago. Then, one could scarcely find an evangelical preacher; now, every one seems so. And the theological faculty appear to be all Christian. In lecturing on German student life, as you cannot remember, thirty-five years ago, I ventured to predict that it must come to this. How glad I am to find it. The Luther festival has brought into prominence justification by faith alone, and the living personal Saviour. With these even the mass of the people seem to be inter-penetrated. Formerly not only the doctors, but even my washerwoman said, the winds blowing and grass growing, and so forth, are God, and there is none else. Different now. I hope the change is really as great as to me it has seemed within the last few days to be. Many have, with the poor, gifted Henry Heine, at the last returned, as he says, "like the prodigal to the Father, from the swine-troughs of Hegelian philosophy." I wonder if we shall have to come back here to learn our religion, when we too get weary of these swine troughs that were shipped over to our side, when the Germans had done with them. We have also had some troughs more British, materialistic, atheistic, positive, which Scotch people won't long endure, the national philosophy being—the best kind of it, that is, I always think—common sense.

I do not know, however, if there are any such mighty hunters after truth here now, as there were giants in the German earth in those days—Schelling, Neander, Tholuck, Müller, Hengstenberg, all of whom I knew, all dead. Only a philosophic Erdmann and an æsthetic Ulrici, a great friend to me. How glad the latter has been to see me. A noble Christian heart, but not so sanguine of the good time coming as I am myself.

I have been going into domestic life a good deal, and what I have seen of it is very beautiful, pious, simple. With my knowledge of the language I can mingle with all classes.

The chief point of my excursions has been Eisleben, Luther's birth-place, where I was present at the festival on

10th November. I have also been in Weimar, the town of
Goethe and Schiller ; Erfurt, Luther's college and monastery ; Leipsic at the University. And what music, especially
church music, you hear everywhere. But the days are too
dark and short and cold for such an one as Paul the aged to
journey much, and the candle dips at night too dim to write
by.

On his return from Germany, he sent to his friend,
Mrs. Hannay, Bridge of Allan, who had lost a son,
his translation of the song in the following legend,
with the message, " I will send her the legend afterwards." It was never sent, but the letter was found
" afterwards " in his desk fully written and addressed,
and so came to her for whom it was intended as a
voice from the dead.

To Mrs. Hannay.

I send you a song improvised from the German, though
you can read the original. I found it two weeks since in
Saxony, and thought at once of you and Mr. Hannay, and
dear little Georgie whom I never forget.

It is founded on an old myth which had little outward
truth in it—but great deep inward truth of feeling—of a
mother's indestructible love and sorrow of heart, of which it
is the poetical outcome, and the comfort which at first is
very thin and shadowy brightens into firmer reality in the
change that Christianity wrought on these old myths.

In Norse and Teutonic mythology, Frau Berchta (Bright)
the white lady, sometimes called Holda (the benignant),
Alma Mater—it is she that announces death in royal houses,
as at Berlin, and sometimes as a heavenly vestal, serves up

the mead and sparkling wine at the banquet of the Æsir
(who were not teetotallers. Odin was above hunger and thirst,
but noble Thor could eat ten stots and drink the ocean up,
and the rest were "drouthy neebors" enough, and drank
from horns that could not be set down till empty). Sometimes in the weird beauty of a Valkyry, down she rode with
her floating tresses, to choose the slain heroes on the battlefield for Valhalla, and bring them to join the "Noble Army of
Martyrs"—the *Einwohner* in Odin's Hall. But specially she
took charge as no other did, of the dead little children, took
them out on evening walks, or on little joyous races down
the Milky-way, over mountain and stream and meadow, and
through the woods in the moonlight or the quiet darkness—
no doubt by day as well, but as then they came down by the
Bridge Bifrost (the Rainbow), the daylight was their invisible raiment—and men and mothers could not see them. It
was at night they could be seen (as the stars are through the
dark) and even talked to, when passing in procession with
Frau Berchta, like a class of Sunday school children with
their lady teacher through the streets. The incident on
which the song turns took place, says the old legend, in
Thuringia, where Frau Berchta with special loving care tends
and fosters the *Heimchen*—the sweet little dead children.
I do not stay to quote the legend which in its original form
is very homely and truly beautiful. As it passed from
heathendom through *Ragnorök*, the judgment of the
gods (for they knew their doom, through the advent of
Christianity, was coming—their wonderful Sibyls, the weird
sisters, had told them, and their Scalds had sung their Dies
Iræ, *and it came*),—the legend in the hands of the old
Catholics replaced Frau Berchta by the Virgin Mary, and she
again was replaced among Protestants by the Holy Child, so
that much evangel gets imported into the myth, and the song
became almost purely Christian, while retaining the fine old

"motiv" of the *Jar.* They too had their "lacrymatories."
David gives God one, "Put my tears into Thy bottle" (so
translated).

The Jar of Tears.

A mother's heart with anguish bled,
    Her eyes were red with weeping,
For her dear little child was dead
    And in the churchyard sleeping.

By night she sought the open air
    To soothe her spirit wounded ;
Lo ! Christ the Child was passing there
    With babes in white surrounded.

In lustrous white the children shone,
    Their heavenly raiment wearing,
And on their foreheads every one
    A crown of glory bearing.

Her own dear child among the rest,
    She saw him halt and tarry—
" My child ! why keep'st thou not abreast ?
    Hast thou some weight to carry ? "

Ah yes, a jar of tears I bear,
    Heavier than any other ;
Because thou shedd'st so many a tear
    For me, my darling mother.

" My night-dress too is drenched with them,
    And I am kept from sleeping,
Oh, mother mine—thy sorrow stem,
    And cease thy heavy weeping.

(The legend says the mother wept no more after that. The

child had said :—"Frau Berchta, die mich liebt und küsst,
sagte mir du kämest auch einmal zu ihr und da seien wir
wieder zusammen.")

> "Thou too shalt see the children's land,
>   And all with Jesus find us,
>   Where no tears touch the happy band
>   But those *you* shed behind us."

There is a kindly quaintness in the *Jesulein*—little
Jesus—which one cannot translate like the *Mutter Meine*
which is also very German.

Even after Mary came, the unbaptized children were still
given to Frau Berchta. Mary would not have them, and
the mother's heart revenged itself upon the Church—common
sense revenged itself upon the theologians and orthodox
that held opinions like Peter Davidson of Arran, on dead
infants unbaptized, by giving them all back to the heathen
goddess, Frau Berchta, to take care of them, as she most
kindly did—the good Frau Berchta—receiving the poor
little outcasts, more Christian than the Church and Mother
Mary herself, that knew not "what manner of spirit they
were of."

You will think this letter quite a characteristic play of
fitful thought. If there is anything in it at variance with
the deepest, softest, holiest feelings of a Christian mother,
whose bereavement is never past, but always present, you
will kindly tell me, that so I may never write you or any
other so again. But next to God Himself in heaven, the
sweet, innocent, dead children have a wonderful attraction
for me, and I never think of them without thinking of you
and Mr. Hannay since you laid your darling of the little ones
in the beautiful Logie churchyard.

Fond of old myths and melodies of the true human heart
in all times, and the response the King of Truth has given to

them—like Richard in the Tower, and Joseph to the dreamer in the prison—I have been writing this in a dreamy mood quite undecided to send it. If it comes, you will know that the beautiful photograph of your two girls has often looked up to me saying, "You have never thanked mother for it in a letter;" let me do it now, with love to Mr. H. and family.

CHAPTER XIX.

𝕿𝖍𝖊 𝕰𝖓𝖉.

DR. ROBERTSON had to pay the penalty of spending a succession of winters in a northern climate, and of the too frequent preaching and lecturing into which he was drawn. His popularity was even greater in his weakness than in his strength. The Church seemed to regard him as one given back to them from the dead; and demands for service poured in on him from every quarter. He used to say playfully that he could not find time to preach, amid the endless labour of declining invitations to do so ; and that, if he accepted all the invitations which came to him, he would preach oftener every Sunday than there are days in the week. The occurrence of the Luther celebrations at the close of 1883, led to a renewed demand for his lecture on the Reformer ; and as, like all his productions, it had grown with the years, its delivery involved a serious strain. He had of necessity learned to say, No ; but after he had said it, or thought he had said it, to all the requests which reached him, there was enough of work left to overtax his strength.

A crisis came in February, 1884, when, after preaching at a ministerial jubilee in Glasgow, he was seized with severe hæmorrhage which weakened him and kept him to his room for several weeks. He was able to return to Westfield in March, but all his public engagements had to be cancelled and he never fully regained his strength.

He was not therefore idle. He had come from his visit to Germany deeply interested in an institution which Tholuck's widow was founding as a memorial of her husband, and he was earnest in commending the object to the sympathy of his friends.

To the REV. DR. BOYD, Glasgow.

WESTFIELD, 4th April, 1884.

. . . It is a little Hall of Divinity and of entrance to the German Protestant Church, the pulpits of which it is at all times desirable, and perhaps in present times not impossible, to fill with an earnest evangelical ministry. It is a chamber in the wall with a bed and a table and a candlestick for each of a few, that is seven or eight, sons of the Prophets, provided by the widowed lady of Dr. Tholuck, after the manner of the Shunamite for Elisha, or the good Madame Cotta of Eisenach for the poor street singing school boy, Martin Luther. It is also a chapel for preparatory pious exercises—a weigh-house so to speak through which young men are passed on to the ministry, if not found wanting, and a vestibule and vestry in which they are robed, before preaching, in gowns evangelical, as nearly as possible of the Geneva cut. It has a threefold interest, from Dr. Tholuck in the past, his widowed lady in the present, and the young ministry of the Church in the future. . . .

The memory of Dr. Tholuck, the most spiritual of all our learned Teutonic masters, is very dear and sacred to those who have sat, as I have, at his feet, in the gas-lit lecture room on winter mornings, or walked with him at noon on the white roads under the poplars, or come at evening to his "Hours of Devotion," when in the shaded lamp-light in his own rooms, his face shone with a heavenly light and his voice trembled in music in the felt presence of God. And had you only heard him preach on early Sabbath mornings in the University Kirche—his sermons were simply the best, the broadest in sympathy and most moving in earnestness that I have ever heard. Almost single handed in Halle, he had to fight against that Pantheistic Hegelianism of the left, that was walking its daily rounds of defiance on transcendental heights, and leading captive silly fellows, young and old, by charm of a philosophy without common sense, an ethic without morality, a theology without God. . . .

In the early summer, intelligence reached him of the death of Dr. Angus Smith, with whom a friendship that was formed so far back as the time of the Dreghorn preachings in 1859, when Dr. Smith went to hear him and see the work he was doing, had in recent years been growing closer.

To Miss J. K. Smith.

WESTFIELD, May, 1884.

I had thought the dark cloud was passing surely, in the silence away, when suddenly, like a thunderbolt, the news has fallen, making me unconscious for the time of almost everything but the beautiful opening in the heavens, the serene sky over him—and the heavy rain on the face of your own saintly love and devotion to one of the very noblest of

men ! Of the truly great men in science and literature that
I have lately had the privilege of knowing well, your beloved uncle was (I often thought) the very best; and the
closer our acquaintance grew, the dearer he became to me,
who saw in him the extraordinary union of scientific insight,
faithful laborious industry, and romantic poetry ; and the
movements of an almost superhuman strength of genius, and
generosity, clothed in the softness of a woman, the humility
of a saint, and the simplicity of a little child.

To Mr. Robert MacLehose.

WESTFIELD, 19th May, 1884.

. . . It is some weeks ere this place is truly at its best,
as well as truly rural, and I am here over summer for anything I know as yet. The weeping weather is, I hope,
departing, after going in mourning for many months: it is
putting on green caps and tree blossoms over its crape of
firs and cypresses, like a young widow looking out for a
change in her condition, and taking up with the young year
at a decent time after the old one. . . . I have lost a
noble friend, a man of rare gift, and soul, and generosity, in
Dr. Angus Smith.

Dr. Robertson found an increasing pleasure in
fellowship with his young colleague, Mr. Dickie, who
sought as far as possible to continue the work in
Irvine on the lines that had been laid down by the
senior pastor. Many letters passed between them, and
when sorrow, or special joy, came to the new dwellers
in the old manse, the letters from Westfield breathed
fullest sympathy. On the death of Mr. Dickie's brother,
Dr. Robertson wrote :—

To the Rev. William S. Dickie.

Westfield, 3rd June, 1884.

. . . From our close and affectionate association in
the pastorate, dear Mr. Dickie, I feel as if entitled to the
privilege of sympathy with you, almost as if I were one of
yourselves; and my thoughts naturally run out specially to
Aberdeen and Alva,[1] as well as to Irvine, where, in the old
manse, the young faces of brother and sister, always beaming
with kindness to me are now clouded with tears. . . .

My fellowship in suffering with you, you will believe the
rather that I can say, "*Haud ignarus mali*," rather than
"Unoccupied by sorrow of its own, the heart lies open."
As a brother bereaved, and bereaved five times over in
succession, I returned into the pulpit you now so ably
occupy, in the spirit of the words, " The voice said, Cry,"
etc. The shadows of these bereavements (others, too, as
close) should have been as that of Nathanael's fig tree, in
which he saw the gleam of the golden footsteps of the
"ladder" that rose into heaven more widely opening. So
will this be, I am sure, with you. The first time, I had not
worn the pulpit gown many months when the wrists had to
be frilled with crape and white. I remember to have
preached on "Blessed are the dead," etc., saying on the
"yea," that as Nature had put a special emphasis on
the grief, so the Holy Spirit put a special emphasis on the
consolation. He will comfort you concerning your brother;
and the " Brother born for adversity" will Himself be
hostage to you for the brother dead, till He restore him to
you. And the hearts of all your good people will flow out
towards you, like a warm fountain opened afresh, as they
always did to me. In silent intercession and affection, more

[1] Mr. Dickie's father was minister in Aberdeen, and his brother a
minister at Alva.

felt than uttered, they will share your burden and make your grief their own.

To Mr. William M'Call, Irvine.

Westfield, 3rd June, 1884.

. . . My crest is a phœnix—type of resurrection. It used to be a cross held up and surmounted by a crown, with the legend *Sic itur ad astra*, " This is the way to the stars ; " and so I would have it still, but some one having profanely written that motto on the Edinburgh gallows, and my impression having run out, I took the phœnix. The legend— *Post funera virtus*—intimates that the dead march to which life is now come, means, if all goes right, a triumphal march to the resurrection, which is our joy and crown of rejoicing through Him that loved us. . . .

I like your thoughts on this "fair world." " Most beautiful world," says old Mr. Graham of Skelmorlie, " I'll stay in it as long as I can." He is gone eighty-seven, and quite fresh !

Some ask, Is life worth living? Profane question ! Just listen to the birds ; the lambs—merry creatures all—10,000 answer, Yes! And children home from school, where perhaps they have been crying over their lessons ; and crowds on crowds, on the streets, on the seas, everywhere ! Who ever says, No? Some pessimists in this horrible age of high culture have got to say it, but they should by no means be allowed to go at large. Even in circumstances of misery extreme, all that a man hath will he give for his life. I have sometimes reaches of dyspepsia and other pain that seem to take the life out of life. But endurance itself is a new life, and we must not only hope, but live in hope, or we might be of all men most miserable. I hope you are both healthy and happy. I cannot boast great things of my health, but though I lose it, I never give up the ghost of happiness.

To a YOUNG FRIEND on the eve of his Marriage.

WESTFIELD, 20th September, 1884.

DEAR GOLDEN YOUTH,—Like a picture of Rembrandt
in which a bright red light plunges all the rest in darkness—
like a picture of Coreggio, in which the light shines all from
a face, such, oh, young man, is the life of thee become,
" of imagination all compact." Like a lover in Shakespeare,
do you ever reflect on the absurd realities of life? Do you
ever think of this vulgar world with such a prosaic person in
it as the hermit hidden in the woods of Calder?

If you forget me I don't mind quite so much if your sister
remembers to fetch you here to do your penance on the
bread and water of a monastery, for the intoxication of love
in which you are habitually indulging, to meditate in the
fields, and attend on ordinances, and see if you cannot keep
staid and sober, over at least one Sunday in October. You
see how thoughts run to rhyme, the rude ore melted into
shining liquid at the magnetic, the electric touch of your
ecstatic frame. Whenever one gets into the charmed circle,
one falls a-singing—

> Now the year, grown somewhat olden,
>   Steals the silver spoons
>   Used at lunch in summer noons ;
> Yet replaces them with golden,
> For the feasts and banquet holden
>   Under harvest moons.

So that if you don't come the sooner, though the colours are
still brilliant, the situation, outdoors, will not be quite so
pleasant for any sketching that might be undertaken by the
fair artiste. Besides that, in any case, the vision of bright
happy faces ought to dawn without too great delay on old
eyes that see many guests, but none more welcome than

yourselves. It may seem tame enough truly, and wearisome, to come to such a place and person, at the darkening of a brilliant holiday you have been spending in some richer rural spot, and with all the scent and sunshine of the summer hanging round you. But if you would only stay long enough to give me the chance, I would do my best to make the trial and the contrast as light as possible. When *can* you come?

To Mr. David M'Cowan.

WESTFIELD, 28th Oct., 1884.

Have you read Rutherford's (Newlands) "Joints in our Armour"?[1] He seems to make Wellington New Church one of them—*i.e.*, churches that migrate UP from the poorer to the richer streets. He gives, very sadly, the diagnosis of the disease of which he thinks our Church is in a bad way, or indeed among her sisters dying. Denominationalism is, but what of the reality? May not *saints* increase while *sects* decrease—or even mount in number through the fall of the membership? Saints are brothers in heaven, but only sitters on the communion roll; and saintship is not let out at the seat-letting. Souls and goodness may be full weight in the balance, while silver and gold are weighed and found wanting. No man knows the financial statistics of our Church better than you do, or their real value in such a reckoning. You used to say that the size of a church for instance, was no true measure. There might be much padding. Do you think we are true to our upward motto, Excelsior?

To-night they have been holding a political meeting

---

[1] A brochure published in these days by the Rev. Robert Rutherford, Newlands, in which the amiable and accomplished author sorrowfully points out what he believes to be signs of decadence in the United Presbyterian Church.

2 F

in Dr. Wardrop's church. Mr. Archy Corbett, who was here some time ago, was unable to come, but your Mr. Cross is speaking and some Edinburgh advocates, with a torch procession following, for which Mr. (the elder) Thornton has contributed two hundred-weight of ropes, though he disapproves of meeting in the church, as to-morrow is the sacrament ! Our " Fast " here has long gone (seeking drink enough) to the wall, and the old-fashioned " Saturday preachings " are thus replaced by tar ropes and Radicals. Is this an improvement in the direction of religion in common life, or another very clear " joint in our armour " ?

Among his many visitors at Westfield in the summer of 1884, none was more heartily welcome than the pew-opener of Trinity Church, Mrs. Campbell, better known as " Susie." She lived among the fisher-folk down at the harbour, and once and again, after her return home, she sent a present of herrings to Westfield.

To MRS. CAMPBELL, Irvine.

WESTFIELD, 28th October, 1884.

I guessed they had come from you, for, of all the world, you most to me unite in you the memories of the church and of the sea. What old familiar face and figure should rise up before me, standing in the church door, under the canopy of crimson curtain (like a statue of a saint in a niche)? Who but yourself should rise up at once before me, when lo! from the western sea a shoal of the finest herrings comes, sailing in a firkin, to the hermitage door of the old minister ?

Often I put on my wishing cap and wish myself back about the " Briggate Heid," but I have never been caught tripping beyond Glasgow since I tripped a foot and fell at a jubilee, tumbling into bed. "Humpty Dumpty had a great fall." However the summer, which is a good doctor, set him up again; and if the winter, with watery eyes and white hair, should see him preaching once more, no doubt the ghost of his old voice must revisit the cloisters of Trinity.

They tell me it is now so beautiful you would never know it to be the same that stood behind the houses in the *kail-yards*, like some good people that show all the finer when their houses and lands are taken away, because you see them better as they really are.[1] But there are also good people who may have no wealth of houses or lands to lose, but they may have warm hearts which they can never lose; who can search the depths of the sea for gifts of their generosity, and send presents of herrings to their old minister. If you know such a one, tell her that every morning a herring is drawn across my path and draws my thoughts away, as willingly they follow, to the opening of the church doors and the little figure that opens them; and somehow I think of Peter that had the keys and that also caught the fish with the money in its mouth, so that the two things have been united before, and thus I hope and pray that you may surely have the key of the unseen Church and let yourself in, in secret often. And with many thanks for the message of kindness (more precious than money) that I have found in the mouth of every fish you have sent, I remain, etc.

The winter of 1884-5 was one of unusual severity. Dr. Robertson's letters are full of references to the snow, in which his great St. Bernard seemed to find

---

[1] At this time some houses that stood at the foot of the hill on which the church was built and partially hid it from the street, had been taken down.

peculiar delight, but which kept himself for the most part a close prisoner. Tidings reached him from Irvine of one after another of his much-loved people, whom the cold had stricken down, and it was a great grief to him that he could not go to attend their funerals and to comfort the mourners left behind. He occupied himself writing letters of sympathy. From one of these some extracts are given :—

To Mr. John Wright, Irvine.

Westfield, December, 1884.

I had been with you in thought over Sabbath in your little church in the house, when the silent and motionless slumber in the white night-dress—in the coffin of earthly life, the cradle of immortality—preached you from that dark pulpit the most affecting sermon you ever heard, or will ever hear, on the blessed childlike sleep, the rest and sleep in Jesus, the Sabbath of the holy dead ! while in the Trinity Church that she so loved, behind your windows, under the storm and darkening of a December afternoon, they were showing the Lord's death till He come.

The thoughtful, listening sorrow of three faces seemed to haunt me—your own, your son's, your sister's ; and the silence of that other face, most eloquent of all, that lay beneath its snow-white veil, that I had often seen and specially marked, aglow with love and hope at the Lord's table, and that we shall not see again till we behold it shining in the transfiguration on the holy mount, when the Lord shall surely come !

She carried a placid light in her face that seemed to me no fleeting play of features, but a steady shining from within. Even the dread of sore suffering could not quench it, not even the certainty. It might darken but could not quench it in her heroic heart. The shadow passed, the light returned, and I am very sure I have seen it breaking into a brave smile when the hidden pain was in her bosom and the hidden tear beneath her shining eyes. And though it has now vanished with her life from the broken lamp she has left behind, it still remains in your remembrance as a beautiful after-glow upon the mountains, when the sun has set and her life ascended like a star to walk with the Lamb in white—the Lamb who was and is her light, with the Lamb's shining company.

Dear Mr. Wright, my dear old friend, John Wright, I will call you, I am sure you do not grudge her her escape into the perfect light and joy. She has found the wings of a dove to flee away and be at rest.

At the end of December he preached for the first time since his breakdown in February. The occasion was one which specially enlisted his sympathy. It was the ministerial jubilee of his own and his father's friend, Dr. Frew of St. Ninians. At the close of his sermon he recalled the days of other years :—

Long ago, when I was still a stripling scarce from school, not yet entered upon the study of divinity, I used on Sabbath mornings to pass, in going down from Plean Muir in the uplands to the Secession Church, as it was then called, in Stirling, your iron gates first, when they were opened for the forenoon service, and only one or two old persons from the farthermost districts had arrived, and the elder was reverently laying out the collection plate. When I returned in the afternoon the gates were closed again and the service was over, but I knew that in the interval a youthful preacher with impassioned eloquence, had been enchaining and charming the hearts of all, and not least of some boys who were my acquaintances, and who used to tell upon the Mondays what wonderful sermons they had heard.

Miss Smith, the niece of Dr. Angus Smith of Manchester, having sent him a sketch of a monument which she proposed to erect to the memory of her uncle, he wrote her a letter, in which he recalled the chief features in the character of his departed friend, and at the same time gave expression to some of his own characteristic thoughts on life and art. Some extracts are given :—

To Miss J. K. Smith.

Westfield, 8th May, 1885.

. . . It seems to me that love and sorrow, such as yours, must, to such as you, supply the finest artistic inspiration that can be had for such a work, implicitly to be trusted, and not to be improved on, at second hand. "The first crush of the grapes," as Dr. Chalmers said, "is always the best;" and as he knew from his own experience when he tried to re-write, and spoiled what he had done as well as possible (like Michel Angelo) at the first stroke. Second thoughts, especially when supplied by another, make such an amendment, as is made upon a motion at a public meeting, when the motion is lost.

My friend Zarrocchi, sculptor, Siena, has made the most beautiful monumental statue I know, the Angel of the Resurrection holding his trumpet and watching with his eye on heaven for the signal to blow. He made it many years ago for his young beautiful wife, who died early. He was poor, and the marble poor; but though you offer him any money and the whitest of Carrara marble, he cannot repeat it. It may be twenty years since, and he was a good Christian then. To get him to give you the statue again, you must give *him* again his faith and his sorrow. . .

No Saxon could go through his (Dr. Smith's) round of duty and earn his reward more faithfully than he, but he also lived the higher life of tender melancholy, relieved with bursts of mirth, which is the atmosphere and inheritance of the greatest minds—which comes with more of childish frankness perhaps in the Scandinavian, and more of weird and wayward sadness in the Scottish Celt.

Not all scientific men know, as he did, that all the lights of suns and electricities, not less of science and philosophy, are only shadows of the light of God through which we can climb only with clean hands and pure heart to the Fountain, where " face to face the pure in heart see God." . . .

The questions of Immortality and Resurrection are no mere questions as in Chemistry, as to whether certain sub-stances broken asunder can be preserved separate, and afterwards reunited, and, if they have been living organisms, recall the old life. To him the question went far deeper than that. Can sin be removed, and that great stone rolled away from the door of the sepulchre? This is what his Saviour Jesus Christ has done, and he knew it, and if he being dead may yet speak through silent stony lips, might they not best speak to any scientific doubter who visits his grave with a heart opened by sorrow, of that Saviour Jesus Christ " that hath abolished death "?

To MR. GEORGE BROWN, Irvine.

WESTFIELD, July, 1885.

I have preached twice this year at Bridge of Allan and in Mid-Calder—in the latter ten days ago, reopening after repair, that rural edifice where Mr. George Crawford (of Irvine, George with tutorial memories) is now conducting, I believe, a very able and acceptable ministry.

A son of Mr. Dunlop, Snodgrass, was his guest on his re-opening occasion, and he carried my thoughts all through the service away back to old Irvine, where we sometimes had a midsummer Sabbath as beautiful as that was—a congregation as good, and somewhat less primitive, with your pew in the south transept never empty, or out of sympathy with the pulpit. And though our river under the bank in front does not run through a valley so fruitful and rich as the Almond, yet *there* is no view to be compared with that we had, in the intervals, on mornings and evenings, from the frontal corridors of Trinity, over the town and the harbour—away into the depths of darker and lighter blue, out of which and into which the emerald of Arran, sparkling in the sunlight, rises. I seemed to hear the bells of Trinity Church, the choir, the voices of the whole congregation, and the deep silence in the time of prayer, out of which rose a solitary voice with tremulous wing seeking to ascend, and I did, as I often do, wish myself amongst you.

In the summer of 1885 he was very happy. He went as the guest of his friend, Mr. M'Cowan, to Grantown in Strathspey, where he drove about in view of the Cairngorm Mountains, " enjoying large draughts of the celestial wine of the air of the pine-woods, which seems true medicine for one's often infirmities and stomach's sake ; " and where, too, he attended a meeting of the Presbytery of Abernethy when it was occupied with a famous dispute about a churchyard, " the drollest meeting of Presbytery I ever saw or heard of." On his way south he halted at Kingussie to visit his friends, Principal and Mrs. Douglas, where he was charmed with a band " of

Kafir girls of English ancestry," who sang to him
" Kafir hymns with the click, over and over again."

He returned to Westfield to receive a visit from
George MacDonald and his family—a party of six—
who had been in Edinburgh giving their representation
of the "Pilgrim's Progress," all of whom he found
" after their measure, like the father, singularly good
and gifted, but moving on very singular lines that run
toward mysticism."

Dr. Robertson was greatly interested in the marriage,
at the end of July, of a young lady of the congregation,
whom he had baptized and taught, to his colleague,
Mr. Dickie.

To the Rev. W. S. Dickie.

WESTFIELD, 20th July, 1885.

I have sent you in five volumes (revised version) the Book
that seems most suitable as betwixt you and me at any time,
and therefore specially so at such a time as this, as it begins
with a marriage in one Paradise, and ends with a marriage in
another, when the Bride hath made herself ready—the Book
out of which I tried to feed the older flock of our co-pastorate,
and from which you are now feeding the younger to better
purpose.

I hope that not a few of the former have found their way
to the Good Shepherd, and the heavenly fields and fold
under my ministry ; and that many more, please God, are
finding, and shall find, in the blessed future, their way under
yours. May we rejoice together when God writes up the
people.

The church belongs to neither. We are her servants for
Jesus' sake. He that hath the Bride is the Bridegroom, and

in bringing souls to Him to hear the Bridegroom's voice, our joy is fulfilled.

I am sure your bride, whom I have loved in a most grandfatherly way since ever she was a baby, will let me regard her as a daughter, as you, since ever I have known you, have truly been a son to me.

He went to Irvine to officiate at the marriage, and again to preach twice on the first Sabbath after his colleague's return with his young wife. The sermons that day were his last to the congregation he loved so well and had served so faithfully. Though both of them were on subjects on which he had preached long before in the days of his young ministry, they were enriched with the learning and experience of the intervening years. Quotations from Savonarola and descriptions of the paintings of Fra Angelico and Leonardo da Vinci were aptly used to illustrate his themes. It was afterwards noted that the text of the afternoon sermon was this : "Giving thanks unto the Father, who hath made us meet to be partakers of the inheritance of the saints in light."

Only on two other occasions did he preach in Scotland, and on one of these he was again led back into the sacred past. It was the celebration of the jubilee of the congregation of Bannockburn in the founding of which his brother Andrew had so large a part.

In the later autumn he went into Northumberland to officiate for the son of an old friend. On his return he visited his sister at Bridge of Allan and preached for her minister, Mr. Muir, his famous sermon on John the Baptist. He then started for Ventnor, in the Isle of Wight, to baptize the second child of Dr. and Mrs. Williamson, Mrs. Williamson being the Janet Bruce of other days, the only surviving child of his dear friend and kinsman, Dr. William Bruce, who had passed away in November, 1882.

Before leaving London he preached what proved to be his last sermon. It was at evening service in the church of his friend, Dr. Walter Morison, formerly of Ayr, to whom he wrote on his return.

To the REV. WALTER MORISON, D.D.

WESTFIELD, 5th December, 1885.

. . . The pleasure I had in conducting vespers in your chapel did not arise from any virtue in them, or in him that did administer them ; but from the happy thought that I was doing you a service, or at least trying to do so, when you were not there to see how poorly it was done. If I brought flowers, as you say (and I must not contradict you), I daresay they were withered enough, as flowers at evening that have not been freshly cut may be. The bloom, the fragrance, the aroma, the dewy sparkle, the rainbow tints that come and go, must have fled on the wings of the morning. . . .

During Dr. Robertson's absence in the south, a great sorrow fell on the whole neighbourhood of Westfield, in the death of Dr. Smith, minister of the parish of Kirknewton. It is evidence of Dr. Robertson's neighbourliness and catholicity that on his return his first visit was to the stricken manse, and

that the bereaved kirk-session sent him a request
that he should preach to the congregation in its
sorrow. His too frequent winter journeyings and
preachings had already begun to bear fruit, and
he found it impossible to comply with the request;
but, in declining, he paid a warm tribute to the worth
of the departed pastor. "Had Dr. Smith," he said,
"been less faithful, less studious, less saintly and
loving, less of a restless seeker of souls and self-
sacrificing brother of the poor, and a less noble man
of God than he was, he might have been among us still.
But his reward seemed impatient to meet him, and
'suddenly, behold a chariot and horses of fire.'"

Another death deeply touched him in that dark
winter. Mr. MacLehose, publisher to the University
of Glasgow, the early friend of Daniel Macmillan, and
one of the most notable figures in the city, into the
"dusky lanes and wrangling marts" of whose com-
merce he laboured for fifty years to shed the benign
light of literature, was suddenly stricken down. Dr.
Robertson would not be restrained from coming, on
a most bitter day, to attend the funeral. The following extract refers to his last interview with his old
friend:—

To Mrs. King, London.

Westfield, Christmas Day, 1885.

In passing hurriedly through Glasgow I saw the late Mr.
MacLehose, and gave him your greeting, with which he
seemed much gratified. They say he took delight in every
book that passed out through his hands, but he had a

special and marked delight in yours.[1] He was repeating it
warmly as before when some one said I had come from
London to vote for Gladstone.[2] He said, " Noble ! off—
time's up—don't miss the train." So his laudatory words of
you and the Memoir were among the last I heard him speak.

To Miss M'Call, Irvine.

WESTFIELD, 30th December, 1885.

The best of our church I used to think, if the trumpet
should sound on a Tuesday evening, would likely be found
at the prayer meeting. One stormy night I remember,
when, in the music at the close of the sermon, we sang
Evening Intercessions ("When the sailor on the deep ").
Over the pleading music, that rose and fell in the voices of
those that had brothers, cousins, and other friends at sea,
the slates rattled, the snow rustled and sighed round the
high windows, and it hung like white sheets in the wan moonlight as we parted at the "Briggate Heid." And do you think
I can forget this when I lie awake on stormy nights, and think
of my own children (as many of them are by baptism) at
sea ; and try to get nearer to One who watched on a midnight mountain when the fishing boat was struggling on the
lake below, and who still upon another mountain intercedes
in the bright light over the storm. I pray that on His heart
be written also the name of your dear nephew, Alexander.
Did he sail yesterday ? For it did blow hard last night as I
lay awake and listened, and thought of the church on the
hill and the ships at sea. Nothing interests me more than
to hear, as you kindly let me, of our boyish mariners, as
well as others older, and their movements. They are not

---

[1] " Memoir of the Rev. David King, LL.D."

[2] This was before Mr. Gladstone had introduced his Home Rule Bill.

perhaps so numerous as once, when I used to say that my congregation was like our Queen's dominions on which the sun never sets; but on being separated from you on shore I seem to come nearer to those at sea. I hope the present race will follow in the footsteps of those old disciples that have walked on the water to go to Jesus, and been hidden from all tempests in His bosom; and, when the storms of life are all over, have been hidden also in the "remarkable hiding" of the grave, it may be a wandering sepulchre suddenly opened for burial by God Himself, as Moses was buried, no man knows where. "But now they are glad because they be quiet; so He bringeth them into their desired haven."

Mr. Alexander M'Dowall, nephew of Mrs. James Robertson of Newington, having been in Wales, and much interested in the *hwyl*, or "sing," with which Welsh ministers preach, wrote to Dr. Robertson :—

Now, you will remember your brother sometimes "sang" in preaching. I have heard him, and I think the notes were either *do, ti, la,* or *mi, re, do.* I think he was often unconscious of this. What I would like to know is, "Where did he get this 'hwyl'?" Was it a common practice in the Secession Church? I fancy I have heard of others doing it. Or was it merely a natural mode of expression for a music loving nature, as his, I think, was?

Dr. Robertson wrote a long letter in reply, in which he entered into a discussion of Hebrew and Greek music, and of how their influence can be traced in the services of the Christian Church. Such portions of the letter as are likely to interest the general reader are here given :—

To Mr. Alexander B. M'Dowall, London.

Westfield, February, 1886.

Your " Uncle James," who had both the " unction" and the " sing," learnt his song from Dr. Smart of the " Back Row," Stirling, a Burgher minister of the patriarchal order (now extinct), upright in form as in character, wearing the snowy mitre of age ere *I* saw him.

He *" served the tables "* at the Sacrament from the precentor's desk (two or so out of perhaps six or seven), and "sang" his meditation right through with variations, but what I remember best is such as this :—

do	re	mi	re	do
He	hath	brought me	into His	banqueting house
la,	sol,	do	la,	sol,
And His	banner	over	me	was love.

The first *allegro*, the second (lower) *affettuoso*, and sometimes very full of heart, so that the old men would shake their heads from side to side and the women cry. When returning to the natural (or *discrete*) voice at the words, " Trusting that these are your sentiments, I will now proceed to put into your hands," etc., we children would nudge each other and say, " The boat's run aground." I daresay he intoned with as much variety as your Welshman, but Smart was no *improvisatore*, and the above (which I have written on no key, but with a rough indication of the intervals) is something like a cartoon of his usual " sing-song," which was, however, very telling.

The alternation of this recitation with the *Coleshill* sung *en masse* by the procession of communicants coming and going was very effective (too operatic you would say), the precentor " reading the line " of the psalm (commonly the 103rd), sung in successive fragments when the tables were changing guests,

the first line on resuming being *spoken* on the key note, the
rest all recited in the singing voice, and the minor third
above the key note, which gave it a slow, solemn, weird
effect, but far richer than anything we hear now, with our
waltzing hymns and jumpy demi-semi-quavers. In *Coleshill*,
as sung in a Free Highland kirk (in Iona), I recognized the
tones of the old Ambrosian chant, still preserved, and said
to have been brought from the east. When I was in Italy in
1842, the priests in the cathedral chanting the *canto fermo*
seemed to me to be repeating old Dr. Smart. But on closer acquaintance with the Gregorian, I would side with your Principal Edwards. The church music of Cymry and Celt is
older than Gregory and possibly of oriental origin, coeval
with the first introduction of Christianity; or more likely a
native outgrowth (partly conditioned by foreign influence) of
the very musical souls that had their bards and harpers from
the oldest time. We are too late to hear the singing of the
Blue coat boys or the wail of Mona, but certainly in music
"Taffy" had no need to be a "thief."

Yet, on hearing the priests chanting in 1842, it *did* occur
at once to me that Dr. Smart's chant might have floated
down from the Romish Church, through the opened gates
of the Reformation, even into Ebenezer Erskine's church in
the Back Row! and, going further back, it may have come
down from the Hebrew into the Christian Church. You
know how the "accents" in the Hebrew Bible are believed
to represent the vocal inflection—or, say, the music. Of
course, being no older, at any rate, than the Mazoretic
points, they could only, though rightly read off, give the
Hebrew music that was used in the Middle Ages. And
who could read them off? Should they lie dumb, like the
truly dead language of Etruria, or be made to speak again, like
old Runes and Egyptian hieroglyphics? In the *Times*,
thirty years ago, I read that a Professor S. Haupt, Leipsic,

had found the key. I wrote for it, and found he made
these accents to be fragments of an old Semitic alphabet,
used somewhat after the modern manner of sol-fa. On
applying it to the blessing of Aaron, in Numbers—

do, re, mi, re, mi, do
ỳbar - rek' - ka   Je - ho - vah.

—a chant is produced—shall we say *re*produced—much more
like old Dr. Smart than that given (as Hebrew, I think) in
our U.P. Hymn Book. Strange ! if old Smart was chanting
the hope of David or the benediction of Aaron in the very
same tones as they did themselves. And yet, the truth is,
as you well say, that the simpler forms of musical expression are the natural outcome " of man's loving nature and
devout spirit," in all ages and all the world over.

With the advent of the new year (1886), the cold
had become more intense, but, as this compelled Dr.
Robertson to husband his strength and guard against
exposure, he remained comparatively well. Some
ladies who were going to Florence visited him in
February, and his sister went from Bridge of Allan
to receive them. Their presence and their plans led
him to talk much on the familiar theme of Florentine
art, and he spoke with all the fresh enthusiasm which
new and sympathetic listeners never failed to awaken.
He was looking forward hopefully to the approaching spring, and planning a long journey, with vague
ideas of at length seeing Palestine. At the close of the
same month, he paid a short visit to his sister at
Bridge of Allan, and then laughingly said that his
" good condition of body was largely owing to his

heathenish neglect of ordinances, for he had never ventured the long walk to church all winter."

The following extract is from a letter written in these days to a young artist—niece of Sir Noel Paton and Mrs. D. O. Hill—who had written playfully upbraiding him for not having called for a long while :—

To Miss J. Maud Roxburgh, Edinburgh.

Westfield, 3rd March, 1886.

Do you know, from my lonely convent in the snow (where, with my noble St. Bernard, who gets dreadfully excited when a new storm is coming, and he wants out to find the man in the snow, I am in jail like Bunyan, nevertheless) I travel away to the " House Beautiful," and the " Delectable Mountains " at will. I have a sledge which I call " The Dream," with horses always in harness, and you cannot think how often (driving silently in the snow) I have halted of late before the gate of Newington Lodge. No doubt you have many splendid chariots like Cinderella's, but it is not likely that you have ever returned from any brilliant city assembly by Westfield way; though I do think I have often heard the silver tones of your little bells in the frost and the moonlight, floating over the funereal woods, with their plumes of snow. Next time I must open the window and call " Who goes? " as the monk in a strange picture of Aricaquas, where, however, the parallel ceases.

I hope your feelings are not hurt by being classed with Cinderella. She is a great favourite of mine, a sweet, gentle Christian girl, who sings Keble's hymn, " The trivial round, the common task," etc., and erects the most ordinary offices of household work, even in the kitchen and the cellar, into a holy dignity and real artistic beauty, drawing down upon the work of her hands, through a window in the end of the 90th Psalm, the beauty of heaven itself. . . .

As to the question you raise, of " Eastward or Westward Ho !" I am truly " stepping westward," in the evening shadows ; but turn and look eastward with my aged eyes to see you climbing the beautiful slopes of the morning to those noon-day heights of art your gifted aunt, Mrs. Hill, has long occupied. . . . There are said to be glimpses of beauty in your line that can only be had through the windows of pain, somewhat moistened and dim. I hope they may always come to you some other way; but no doubt sufferings *are* windows through which to look out to things unseen, if we don't keep the shutters up.

To MISS MIDDLEMAS, Edinburgh.

WESTFIELD, 17th March, 1886.

I have scarcely been abroad all winter, excepting to funerals of one and another whom the season had smote down. Once I was in Edinburgh to visit Dr. Knox on his last Saturday evening, and when the Sabbath morning bells were ringing he had gone up to church.

Already, by the almanac, the spring must be at the door, but cannot get in for the snow.

It is lying quite deep still all around, and to-day the storm seems renewing itself fierce as ever. Pity to the suffering poor ! What black distress and death are smothered up from sight by the great white hypocrite that is descending now in footsteps as noiseless and innocent as the angels! The most beautiful may be the most deadly —the sisters with the vials of wrath came out of the Temple clothed in white linen, with golden girdles, the prettiest dress of all.

But the good snow is no false beauty. She is doing

God's work faithfully all the same, though in secret, as the loveliest, the most God-like always do. On her white brow is written, " Wait a little and see ! " She has come down to keep our mother earth warm in the shadow of the great white wings till suddenly a greener summer shall start up, as I have seen it in the Engadine. " He giveth snow like wool "—warm and white like the downy fleece of lambs.

To Mrs. Corry.

WESTFIELD, 23rd March, 1886.

I did not write you sooner, because, for one thing, I did write you very soon ; and the letter, broken off by a little illness and resumed, grew and grew into no letter, but a lecture on Celtic art, or rather Irish art, in music, poetry, and picture—a fresh subject that charmed me, but which I have very partially worked as yet. If ever it be worked out as I hope, I shall send it to you. . . . The distinctive feature of Irish art in music, fiction, and poetry, seems to me to be a certain pure, pathetic delicacy. I can trace it in the music of old harpers, the songs of the bards, the beautiful illuminations of MSS. (the most delicate in the world) a thousand years ago. . . . This, at any rate, is the direction in which Celtic art outstrips her sisters—that of pure pathetic delicacy. I do not know how technically to express it. Indeed, words cannot do that, music may, but music of a rarely gentle kind, like that which might be played at a Celtic fairy's funeral, or the tones of silver bells heard ringing overhead when the beautiful die young, or the liquid hallelujahs heard in far-off dream in moonlight, between stars and snow, that are said to be no language of the earth, but voices of the angels in mellifluous flow.

You tell me you were Irish both, but you did not need. Already I knew it when I first saw you together in your sweet little room in Cambridge, and carried away with me a sense of something that, for want of another word, I must call "charm," that belongs to the Irish—not to all of them, or even perhaps to many in a high degree, but only to be found in its true type within the race, and never genuine outside of it. . . . I can distinguish it at once from every other racial style—from Saxon common-place, or Norman show, or round-faced German prettiness, or Norse weird phantom figures, carrying funeral lights across the frozen fiords, . . . from all of them, I think, the Irish style, with which the Scottish Highland coincides, may without difficulty be marked off. Manly, yet intensely womanly, yet intensely child-like, in its wonderful facility of passing from one mood into another, and its opposite, it springs from deepest pathos to heights of merriment, to plunge again into a melancholy more profound. If the fingers that touch the harp also wield the shillela, if the voices that dance, as with twinkling feet, through the delicate turns of Irish melody can also march shod with the "brogue"—this shows the breadth and richness of the Irish nature, that may seem inconstant or unsteady, but it is the inconstancy of motion and the restlessness of life, full of longings that are readily awakened and as quickly disappointed, and of contrasts that no more destroy each other than shadows do the light of a picture, or discords the beauty of a song.

Our Anglo-Saxon race, they say, shall dominate the world, and perhaps it is the mightiest after all, and the most royal of the races. But in order to be perfect it must absorb the Celtic element, which it does not by birth possess—the racial charm, as I have called it, which is not merely personal, but runs through all the arts of music, poetry, and fiction, and stamps them with its threefold stamp—its trefoil type of delicacy, purity, and pathos.

In the middle of March, he wrote to his sister that he had at last "walked through the snow to West Calder Church and had come to grief, but was all right again." She was not sure about the latter part of the sentence, and went through at once to bring him home with her. She found him planning visits to his friends Mr. J. T. Brown and Mr. M'Cowan, after which he would go and settle down at Bridge of Allan for a time. The visits were never made. He only went for a day to Edinburgh, and, driving from place to place, called on almost all his chief friends in the city. Several of these remembered afterwards that there was something about his manner which indicated a consciousness that he was bidding them farewell.

For a time, after his arrival at Bridge of Allan, he appeared bright and buoyant to outsiders, and wrote as of old, making light of his trouble.

To the REV. JOHN KIRKWOOD, Troon.

BRIDGE OF ALLAN, Tuesday Night, March, 1886.

I am at present preaching or engaging to preach nowhere, but doing battle for a little with a small rebel which Dr. Haldane, I think, is empowering me with powder, if not with shot, to overcome. I am counting kin, afar off to be sure, with the grand Prometheus who has the vulture preying, not on his heart, but his liver ; and though my bird is a very small one and my sunshine not turned to gloom at all, nor my good temper to grumbling, nor my comfortable couch at Bridge of Allan to a rock of Caucasus, all the same I am in my little measure a Prometheus Vinctus, and not unbound as I would like to be, so that every invitation, even from creditors such as you, I am declining.

From the first, however, those who loved him best saw an indefinable change in his look and manner. He frequently said himself, " There is something new in all this, and that walk to West Calder did it; but Dr. Haldane will soon put me all right." During April he was out every fine day, but his wonted attempts to baffle illness seemed no longer to avail. In the beginning of May serious complications were discovered and a consultant was called in. Dr. Robertson's spirits fell, and he said, with an unutterable look, which will be long remembered : " This is *very* serious." About this time he gave his sister these verses on

The Mystery of Pain.

Oh ! Life it is a mystery
   That goes from pain to pain,
In grief we're born, in grief we die,
And what brief space betwixt may lie
   Is filled with tears like rain.

From mystery to mystery
   We came, when life was born,
And when this little day shall die,
Who knows what wild and angry sky
   May rise to-morrow morn ?

We only know that yesterday
   We went a happier road,
For tones of sweetest music play,
Far up behind us, on the way
   On which we came from God.

The silver sound of harps that seem
  To have been heard before,
And flashing golden gates that gleam,
But crossed with swords of cherubim,
  And opening never more.

We know this life runs downward fast
  Through darkening days to death,
The present sadder than the past,
The saddest above ground the last,
  And who knows what beneath?

Thou know'st, oh ! Christ, Thou say'st to me
  That I shall live in dust ;
I do not know how this can be,
Like all the rest 'tis mystery,
  But in Thy word I trust.

For Thou hast read through pain, and now
  The secret dost reveal,
With crown of thorns upon Thy brow,
Thou livest and wast dead, and Thou
  Dost open every seal.

Life's chequered seals of white and red,
  And Death's black seal, and lo !
The harps are sounding overhead,
And through the portals of the dead,
  To higher heavens we go.

Into our heart of grief to look
  The Lamb of God was slain ;
He on Himself our sorrows took,
And straight the bitterness forsook
  'The mystery of pain.

He soon rose into his former brightness, and no dark shadow was ever seen again. It seemed as if the brief period of depression was his Gethsemane, from which he emerged brave and strong to drink the appointed cup. His voice was as bright and natural as ever, his humour always at hand, sparkling and irresistible. But she who watched by his bedside tells of "weary nights of pain and agony, of slow but sure decay; and yet," she testifies, "there was never a murmuring word or complaining look. Surely it was born of Him who bore the cross for us, and yet opened not His mouth! It was the 'mystery of pain,' for through it and above it the spiritual life was growing and shining with even more than wonted beauty, as one by one the earthly garments were dropping off, and he put on the immortal garment which now he wears."

As soon as the first streak of dawn came in at the window he would say, " Sing me a psalm ; the birds are at theirs." According to his mood, he would ask for a " penitential psalm," or a " psalm out of the depths," or a " psalm of thanksgiving." The 145th was a special favourite. He would say of it, " The finest morning hymn I know. How often I have given out to my people, ' Good unto all men is the Lord.' Strange to say *that* in a world of suffering, and for David to say it, who knew more than most men what suffering was ; but he was a grand man David ; he could look on all sides of a thing. He was a poet, and that kept him from being a pessimist." When

Psalm lxxvii. was read to him he said, "That is a fine psalm, although it was Asaph's; but do not read me any more of his. They are too sentimental. He did not understand real trouble, or cry out of the depths as David did. Read the 32nd—the psalm I liked best of all to preach from, with the grand evangelical element in it. We cannot do without that at any point of our life, least of all at the end."

He often asked that the 8th chapter of the Epistle to the Romans should be read to him, and on one occasion said, "The whole strength of Paul is put into that chapter. He need scarcely have written anything else; it takes in earth and heaven, things created and uncreated, human and divine, from the lowest rung of the ladder—the 'groaning of the creature,' up through the intellectual, the emotional, and the spiritual; it leaps across the finite on to the infinite love of God, which is in Christ Jesus our Lord."

At the end of May the shadows began more visibly to lengthen. A severe attack of hæmorrhage came on, and the paroxysms of pain were more frequent. Professor Gairdner was brought to see him, but it was too evident that the end was approaching. Yet his vital power seemed even then to assert itself, and hope would sometimes rise in the hearts of the watchers, the rather that, as one of them expresses it, "his ever ready humour would run over with its kindly help both for himself and us." "I do not know what men do who want humour," he would say; "it is a wonderful help."

His life-long delight in the sunshine and the summer was not abated. He would often say, " We are going up to summer now." "This is a beautiful summer morning," one said on entering the room. " I know that," he replied, " by the step of the children outside. There is a girl passing just now ; she knows it is summer." " How do you know it is a girl?" was asked. " Because she is dancing ; a girl always dances when she runs. You'll seldom find a boy do that."

Till near the end he sat up several hours daily, surrounded by books gathered from several libraries, but there were signs of quickly failing strength ; and on the 15th of June, when his sister was helping him into bed, he suddenly fainted in her arms. Help was instantly at hand, and when he had recovered consciousness he was lifted into bed, ambulance fashion, by four. When the three helpers had retired, he looked up with his pale face and repeated to his sister, in sadder tone than usual, the words—" When thou wast young thou girdedst thyself," and added, "you know the rest ; " but evidently fearing that what he had said was too trying, he quickly glided into another vein—" What an interesting group you made as you so gently lifted me up. If I had been a painter I would have dashed you off, especially Mary H.'s face, with her combined look of terror, sorrow, and affection. I will take the photograph of that group with me into the other world."

He never rose again, and the doctor allowed his friends to see him freely. Some of them brought him

daily gifts of flowers.   "I do not need to go to heaven
for angels," he would say; "I am surrounded with
them here, and I much prefer them in human form."

"I am losing count," he said at another time, "of
the days and months since I have got into the vestibule of that world where one day is as a thousand years
and a thousand years as one day."   He asked for the
parting of Elijah and Elisha to be read to him, and
when it was finished said, "They went on talking,
these two, as long as they could, and I do not think
it would be all about heaven.   Elijah was too wise a
man to give up his interest in earth before the time,
and so I would like to mix everything up.   There's
Mary (Miss M'Dowall, who had just then entered the
room), she'll read me a bit of the papers ; I would like
to hear what that Gladstone is about."

On the Sabbath a week before he died, after a time
of great weakness, when they thought he was passing
away, he said to his sister—"I think the gates are
closing in.   I am only sorry they should be shutting
you out alone !   I wish I could come back and talk
with you and tell you all about it ; but you'll soon be
wanted over there, and I'll come and bring you."
Some one in the room repeated, "God shall wipe
away all tears from their eyes ;" when he said, "That
will be an easy thing to do in heaven, but I hope He
will wipe *her* tears away."   He asked that the English
Church service for the day should be read to him, and
remarked on the extreme beauty of the prayers.
Then he said, "Now read the 'Order for the Visitation

of the Sick.'" When his sister reached the sentence, "Then shall the priest say, I absolve thee," she stopped. He looked up and said, "Why do you stop? Go on. It *is* awful nonsense, but I can put the right interpretation on it." So she read to the close, when he said, "What a dangerous and pernicious passage that must have been to many a soul."

On being asked if he was suffering much, he answered "Only bodily pain. I have been all my life the victim of a threefold pain, physical, mental, and spiritual. I hid the two last under the first, and few suspected them to be there at all, but they have gone for ever, and nothing is left except physical pain, a thing not worth speaking about."

He said once to the Rev. Mr. Muir, who saw him daily, "They say there's an enemy in this valley, but I have never seen him. Everything is so smooth and easy that I am afraid I may be deceiving myself. Do you think that possible?" Mr. Muir's reply was, "I do not. If it were not so, He would have told you;" when, with great emphasis, the response came, "God bless you! *You* know what to say to a dying man."

"How long have I been ill?" he asked on another occasion. The number of weeks was given. "And you have been watching night and day all that time! How much better off I am than Christ was! *He* said, 'Could ye not watch with me one hour?' A weak set of men those disciples must have been, but there was not a woman among them."

They often read to him his favourite hymn, "O
sacred head once wounded," and on one occasion
he said, "When you all thought me dying, fifteen
years ago, I asked that I might go in at the gate
with that hymn ringing in my ears. You won't
forget that now, *you understand.* Now read me that
passage, 'I am now ready to be offered.'" At the
verse, "Henceforth there is laid up for me a crown,"
etc., he interrupted, "No, I cannot say that, I cannot
follow Paul into the third heavens. I would rather
take my stand beside David or fallen Peter, or say
with the publican, 'God be merciful to me a
sinner.'"

Two days before the end when he was asked, after
seeing some friends, if he was very tired, he raised
his voice and said, "I could preach yet ; I could say,
'Able to save to the uttermost all that come unto
God by Him.'" It was his latest effort to speak
aloud, but they could hear him from time to time
whispering such sentences as, "The night dews fall
not more gently than this," "He giveth His beloved
sleep,—it is not *very* impudent of me to say *that*,
is it ? "

On the Sabbath morning he had constantly
repeated attacks of hæmorrhage. In the intervals
his sister bathed his face and hands. He whispered,
"First a baptism of blood, then a baptism of water,
but I have a third before me, and how am I strait-
ened till it be accomplished." His niece had
repeated

> " Jesus, Lover of my soul,
>   Let me to Thy bosom fly,"

and a little while after they heard him whisper,
" Jesus." The last verse of his Engadine hymn was
begun :—

> " Up, then, my heart,
>   To Thee, my Jesus only,"

but, with an almost impatient gesture, he said, " No,
not that." The desire that had come into his heart
fifteen years before had returned. It was the grand
Passion Hymn he wished to hear :—

> "Jesu, all grace supplying,
>   Oh, turn Thy face on me."

" Yes," he said, with a smile, " *that* will do." " It
was," says his sister, " the last. Like a tired child,
sinking to rest, he gathered up those beautiful
features, that grew sublime in death, and, as the
church bells began to ring for afternoon service,
he passed within the gate," on June 27th, 1886.

On Thursday, 1st July, amid the full blaze of
cloudless summer, we bore him to St. Ninians, and
laid him beside his kindred. His name has now been
carved on the granite monument, that, in the likeness
of a Gothic church window, he had set up to mark
their resting place.

END.